KNIGHT OF THE DIVINE WIND

Also by Barnaby Williams

STEALTH BOMBER
SOLDIERS OF GOD

KNIGHT OF
THE DIVINE WIND

Barnaby Williams

Macdonald

A Macdonald Book

First published in Great Britain in 1991 by
Macdonald & Co (Publishers) Ltd
London & Sydney

British Library Cataloguing in Publication Data
Williams, Barnaby
Knight of the divine wind.
I. Title
823.914 [F]

ISBN 0-356-18998-8 (HB)
ISBN 0-356-20543-6 (PB)

Typeset by Leaper & Gard Ltd, Bristol
Printed and bound in Great Britain by
BPCC Hazell Books
Aylesbury, Bucks, England
Member of BPCC Ltd.

Macdonald & Co (Publishers) Ltd
165 Great Dover Street,
London SE1 4YA
A member of Maxwell Macmillan Publishing Corporation

For my daughters Abbey and Philippa, with love

ACKNOWLEDGEMENTS

With Thanks: to Nick, Barbara and Julia, Imogen and Debra; to the Reverend Stanley Snelling for his encyclopaedic knowledge of the Church; to Dr Peter Dorrington-Ward for knowing who to call and to Professor Bowen, Head of Forensic Pathology at the Charing Cross Hospital, for a most enjoyable excursion through the pulmonary-vascular system with a view to its sabotage; to Walker Smith, oldest resident of Adamstown, and to John Brown, Postmaster; to William White and John Buchan, of CRAY Research, for expert navigation through reverberating electronic circuitry; to Chris Donnelly, Special Adviser on Eastern European Affairs to the Secretary General of NATO, for knowing more about the Soviet Union that just about anyone else, and for sharing that knowledge; to Tim Adams for making the best Shiraz in the world; to Abbey for the cooking; to Philippa for the coffee, and to Anne for everything.

SEE CUBED EYE — C³I.
– COMMAND

N. STREET, WASHINGTON

In Georgetown the Vice-President slept, his rest guarded by eternally vigilant electronic walls and secret-servicemen. Even in repose his hair was neatly barbered, his jawline smooth. In the adjoining twin bed his wife's mouth was slightly open, her face for once revealing the cost of marrying into Washington's fast track. Tom Barnet had been a freshman in the House class of '78; once in Congress he understood what the grey-haired, old-fashioned 'pols' of the day had not, that Boss Tube and PAC-Man had succeeded Boss Tweed and the bagman. A video politician, he was telegenic and pithy, could reduce a complex subject to the political equivalent of a one-liner and have it on a video feed to stations across the nation in time for the nightly news. It was a new Washington, carved up not by deals in smoky rooms but by sectioning the public and finding its hot button, where 'participating' with the Political Action Committees was the euphemism for getting into bed, where the bagman had an Ivy League degree, a Jaguar sedan and the best table at Mel Krupin's.

Barnet's skill at personality politics and staying ahead of the power curve took him out of the House and into the Senate, and six years later to a run for the Presidency. A natural showhorse, he was the ideal junior partner for Governor Hawkins, one of the workhorses of political life. In a close race they triumphed on November 4, but for the Vice-President the honey of success soon turned to gall. Once in the White House Hawkins made sure Barnet put his skills to use welcoming delegations from Zaire and Belize and opening drug rehabilitation centres

3

while he got on with the business of running the country. Hawkins' opinion of the new breed of politician was unrepeatable, and freely available.

The secure phone with its three-digit KY scrambler number rang. The device was proof against the Soviet Cosmos satellites that hung 22,175 miles up over the USA, sucking in the microwave transmissions of the nation talking. Barnet awoke with his heart suddenly thumping. When you were in the number two slot, the phone never rang in the middle of the night. It was still dark, and he checked his watch. Dawn was still an hour away, and he picked up the receiver.

'Tom, this is Ed.' Barnet recognized the voice of his own top aide, Ed Reisch. Despite the hour his voice was crisp, and Barnet sensed the energy and excitement coming down the line.

'Tom, the President's dead.'

'I'm not sorry,' Aileen Barnet said coldly. 'The old bastard enjoyed humiliating us. He turned it into a goddamned art form.'

'Ed said his wife found him. Lying on the bathroom floor, stone-dead,' Barnet said wonderingly.

'A heart attack does that. That's how my Uncle Silas died. We *won* the election for that old bastard,' she said, still brooding over the pain of the past two years. 'You worked the PACs, you were so good on the tube ... and what reward did we get? *He shut us out of the loop.* Having to stand and be condescended to by some Senator's wife because her husband's read the latest NID and we haven't. Freezing my ass at the airport while some black man inspected the Marine guard ...'

'The traditional value given to my job is something less than a bucket of warm spit,' said Barnet absently. 'I can affirm it is worth a lot less than that.'

His wife turned from looking in her wardrobe for the correct dark suit to wear. There might be joy in her heart, but there would be the badges of grief for the

4

cameras. Barnet stayed sitting on the edge of the bed in his shorts, still stunned by what had happened.

'*Your job?*' she said sharply. 'All that's changed. Now that old sadist's gone to his maker.'

'Sure,' he agreed slowly. 'I'm President. I'm the new President. You know, the CIA's going to think the KGB sent in some assassin or something.'

'Never mind about the spooks,' she said impatiently. 'Yes, you're the new President. But for how long? *There's an election in eighteen months.* Do you want to be a one-shot wonder? You want to go on the rubber-chicken circuit the rest of your life, telling people what it was like to be President for a year and a half? This is the golden moment; you've got to get out there, start running today.'

She went over to him and tilted up his chin so that he looked at her.

'You owe it to me, Tom,' she told him, and he nodded. The list was long, from the weeks on the road, the endless campaign, the children whose neglect you paid for with expensive schools, cheques and trouble, the affairs the press never knew about but which she did, the weekly trip to the airport to shake hands with one more aid-seeking president from the Third World and the tour of the capital with his wife. The lines in her face were not happy ones, and the humiliation of the past two and a half years had deepened them. It had been her money which had paid for his career in the beginning, but that was the least of it.

'Yes,' he said.

'Call Tony Jacobs,' she said. 'He'll know what to do. Call him now.'

Barnet picked up his scrambler phone, tucking it under his chin while he ran his finger along his file of personal numbers. While pressing the buttons he suddenly looked up at his wife, who was holding a formal Karl Lagerfeld dress against herself as she stood by the mirror.

'You don't think the KGB did take out the President, do you?'

5

ANNAPOLIS, MARYLAND

Mutual Assured Destruction – or MAD – guaranteed no winners from a war in which both sides had turned each other into radioactive wasteland. However, as every general had always known, there was no substitute for winning. Winners got to do everything, from enjoying the losers' property and arranging their new way of life for them to writing the history books to justify what they had done. So there had to be a way to win a nuclear war without being annihilated yourself. There was: it was called 'decapitation'. The concept stemmed from the probability that a nuclear war would begin with the killing of the head of state. The 'decapitation' doctrine took this basic premise one logical stage further and presumed one lightning nuclear attack on the nucleus of command – in America the NCA, the National Command Authority – to eliminate the national leadership and the nation's ability to continue fighting the war.

The most obvious target for such a pre-emptive strike against the USA was the capital, Washington. Two practical considerations stood in the way of executing such a plan, however. Firstly, the difficulty of gathering all the thousand-odd prime movers of the nation's leadership geographically together in the capital at one given time. Secondly, the problem of preparing one's forces for a strike whilst under the unblinking, basilisk scrutiny of the vast American intelligence network with its ahead-of-the-art technology that gazed, listened and felt everything within the USSR that it considered its business. The analysts who tested the Soviets' willingness to go to war were provided with everything they needed –

PHOTINT, RADINT, COMINT, ELINT – in fact all kinds of TECHINT, not to mention super-sensitive HUMINT from the moles and spooks burrowed into the fabric of the enemy society.

That day the great and powerful gathered, streaming into Washington to pay homage to the dead President, to make sure they were there, counted among those close by when the Vice-President took the oath. No one was thinking of war. Preparations for war were as unmistakable as they always had been, and the nation rested contentedly at DefCon V – all except SAC, the Strategic Air Command, which never admitted to anything more peaceful than DefCon IV. But preparations for war involved unprecedented activity among the fleets of strategic bombers the property of the USSR, and involved great increases in the sailings of nuclear-armed SSBN submarines from Petropavlovsk and Severomorsk. It was easy to miss one single *Blinder* inter-continental strategic bomber among the many. The analysts knew when the big submarines left port, they had pictures of them heading down the sound on their desks within the hour. But a submarine was a stealthy weapons system; where it went after it slipped beneath the surface was another story.

The *Vladimir Illyich* had left the Atlantic now, and travelling through Chesapeake Bay had passed Point Lookout earlier in the morning on her way up the intra-coastal waterway towards Annapolis. Out over the Atlantic, Colonel Zaikov's *Blinder* had left its last Ilyushin IL-76 tanker far behind and with wings swung back had accelerated to trans-sonic speed, skimming a mere one hundred feet over the ocean on its run-in to the target, staying well below radar. Nothing showed on the 'scopes and the NORAD interceptors remained on the ground. Zaikov and his crew had trained for hundreds of hours for their role, and furthermore knew that this was a one-time, one-way mission. They had determined to do it right, to demonstrate to the Yanquis what the men of the Soviet strategic air forces were made of.

The reviewing stands were full of the great and powerful, and there was a buzz through the movers and shakers as Barnet's motorcade was seen. As they drew up he glanced at his watch. For an occasion like this, timing was of the essence. He got out, followed by his wife, and they walked up the steps to the podium in a swarm of secret-servicemen, waving and beaming. The flags were flying, the sun shining. It was a glorious day.

Silence fell over the great assembly. Everyone was looking out over the water. In the air, over to the east, a speck was moving. Half a mile off-shore, the water suddenly seethed white, and vast, a leviathan, the gigantic submarine the *Vladimir Illyich* rose to the surface with foam streaming down her flanks. A great roar of excitement broke from the crowd. The speck in the sky came jumping out of the frame, and as Zaikov pulled back on the yoke the *Blinder* bathed the assembly in the perfume of burned kerosene and the shattering bellow of its four Koliesev Type 57 turbojets on full after-burner.

The bomber vanished into the expanse of the sky as Zaikov came back on the throttles and prepared the aircraft for approach into Andrews AFB. Out in the waterway American and Soviet flags broke out from the sail of the great *Typhoon* as the crew prepared to take on the lines from the tugs that were to convey the enormous craft to its permanent mooring in the Monument to Peace. They were all there: the *Ohio* class SSBN, the Typhoon, the SS-X-24 and Atlas ICBMs, the IRBMs, the AS-2 and AS-4, the Boeing ALCM, the depth-charges and the shells, the mines, missiles and bombs and their delivery systems, the whole panoply of horror of nuclear Armageddon. By the gates to the Monument, impaled on a concrete plinth, they had one of the only ten B-2 bombers ever built. It was the most expensive piece of statuary ever constructed. The whole comprised a testimony to the achievement of the late President – the disarmament treaty with the USSR.

President Barnet, newly sworn-in that morning, stood

tall and handsome on the podium. He held up his arms like an evangelist.

'My fellow Americans,' he exulted. *'We have peace in our time.'*

They came to their feet as a multitude, baying like a football crowd.

THE TREATY ROOM,
THE WHITE HOUSE

Ed Reisch and his boss paused in the corridor.

'I've let you keep Hawkins' meeting with State and the NSA. I think it's important. But I'm rearranging everything else; I'll have your new schedule by tonight. MacGregor at State was Hawkins' main man, he used him to deal direct with Yanov. I think we'll move him sideways. The NSA, Kuusinen, was shut out by Hawkins. But he's good. I think we'll use him. We'll have to move fast to get our own stamp on things.'

Reisch cocked his head at the Treaty Room door. '*He* knows that. We mustn't make Carter's mistake. He let it drift, thinking he had time. You haven't, you have to hit the ground running.'

Short, crew-cutted and with a face like a pugnacious bulldog, Reisch lived and breathed politics. He had never wanted another life. Early involvement at high school had taught him not only that he had neither the size nor the charisma to be the man in front of the cameras, but also the more useful lesson that the big man depended totally upon those behind him, that the manipulators saw more of the game: sometimes, had more of the power. Reisch, whose skill it was, settled for the reality rather than the appearance like a beast sinking its fangs into flesh.

Having made it to the top of the greasy pole, he was the new Chief of Staff to the new President and now the only task was to stay there. He held open the door. Tony Jacobs was sitting in a bentwood swivel armchair by the massive walnut Cabinet table; he rose respectfully.

'President Grant used to sit in that chair,' said Barnet.

'I know,' said Jacobs. He was a slim, compact figure in his forties. When he had been in advertising he had found out what appealed to the public; in political relations what mattered to those in power. He had married the two, and now there was no one in Washington who would not take a call from Tony Jacobs.

'In this town I guess we all like being close to power, whether it's past or present. When I was waiting for your predecessor in this room I used to like to sit here, or at the table, just soaking up the history of it all.'

'You planned the campaign with President Hawkins here?'

'We had meetings, yes.'

'That's why I thought we'd meet here. I want you to do the same for me.'

Jacobs nodded thoughtfully. The King was dead, and the King would live for another eighteen months – but longer if he won the election. Jacobs was Kingmaker and Rainmaker, the ultimate campaign consultant.

The two men sat across the leather-topped Pottier and Stymus table and Reisch sat beside the President. Behind Barnet were portraits of Grant and Johnson, between him and Jacobs rested the stand with its inkwells and pens, the ceremonial of treaty.

'Mr President, before we discuss your upcoming bid for election, may I ask to what extent you were a party to high politics under the administration of your predecessor?'

'Let me put it to you this way. Ed here is my new Chief of Staff in the White House. He has been at my side in both Congress and Senate. My power within the previous administration was such that I was able to get him an office in a closet on the fourth floor of the EOB.'

Jacobs nodded soberly. Such was the power of access to the President that White House staffers would rather take a cupboard as an office within the surprisingly small White House West Wing than suffer isolation in a suite in

11

the Executive Office Building across the road. The fourth floor was known as Death Row, usually for those on the way out.

'I have encyclopaedic knowledge of the small talk of leaders of the Third World,' Barnet said dryly. 'President Hawkins saw to it that I met practically every one who came to Washington. I had good access during the election, but that ceased to be effective on November 4. I protested about it to Al Carnera, Ed's predecessor, and he said maybe I should make an appointment to see the President if I had something to say. That's when I knew Hawkins was cutting me out of the loop. If I needed any further evidence of his regard for me, I got it through the endless stories. This is a leaky town, and you get to hear everything. I don't know whether I prefer the one Hawkins liked best – you know it? "What are the most frightening words in the dictionary?" The answer being: "Tom, this is the President. I'm not feeling too well."'

Barnet smiled grimly. 'Either that or the remark I had passed on about ten minutes after it was made. Henry K. is supposed to have made an observation about life at this level and said: "You don't have time to learn. You just expend all the intellectual capital you accumulated before." The late President's comment being: "That gives the Veep the life expectancy of a thirty-second sound bite." That one got a good laugh from all Hawkins' boys, I heard. Well, they'll be laughing on the other side of their faces now.'

Jacobs nodded. The mansion vibrated like a disturbed hive as Hawkins' staffers made a hurried departure to alternative employment and Barnet's men took over in a frenzy of joyous office-cleaning.

'The late President was a very old-fashioned politician,' said Barnet. 'I know he despised the new guard, people like me. He was wrong. I intend to show all the people like him, and the American people in general, that my skills are not restricted to the politics of a bumper-sticker slogan – as he liked to sneer – but to the command of government itself.'

12

Beside Barnet, Reisch allowed his hand to drop to feel the black horsehair of the Polk heart-back chair he was sitting on. Jacobs is right, he thought; in this town we love even the historical trappings of power. I've been trying to get in here since I was in high school, and we're not leaving now.

'You're right,' said Jacobs. 'President Hawkins was a very old-fashioned man. He reminded me of Lyndon Johnson, certainly in his personal relations. Johnson once asked one of his aides why people didn't like him, and the aide – who must have been quite courageous – said: "You're not a likeable man, Mr President." But Johnson knew how to get things done. Far more than Kennedy, who was strong on style and weak on performance. That was Hawkins, too. He was short on charisma, which was why he brought you in.'

'On your advice?'

'I approved,' Jacobs answered equably. 'All the indications were that the mix required a glamour politician to offset the negative elements of Hawkins' presentation. It worked. But let me continue. Hawkins, like Johnson, could get things done. He did. What most people do not realize, and what will probably remain pretty much secret, is that Hawkins came into office with a single agenda – simply to halt the slide in American fortunes. To Hawkins all was clear. The cause of the decline in American competitiveness, of the yawning trade gap, the weakening of the dollar, was excessive investment in the military.

'Hawkins had been around a long time. He was a combat soldier in World War Two, and he went into politics when he came home. Yet he didn't get bogged down in the detail of it all; he still managed to keep his head up and see the broad picture. I recall an article he wrote as long ago as the early Sixties, in which he identified the emerging multi-polar world – western Europe, China, Japan, the USSR and the USA – and he said that they were the five who would determine the economic future and, *because economic power was the key to other*

13

kinds of power, the future of the world in other ways.
Hawkins understood Great Power politics. He'd read
some history in his time, he'd been around when the
British went from being Number One to a basket-case,
he'd run a big state successfully for twelve years. He
thought Reagan was crazy diverting so much of the
country's resources into defence while our competitors
spent less – Europe, China, Japan – especially Japan –
and invested the change where they could beat us. *Because economic power is the key to other kinds of power
and determines the future of the world*, yes? The economic pie is only so big, and it has three slices: guns,
butter and investment. We've been cutting it with two big
wedges for the military and the consumers – buying
imports – and a small one for investment. Hawkins knew
that in the long run this would lead us to the position of
the Spanish. You've heard of Spain? Nice place, bull-
fights, *paella*, cheap holidays. Once the greatest empire
on earth. They did what we've been doing. The *only* way
to get back on track is to shift resources from non-
productive military spending into investment. But any
President who tries it will get cut off at the knees for
being a Commie-lover, for all they have to do is point to
the Evil Empire out there, right?

'Or do they? Hawkins sensed that the Soviets might be
thinking just the same way as he was. Especially with the
growth in the real cost of weapons systems – the fact
that the Air Force's next bomber would consume the
entire Pentagon budget on its own, *for one copy* on
current trends – and the Soviet economic pie being so
much smaller than ours meaning they have to squeeze
both butter and investment to get the military wedge big
enough. He thought President Yanov would deal, and he
did. In effect they agreed that the Cold War was over,
that the USA and USSR had never actually gone to war
with each other and never would. It wasn't total disarmament either – both leaders could turn around to their
generals and point to the 50 MX and *Satan* ICBMs, to the
twelve *Ohios* and *Typhoons*, to the two wings of B-1s

14

and *Blinders. But that was all bought and paid for.* What both sides got rid of was "the too vast orb of their fate" – the upcoming defence projects whose cost was measured in trillions. Both sides still have more conventional forces than anyone else – Europe's defensive and NATO, the Chinese are keeping the military spending down for long-term growth and the Japanese are strictly interested in their financial and industrial ability to shaft everyone else on earth. Neither us nor the Soviets have much to fear. With the conventional forces we have we can organise things to suit us in the rest of the world, as we proved when we kicked Saddam out of Kuwait. What it does is give both sides a chance to get back in the race, to avoid the fate of other great empires who got their proportions of the pie wrong.'

'I understand all that,' said Barnet. 'Hawkins simply went over the heads of all the vested interests and appealed to the public. He brought me in because I was a television animal, but the old bastard used the networks like a pro. He got what he wanted and the "Iron Triangle" couldn't do a thing about it. But how does this affect me?'

'Well,' Jacobs said slowly, 'you took a lot of your support from the "Iron Triangle". In the Senate, you were a part of it, one of the three legs – the military services, defence contractors, Congressmen and Senators from districts and states where military spending is heavy and visible. We had you on board for the election most certainly in part because you were there, you were PAC-Man, you brought in the money.'

'And once the election was won, you shut me out of the loop.'

'The President did,' Jacobs said mildly. 'After all, who was he going to put the shaft to in the biggest possible way but the Iron Triangle? Military spending had got to the status of being a sacred cow, and he was going to gore the biggest ox of all. And you were their man.'

'But I say again, how does this affect me?'

Barnet's very restlessness made him successful –

15

Washington was a town with an attenuated attention-span – and he disliked sitting for more than short periods of time. Now he got up from the table and went over to the window, resting his hand on one of the side chairs there as he looked out. The chair had a miniature portrait of President Van Buren painted on the crest rail. Aware that his grip on the highest office was fortuitous, and knowing that Jacobs for some reason thought it precarious, he realized just how much he hungered to be there for four, eight more years, to have his portrait on the wall, on the crest rail of furniture.

Jacobs had paused courteously as Barnet peered outside. 'Go on,' Barnet told him.

'I have just had a poll taken. You might have thought that you would have benefited from public sympathy following the death of the President, just as Johnson did after the assassination of Kennedy. I'm sorry to say that it doesn't look that way.'

'Why not? Hawkins was their darling, didn't he bring them peace in our time?'

'The public has a short memory; it has taken peace for granted. What it is now feeling is aggrieved. The recession is beginning to bite. Inflation is up – as is unemployment. And it's coast-to-coast. It would be. One of the Iron Triangle's best ruses was spreading their contracts throughout the states of the nation, to make it politically impossible to cancel. If I remember, Rockwell really began that with the B-1. They tied in 48 states to eliminate political "turbulence". But Hawkins did the impossible; he rolled back the growth in defence spending, and one result is that there's a recession and people are hurting. If he had run in eighteen months, he'd have lost. Not that he had plans to.'

Barnet was dumbfounded. Like most of the shakers and movers of the city, he loved it. Old unsuccessful politicians didn't go home to their native states and fade away, they stayed on inside the Beltway and found themselves jobs doing something. And to give it all up voluntarily was unheard of.

16

Jacobs smiled wryly at Barnet's horror. 'The late President was a patriot. He came to do something and he did it. In three to four years time the rottenness will be purged from the economy and we'll be beginning to compete again. But there's an election to fight between now and then.'

Jacobs paused, running his finger over the smooth hide of the table-top.

'I share the attitudes and desires of most people in this peculiar and special city,' he went on. 'I am interested in winning, and I do win. I am called Kingmaker. But a part of my success depends upon winning. I have been consultant to two victorious Presidents. Since I am desired by all candidates, I can pick the man I consider most likely to win next time, and so increase my reputation for infallibility. If I back a loser, my own stock will fall. You are unlucky, Mr President. The last year of a presidency is consumed by electioneering. You have but six months in which to stamp your authority on your position. You cannot materially alter the economic situation, which is due to get worse before it gets better. You are the beneficiary of the public's anger at Hawkins for hurting their pocket-books.'

Jacobs looked up at Barnet, tall and handsome by the standing candleabra alongside the mantel. And a loser.

'I do not see that you can win in eighteen months' time,' he said, pronouncing judgement. 'Unless you have access to some hot button I do not know about, you will be defeated in the election for President.'

17

ZHUKOVKA-2, MOSCOW

The young girl shivered in her light bridal finery as she laid the wreath at the foot of the concrete plinth, the T-34 tank vast above her, its carcass oozing the rust that stained the edges of her white shoes. While the two teenage *Komsomol* guards goose-stepped along the rim of the war memorial, clutching their Kalashnikov assault-rifles, the happy couple posed for a ritual photograph, their marriage now properly sanctified.

Below the site the police who infested the roads around Moscow were busy stopping motorists, swaggering into the centre of the Uspenskoe Highway, slapping their boots with their truncheons – burly young men, ex-National Servicemen, asking this, scrutinizing that, telephoning here, radioing there in a strange and complicated patriotic dance designed to ward off evil. The drivers were patient, they too were participants.

No one planned to stop the Zil as it hissed along the centre 'Chaika' lane at a steady eighty miles an hour. Its passage blew a fine spray of dirty water off the road, which the wind carried, lightly covering police and drivers, the newly-wedded couple from Beskudnikovo and their guests with Marxist impartiality.

In the back of the limousine Vyacheslav Mazurov poked his head out from the warm astrakhan collar of his coat like an elderly turtle emerging from its shell. The spring sun hung low over the birch and pine that lined the government road. A walled compound had been cut into the forest at the highway's edge; there was a dacha crouching inside. Outside the gates was parked a very rare car, a Volkswagen Golf. Mazurov grunted at his driver as they approached and the huge limousine, reminiscent of a 1960s Lincoln, carved across the damp road and pulled up alongside. The fedora-capped driver opened the door for his passenger and the old man got out, moving stiffly, and climbed into the little hatchback.

'You can go,' he said. The KGB chauffeur bowed, climbed back inside and with a rumble from the huge V-8 engine turned and headed back into the sprawl of Moscow. Nikolai Serov, sitting behind the wheel of the Golf, looked enquiringly at Mazurov.

'My car?'

'I didn't want him talking to the man who employs him.'

Serov, who was a young and ambitious politician in what he hoped was a new Russia, looked anxious. The marriage of the two was a strange one. Serov had wanted Mazurov's dowry, but feared his past.

'Let's go to my dacha,' said Mazurov. Serov started the engine and pulled away from the house in its compound, as clean and silent as a museum.

'A strange place to want us to meet,' he remarked tentatively.

No one had lived there since 1953. Dalynaya had been the home of Iosef Vissarionovich Djugashvili, who had preferred to be known as the Man of Steel, Josef Stalin. His successors had shot the only man who desired to pick up his bloody mantle – thrice-accursed Judas, Beria – and quietly left the dacha to the attentions of the caretakers.

'It seemed appropriate,' said Mazurov, who had a gallows' humour, and the expression of worry on Serov's face tightened.

'I remember when a summons there meant a car ride along this very road, the sweat of fear slowly seeping into your clothing, never knowing if the car sent for you was to bring you home or to a grim place prepared for you.'

'Yes, yes, but that was all in the past.'

'The past is always with you. It never goes away.'

19

The little car hummed along the road, its heater working busily.

'I saw Nikolai Kaganovich on the airplane,' said Mazurov.

It had been an extremely long day. An Arctic wind had knifed down the Gulf of Finland, penetrating the thick clothing of all those standing on the platform on the small island of Kotlin off Leningrad. They had stood stoically, Mazurov and his ilk, as the American submarine surfaced, and the B-1 bomber pilot attempted to split their ear-drums and doused them in burned kerosene before crackling away to land at the *Krasnoye Selo* air base. They had stood while the American ambassador and the President had made equally long-winded speeches. Mazurov had had more experience than any at the art of standing stock-still in line at bleak places like the Lenin Mausoleum while squads of rockets rolled, companies of troops marched, battalions of gymnasts tumbled and regiments of the red-bannered working people flowed across enormous concourses like Red Square under the vast, curiously mediaeval tabards and portraits of the Party. And now there was a difference, for the Party was no longer one and figures from the past had emerged on stage, as though the dictatorship of the proletariat had been but a dream. Still Communist, the Reform Party stood at the centre of the group, taking its position from its leader, who had another job, and on the one side stood the radicals, the Democratic Party, with at its head Nikolai Serov – with at his back, as king-maker and grim bodyguard, Vyacheslav Mazurov. To the right of the Reformists were the bulky figures in Red Army uniforms. And most astonishing of all, the man from the Zagorsk Monastery, the Orthodox Patriarch in his glorious vestments, backed by his priests. Above them all, the tsar and leader of the Reformists, President and General Secretary Yanov. When it was all over, they got on the Tu-154 to go home.

As the Kusnetsov turbofans came back to cruise and the jet levelled off at altitude, he had seen Nikolai Kaganovich rolling down the aisle towards him. Nikolai had done well, been one of those Andropov had promoted along with Gorbachev, and now that Yanov held the reins he was riding high, a Central Committee man.

'A long day, Vyacheslav Alexeyevich,' Kaganovich called pleasantly. He raised his tumbler of Chivas Regal as he passed. 'And a cold one.'

The old man heard the creak of the seat as Kaganovich eased himself down, and the tinkle of ice as the glass was placed on the seat-tray. There was a rustle of paper as he took out a magazine to read. Then Mazurov's thoughts of home were interrupted by the whisper of his companion behind him.

'The President is a child of the Twenty-Second Party Congress,' murmured Kaganovich.

Mazurov understood the allusion perfectly. The Twenty-Second had been the most anti-Stalinist gathering ever convened by Krushchev after his famous 'secret speech' denouncing the tyrant. The new guard of whom Gorbachev had been leader were all 'children' of that Congress, President Yanov foremost among them. Mazurov waited for Kaganovich to go on.

'They in the West think that that means Yanov wants to make *rodina* a democracy. Free elections, Coke and hamburgers for all.' Kaganovich gave a brief chuckle at the stupidities of the Western public.

'You and I know that is not so. Yanov agreed to end the Cold War in order to keep our nation great. For either we are a Great Power or we are nothing. The old ways threatened to leave us in the past, but to become modern we need help. Help from the West. But to get that help he must show them that the new road is one they can sympathize with, one which will keep the cheap dollars coming, bring in the technology, the management techniques. All rides on this.'

Ice clinked in the glass behind Mazurov's head.

'He needs a symbol.'

The jet banked slightly, obeying some radio beam from the ground guiding it home, and again Mazurov

21

waited for his companion to go on.

'He needs an old Stalinist to denounce,' whispered Kaganovich.

'There are many, old and not so old,' Mazurov said stonily. 'Let him look out at the cars as he drives down Kutuzovsky Prospekt and he will see many a portrait of the man who was once our leader.'

'It is part of our character. The *narod*, the masses, have this nostalgia for a strong boss, for a "broad back". But in the West they do not remember Stalin as a great leader but as a great murderer. President Yanov is going to use the next Party Congress to reassure them. He will complete the denunciation of Stalin begun by Krushchev, moved on by Gorbachev. And to make his point clear, he will ruin an old Stalinist, one who served him.'

The ice in the glass tinkled again as Kaganovich drank.

'He will denounce you. It will be the ultimate proof that the Soviet Union is "okay", "one of us". It will be very good for business. And, of course, it will serve the very real purpose of ruining your little party, your Democratic Party. Yanov, you must remember, is a Leninist. He wishes to make the system work better, not to create a democracy.'

'A show trial?' Mazurov said doubtfully. 'Some pictures of me in exile, running a power station in Irkutsk?'

'A real trial,' murmured Kaganovich. 'Real charges. And a real verdict. As I said, Yanov wants to give the West proof. What is more real than blood? Did not the Rumanians know that when they put Ceaucescu up against *his* wall?'

'He plans to have me shot?' Mazurov asked in amazement.

'Did you not do it to others?' Kaganovich said softly, and Mazurov said nothing.

'Why do you tell me this?' he asked a few moments later.

'You were different from most who served the monster. Where you could, you saved a man. Perhaps you were just like one of those explorers, putting down caches of food on your journey against the day when you might come back that way in need. You laid down favours owed.'

The airliner's chair creaked as Kaganovich pulled himself to his feet. 'You knew my father. So now I return your old favour. It is a little time. Make of it what you will.'

Then Nikolai Kaganovich was walking up the aisle back to his job on the Central Committee.

'Farewell, Vyacheslav Alexeyevich.'

So it was to be done, and the little man rid of all the old men, the last sacrificed to the god of the Western public who held the Soviet leader in an esteem they did not grant to their own rulers. It was his world now, just as long as he could ride the tightrope, keep all the balls in the air. Maybe he could. The bombers and rockets and submarines had all gone west and east; the gifts had been exchanged, now both sides waited to collect the real benefits. It was certainly important enough to sacrifice an old man for.

Mazurov was President of the Academy. It was a position without power, he existed as a totem. He had wondered for some time why Yanov had retained him in the role – now he knew. He had value, he could be sacrificed and his blood spilled to atone for the sins of the past, his guts pulled out and read to the West for runes of the future.

The pilot came back on the power and the nose of the Tupolev dipped towards Moscow.

In the speeding Golf, on the Uspenskoye Highway, Serov's knuckles were white on the wheel.

'You will be our ruin,' he whispered. 'Your past will kill our future.'

THE ROOSEVELT ROOM,
THE WHITE HOUSE

As they left Jacobs and went down the long, carpeted corridor, Reisch was struck by the pervading calm of the West Wing. He could not imagine voices being raised, or people shouting. Barnet had at least had a form of residence within the centre of real power in the mansion during his term as Vice-President, occupying a small, dark office which had once been a washroom in the Hoover administration. Reisch's exile in the vast marble-lined mausoleum of the EOB had been so total that he had spent half an hour that morning poring over a ground-plan of the mansion in order to avoid the embarrassment of the new Chief of Staff having to procure directions to get about.

He steered them successfully to the Roosevelt Room. Reisch had heard that the late President had disliked large meetings, preferring to work through small gatherings of those who could get things done. When they went in he saw that it was so, for apart from a single white-coated steward standing attentively by the breakfront bookcase only two men were in the room, but they were important. MacGregor and Kuusinen were among the real heavy-hitters of the Hawkins administration.

Craggy, dour, Scots and former CEO of one of the biggest corporations in America, MacGregor was the man Hawkins had used as Secretary of State to force through his Arms Treaty over the heads and against the wishes of the packs of vested interests on both sides of the rusting Iron Curtain. Kuusinen was one in a line of

24

Europeans in the National Security Advisor's role that went from Kissinger through Brzezinsky, first-or second-generation immigrants, men with doctorates in history and political science, chosen for their ability to understand the Russians. Kuusinen understood them better than most. A Finn from Karelia, he had a yellowing photograph of a boy not yet ten standing amid snow-covered pines, grasping a captured Degtyarev machine-gun almost as tall as himself. It hung on his wall at home. The boy was himself, the war a vicious footnote in a worldwide contest nearly half a century before, the enemy Russia.

As Barnet and Reisch came in, Kuusinen rose from the sofa under the Bierstadt oil of the Yosemite valley were he had been peering at a model of the *Bonhomme Richard*, and MacGregor came forward from the wood fire under the mantel where he had been warming himself.

'Good morning, gentlemen,' Barnet said briskly. 'Let's sit down.'

Although the meeting was small, it was set in the fashion of the White House, with heavy pitchers and water-tumblers on the table, crisp fresh pads of lined paper, new sharpened pencils and place-markers set in silver signposts so that everyone knew where to sit. Barnet sat at one end of the long reproduction Chippendale table with Reisch at his right, Kuusinen alongside him and MacGregor to his left. Taking a brief, encompassing glance around as he circled the table to get to his place, Reisch noticed that the room had retained its aquatic feel. It had once been known as the Fish Room when it housed victims of Franklin D. Roosevelt's angling trips, and although the sailfish displayed by John F. Kennedy had gone to storage in the vaults Hawkins had displayed similar examples of his own prowess on the walls. Although Reisch knew nothing about fishing he was something of an expert on political history. He had caught Potomac fever early in life. Aged eight, he had made a pilgrimage to the guided tour of the mansion and

25

had emerged with a piggy-bank's armful of memorabilia about the place and an ambition. All his friends wanted to be football stars; he wanted to play in a bigger game altogether.

'Mr Kuusinen, Mr MacGregor. I am Ed Reisch. I shall be organizing the President's schedule so that all senior members of the administration get a chance to talk to him, and we will arrange meetings to plan our strategy for the coming months. I've retained this meeting as it semed a good opportunity for you three to convene, and furthermore it was arranged to discuss something rather important. Mr MacGregor, do you want to have the ball first?'

'Thank you, Mr Reisch.' MacGregor's voice sounded like gravel sliding out of a truck. 'In a word, Mr President: Japan. This meeting was convened by President Hawkins to discuss what to do about the Japanese. The Cold War with the Russians is over, but it appears to have been replaced by another conflict of a different kind with a people who are ostensibly our allies and former pupils. After 1945 we spent a lot of money and granted a lot of licences to rebuild the Japanese economy. They have benefited greatly from the lack of any necessity to invest in armed forces of significant dimensions due to the shelter of our own nuclear umbrella. I don't have to point out the competitive advantage it gives any economy, let alone one like theirs, to be able to devote practically all resources to industry. Since 1945 I would say that our attitudes towards them have gone from slightly amused approval as they produced flimsy imitations of our goods, enjoyment as they started making good and cheap equipment – which we bought – annoyance at them and at ourselves for letting it happen, as they took over from us in some areas, to what we have today – which is downright alarm as we sense some kind of overall global thrust of the Japanese to seek domination over a much broader front than we ever thought they wanted.'

MacGregor paused to drink a little water. In the grate,

26

the pine logs popped softly as the sap burned.

'Let me go over what seem to be the most salient points in a little more detail. I'll begin with their trade. It goes without saying that they run enormous trade surpluses – $100 billion-plus in the past year or two. But it goes a lot further than that. Their economy is practically impervious to foreign products, and not only do they thus export far more than they import – apart from raw materials – but their exports combine with this outright protectionism to undermine the industries of ourselves – and of other Western nations. Since 1945 we have assumed that the Japanese economy was of the kind we understand – that is, one of the "capitalist, free-market" economies. Like, let me say, the other nation we defeated back then: West Germany. West Germany also enjoys very large trade surpluses, but there is no doubt that her economy is of the kind that we understand. She practises competitive trade, as do we ourselves. That is, she imports manufactures of the same kind that she exports. It is beginning to become apparent that the Japanese do not do this. Their trade one may term "adversarial trade". It appears to be designed to drive its competitors out of business.'

A small case on the wall opposite Reisch contained the gold medallion of the Nobel Peace Prize awarded to Theodore Roosevelt in 1906. As MacGregor paused to clear his throat the thought flitted through the Chief of Staff's mind that they'd have to find a place for the one they'd certainly give Hawkins. Maybe they'd put it alongside that one. Then they could call it the Peace Room and clear all the damned fish out. Now MacGregor was talking again, and Reisch brought his thoughts back to the war they had and forgot about those that were history.

'If this adversarial trade of the Japanese was limited to driving us out of the trivet-manufacturing business I daresay we could take the blow in our stride, but it is most certainly not. Really crucial areas of modern technology like consumer electronics and semiconductors

27

have been taken over by Japanese firms. These are crucial in that they form the bases for more specialized industries. If electronics make up the "third industrial revolution" then we are in grave danger of becoming "de-industrialized" and reduced to the level of a supplier of foodstuffs, raw materials and labour. This is a colonial status we have not known for over a century and a half.

'The history of how the Japanese destroyed our semi-conductor industry is an enlightening one. It took place in the 1970s and 1980s. They borrowed heavily from our own technology to begin with, since we were the leaders in this field. They were then able to make use of all their native advantages – a protected home market, MITI support, better quality control and a very favourable yen-to-dollar ratio. The *coup de grace* came by the use of "dumping" at below-cost prices to drive American companies out of the production of semiconductors, whether of the 16k RAM, 64k RAM, or the later 256k RAM. The Japanese firms were able to do this because they were all parts of very large conglomerates – their *gurupu*: the successors to the pre-war *zaibatsu*. Most of the giant corporations we are familiar with over here – Mitsui, Mitsubishi, Sumimoto, Komura – are *gurupu*. The part of the conglomerate selected as a temporary loss-leader was able to pour money into dumping their semi-conductors, supported by the rest of the group in the sure knowledge that eventual monopoly was theirs.'

Seated at the head of the table, Barnet recalled that MacGregor's informal title around Wall Street before he put on his government suit had been 'the Killer Whale'. Probably few people in any administration had ever had so much first-hand knowledge of leverage, gearing, unfair competition, asset-stripping and all other aspects of business predation as MacGregor. He was certainly the best person to advise them of the sins of the Japanese.

'The story of the Japanese acquisition of the monopoly of the semiconductor industry – used in everything from the calculator there on the table to an

28

air-to-air missile on one of the jet fighters that defend our skies – is an enlightening one. It seems that given their current advantages, once they have obtained the requisite technology Japanese industry seems to be capable – with a concerted effort, and through the use of adversarial trade – of out-competing and taking over from the original inventors and developers in any field. This is very significant when you consider the overall pattern of pursuits of the Japanese which has been emerging in the past few years, and the extent to which they have damaged our economy.'

'Quite a lot of our damage is self-inflicted,' Kuusinen said in his soft, rising-and-falling accent. 'The beginning of the Eighties is the place to look. Up until then we'd spent the twentieth century amassing the greatest agglomeration of wealth and prosperity in history. In 1980 the world owed *us* over \$150 billion. Six years later, not only had we spent the lot but *we* owed the world practically \$250 billion. Back then, we dug the pit we're in now – the mess we're trying to get out of.'

'Exactly,' MacGregor said triumphantly. 'The Eighties were when the adversarial trade of the Japanese became fully effective. What happened after the New York and London stock market crash of October 1987? Not only was the Tokyo market hardly affected, but a few months later stock prices reached new and by our standards amazing heights – when measured against corporate earnings. This was preceded in 1986 by the moves of Japanese firms – nearly always spending significantly more than warranted by market value – to invest very heavily in foreign real estate and to buy foreign banks and corporations.'

'I agree that what the Japanese are doing is a matter for concern,' said Kuusinen, 'but I still say that we can take some of the blame for the economic mess. You don't have to look too much further than "Voodoo economics" to see where it started. And if you made your points to a Japanese official he would say that the USA should put its own house in order, that we should stop being lazy and recognize our "advanced nation disease" for what it is. I've heard them. For about two decades, all we heard was a refrain that what was necessary was for the West to have patience with Japan, that they understood the need for adjustments and were speeding up their efforts to achieve "internationalization". That is, opening up their own market. But it hasn't happened. They are extraordinarily skilful at avoiding implementation of any bilateral trade agreements. My favourite was the banning of European skis from Japan because "Japanese snow was differently constituted from that in Europe". You don't hear that message of patience any more,' Kuusinen said thoughtfully. 'What you get are retorts to put your own house in order. I've said that we have to take some of the blame, but I think I'm in agreement with Hamish that it's more than putting our own house in order. The Japanese don't seem simply to be "beating us at our own game", they seem to be playing a different one altogether.'

'I agree,' said MacGregor. 'One can understand a desire to get rich. Our own country was made great by poor men doing just that through their own efforts. But the Japanese amassment of wealth is not translated into noticeably superior living conditions for the citizens that produce it. Measured against an average income, the cost of living is cruelly high. Their houses are not only small and most cramped – and only about a third connected to a sewerage system – but incredibly expensive. Their commuter trains could be in New Delhi, so crowded are they, and they have to spend hours a day on them. The roads are totally inadequate. In short, the deficiencies in the infrastructure of daily life leave the people of what is perhaps the strongest economy in the world today with a standard of living below that of a far less wealthy European nation. This is significant. For the adversarial acquisition of ever-greater foreign market shares and businesses has been financed by the suppression of the living standards of the very people making the wealth. The last adversary we faced who

30

financed his aggression in such a manner was the USSR. That particular conflict now seems to be over. I guess it's just the Lord's way of keeping us sinners busy that He don't let us rest, just sends us another.'

MacGregor's face, seamed as a rock-fault, cracked into a wintry smile at the whimsicality of the Almighty. Then he was serious once more.

'But conflict it is. And quite as weighty as the one with the Soviets. It isn't military, but that doesn't mean we aren't going to have to marshal all our national resources to meet the challenge. At the end of the day, it is economic strength that counts.'

'Okay, Hamish,' said Barnet. 'So what do we do?'

'Before we decide what to do, we have to sort out a couple of problems – two aspects of it all that are in fact related. The first is the sheer difficulty of communicating with the Japanese. I don't just mean the language – a lot of them speak good English, and we have our expert guys who are fluent in Japanese. But I do mean communication, and at all levels. At the top, we take it for granted that any government with which we deal has the power to take responsible decisions. Diplomacy would be impossible without the basic assumption that a foreign government can cope with the external world simply through changing its policies.'

MacGregor shrugged so that his double-breasted suit fell in folds around his shoulders.

'When you deal with the Japanese government you are driven to the realization that this is not so. The history of the past quarter-century has been one of making deals and agreements with the trade minister, or the foreign minister or the overseas delegation, or even the prime minister – which they are then unable to deliver on. I received a report the other day which basically said that none of the officials we dealt with had real power, that real power was invested within the Japanese "system", whatever that might be, and that probably the most powerful person within that system was a retired industrialist, the former president of Komura Industries,

31

who we never talk to anyway because we don't know who he is or his position within the scheme of things.

'The worst thing is that they have been getting away with it! Our own turnover of government and administration is sufficiently fast that we have a relatively poor institutional memory. If you read the history of it all you find again and again guys on our side celebrating some "breakthrough" or other that the Japanese had in fact agreed to a year or three back. And they don't deliver on that breakthrough any more than they did on the first, or any of the host of others.

'This leads to the second problem we have to solve before we can get something done. At all levels, our own intelligence regarding the Japanese appears to be faulty. I have access to whole cohorts of specialists on Japan, men who when not holding forth at this seminar or that conference to improve "mutual understanding" will advise me on any aspect of the country and its actions that I choose. They are invariably wrong. They have, for example, assured my predecessors for the past quarter of a century, as well as myself today, that Japan was at the crossroads. Change, the opening up of their market to foreign products and influences, the flowering of individualism, the smooth meshing of Japanese institutions with the outside world – it has always been just around the corner. We have been urged to be patient; it is sometimes suggested that it is our fault, not theirs, for being too impatient with a nation that is trying hard to conform.'

MacGregor stared angrily at the other men around the table, his craw filled with the undigestible opinions of men he despised.

'Hogwash and baloney! We have been paid off for a quarter-century by soft words and no action while the Japanese have built themselves up into the formidable neo-mercantilist power that they are today – entirely due to the forbearance and protection offered by the USA. My friends, it is time for it to stop. Japan lives in the real world, the same as the rest of us. It is time for them to become part of it.'

'They are expert tacticians,' observed Kuusinen, 'and have been for a long time. Within our own lifetimes, the middle-rank officers in Manchuria displayed outstanding tactical skills. Their strategic vision was less impressive. What they were doing was beginning the Pacific War. Their actions were not ultimately guided by any overall strategic plan that took into account the world outside China, nor realistic provisions for a war with the United States.

'It seems to me that we and they are in something of a similar situation today. Once again the Japanese have proved themselves tactically brilliant. All those people in MITI, the Ministry of Finance, the banks, the *keiretsu* and *gurupu* companies, the business federations and all the other institutions that have ensured this terrific social discipline that keeps the workers at it so hard – and which have enhanced Japanese productivity and export prowess to its present pitch – have in fact far outdone what the Japanese military did in China in the 1930s. But once again they do not seem to have any grand overall strategy. Historically the Japanese have been remarkably bad at foreign policy. One often gets the impression that they would much rather shut the world out as they did for centuries before Admiral Perry arrived. But they can't. They require the world; they pay their way by exporting their wares to the world. As Hamish has said, they are in the world but not of it. The result is that not having taken the world's reactions to their actions, they now face great uncertainty to their position. Because unless the situation is altered, the day will come when we, the Europeans, the Chinese and everyone else will say "enough!" As National Security Advisor I would find such a situation alarming, since the relationship between the USA and Japan is indisputably one of the most strategically important in the world.'

Behind Kuusinen the tall Victorian grandfather clock ticked smoothly and steadily, the face of the moon rising over the clock-face and peering down on his balding head. While the Finn took a sip of water, Reisch eyed a fish on the wall whose gaping mouth and shining varnish particularly repelled him. All he wished to know about fish he could find on the menu at Joe and Mo's. From time to time he had had Barnet go out to some stretch of water to look suitably bucolic for the electorate, but they were neither of them country boys. They liked it where they were, inside the Beltway.

'With regard to our bad intelligence, it is fairly easily explained,' Kuusinen said, and Reisch focused down again. 'For a start, much of the foreign criticism has been defused by the use of money. No country on earth has ever spent so much on officially recorded lobbying expenses as the Japanese spent in Washington in the 1980s. Furthermore, the Japanese government and corporations have hired the best lawyers and former US administration officials to defend their position. The research of the Western academics who concentrate on Japan, and whose efforts Hamish dislikes so much, is funded by Japanese institutions. It is an illusion to think that this does not affect their analytical powers. Both businessmen and scholars are peculiarly dependent upon personal contacts and access to various institutions, and rapidly become very much aware that a genuinely critical stance will close a lot of doors and lead to a lack of personal advancement within their field. Money, a need for access and quite a degree of political innocence has produced a large number of people who are – wittingly or otherwise – apologists for Japan. They have had to become part of the Japanese system in order to function within it, cannot risk their position by producing genuinely critical analyses and are therefore unreliable informants.'

'What of this retired industrialist, Komura? How come he has so much power? Can we deal with him?'

'I don't know, Mr President. But I know a guy who could tell us. Ex-CIA man, half-Japanese himself. Quite a character. He was a fighter pilot in the Second World War, got shot down, managed to escape from a Jap camp and rejoined his squadron. Near the end of the war

34

he came across Komura in a Zero fighter plane and shot *him* down. At war's end he was recruited by the Counter-Intelligence Corps on account of his ability to speak Japanese, and he stayed in Japan for most of the occupation. Was heavily involved there, first with CIC and then CIA. The guy knew Komura personally, probably understands how the place works better than any of Hamish's college professors. His name's Thrale, K.K. Thrale. I could sound him out if you like.'

'Okay. Have him produce a report for us. You deal with it, Lief. Ed, have us meet again next month.'

As Barnet shifted to leave, MacGregor cleared his throat as though at a meeting of petty shareholders.

'Maybe we should gather a little before then, Mr President. The latest word on the Japanese is that they're seeking to buy USF & G, and the Ford Motor Company.'

'And the significance of that?'

'Ford is more emotive. Real American heritage, the Model T and so forth. But USF & G is a threat. Economic power is the key to all other forms of power – to ultimate power itself. The Japanese are targeting Western financial institutions. They are using the massive profits that they have made by consolidating their conquest of international market shares for finished goods – not for investment at home, where the expenditure of such funds would solve a number of problems, both domestic and international, but by the adversarial acquisition of the very muscles and sinews of our Western economy.'

MacGregor was speaking slowly, as if to someone unversed with the truths of life.

'When they "liberalized" their financial and capital markets it was not – as always – in order to allow the outside world to compete with them, although – as always – this was what they suggested. In fact, it encouraged and strengthened the Japanese banks, security houses and insurance firms, enabling *them* to compete better in the money markets of the world and to give their trading companies a great new field for foreign investment.

35

'All of this carries considerable political significance. The Japanese are attempting to get a lock on the world's financial markets. If we allow it to happen, then our ability to counter the unilateral economic victories of the Japanese will be much limited. In effect, they will have won the war. *We are in the middle of a war, Mr President.* It is undeclared, but if you read a little history you find the Japanese never bother about that, they just go ahead and strike when ready. *They* are the ones with the ball. They have been clear-sighted in their aims and the assessment of the possibilities inherent, and are going for it. It is time for us to react.'

'So what can we do?'

'You're the President,' barked MacGregor, his underlying contempt for Barnet rising near to the surface like a whale travelling at speed. 'Take charge.'

Barnet nodded in a chill manner and rose, the others with him.

'Ed'll be in touch,' he said.

MacGregor stared at the heavy, panelled mahogany door as it swung to behind Barnet and Reisch.

'Off to get re-elected,' he said derisively. 'If the sorry son of a bitch doesn't get his ass in gear he'll come back to be president of the American branch of the Greater East Asia Co-Prosperity Sphere. You remember that, Kuusinen? Imperial Japan's version of empire. Killed a few million, as I recall. Co-prosperity....'

MacGregor rose to leave.

'I'll say one thing for the little bastards. They have a genius for dressing up something nasty as something else. And they smile while they're doing it.'

ZHUKOVKA-2, MOSCOW

In accepting Gorbachev's invitation to become President of the Academy of Sciences, Mazurov had not found approval for the technicians and bureaucrats of the new era any more than he had enjoyed rubbing shoulders with the bloodstained *kulaks* who had inhabited the Politbureau of those days past. When he had been shuffled sideways he had asked for, and retained, his dacha in Zhukovka-2, better known as 'Academic Zhukovka', rather than go to Zhukovka-1, 'Sovmin', with the Cabinet Ministers behind their brick and iron fence. He preferred the looser, more informal settlement with the scientists, musicians, writers and composers. It was a small vanity too, a conceit, that the old man felt he was one of them and not one of the others, because he had studied at the Plekhanov Institute and had been a member of the Institute of Red Professors. A long time ago, and before he had become a part of the real world, Mazurov had been an academic.

He was under no illusions that the party élite had allowed him to stay among the cultured simply because he felt an affinity with them. They had done it because you did not cross any man who had been head of the KGB. More than most men, he was someone who knew where the bodies were buried.

'You will ruin us,' Serov repeated. 'I should never have allowed you to join us.'

'Without me your little party would not be where it is. You had to have me. But getting into bed with someone like me means more than just a good night's sleep.'

'Surely,' Serov retorted. 'But there is a difference

37

between being screwed and being shot.'

'True,' murmured Mazurov.

Serov took the turning past the concrete and glass blockhouse, manned by the grey-uniformed police, who moved with binoculars and guns flapping to block their path but waved them through obsequiously once they saw Mazurov crouched in the passenger seat like an elderly vulture.

'Why did you join us, really? Someone like you, you should have been with the old guard. I was so grateful to have you I was afraid to ask.'

'I am a Russian, not a Communist,' Mazurov said simply. 'Communism has failed Russia, has killed millions of her people, scarred the face of her land, polluted her rivers, her air, her very soul. The new way offers a hope of ending all that. For centuries we have been importing Western artefacts, Western technologies without taking the substance. Ever since Peter the Great. First-class cavalry regiments galloped through mud-hut villages. One of their leaders once described the Western democratic method of government as the worst of all – but then he added, "except for all the others". For also I am, in my own way, like our tsar, President Yanov. I want Russia to stay great. Communism, whether reformed or not, will simply preside over our country's downfall.'

'Yes,' Serov said sadly, 'but unless there is something we can do, *you* will preside over *our* downfall.'

The Golf crunched gently to a stop outside the comfortable, rambling, two-storey wooden house with its gables and view over the Moskva River. Mazurov had spent most of his free time there for years. He wondered who Yanov would give it to, once it returned to his gift. In theory Mazurov owned it, but such niceties would not survive such a fall as his. For him and those of his, ruin would be total, Mazurov knew. He had done it to others.

'I am good for more than standing on parade-grounds,' Mazurov said savagely. 'Aye, or before the television cameras in a dock while Yanov tells the world of the sins of the past.'

He went up the steps, holding on to the rail and moving carefully, with Serov following him. The door opened and Rai, his housekeeper, stood waiting.

'Welcome back,' she said. 'I was watching on the television, it was cold out there.'

'Cold indeed,' he agreed, 'but warm here, and good to be home.' He turned to Serov. 'Your boy Yuri – have him come out here. My grandson Otari is joining us. I called him on my car-phone in the Zil. Rai, show Serov the phone. And bring us drinks, in the library.'

The middle-aged woman smiled and bustled away. To work for the *nachalstvo*, the real élite, was a hard-won privilege which brought rewards in the form of access to their own special stores and dacha complexes. Even the servants of the bosses lived better than the proletariat whose dictatorship it was.

Mazurov went along the polished wood corridor to his richly-furnished library. A fire burned welcomingly, chairs were set comfortably around its hearth. Books lined the walls. The old man still loved to read; it had become a major interest now that he had more time in his old age. The Russian classics were there, together with Plato, Hegel and Kant. Mazurov had read Peter Cheyney and James Hadley Chase to polish his English, and had Oscar Wilde and H.G. Wells together with English editions of Cervantes. It was the family tradition to present books as gifts for birthdays or other special occasions. He liked to read history, and volumes in both Russian and English sat on the shelves – Solzenitsyn, Medvedev and Souvarine alongside Gilbert, Braudel and Kennedy. His taste was catholic and he allowed Hobsbawm to rub shoulders with Howard, Kolakowski to argue silently with Deutscher, although sometimes when irritated with Hobsbawm or Deutscher the old KGB man would feel the itch to educate them as to the true nature of Marxism.

Serov made his call. 'He's coming,' he said.

The housekeeper brought a bottle of Scotch whisky, and steaming tea in a tall glass set in a metal *podtsakan*, with lemon and a long spoon. She left quietly, shutting the panelled door behind her. Mazurov pressed the slice of lemon with the spoon and raised the glass to smell the tea's bouquet, while Serov poured himself a drink, his expression of fear giving way to one of hope as he saw Mazurov putting events into motion.

Both men owed their privileged positions first to Lenin, who had decreed after the Revolution that those of value to the state should receive more food and pay, and even more to Stalin, who developed the principle into a system. An entire department of the Party Central Committee, blandly called *Upravleniye Delami*, 'the Administration of Affairs', now minded business for the power élite. For men like Mazurov, it had become hereditary. He was an aristocrat, and able to procure privilege for his family just as easily as a *seizième siècle grand duc*, although he was cautious as to his manner of using his great *blat*. For him it was the connections, the smoothing of the way; he never made General Shcholokov's mistake. Brezhnev's drinking-buddy had thought himself so secure he had procured sixteen Mercedes and Volvo limousines for members of his family, while Mazurov went no further than smoothing the way for a Zhiguli. Being discreet meant not having to don full dress and medals and put the barrel of a Kalashnikov in your mouth and pull the trigger.

The first thing Mazurov had done on climbing into the Zil at Vnukovo-II, the élite's private airport outside Moscow, was call his grandson Otari. And if it was true that with their billion-rouble satellites the Americans could hear a man break wind on the other side of the world, they would make little of the President of the Academy inviting his young relative over for a drink.

Mazurov was a patriarch. His wife had died a few years earlier after some fifty years of marriage, but she had left behind her seven sons and daughters, and Mazurov was a grandfather more than twenty times over. Otari was the son of his daughter Masha.

Yuri was the son of Nikolai Serov. When he had been of age to go to school, his father had naturally seen to it

40

that the boy went to the good school in the Tusino district. It was when the young man started putting in a string of grade 5s that his family and teachers took notice, and he was entered in the great annual academic Olympiad to determine the handful of stars that would gain entrance to the half-dozen specialised *phys-mat* (physics and mathematics) schools across the country. Yuri was one of the few among the million-plus entrants not to be disappointed, and went through the school in Moscow all the way to tenth grade and on to Moscow State University to study computer engineering. He turned out to be that rare thing in Soviet society – a man with a natural bent and aptitude for computers, and the different way of thought that their emergence had brought with them. He knew that somehow he had escaped the stultifying effects of Russian tradition which raised such psychological barriers among the vast majority of his countrymen, but he was not sure how, or why.

The pitfall which awaited him when he left State University with top honours and a desire to do post-graduate research into artificial intelligence was that it was an area in which the Soviet Union lagged far behind the two front runners in the field – the USA and Japan – and that those in authority would be very reluctant to let so valuable a member of Soviet society loose in the West lest he never come back. It was here that the influence of having a father on the Council of Soviets was used, and he duly enrolled at the Massachusetts Institute of Technology. When allied to his exposure to the technology of the West, his natural talent was such as to land him a professorship at Moscow State within four years of his return. Now he combined research with teaching.

What strings Mazurov had had to pull for his grandson consisted more of soothing the feelings of outraged teachers, and later mothers. All were glad when the young man had graduated from the Komsomol to the army like a larva to an insect. When they heard that he had been selected for service with the *Spetsialnaya Razvedka* straight out of basic training, few were surprised. All knew the Special Forces soldiers were nothing better than animals, anyway.

Mazurov heard the rasp of an exhaust outside, and peering through the library window he saw a boxy white Zhiguli, the Soviet-built Fiat, pull up among the maples, firs and birches outside. A tall, athletic young man got out, broad-shouldered and with hands like kettles; he saw Mazurov peering out and waved cheerfully. As he strolled over to the door they heard the softer exhaust of a small Peugeot. Like his father, Yuri favoured all things from the West, from their system of government to their cars.

Rai showed the two young men in, a motherly, beaming figure.

'We will eat after the drinks. Bring beer for the boys.'

The relatives embraced. Mazurov's grandson had the same wide-set grey eyes and hawk nose, but Serov's son was like his mother – small, with a permanently-enquiring set to his round face. Otari was tall and, while he did not share his troops' fetish for body-building, powerfully made.

'It is kind of you, Papa, to invite us here,' he said. He was always extremely polite and respectful to his grandfather. 'And so soon upon your return.'

'Some things happened out there ... I needed to ask your advice,' said Mazurov. 'But sit, and pour beer. I was glad to find you home on leave. You are still in Germany?'

'They have moved me from Furstenburg. Now my unit is at Zheltyye Vody, near Kirovograd. The work is the same.'

The four sat down around the end of the long table that ran down the middle of the room. For Mazurov the library filled the role of the kitchen, the traditional gathering ground of Russian family and friends, now that his wife was gone. Yuri and Otari were dressed in their best, Otari in real American Levi's and Nike trainers, British

Marks & Spencer checked shirt under a blue naval 'woolly pully' (a habit copied from his British counterparts), and Yuri American throughout. He favoured the look of his Ivy League colleagues, and was in flannels and houndstooth jacket. The taste for Rolling Rock beer was his, one in which Otari – who shared the enthusiasm of Special Forces soldiers worldwide for a relaxing drink off-duty – was happy to acquiesce.

'When you were here some time ago, Yuri, you were talking of this craze for word-machines, for small computers,' said Mazurov.

'You know, sir, that the hottest thing for the *vlasti* now is one's own personal computer. Only the military and the *vlasti* are allowed even access to computers, of course,' Yuri Serov said respectfully. 'Most keep records on their computer and write letters to all their friends so that everyone can see they are using tractor-feed paper. Okay. But they all have problems learning how to work the Apple or the Amstrad; most can't read English and so can't use the manual, which isn't particularly user-friendly even if they could. And they can't call up the local store to have an instructor sent round because their nearest friendly dealer is in San Francisco. So – if you're in Moscow – you call on us at State. Most of my students, if not all, make plenty of roubles *na levo* giving instruction.'

'And did you not say that sometimes you do this work yourself?'

'Yes. Occasionally we get a call from a fish big enough to expect more than just a student through his front door. So sometimes the professor himself goes. Me. It does no harm.'

Mazurov and Serov both nodded. It was always a good thing to store up favours owed by the rich and powerful.

'Did you say you did this for Aleksandr Borodin, the Chinese expert?'

'That's right, sir.' Yuri was patient; he understood that his father's political colleague was driving somewhere and he was content to call out signposts when asked

43

and wait to see his destination. 'He has a nice apartment over on Aleksey Tolstoy street and does work there in the evenings. Like most of us, he realized some time ago that a word-processor would be useful – though you'd think he'd use ink and brushes! Everything in the place is Chinese, he even wears Chinese clothes at home. Anyway, he got a little Amstrad PC 1640 with a colour display – the Amstrad's really popular since Boris Yeltsin used his to write his memoirs – and it's quite adequate for what he wanted. He speaks English, so he'd managed to get it up and running, but he was annoyed because he kept having to put floppy disks in and out, and basically he needed more capacity. He planned to store all his files electronically, you see. So he did what he should have done at the beginning, which was call me. I got hold of a hard card with 30 million bytes capacity and came over to his place and fitted it for him. He was very pleased, gave me a glass of Chinese wine and a nice jade – or *yu* as he called it – figurine. I installed *WordStar* for him, he's happy, and basically we're friends. He's called a couple of times since to ask some questions about organizing his files.'

Yuri paused to drink some beer, and Mazurov inhaled the aroma of his tea.

'My advice is sought by more than just men who want to play with word-processors, of course. For the past five years I have been involved with an on-going programme to advise the military on the use of their computers. Within our country it is the military who use computers more than anyone else – the exact opposite of the situation in the West. Within the past year I have had secret meetings with two big-shots to discuss the subject of chess-playing computers. They were General Ogarkov, GOC Far East Military District, and a man called Kirill Suvurov.'

'I know Suvurov,' grunted Mazurov. 'He's GRU. Boss of their technology-gathering. So why does Ogarkov want Suvurov to steal a chess-playing computer?'

'For the same reason the Pentagon's Defense

Advanced Research Projects Agency DARPA has been funding the development of one called Deep Thought at Carnegie-Mellon. Chess is the oldest board war-game. The American military believe such a computer to have war-winning potential. They're right. It was their use of a computerised C^2 system – lashed together from developmental systems and modified commercial hardware – that enabled them to be so effective in their 'Desert Storm' war against Iraq. The air tasking order for each day encompassed every single combat and support sortie, the pilots loaded mission plans in seconds via data cartridges, they simply hit the Iraqis like a fire hose. But it was the computers that enabled them to do it.'

'I served under Ogarkov in Afghanistan,' Otari interjected helpfully. 'He's a *modern* general – flexible, quick-thinking, not hidebound like the old Hitlerite war types. Ahh ... we had more than a few of those to suffer under in the beginning. Rolling offensives to Berlin against mountain guerrillas.... There was plenty of blood spilled before we got good commanders – our blood – then we turned things around. Ogarkov's the best general we have, I can tell you that. And he'd love a computer like the one Yuri is talking about. It's the kind of quantum jump in military technology that comes along about once a century. Or more. Bronze swords against flint axes. Spears against machine guns. That kind of thing.'

'This American computer was what Ogarkov and Suvurov were interested in?' Mazurov said to Yuri.

'That or others like it, although really there's only one competitor, about which we know very little – except that there's a very odd story going around in the chess world.... You see, a few months ago a man called Timmo Larsen was found hanged in a Tokyo hotel room. Suicide. He happened to be the world number two chess player.'

'And?'

'The headquarters of Komura Research is in Yokohama. It's *their* computer that's the only competitor to Deep Thought that we know of. It's called *Coral Spear*.

45

And the story in the chess world is that Komura had their project up and running finally and approached Larsen with a challenge, to play *Coral Spear*. They deny it, they say it's simply a coincidence Larsen died in Tokyo. But the chess players say Larsen must have played *Coral Spear*, and lost so badly he lost his mind and took his life.'

Mazurov grunted and Serov sat quietly nursing his drink, waiting to see where all of this led.

'To return to Borodin, the Chinese expert. You said again that he wanted his word-machine to store his files as well as prepare reports and so forth?'

'Sure. He's in love with the new technology, it makes his job so much easier.'

'And these files are in the machine?'

'Stored electronically, on the hard card I fitted for him. And somewhere he'll keep copies he'll have made, on floppy disks.'

'And he can summon up any file at will, just as though he were in front of a filing cabinet?'

'That's it. He has to use the passwords built into its security, of course. And if he wants to make a copy for someone to read, he just moves over to Printing in *WordStar* and runs it off on his printer.'

Just then Rai came in, pushing a trolley. She began to set the table, laying plates, cutlery and glasses on a red and white checked tablecloth.

'Enough for the moment,' said Mazurov. 'Let us enjoy the food.'

Rai had prepared *zakuski*, Russian *hors d'oeuvres* that in fact could make up an entire meal. Traditionally the diners would consume the dishes – normally served as a feast – to the accompaniment of toasts, each followed by a shot-glass of chilled vodka: salt herring and vodka, caviar and brown bread and vodka, red beet salad and vodka. However, late in life Mazurov's doctors had limited him to two shot-glasses of vodka daily for his health, and he took them at the end of the day, usually with some spoons of jam. It was a traditional way to end a meal. So instead, as they consumed the delicacies they drank spicy red Georgian wine.

When there were but plates littered with scraps of salami, smoked salmon, pickled cucumber and marinated mushrooms, Rai reappeared. She cleared the table in order to place a dish before them.

'Ice cream!' Serov exclaimed approvingly. The cold dessert had become an instant craze in Moscow, with a British-built plant churning out thousands of gallons a day.

Mazurov fetched a bottle of plum vodka from the cupboard and they settled back to drink it to the accompaniment of spoonfuls of unboiled jam. Mazurov poured four barrel-shaped glasses and they tipped them back. Glasses were always drained at a gulp. In the ninth century the Russians had decided which religion to embrace, and had rejected teetotal Islam out of hand. 'Drinking is the joy of Russia,' the prince had declared. 'We just cannot do without it.'

'The Polish vodka is good,' said Otari. 'They do one with buffalo grass, and another with pepper.'

'You have been to Poland?'

'Twice ... when the union was making trouble. Solidarity. It was thought that we might have to restore order and so some of our units went in there ... secretly, undercover.... Walesa, the other troublemakers ...' Otari's voice trailed off, but the implications were obvious. 'Those Poles! They want American wages, but they work the same way as we do here in Russia!'

With fine food in their stomachs and drink on the table the young men looked content, Mazurov noticed.

'It was good, the meal?' he enquired, and was rewarded with rolling eyes and hands rubbing midriffs.

'*Lyuks*,' said Yuri, referring to the luxury of it all.

'That is good,' he said brutally. 'We should enjoy it now, for it may not come again.'

Both looked at him in alarm.

'I heard some news from an old friend on the aeroplane coming back today. He informed me that I am to be a kind of sacrificial goat, offered up to the Western public as a Stalinist token, a gesture of goodwill to prove that Yanov's regime is liberal, to be trusted and suitable for more offerings of their aid. It will involve more than me; it will involve us all. If I am gone and disgraced, there are many hyenas out there whom I cut down in the days of my prime and who will then seek to do to my shade and mine what they feel I may have done to them and theirs. Your father, Yuri, will not be immune. My disgrace will be used to pull him down as well.'

He stared at the three others, and they back at him. All knew quite enough about Russian politics to know that every word the old secret-policeman said was true.

'You remember Viktor Grishin, once boss of Moscow? The time was you never saw Viktor without a fleet of black Chaikas and dozens of aides all around him. Viktor had aspired to be tsar, he was a symbol of the old order and Gorbachev broke him to demonstrate the power of the new. I myself saw him the following winter, stumbling along on a snow-bound street in an old woollen coat with a Karakul hat on, like a pensioner. He had a small bag of shopping, he was going back to his two-room apartment. Viktor's sin was ambition. For me, there is a firing-squad. For you, Otari, command of a platoon in Novaya Zemla ... if you are lucky. Or maybe they'll just take you over the wire in Zheltyye Vody, let you dig at the clay plant until your hair and teeth fall out. You, Yuri – maybe schoolteacher in Chelyabinsk. Maybe not. With a scientific background they might use you in the Fleet, changing the active zones of the reactors in the submarines. I believe most men last a year or so doing that.'

He looked intently at the others. 'Unless we stop Yanov from doing it.'

'How do we do that?' Otari asked quickly.

'You have to understand that in the days of my power I was not one of the old guard who resisted all change. I was not in the Chernenko camp, for example. I saw that if we wished to remain powerful we would have to change, and that younger men were the instrument.

Looking at them I saw Gorbachev, for example, and also Yanov. The two ablest of new leaders, able to dissemble in the Western manner. While I was still powerful, and Yanov on his way up the ladder, I was offered a piece of information with which to damage him. It was something which today would ruin him in the eyes of the liberal Westerners, for whom he appears as one of them but simply in Soviet guise. They do not know how wrong they are. Few know, for they are not told, that Yanov's appearance as a besuited Moscow politician was a late move. Yanov's early career was GRU.'

Mazurov reached out and poured more plum vodka.

'I rejected the offer and destroyed the information, as I believed it in the interests of both *rodina*, our mother-land, and myself that Yanov should continue his advance. I was, up until today, correct.'

He raised the shot-glass and they all drank.

'These word-machines. The files are protected by passwords, you say?' he said to Yuri.

'Yes. Although of course the main concern of those in charge in our country is less the fear of Western organiz-ations – that of unauthorized access, that is, "hacking in" – than the fear that operators and users will break *out*, and transmit data when unauthorized to do so. That's why Borodin's allowed to have his word-processor, curi-ously enough. It's not a modem, he can't communicate with anyone.'

'So no one can get at his files except Borodin?'

'If someone was sitting at the word-processor, they might be able to hack in, yes, given enough time.'

'Could you do it?'

'I? Ah, well, yes, I could.' Yuri had the grace to look embarrassed. 'I installed it all, and I'm afraid I succumbed to a temptation common to people in our business, who are ... obsessed ... with information. I put in a master key. I can read his files any time.'

'The man who offered me that information was Alek-sandr Borodin. I believe that his file will be stored within the word-machine in his apartment. I want you to get it for me.'

HUAI RO KHI RIVER, THAILAND, 1943

Monsoon drizzle fell from a dirty yellow sky on to the ramshackle atap huts of the work-camp, the men crawling back from the river and the half-completed railway embankment and bridge nearby. Evening was approaching, the harsh cries of *speedo* had died away and the men were returning to the camp. They were Europeans, all emaciated and shivering with cold or fever. When they had surrendered at Singapore their British army clothing had been new; now it hung in rags. Most wore tattered shorts, some had fashioned *fundoshi* underpants for themselves after the manner of their guards. None of the men moved quickly. Of those who could walk, most had the swollen legs or stomach of beri-beri. Those whose feet had rotted away propelled themselves along by use of a bamboo pole, slithering on their backsides. The British, whose humour Thrale had difficulty in understanding, called them 'gondoliers'.

Thrale stood out amongst the wreckage. The damp had not yet rotted his clothes, which were those of an American aviator. He was not yet starved; he was not part of the teams working to their deaths to build the railway for an emperor they would never see. As they shuffled and slithered by he stood talking to the camp commandant, a Japanese Captain, translating for the senior British officer, a Lieutenant-Colonel in the Army.

With his job done, Thrale made his way through the camp. The returning men were dragging the bodies of men from the huts where they had died in the day and

50

taking them to the hill where a great funeral pyre was burning. Thrale headed for the opposite side of the camp where the 'wards' were. They were huts and simple canvas structures. He gave the isolation ward a wide berth; its corpses were piled like logs waiting to be carried to the pyre that burned night and day. Passing at a distance he could see the dying lying on rough bamboo platforms slimy with excrement and vomit, and smell the rot and death on the air.

He went into a ward where dim fires were burning in the aisles and the darkness lapped around him like a foetid tide. Small islands of light stood out where men had made little lamps from twists of cloth propped up in tins of palm-oil. He squatted down beside a man, who, although thin and with a grim pallor, smiled as he recognized him. His face lit up and he fished in a bag beside him with a hand like a claw.

'Hallo, old boy,' he said. 'I've got something for you.'

ADAMSTOWN, MARYLAND

The screams came across the night air, and in the house nearby bedclothes thrashed in alarm and a light came on to illuminate a man and a woman of middle age thrust suddenly into wakefulness.

'Jesus ...' the man moaned. The noise from the house next door ceased and he pushed himself out of bed to peer over the adjoining yards. A solitary window glowed through the dark. He went back to sit on the edge of the bed.

'I sure wish Mr Thrale would take some sleeping tablets or something,' his wife said shakily. 'These nightmares of his don't seem to be getting much better.'

'He's lost his wife, honey; he ain't to blame. And he was in one of them death camps in the war. He escaped, you know. Ain't many did that. He was a hero, went back and fought for the rest of the conflict. But in them camps, they were there to build a railway for the Japanese. A man died for every sleeper laid, Elias was telling me at work.'

He got back into bed and switched out the light. The couple prepared themselves to go back to sleep.

'It's the way he screams,' the woman muttered. 'You'd think he'd woken up to find someone had been murdered next to him in his bed.'

GEORGETOWN, WASHINGTON

Ed Reisch had lived within the Beltway a long time. In '78 he'd had a game-plan; they'd held on to the ball and with the clock running out on the five-yard line Barnet had seen daylight and gone for the hole. Winning the election meant Reisch got to ride in the victory coach to the most important place in the entire universe – Washington DC. Reisch was so proud he went out and got a home better than he could afford, a pretty little house in the nicest part of Georgetown, across from the P. St Bridge where rows of them in tree-lined and brick-paved streets re-created smart Georgian London. He'd gradually grown into it as he and Barnet became fixtures, as he skilfully exploited the powers of incumbency to fight off challenges to Barnet's seat in Congress, building up his war-chest to frighten away would-be contenders, having his man work the political action committees, forge links with the Iron Triangle. 'Participation' was the euphemism for getting into bed, sometimes with the strangest of companions. Reisch worked Barnet like a pimp with a good whore.

Reisch's own personal game-plan called for staying within the Beltway for ever. He'd understood the changes in the system that took place in the Seventies and Eighties, realized the necessity for running for office 365 days a year. Barnet spent so much time on the late 727 going back to his home state to work his constituency that he'd had affairs with three of the stewardesses. That was the other thing about being inside the Beltway: the adrenalin which you craved, and which was what kept you going, was not conducive to marriage. Excellent for high-boost sex, however.

Reisch's quarterbacking kept Barnet on a roll. He was a winner, all the way to the White House. Given the fortuitous blockage of a pulmonary artery in the incumbent, to the Oval Office itself.

When he went home that night, Reisch should have been a happy man. The game-plan had worked, it had got him where he wanted. But Reisch wanted eight more years, not eighteen months. Washington was littered with the bones of the political dead. Reisch and Barnet weren't new guard revisionists any more; they were old pols, the ones the hungry young men and women wanted to unseat. Once it was over, what was there? Plenty of money, sure. Barnet could make a good living on the rubber-chicken circuit. Maybe he could team up with some other half-successful ex-President and run his own version of the Jimmy-and-Gerald double act. As for Reisch, there'd be plenty of opportunities in the media, in business.

It would be a form of hell. Reisch wanted to stay where he was. He went home, slipped his key in the lock and went into his little house, troubled in mind.

Hearing the click of the door, someone rose lightly from the cream leather sofa under the Hockney print, ran forward and kissed him on the mouth.

'Welcome home, Mr Chief of Staff.'

Reisch had a live-in lover. For years he had catered for his sexual and emotional needs through short-lived liaisons with other similarly driven denizens of the political world within the Beltway, but that had all changed. He had met Ala at a party on N. Street shortly after Hawkins had chosen Barnet to be his running-mate, and had been immediately attracted to the exotic looks, the soft pony-tail of dark hair, full mouth, sloe eyes. They had become lovers that night and for Reisch, running as fast as he could in managing Barnet's campaign, their coupling had been magical release. Ala provided him with the support he required throughout the election, often flying long distances and taking time out from the advertising agency to be with him. When his team were in the White House, Reisch made the decision and Ala moved in with him.

'Hallo, darling,' he said. He stroked the dark hair briefly, touched the corn-coloured skin. His lover was from the Philippines.

Drinks were prepared and he sucked eagerly at his glass. The eyes looked at him sympathetically.

'Was it a tough day?'

'Hell, not the job. I've been practising a long time for that. We just got some bad news.'

Reisch, as watertight as they came with the rest of the world, told Ala everything. It was his release from the pressures that would otherwise have destroyed him.

'What can be bad, the first day in the job?'

'Being told you have it on very temporary loan,' Reisch said savagely. 'We saw Tony Jacobs, and he says we'll lose.'

Reisch related the story, then put his glass down, the good taste of gin and martini in his mouth.

'I'm going to take a shower,' he said. 'There has to be a way to turn this around. We have to make Barnet a hero to the public, not the architect of their misfortune. I just don't see how to do it, is all.'

'I have supper prepared.'

The stinging hot water and the alcohol seeping into his veins both relaxed and stimulated Reisch. When he went into the bedroom, drying himself, he was aroused.

Ala was lying on the bed, naked except for a sheet. Reisch dropped his towel and slipped in alongside. They kissed.

'You understand me so well,' he said. 'You always know what I need.'

By the side of the bed were appliances, things made of rubber, and Reisch reached out. Ala stopped him with a gentle hand.

'We love each other. Do you trust me?'

'Yes,' Reisch said huskily.

'I trust you.'

Ala slithered on Reisch's stiffened body and with

delight he felt the nibbling and caresses of teeth and tongue. Then his partner rolled over with his face to the pillow and Reisch mounted him from the rear.

Auto-immune-deficiency syndrome had made a devastating difference to the lives of men like Reisch. Even back in the halcyon days when a dose of anything nasty could be cured by a trip to Doctor Fixit, Reisch had been far too discreet to get involved with the sexual mayhem of the steam-baths. However, in a city like Washington there was enormous opportunity for meeting like-minded people of the same sex. As Reisch had realized long ago, politics was the best profession there was if you were gay. To be successful you needed to be in politics all your waking hours, seven days a week. Even the bare minimum of time given to service a wife and family was time out from the game. If you were gay, you had none of those problems and could enjoy liaisons with people of similar persuasion and profession. Washington was packed with them, as Reisch knew. He knew also that like himself, they were terrified of AIDS. The prospect of getting killed making love was not an aphrodisiac. Hence the devices for 'safe sex'.

Lying back on the sheets with his lover, both smoking a satisfying cigarette, Reisch knew that led by Ala they had made a commitment. He was happy.

'You want to turn things around, for Barnet,' Ala said. 'Make him hero, not villain. That's easy.'

Reisch was instantly attentive and alert. He was an administrator *par excellence*, an organizer of people and programmes to a high degree. But he was not creative to the same extent – the qualities were not compatible. Ala's idea of a schedule was to arrive within half an hour, but creative he was. His advertising agency paid him well for his concepts and Reisch had found that by bouncing ideas off him he got results.

'Give.'

'Do what they all do when they're in trouble. Externalize the problem. Find a villain. What did that dictator down in Argentina – Galtieri – do when things were bad

56

for him? Invaded the Falkland Islands, took them away from the Brits. Now if he'd succeeded he'd have been a national hero, there in the palace till he died. Right after his troops went in, wasn't there national rejoicing?

'Now he got unlucky. He was up against Mrs Thatcher, and she sent *her* boys down and they took it away again. So Galtieri does not pass Go, does not collect two hundred bucks and goes to jail. But what about Mrs Thatcher? *She* was in political trouble at home when Galtieri invaded. But she won the war, and the result was she was winning elections for years afterwards. Defeating an external villain made her enormously popular at home. All Barnet has to do is the same, and he's got it made.'

'I don't think we'll find any foreign power obliging enough to invade us within the next six months,' Reisch said dryly.

'What do you mean? There's a nation out there doing it right now; they've been doing it for years.'

The young man turned to face Reisch in the half-light and the sheets rustled. 'The Japanese.'

He let the words hang in the air for a moment while Reisch absorbed them.

'They're tailor-made for the task. They attacked us before at Pearl Harbor. In a righteous war we defeated them, and used our advanced technology to bring the conflict to a close before even more lives were ʌost. Afterwards we helped them, restored their economy and fortunes. Now how have they repaid us? By invading us economically, by not allowing fair competition in their land while reaming us out here – putting good American firms and people out of business. People don't like it. If things are tough for Barnet, what he needs to do is paint the Japanese as the bad guys. Then *do* something about them. The people will love him.'

'God, yes ...' Reisch breathed. The concept was beautiful in its simplicity. 'MacGregor over at State was griping about them today ... I think you've got it.'

'Remember, darling, think visually. The right image is

57

worth ten thousand words.'

'Yeah. I think I can make a start on that.' Reisch swung his legs out of bed and picked up the telephone. 'Did you say the supper was ready? Let's eat, then we'll go out. I'll have something to show you. Hey, Franco? This is Ed Reisch. I need to ask a favour....'

THE METROPOLITAN CLUB, 1700 H STREET, WASHINGTON DC

Thrale attracted no attention in the club. The blue-bloods, movers and shakers whose second home it was had got used to the Japanese. The lawyers who haunted the place, English wing-tip shoes agleam, rather liked them, as did the old pols, for they brought yen in sack-fuls for the lawyers and pols to present them in a good light in the nation's capital.

In his old age Thrale looked indisputably Japanese. He thought of himself as American as mom's apple pie, but *his* mom had come from Osaka.

Lars Kuusinen had logged wood on the Kemijoki River, but his grandson was new power in Washington and the Met. adopted him as one of their own. Thrale they let in because they thought his pockets were stuffed with yen.

They intercepted each other in the lobby, and went up to the dining room on the fourth floor. There silver cutlery clinked on imported plate, the hum of the whole blotted out anything but the conversation of one's dinner-partner and people could do business.

'Good to see you again,' said Kuusinen, peering over his ivory menu.

Thrale smiled. 'Do I call you "sir" now? I've been boasting to the other guys on the technological espio-nage team that the National Security Advisor used to work for me.'

'I'd thought that you'd retired. What are you doing back out at the Bureau of Public Roads?'

Kuusinen and Thrale had worked together in the days

when the Central Intelligence Agency could only be identified by a sign out in the Virginia woods pointing to a mythical Bureau of Public Roads. The name had stuck.

Thrale shrugged slightly. 'You know I retired, Admiral Turner saw to that. I went to work on my own account. I could see that Japan was the coming nation, and since I'd spent about ten years there heavily involved with its post-war construction I decided to put my rather specialized knowledge to work. Eighteen months ago my wife Keiko and I decided we'd made enough to retire on and I sold the consultancy. Shortly afterwards Keiko died and retirement suddenly became very unattractive. I had a word with a few people in the Agency and, the circumstances of my enforcement retirement notwithstanding, they were good enough to make me a consultant with the Technology Transfer Assessment Center. When I had my own consultancy I'd mainly been dealing in high-tech, and after I left Japan in the fifties I'd had another decade and a half of dealing with the Soviets, so I had the right kind of background. I'm grateful. It gets me out of the house in the morning.'

'I'm sorry about your wife,' murmured Kuusinen.

'It was very sudden. An aneurism ...'

An elderly, soft-shoed steward in his starched beige jacket stood ready to take their instructions. Kuusinen opted for clams on the half-shell and broiled swordfish; Thrale for chicken broth and rare roast beef. They agreed on a bottle of Mondavi Chardonnay.

'You don't find the recent arms agreement has put you out of business?' Kuusinen asked.

'Can't say I do. Treaty or no treaty, those boys in the GRU and Directorate T seem to be earning their crust every day. What about you? Ain't the war over?' He grinned. 'Maybe you're redundant.'

'I'm in favour of arms limitation agreements,' said Kuusinen, who had been a professor of history after being in the CIA and before entering politics. 'But in the long view they're just hiccoughs. Aside from my tabby cat and other domestic beasts, how many animals die of

60

old age? Disease and starvation account for some, and practically all the rest are killed. And in the killing there is a fang or a tusk, a talon or claw. Weapons. The world of nature is simply an armed camp, the scene of weapons competitions that have gone on for millions, even billions of years, and since nature creates weapons in such profusion we humans are but talented late-comers, following precedent.

'I'm afraid I think there's *more* reason to have a National Security Advisor now, not less. We seem to be leaving one era and entering a new. We've had nearly five decades of peace – the Cold War was cold, and what we enjoyed was a *Pax Americana*, not unlike the *Pax Britannica* or the *Pax Romana*. That only happens when one power is sufficiently powerful to impose that peace. Nuclear weapons saw to it that, in effect, war became a luxury that only the weak and poor could afford, to quote one of my predecessors. But what of now? The bipolar world is a multi-power competition again. And what of the pace of technology? Mutual assured destruc-tion kept the peace. Nuclear weapons against nuclear weapons represent the symmetrical response of the threat-response patterns that drive the system of weapons proliferation, to slip into jargon for a moment. However, an adversary weapon can be met with a *counter-response*, some piece of military hardware specifically designed to oppose the threat – a surface-to-air missile against a bomber, for example. The pace of technological change seems now to be so fast that it is quite possible that someone will come up with a totally-effective counter-response to nuclear weaponry. Culture and politics nearly always lag behind military technol-ogy, usually with disastrous effects.'

Kuusinen speared a last clam. 'It will be a much more tricky time. While dealing with the Soviets was not simple, at least you only had one opponent. We must hope that our national servants are up to the task.'

'They seem to be doing a fair amount of flag-waving. I saw a clip on the tube of Barnet's staff coming to work,

61

and there wasn't a Toyota there. That guy Reisch was driving an old muscle-car, a Shelby Ford Mustang, wasn't it? The thing Steve McQueen drove in the cop movie.'

'I think Mr Reisch is doing his best to get his employer re-elected,' Kuusinen said dryly. 'Patriotism garners votes.'

The steward silently gathered their plates. Leaning back to let him do so, Thrale suppressed a yawn and rubbed a jumping muscle at the corner of his eye.

'Pardon me,' he said. 'I haven't been sleeping too well lately.'

'Your wife,' Kuusinen murmured sympathetically.

'Yeah. And the war. My dreams are filled with men long dead.'

The steward brought the entrée.

'So what can I do for you?' Thrale asked.

'The administration is worried about Japan – as worried as previous ones were about the threat from Russia. The threat from the Japanese being economic rather than military, of course. In considering what to do in this economic war in which it finds itself, it is hampered for a number of reasons – lack of institutional memory, faulty analysis, intelligence and so forth – all of which can be summed up by saying that we don't understand our opponents. From our Agency time together I remembered you as someone who had very clear vision about Japan and its people, and who understood the situation very well. Furthermore, the name of Komura Tadaji came up as some shadowy figure of power, and I also recalled that you and he knew each other.'

'Komura? Yes, we know each other a little. Our paths first crossed in April 1945. I saved his life. Not once, but twice, as a matter of fact.'

'April?' Kuusinen's brow wrinkled. 'The war was still on.'

'Right. After I escaped from the camp and got back to our side, I agitated to get back into the war. Don't, at this remove in time, ask me why. How you think when you're very young is a complete mystery when you're half a

62

century older. I was a fighter pilot, and a good one. I could knock the other guys down. And wasn't it a just war? Didn't the Nips start it? It was almost your duty as a good American to kill as many of them as you could. As the Marines used to say: "It is the duty of every Japanese soldier to die for his Emperor. It is your duty to see that he does so." Anyhow, come 1945 I had managed to get myself back into a P-38 Lightning and was knocking a few down again. By rights, the closest I should have got to Komura was dropping a bomb on him, because he wasn't a pilot, you know, he was a soldier. He was an intelligence officer, and a damn good one.'

'So what was he doing in an aircraft?'

'He knew the war was lost – he'd known for some while. But when the time came he was caught in the glue, he was as infected with *kokutai* as the most rabid nationalist, and he was ready to give his life for the Emperor. He volunteered in mid-March when he got back from Okinawa, and five weeks later he was ready. Couldn't navigate, barely land, but able to follow someone who could into sight of American carriers. At which point put the stick forward, yell *banzai* and maybe body-crash into the ship. Anyhow, come end of April he'd drunk his ceremonial water, tied his *hachimaki* round his head, composed his *haiku* – the usual stuff about life being like a flower, in bloom today, scattered tomorrow – and was lifting off from Kyushu on a one-way trip to Nimitz's carriers off Okinawa. Which is where *I* came in. I was leading a flight of six from the 49th Fighter Group. We bounced Komura's section of would-be kamikazes and shot them all down as they were lifting off. I took out Komura and his wingman.'

'I see how you saved his life once – he was about to go immolate himself off Okinawa – but the second time?'

'He managed to put the Zero down, breaking his legs in the process. What I *didn't* do was go back and finish him off.'

'You would have?'

'It was pretty common,' Thrale said frankly. 'Nobody was much interested in taking prisoners. Remember Halsey? "Kill Japs, kill Japs, kill more Japs." If the commander spoke that way you know his wishes got carried out. Or the Marine slogan: "Remember Pearl Harbor – keep 'em dying."'

'So why *didn't* you finish him off?'

'Airfield strikes were so damn' dangerous. Flak. You got in, and got out; you sure didn't go back for another crack. So Komura lived to fight another day.'

Thrale paused to chew rare roast beef.

'You saw him again, though, as I recall,' Kuusinen said.

'That's right. I collected some ground fire and tore the bird up some on landing, and *I* was the one in hospital. While I was in there, Truman dropped the bombs and the whole show was over. Except then we had the business of re-ordering the entire place, and I got a visit from a guy in the Counter-Intelligence Corps. There was one hell of a lot to do. The CIC were getting ready to dismantle the Japanese intelligence framework – top of the list being the *Tokko Ka*, the Thought Police, and the *Kempe Tai*, the Japanese Gestapo. They had to screen the military and political organizations like the Black Dragon Society and the Great Japan Political Society. On the horizon there was the new threat, as the old ultra-nationalist threat faded, of the Japanese Communists. And the problem was, they were real short of Japanese speakers. They got to hear about me, and one of them came to see me just about when I was getting ready to come out of hospital. I liked the guy; he had two degrees, spoke three languages and carried a sub-machine gun. He said if I was interested he could give me the entrance check right then. I could see that the Air Force wasn't going to be much fun now the shooting had stopped – there'd be a lot of retrenchment and bureaucratic bullshit, and I didn't know what I wanted to do anyway – and being some kind of secret agent seemed interesting work, so I said sure. He said he'd make it easy, seeing I was a pilot, and he asked how, if

64

he gave me a barometer outside the Empire State building, I would determine its height. So I said I'd go inside to the nearest phone, call up the architect and offer to send over a nice new barometer if he'd tell me how tall the place was!'

Kuusinen chuckled. 'You always were a sneaky bastard.'

'I had to be. I grew up in California during the depression, when being half-Japanese was not a popular thing to be. To keep my hide intact from the local white boys, I resorted to cunning. I became good at it, I graduated, it was why Admiral Turner had me near the top of his list when he arrived with his hatchet after Watergate.'

'I'm surprised you got into the military. Most of the American Japanese were interned, weren't they?'

'Right, but you're talking about *nisei*, and pure Japanese. My mother was Japanese, but my father was of English stock. My mother died when I was twelve, and by the time of Pearl Harbor most folk had forgotten that I had Japanese blood. When I went to the recruiter I told him my Ma had been Chinese, and since we were all on that Pearl Buck, FDR, "Chinese are the Good Guys" thing, that went down fine. Of course, by the time I was interviewed by the CIC everyone knew different, but by then it didn't matter. I was in the CIC for a long time. Early on, I got to see Komura, who was himself getting ready to come out of hospital.

'We were very polite to each other. When I left he gave me his *hachimaki*, his ceremonial white scarf he would have worn on his last mission. I still have it.'

'A generous gesture?'

'Not entirely. His gift of his *hachimaki* appeared to be the generous gift of one great warrior to another. It wasn't. It represented his deepest and most sincere desire that I, and America, should go off and kill ourselves.'

'Nice man,' commented Kuusinen. 'There are probably still plenty of ex-Zero pilots in Japan, just as there are still plenty left like you, old boys who once were young men in Lightning fighters. But the rest don't metamorphose into shadowy figures of great power within Japan.'

'Who thought in 1945 that Japan would be able to resurrect herself by her bootstraps and become the power she is today? Komura is interesting in his own right, but also because of what he represents. I never saw Komura the warrior again. Just as I was leaving his room, I turned back and said, "This War Last One Hundred Years?" – that was their slogan once they realized they were going to lose – and he bowed, palms flat on thighs, and said, "*Hai*, Ninety-six to go." Then I left, and went back to interrogating the Class "A" war criminals.'

Kuusinen looked at Thrale thoughtfully, ' "Ninety-six to go." Yesterday I attended a meeting at which the problem of Japan was discussed at the highest level. Secretary of State MacGregor was there. He would have been very interested to hear you say that.'

'I've been saying it for years. My mother was Japanese, my wife was Japanese, I worked in counter-intelligence in Japan for ten years. When I left there they put me to work with the Soviet Union, naturally. Who the hell was interested in Japan back then? Wasn't it just an overcrowded little island producing cheap and shoddy consumer goods? When I'd tell anyone in the agency that the Japanese were different – that they thought in Japanese but wrote in Chinese, went to work in Western clothes to buildings of concrete and steel, but came home to put on Japanese clothes in homes of wood and paper, were deeply traditional but were as quickly adaptable to the most radical change as a chameleon was to colour – they'd look vaguely interested, like I was describing the amusing habits of some South Sea islanders. When I would say that the Japanese had a desire for international pre-eminence – they called it *hakko ichiu* – even greater than the British with their empire, the USA or the Soviet Union – this said at the height of the Cold War – that this desire went back into the last century, making itself properly manifest in 1894 when they

66

attacked Korea, occupying Seoul – sinking the Chinese Navy in the process – underlining it by defeating *Russia* in 1904–5 – sinking *her* navy in the process – and collecting Korea shortly afterwards, a strange look would come over their faces. You know how it is when you meet someone who's got a thing about, say, bug-collecting or Etruscan piss-pots, you wonder if they aren't just a little dingy. In the early days I'd go on to point out how they took advantage of good diplomacy – in making an alliance with the British, who were the power of the day – to scoop up all the German-owned islands at the beginning of the First World War – you know, places like the Marshalls and Carolines, all the little places where the Marines had to die on the beaches to get them on their way to Japan thirty years later. In five months in 1942 the Japanese fought with such daring and dedication that they won stunning victories throughout the Pacific. We won the war because our might was ten times greater than theirs. But my point – which I stopped making after a while to guys fully occupied with facing up to the Russians at their most paranoid and perverse – was that the Japanese didn't accept the verdict of 1945. Komura's a good example of that. Just a couple of days after he gave me his *hachimaki* he managed to get in touch, nice as anything. Explained that he was going back into the family business, maybe he could help me, seeing as I was in intelligence? He knew a lot of people. He *was* helpful. He asked me if I could get him some films. He especially wanted *Gone With The Wind* – that and some rice and vegetables, I remember. Within a month he was on the way to being a millionaire, running a cinema in Kyoto, which was untouched by the war. The people were desperate for entertainment; they'd never seen colour films before. He used the money through a dummy company to finance entertainment for the men of influence. It was to pay dividends after 1950. He got in on the underground stock market. With it he was able to finance his operations on the "blue sky market", which were aimed at circumventing SCAP's anti-*zaibatsu* policies. Komura Bussan's subsidiaries were sold off to the public as part of the American plan to promote widespread public ownership of corporate Japan. Unknown to SCAP, however, Komura had enough money to lend to trusted workers to buy shares, which they then agreed to sell back to Komura Bussan at a later date. As fast as SCAP's liberals worked to dissolve the *zaibatsu*, men like Komura were rebuilding it all again. The liquidators would thrash their way through these webs of contracts, through sheets of accounts and loans, the nominee holdings and joint holdings, the family ties and *oyabun-kobun*, boss-follower relationships – all the things that held the business world together, much of which they didn't understand – and as fast as they managed to slice through the connections, the strands silently wove themselves together behind them. Komura managed to save his family's company between 1946 and 1950, at which point of course everything changed and Komura Bussan, like Japan itself, was launched on its upward course. Courtesy of the USA. But that's another story.'

Thrale cut himself some more beef and lathered it with horseradish sauce.

'As I say, that's why Komura is so interesting. He was a warrior, a militarist, fired with the spirit of *bushido*. He lost the war. He returned to his other roots – his *zaibatsu* roots – and went to work among the shattered ruins, still fired by the spirit of *bushido*. Komura Bussan goes back to 1621. Once again it is one of the modern *zaibatsu*. It has interests in banking, investments, industry and electronics. It's now the biggest company in the world, Mr Kuusinen, and the richest.'

Their steward came across the dining room with measured tread. 'A telephone call for you, Mr Kuusinen, sir. The White House.'

'Oh. Thank you,' Kuusinen said, rising. 'Will you excuse me?'

The tall Finn moved across the room and in the power-conscious town there was many an eye that noted

68

his progress. Thrale leaned back in his chair, putting his fork to the centre of his plate. The muscle at the corner of his eye was still jumping and he took another sip of the wine. Booze helped, he thought. Sometimes he made it all the way through the night. Sometimes he woke screaming and sober, straight out of the past.

Kuusinen came back, careful to be in no hurry. He sat down, but left his napkin on the table.

'I have to get back to the office,' he said. 'I'm sorry to leave you. Could you prepare a report for me? I want to know more about Komura – the man. Why is he so powerful within Japan? Our guys are having a lot of trouble coming to grips with what the Japanese are doing, and it's because they don't understand them. If they were able to understand how power is actually exercised there, they might have more luck.'

'I'd be happy to,' Thrale told him. 'It'll be like old times. A change from wondering which electronic widget of ours the Russians are planning to steal next.'

He shook hands with Kuusinen and watched the Finn as he went from the dining room, nodding and giving small waves of his hand to those he knew as he went. With him gone Thrale called for a coffee, which he drank before heading back through the shoals of lawyers, politicians and lobbyists to the front door, where he surrendered his badge to the porter and emerged on to 17th and H. Street. He went back to work.

Thrale's office was on the sixteenth floor: he could see Chinatown. He hung up his coat and loosened his waistcoat. On his grey government-issue metal desk was a photograph. Taken from above, it showed a number of men standing about a long fresh scar cut into somewhat bleak and featureless terrain.

'Curtis!' he called, and his assistant appeared from an adjoining office – a young, bespectacled product of UCLA who regarded his superior with a certain amount of amusement, sometimes tinged with respect. Thrale knew he looked upon him as something mysteriously still alive from a bygone age: a kind of dinosaur.

'Hi, sir,' he said cheerfully. 'How was the NSA?'

'We had a good lunch. Now, what's this?'

'You tell me, sir.'

Thrale was proud of his counter-intelligence origins; Curtis knew it, and never failed to tease him into acting as detective.

Thrale scrutinized it closely.

'Okay, it's an image from a KH-ll reconnaissance satellite, on a relatively low pass.'

'Right. Came in from Fort Belvoir while you were supping with the great and powerful.'

'It's an impact scar in the ground some three hundred yards long. Made by an airplane. The wreckage has been removed. The 'plane clearly hit the ground at a relatively shallow angle, and from the size of the scar in the earth it was not a very large aircraft. But from the impact and length of scar, indicating the speed at which it was travelling, it was probably a military aircraft. A fighter of some kind, but small, or a trainer.'

Curtis beamed. 'Very good. Want to take a guess?'

'Difficult to say. An F-16 is small, so are most trainers – T-38s, the British Hawk and so forth. A MiG-21 is small. Maybe it's a cheap mudfighter of some kind.'

'The boys at NPIC ran the image through their computers.'

Thrale nodded. The CRAYs at the National Photographic Interpretation Center over at M and First by the old Navy Yard were second to none in their crunching ability.

'They came up with a probability. Only a probability, not a certainty, but a possibility, because the aircraft they're thinking of has such distinctive contours. They say it *might* be the site of an F-117A crash.'

'The Stealth fighter? The Air Force has lost one?'

'No, sir,' Curtis said quietly. 'They say not.'

'They haven't? Hold on, then … I shouldn't have had that last glass of wine at lunch. If they say not, and the image is *here*, with us ... Where was this taken, Curtis?'

'That's it, sir. I knew you'd get it. We have this image by accident. They had some problems with the house-keeping of the satelite. While they were getting the electro-optical system of the bird back on line, they shot a series of images at random over the territory below. One of them was this one.'

Curtis Mayer tapped the glossy image with his finger.

'That's Fukhai. Just fifty miles the Chinese side of the Sino-Soviet border.'

THE WHITE HOUSE

Kuusinen would have walked back to work like Thrale, but the Secret Service didn't like it and Reisch had been urgent, so he took his blue government Lincoln. He might have done better to go on foot; the traffic was backed up along 17th Street and his driver took him round to the East Wing. He trekked along the Ground Floor Corridor past the tall oils of Jacqueline Onassis and Mrs Carter hanging by the Diplomatic Reception Room and on to the west end where he vanished into the working part of the mansion under the unbending gazes of Mrs Nixon and Mrs Ford.

He went straight to Ed Reisch's office, where the Chief of Staff worked in his annexe to the Oval Office. With Reisch was a man in his early thirties, small and neat, with alert, intelligent eyes that were darting about. He reminded Kuusinen of the small squirrels in the woods of his youth.

'Lief, this is Dr Fineberg. He's one of the doctors who performed the autopsy on the late President.'

Fineberg nervously nodded his head several times at the National Security Advisor. Now he looked like a squirrel that had mistakenly blundered into a clearing full of stoats and was belatedly considering the outcome of its action.

'Dr Fineberg says President Hawkins didn't die of a pulmonary embolism at all. He says he was murdered.'

MOSCOW STATE UNIVERSITY, LENIN HILLS

The hills looked down from the south-west over the sprawling expanse of Moscow. It was a commanding view from ground level, as the rebels had realized in 1917 when they had emplaced their guns there to lob explosive down upon the government troops below, but attained the authority of the bomber-pilot's cockpit when viewed from 150 metres up in the vast, multi-turreted skyscraper of the university. Otari stared out over the architectural wilderness of the city as Yuri sat at the console of the computer. At his feet figures slid like water-beetles over the surface of the artificial ski-jump, and across the Moskva River gigantic crumbling apartment blocks and bureaucratic fortresses marched along the yawning streets all the way to the Kremlin. Trees crouched like bonsai below. The red-and-chrome star-crowned spires, which for decades had competed with Soviet advertising for space on the roofs, were gone. 'The Ideas of Lenin Live and Conquer.' 'The Communist Party is the Glory of the Motherland.' For Otari, as for everyone else in the city, the anxious exhortations of the party leaders had not been words but simply part of the architecture. Now they were gone, the city seemed strange. Lenin's mausoleum was empty, there was a hole where the great GUM poster used to be, and embittered and crippled Afghan vets infested the Arbat, busking for kopeks.

The long room on the 19th floor housed the magnetic-

73

tape library, computers, mass-storage units, front-end interfaces and numerous accessories of Yuri's computer engineering department. The young professor sat on a black vinyl bench at the console of his IBM 360.

'We're ready,' he said, and the soldier came to perch beside him, huge hands resting like pink crabs on his knees.

'This is the other side of what we do in Furstenberg and Kirovograd,' Otari remarked. 'If there is a war, then our twelve-man groups – like my 35th of the 277th – will infiltrate the enemy homeland – for me, London in England or Beijing, China; I speak both languages – up to a month in advance. My task might be to take out the British prime minister, for example, or SACEUR, or any of the other prime figures who make up the command authority. We're talking about the old war-against-NATO scenario here, but our role is still valid. When we strike, it is speed that is of the essence, to win like lightning. To do so I would be given detailed information about my target – very detailed – how he lives, who he is with, where he goes, what he does. That part I have nothing to do with, so it's interesting to see how it's prepared.'

'I'm inside the files of *Upravleniye Delami's* 360 – they have one like this, I helped set it up, which gives me an advantage in hacking into it,' said Yuri. 'As the Administration of Affairs runs things for the *nachalstvo* in number 32, Aleksey Tolstoy Street, they should have much of what we want on record. I'm surprised they haven't got around to changing the name; he was only an old Soviet hack anyway.'

'Right. Well, let's begin with a list of all the occupants, and then the security staff. The building has a *dezhurnaya*?'

'These are *vlasti.* No duty-woman, round-the-clock security men.'

'Pull all the files.'

Yuri's long fingers danced over the keyboard and green and blue numbers and letters spread themselves over the black typing screen. The dot-matrix printer burped and began to chatter noisily as it dragged paper around its toothed wheels and sped to and fro, spraying information as it went.

'Architecture. Plans of the block.'

Neatly-drawn lines appeared – courtesy, it said, of L.B. Chernyshev – and were transferred to paper.

'Security of the block, and of the apartment. Locks, alarm systems.'

'Looks like they rely on the guards at the entrance. No electronic security, just stout locks.'

'There's only the one entrance. It's not unreasonable, it makes our lives easier. British Chubb locks, I see. Okay, I'll take a look through all that.'

Otari watched as Yuri disengaged from the Administration's computer.

'That's a clever piece of stuff,' he observed.

'With their CRAYs and IBM 3033s the Americans would consider it out of the technological ark,' Yuri said rather wistfully. 'But I'm fond of it.'

As he prepared to leave the computer his hands touched the controls in an unconscious caress.

'You really like it,' Otari said in surprise.

'It's alive,' Yuri said rather defensively. 'Some people keep pets. This is my work.'

'What do you mean, it's alive? It's a machine.'

'Life doesn't necessarily have to be based on hydrocarbons. It's entirely possible that other biologies could be based upon electronic reverberating circuits or even photonics. Life on earth started as inorganic crystals and could well be based on crystals again, exploiting a range of optical phenomena. I think that the biological world is already characterized by three great classes of life – animal, plant and machine.'

Yuri smiled up. 'But you mustn't get me started. I can talk about artificial intelligence all day.'

'I don't understand them,' said Otari. 'If I'm honest, I don't *like* them. They don't seem Russian to me.'

'To you and most of our countrymen,' Yuri agreed sadly. 'But they are the tool of the new age. The computer is a defining technology; it collects and focuses different ideas and concepts in a culture into a bright and piercing ray. Out there – out in the West – they are redefining man's role in relation to nature. It's a different world. It's why my father is right, we must slough off the centuries of autocratic rule – we need to rid ourselves of all vestiges of Communism itself. Communism as an ideology could never co-exist with another ideology that promises to lead to a different destination. One had to go.'

He looked curiously at Otari. 'How are you in the army managing? If the CPSU is dead, what ideology drives the soldiers? What will the political officers do, without a rationale?'

'I don't think most of us would agree with you completely. We want a revival in the economy, the same as you, but trying to become Western will not do for us. I wear Western clothes, but I am not Western, *I am a Russian*. The way ahead must be a Russian way. The Western countries are not as we are – they are gregarious, cosmopolitan and multi-ethnic. We are homogenous and self-directed – even if we adopt a market economy – as well as monolithic.'

'Only if we get rid of the non-Slavs,' Yuri said softly, 'which means no Soviet *Union*.'

'We can do without them, they were subject races at best. The Red Army remains what it always has been, which is the main repository of *Russian* national ideas. Have you not seen how army and church now march together? The priests and the soldiers together represent the essence of all that is Russian. We in the army have been blamed for much since the CPSU began to crumble, but we will overcome, the people will look up to us again – not because we are Communist but because we are *Russian*, and *Russia* will be great again, not the Soviet Union.'

He peered down at the keyboard of the IBM.

'Perhaps we should change the subject,' he suggested with a disarming smile. 'In England they say "don't discuss religion or politics", and I have done both. Why can't you just talk to this machine? Why do you have to type everything out?'

'Because by typing the commands, or information, the computer knows exactly what you are saying. If you could speak to it, it would have enormous trouble knowing where one word began and another ended, for example, or the difference between different words that sounded the same: like *their* house over *there* that *they're* moving into. Different national or regional accents would confuse it. But it'll come. The Japanese are investing most in the research because their own language is so ill-suited to the current method of presentation. When it happens it'll probably be a Japanese computer that talks, and that you can talk back to.'

Otari began folding up the sheets of paper and carefully tore across the base of the last one to free the pile from the printer.

'Let's go, then. I'm going to show you how to reason with something quite unintelligent and quite obstinate. A lock.'

THE OVAL OFFICE ANNEXE, THE WHITE HOUSE

Dr Vernon Fineberg wrung his hands nervously. Reisch was looking at him with the expression of the powerful throughout time when gazing upon the bearers of bad tidings, while Kuusinen was trying to absorb the idea that the head of the state he was sworn to protect might have been assassinated.

Reisch suddenly seemed aware of the effect they were having on the young doctor and immediately softened his manner. One of his skills, after all, was the massaging of people.

'Leif, Vernon here has come to see us off his own bat. It's not at all an easy thing for him to have done. Let me rephrase what I said. He was on the three-man team that conducted the autopsy on the late President. In charge was Professor Cameron, head of forensic medicine at Washington General Hospital. With him was his senior registrar, Dr Cale, and Dr Fineberg, who is the junior registrar. Now I'll let him take up the story.'

'Mr Kuusinen, sir,' Fineberg began nervously. 'You have to understand that Washington General is an old and prestigious establishment. It is axiomatic that our forensic department would conduct the autopsy should an incumbent President die. In charge is Professor James Cameron. Venerable, respected, loaded with honours, a pioneer of his time. *Of his time.* Professor Cameron is old. His mantle of authority is so magnificent that he has been allowed to stay on in office well past normal retirement age.

'Below the professor is Dr Cale, the senior registrar. Cale has just gone up a grade because his predecessor, Simon Bartlett, recently died. Cale is very happy about his promotion because he is now in line to succeed Professor Cameron when he retires next year. He is ambitious and cannot believe his luck. He *is* lucky because he is not that talented a pathologist – not like Simon Bartlett, who really was. I tell you these things not to acquaint you with the office politics of the department but because they have a real bearing on what I am to say.'

Fineberg's eyes flicked from one to the other of the two powerful men in the room – the squirrel assessing whether his words were sufficiently interesting to satisfy the appetites of the stoats.

'The considered opinion of Professor Cameron, delivered with all the weight of his half-century and more of practice in the art of forensic medicine, was that President Hawkins died of what is known as a pulmonary embolism. This is a condition caused by a clot of blood forming somewhere else in the body – usually in the legs – and then breaking loose from its site of formation and travelling through the bloodstream until it becomes lodged in an artery further along the cardio-vascular system. A clot of blood that has formed in a leg vein and then broken loose has a clear passage from its site of origin through the right side of the heart. It is after this point that it becomes lodged – in the pulmonary arteries, the arteries of the lungs. A large clot will come to rest at the division of the pulmonary trunk, and will lead to death within a few minutes. In the old days it was a cause of death among a small proportion of patients following surgery, but nowadays with the practice of getting patients up as soon as possible afterwards to avoid the blood stagnating in the legs it has become a rare cause of death. However, Professor Cameron has seen many people who have died of it in his time, and has even written a monograph on the subject.

'He reached his conclusion through a practised and

79

reasoned line of argument, successively looking for and eliminating heart attack, valve disease, myocarditis, grave stenosis – narrowing – of the aortic valve, ischaemic heart disease and so forth. He arrived at the verdict of pulmonary embolism. The circumstances were classic. The soon-to-be-dead man awakes with a feeling of impending doom. He has a desire to empty his bladder – in a hospital the classic sign is the patient calling for a bedpan shortly before losing consciousness and proceeding to death. Professor Cameron invoked the image of the late President awaking in such a state and hurrying to the bathroom. There he lost consciousness and fell to the floor, cracking his head on the basin on the way; there was a graze on his forehead. There he died within a few minutes. A little while later his wife awoke, aware that her husband was not with her, and found the body.

'Professor Cameron conducted the examination, assisted by Dr Cale. I performed my function, which was to take notes. Nevertheless, even from my relatively distant viewpoint I was unhappy about, and disagreed with, Professor Cameron's verdict.'

'In what way?' asked Kuusinen.

'Three specific points. Firstly, the clot itself. An ante-mortem clot – that is, one which has formed elsewhere and is itself the cause of death – is constituted differently from a post-mortem clot, one that has formed after death. Not only is it differently constituted under a microscope – the platelets and fibrin and white and red cells are all intermingled – but also it looks different to the naked eye, when it has a certain rough appearance – having taken on the characteristics of the walls of its parent vessel – whereas a post-mortem clot has a smoother appearance and under a microscope it can be seen that the red and white cells have coagulated in layers, white over red. Classically, this clot has a shining surface, and in the trade is known as a 'chicken fat' clot. This said, the difference can be difficult to spot, even for a trained eye.

80

'My second objection is that President Hawkins did not seem to be the right colour. I thought that he should have been properly cyanosed – purplish-blue colour – but he was not. He was not pink but equally he was not, to my eye, properly cyanosed.'

'What is the significance of that?' asked Reisch.

'It usually indicates some interference with the blood. Someone who has died of carbon-monoxide poisoning is pink, even after death. Someone who had been assassinated by cyanide is pink, even after death. President Hawkins was not properly cyanosed.'

There was silence for a few moments while Kuusinen and Reisch thought about it.

'Did you raise your objections?' Kuusinen asked.

'No, I kept my mouth shut and took notes. You have to realize that hospital medicine is most hierarchical. Professor Cameron is a full general and I am a lowly lieutenant. Furthermore, the professor has always been autocratic, and of late is worse. Had I brooked his authority in any way, he would have simply ordered me from the room.'

'What about this Dr Cale? Did he not see anything wrong?'

'The two things that matter about Dr Cale are that he is both ambitious and a poor doctor. The first quality means that rather than risk his prospects of promotion he would agree with Professor Cameron, whether the professor stipulated that a man had died of pulmonary thrombosis or an ingrowing toenail. The second means that he probably wouldn't recognize the difference between the two.'

'You said you had three objections?'

'Yes,' Fineberg said quietly. 'The third is that our late Senior Registrar, Simon Bartlett, died six months ago. Professor Cameron conducted the examination and found that, in similar circumstances to President Hawkins, Bartlett had died of pulmonary thrombosis.'

Fineberg looked from Reisch to Kuusinen and back again.

'When I was at college I always understood that three strikes and you were out.'

'Didn't Professor Cameron think it was strange?'

'No,' Fineberg said levelly. 'I reminded him about it afterwards, and it was clear to me that he had forgotten all about it.'

'*Forgotten*? How could he forget?'

'Professor Cameron is suffering from the onset of senility. A man is only as old as his arteries, and his are furred like old lead piping. A once-powerful intellect has been dimmed. Body and mind do not always agree to die together, unfortunately. Professor Cameron's judgements are now unsound. The fact is that he has done very little clinical work in this past year. He will retire very soon. It is just unfortunate that protocol and procedure demand that when a "great man"' – Fineberg raised both hands to mark the inverted commas in the air with his forefingers – 'like the President dies, then another "great man" of medicine must perform the autopsy.'

'If Professor Cameron doesn't do much work in the department, who does?' asked Kuusinen.

'I do, and Dr Cale.'

'You said Dr Cale wasn't a very good doctor?'

'Dr Cale is qualified for his job; it doesn't mean that he's really good at it. I'm sure there are qualified fighter pilots out there in their F-whatevers that the real Top Gun types don't think much of. I'm sure there are men in politics – senators or whatever – that people like yourselves consider poor operators. And to be fair, for the majority of the work we do, we do not require the deductive skills of Sherlock Holmes or Quincy to determine the cause of death. The dead of the crack wars die like any other casualties of war. The damage caused by a .357 semi-jacketed slug or a baseball bat is clearly evident to the naked eye. You don't require recourse to a microscope.'

'You have experience of more subtle forms of death, however?' Kuusinen probed gently. 'Like pulmonary thrombosis. Or various forms of poisoning.'

'I won the Hawthorne Scholarship and a Gold Medal in Clinical Pathology. I passed top of my class,' Fineberg said, the squirrel suddenly haughty, suddenly sure that in his own domain he was as strong as those about him in theirs.

Reisch picked up his telephone and dialled a short number.

'Charlie? Would you mind coming in here a minute?'

He turned back to Fineberg. 'Vernon, I'm going to have a quick word with Lief here about all this. I want you to know we greatly appreciate your courage in coming to see us. Charlie will take you to get some refreshment and then we'll get back with you. I don't have to tell you not to say anything about this – not to Charlie, not to anyone.'

When the door was closed again Reisch turned to Kuusinen.

'Right now, aside from the good doctor and the President, only you and I know anything of this. This place is traditionally leakier than a sieve in a rainstorm, so I intend to keep the bigot list that length and no longer.'

'No official inquiry?'

'No. For two reasons, both of which are to me valid. The first is that if Fineberg is correct and someone *did* assassinate President Hawkins, and that someone was the agent of a foreign power, then that was an act of war. The American public is possessed of a great reserve of moral outrage for such underhand acts. Consider the national mood created overnight by something like Pearl Harbor. Were the public to know about it, the pressure upon us to find out who did it and retaliate more than in kind would be overwhelming. Now. We *may* retaliate, and more than in kind, but only once we know who, how and why. Which leads me to the second, related objection – if we go public it will be the most certain way to ensure that we *never* find out who, how and why. Our vessel of inquiry will be assembled with enormous effort and time, the bureaucratic infighting to be included on board will ensure that the passenger list is vast, and that most of them will be swarming over the bridge attempting to wrest control from the Captain. The ship will be constantly diverted from its journey by summonses to visit obscure regions of Capitol Hill, and be under constant attack from above and below by hostile elements not included on board. It will founder, a rudderless and drifting hulk after months of futile existence; by which time we may have been forced into declaring war on someone anyway. I just hope the Colombian drug barons did it. No one will object to us bombing them out of existence. But do you agree?'

Kuusinen nodded. 'Our system of government was designed to be suitable for a minor and isolated power in times when the speed of international communication was measured in weeks, if not months. It is fundamentally flawed as a system for exercising power in the Number One nation at the end of the twentieth, technological century. Since the break-up of the New Deal coalition, there has been no clear majority party. The bureaucracies are baronial, and engage in tribal warfare. The PACs exert a malign influence that is not aided by the ticket-splitting habits of the electorate, nor the demands of Boss Tube and the constant campaign. At the highest level the mis-match between the skills required for campaigning and governing mean that the country is run by amateurs. It all makes reasoned policies difficult to formulate and consensus government almost impossible to achieve. There is a great howl of protest every time the deeds of someone like Oliver North surface, but few people point out that this kind of method of doing things – in a covert manner – has become almost the only way to get anything done. With regard to the late President and his postulated assassination, the most vital thing as always is to be able to distinguish between what is important and what is urgent. It is both urgent *and* important that we find out whether he was assassinated. It is important that we find out who did it, and why, and that we take the correct steps in response. It is not necessarily *urgent* that we do so. However, if the fact becomes public knowledge then domestic pressures will force the wrong choice of imperatives upon us. So yes, I agree with you.'

Kuusinen had once taught political science at Harvard. Reisch, who knew it, sometimes wished he would remember that he wasn't still there giving hour-long lectures to his students. Reisch knew the system was flawed but didn't care, since he operated in it well enough to get to the top anyway.

'Right. If we are to find out who did this, we don't want a committee. We want some underhand, smart, sneaky intelligence guy probably not unlike the SOBs who did the job. We go public – or even go further than our short bigot list – and everyone from the CIA down to the Coast Guard will be putting forth their own investigations. The water will become muddy as a spring creek. You're National Security Advisor. The President is minded to let you be our vicar on foreign policy. You're one of the few people to hold down your job in recent administrations who not only actually possesses the qualifications to do so but, in the little doctor's words, are *good*. If Hawkins was assassinated, we'll let you handle it.'

'Thank you. One of your predecessors – Jack Watson, who held your post for President Carter – was once asked how he saw the job in sports terms: was it like a quarterback, which is the glorified image, or was it more like a goalie, or a utility infielder? Or a cheerleader? He replied that the image that came most readily to his mind was that of javelin-catcher. Do I get the feeling that in offering me this task you are also electing me to that potential function?'

Reisch smiled. 'We're also offering you a lot of power.'

'Which carries its own responsibilities,' Kuusinen said wryly. 'Yes, I know. But first, we have to find out if President Hawkins *was* assassinated. Which means letting Dr Fineberg loose on his corpse without anyone knowing. And I see a problem with that. The late President is lying

85

in state in the National Cathedral and due to be buried in the morning.'

'Yeah, that's right,' agreed Reisch. 'We thought that you might be able to help with that, too.'

SOVETSKAYA PL., MOSCOW

The trees that edged the square leaned in on each other to form a leafy tunnel, under which *babushkas* sat on park benches like sacks of cabbages set up for sale. Vast in effigy, Prince Yury Dolgorukiy looked down from his horse on the lines of shining Chaikas and Volgas filling the rim of the square, set in the smartest part of the city he had founded so long ago. The limousines waited outside the best shops and restaurants for those able to use them. An enormous granite statue of Lenin grasping a proclamation glared over the trees at the prince. Once the most popular art form in Russia, he strode forward into a glorious new classless age.

Outside the Aragvi, Yuri waited with the other chauffeurs for their aristocratic customers to finish eating, drinking, shopping or making love. Along the south side of the square were the good shops like the Almaz with its jewellery, and Yantar' selling amber. Across the way was the Beriozka, where they might acquire a chandelier for the apartment or Italian crystal to drink their Scotch whisky from, and alongside the Druzhba bookshop where sometimes even ordinary people could pick up a copy of Turgenev or Tolstoy – provided they contributed to the official sales quotas and bought four or five books on Marxism-Leninism and the Komsomol to keep the classics company.

Two Chaikas away, a veteran polished away some motes that had settled on his car in the patient manner of chauffeurs all over the world. A brass-blonde woman appeared from the Aragvi restaurant with a man ten years her junior at the elbow of her fur-trimmed coat, and the driver slipped the cloth into the side pocket of the Chaika's door. She paused to speak with him and he beamed and nodded. Then she turned away with her escort, who was laden with a number of discreetly wrapped brown paper parcels, and the two came up to Yuri, standing by his own black limousine. He looked his partner in the eye without expression except of enquiry.

'Sir?' he asked.

'*Aleksey Tolstogo*,' Otari ordered. He turned to the bottle-blonde, opening the door for her to get in. 'Number ...'

'Thirty-two,' the woman said huskily. 'I'll point it out.'

They got in, and as Yuri closed the door on the tasselled curtains she settled back on the buttoned-leather seat, crossing her Kurt Geiger boots and drawing a packet of Camels from her Gucci handbag. She had the unmistakable air of someone who has had a good meal and was now ready for dessert.

As Yuri got in and carefully reversed out into the square, the aroma of Georgian champagne and spiced kebab was being overlain by tobacco smoke and a fresh blast of Yves St Laurent directed in the region of her impressive cleavage. Otari leaned back on the cushions with the natural grace of the very fit and, catching Yuri's eye in the mirror, grinned.

Yuri came out of the square, turning north on to Tverskaya, the old Gorky street for the *Bolschaya* ring-road. Stalinist icons erupted from the Moscow Soviet, a vast proletarian Artemis forging a new world with her blacksmith's hammer vanished behind the Number 1 trolleybus, and Yuri urged the Chaika into the traffic flowing up the wide, eight-lane boulevard. The woman's chauffeur, who had gone in front, turned off towards the Central Hotel to put in some time on his own account, working his Chaika as a taxi *na levo*.

The woman resting her beringed hand possessively on Otari's muscled thigh was Aleksei Borodin's upstairs neighbour. She was married to a busy Central Committee *aparatchik* whose job took him all over the USSR. The

88

union had been an arrangement from the beginning: he had the talent and ambition, she – the daughter of second-generation bureaucratic aristocracy – the connections. The couple remained childless, and as they had grown older both had realized that the qualities they had found most attractive in the other were precisely those which were receding with time. Both were *coureurs de jeunesse* – he on his trips around the empire, she at home while he did so.

All of this had become Yuri and Otari's knowledge courtesy of one of the security men at Number 32 *Aleksey Tolstogo*, a one-legged *Spetsnaz* veteran of the Afghan war. It had been easy for Otari to make friends with him, to share reminiscences and a couple of bottles of *Stolichnaya*, especially since the good and famous brand had been reserved for hard-currency export, while those who had fought for the motherland and left a limb behind in the process were left to drink a brand as crude as its name, which was simply Vodka.

Sergeant Vashurkin had been delighted to grouse with a fellow veteran; the two had been 'cousin' within minutes. Trained in the extraction of information, Otari had a run-down of all the block's tenants – like all servants, Vashurkin liked to gossip about foibles of his employers – before targeting Mrs Glotov. An obscene thrusting of the old machine-gunner's forearm indicated her main excitement in life, and Yuri's penetration of her bank account had told them where she did her shopping and where she ate. The knowledge that she lunched at the Aragvi – famed for its Georgian cuisine – with other similarly bored wives hinted that perhaps she had found what folk-lore claimed to be true. The Georgians, who glittered like daggers against the stolidity of the Russians, were reputed to be great Romeos. Wham-bam was what summed up the average Russian male, whereas the Georgians – it was rumoured – had heard of foreplay.

Given this knowledge, it was easy for Otari to become a *Spetsnaz* war hero – which he was – and the son of a wealthy Georgian, which given the fact that he had a chauffeur-driven limousine of his own meant that his 'father' was probably one of the millionaires of the counter-economy. It was also fortunate, he pointed out, that as a widely-travelled man he had had the opportunity to become as skilled in the arts of love as he was in those of death.

Yuri pulled off *Aleksey Tolstogo* on to the landscaped grounds of the tall yellow-brick building with its balconies and picture-windows. He parked outside and opened the door for the two to get out.

'Bring the parcels,' Otari said casually. Yuri took them from the trunk of the car and followed behind as Mrs Glotov wafted them past the security and into the lift. It was not the same man who had been on duty when Yuri had arrived to fit the hard card to Borodin's word-processor, and he was in any case in flat fedora and raincoat, laden with parcels, unrecognizable as the professor at Moscow State.

The block was as he remembered – carpeted floors, smooth Western lift (no rickety, folding wooden doors), discreet lighting, a hallway that did not reek of the ubiquitous carbolic. They came out of the lift on the ninth and Mrs Glotov reached in her bag for the keys to her smart mahogany door. Putting the parcels down in the hallway, Yuri had a glimpse of Finnish elegance which would have had the average member of the proletariat calling for a Communist revolution.

'Wait for me outside,' said Otari.

'Yes, sir.'

The door closed behind them. Yuri thumbed the button for the lift, but when it came he rode down only one flight. In a block for such people they did not have a *dezhurnaya* on every floor, and the immaculate corridor was deserted. He reached in his pocket for the tools with which he had so assiduously practised under Otari's supervision, and began to invade the locks that sealed the apartment of Aleksandr Borodin.

It went just as it had that morning, when he had

turned a Chubb unknown to him in under two minutes, and with a great sense of relief he slipped inside.

He had forgotten how strange the room was. The shell was Moscow privilege, the interior Celestial Empire of the Sun. Ancient Qing ink-slabs, wells and brushes existed side by side with Sony VCR and television. A wooden chair with a tiger-skin rug thrown over it – the seat of a Yansheng Duke – was in front of the word-processor. On the walls hung ancient symbols of power – flags and weapons, gongs, parasols, fans, drums, calligraphy.

Such interest in a foreign culture would have had most citizens of the USSR on a one-way trip to a psychiatric hospital to have their thoughts re-ordered, but in the case of Aleksandr Borodin the exotic possessions were the gift of a grateful employer. Borodin *knew*. About China. He was never wrong.

The room gave Yuri the creeps.

Seating himself in front of the Amstrad, he was in familiar territory and in command. The defences of the computer, and its files, had been designed and put in place by him. As he switched on and the little machine began its normal routine of electronic grunts as it came awake, he heard the first of similar noises coming faintly through the ceiling. He smiled, and then began to plunder the machine as thoroughly as Otari was plundering Mrs Glotov, he hoped – or perhaps, as she was him.

There was something out of place on the desk, a photograph in an old, tarnished frame. A group of people, strangely dressed. They looked worn, and poor, standing outside a hovel in the snow. Jews, perhaps? Zeks?

The glass was not polished; it was smeared. Aleksandr Borodin kissed an old photograph of some strange people from the past and had done so many times.

Yuri put the photograph down. The sooner he was out of the strange room the better.

In under half an hour he was riding the lift back down to the lobby. He gave a wave to the security man and loped casually outside, half a quire of tractor-feed paper folded in the inside pocket of his raincoat. He settled in the seat of the Chaika and felt the sweat begin to dry.

From *Aleksey Tolstogo* a tiny, elderly but lovingly-cared-for Zaporozhets-968 puttered up the drive. Its driver saw the shiny Chaika and veered over to pull up alongside. He was a big man in his security guard's uniform, almost filling the interior of the little mini-car. He stared intently at Yuri, who broke out afresh.

When the guard held up four imperative fingers, Yuri's fine brain went completely blank under the strain.

Irritated at his lack of co-operation the guard wound down a creaking window. Mashina Vremeny blared forth, a thumping bass making the flimsy radio add its own howl to the rock music.

'Gas, yah?' he grunted hoarsely, holding up the four fingers again. 'Forty litres okay?'

Understanding flooded over Yuri, and he nodded weakly. Starting the Chaika, he followed the guard down into the underground car park where the man swiftly and efficiently siphoned off forty litres of state fuel from the Chaika, paying Yuri a rouble and twenty kopecks – about a third the pump price – before pouring it into his own tank.

'I missed my regular supplier this week,' he confided. 'So I was really pleased to see you.'

Driving back up with his riches in his pocket, Yuri's hands were trembling. He parked once again outside the block and a little while later Otari came nonchalantly out. He settled himself casually in the back and Yuri started the engine and drove out to the street.

'Get what you wanted?' murmured Otari.

'Yes. Did *you* get what you wanted?'

'I left her ecstatic but heartbroken,' the soldier said extravagantly. 'A woman who had tasted Heaven, but did not know where she would turn to take it again. I told her I had to return to Georgia.'

Yuri smiled, noticing Otari's forehead was still beaded with sweat. 'It was that tough,' he said.

Otari gleefully smacked a fist like a ham into his palm. 'A veritable assault course,' he agreed, grinning.

They drove straight out to Mazurov's dacha. It was a fine spring afternoon and they found the old man seated on his folding aluminium chair on the second-floor balcony of the wooden home, overlooking the view down the river. Gypsy music was playing, filling the woods of spruce and birch. Further along the balcony Nikolai Serov sat anxiously, immune to the music.

When he saw the folds of paper in Yuri's hand Mazurov called for beers, and both men accepted eagerly: Yuri to calm his nerves and Otari because like most élite Special Forces soldiers he did not drink when he worked and made up for it when he did not. While they sank their first mouthfuls, he looked over the file Yuri had extracted from Borodin's computer.

'Is that it?' Yuri asked anxiously.

'That is it,' Mazurov said with deep satisfaction.

Serov rubbed his son's head with pride.

'Well done, darling. Well done, both of you.'

'Now we are safe,' said Mazurov. 'I will have you make copies on the machine inside. How did you find it?'

'Simple. I had it pull a list of all files that mentioned Yanov – either because he featured in them or was on the "bigot list" of those who could read them. See, that's the first page. Then all I had to do was call up the files and check the information out. Since you had given me a rough date it was quick.'

Mazurov looked down the list. 'Borodin has done much work for Yanov. It makes sense. Now that the Americans are no longer our most dedicated foes, it is the Chinese and Japanese he must worry about.'

Mazurov looked at the entries on the sheet. There was something about them that fascinated him, and Yuri leaned forward.

'This ...' Mazurov's long forefinger pointed to it. 'This one here, eighteen months ago, it is a list of those who may read the file?'

'That's the bigot list. It's obviously top-secret. Five

93

men only – the General Secretary, Defence Minister Dely-usin, General Ogarkov, head of the KGB, Kobulov, and the Orthodox Patriarch, Zossima. That's odd ... why him?'

'*Zarnitsa* ...' murmured Serov, leaning over Mazurov's shoulder. 'It is code-named "Lightning".'

Mazurov raised his eyes from the page to look at the two younger men.

'I must see this file,' he said quietly. 'I have to ask you to do what you did today once more.'

Otari grinned and Yuri felt a fresh stab of fear. *Fucking Spetsnaz* soldiers, only interested in drinking, fucking and killing people, he thought bitterly.

'Tomorrow,' he said.

The two left and Serov turned to Mazurov, his fear re-lit within him. 'What is the significance of the bigot list? And Yuri is right, why the Orthodox Patriarch?'

'The man from the Zagorsk Monastery? Were you not with me at the parade in Leningrad? Did you miss its significance?'

'Commemorating Nevsky's victory? Of course.'

'Priests and soldiers acting together to honour an important event in the formation of the *Russian* state. The Orthodox Church has revived, it is a power in the land once more. Army and Church represent the very essence of *Russianness* in this new un-Communist world.'

He folded the sheets of paper and put them in his jacket pocket. 'The bigot list? It's a Stavka,' he said. 'And a Stavka is only for one thing.'

When Serov had left to spend a troubled night in his apartment on the Lenin Hills, the old man sat lost in thought as the shadows lengthened and the great river flowed beneath him unseen. Wars to end all wars left altered those they did not kill. Like all his countrymen, Mazurov had been changed by the Great Patriotic War against the fascist Hitlerites. Actions which ever since had been viewed by Westerners as profoundly hostile and aggressive became understandable as wholly defensive when seen from within the ring of steel that surrounded the USSR. Afghanistan had not been an imperial venture gone wrong, but a shoring up of frontier defences.

Mazurov recalled the utter chaos which had followed the German invasion of 1941. Soldiers and civilians alike had died like insects, and in Moscow it had seemed for months that the levers of power were connected to no more than thin air. The prospect of being hanged or worse in the near future had concentrated the minds of those responsible wonderfully. Stalin and those top officials he had spared from his massacres moved swiftly to abandon the unwieldy and inefficient system of command of the pre-war years. Just as he sent out priests to the troops to invoke the help of someone who was not supposed to exist, namely God, so did he abandon party-political claptrap in his running of the war. The cumbersome Main Military Council was ditched, and replaced by a General Headquarters, known as the *Stavka Verkhovnogo Glavnokomandovaniya*, or Stavka. Mazurov was well-familiar with this history as he – as first secretary of the Komsomol in the Ukraine – had had to report to it, and also deal with the Stavka representatives sent out to carry the strategic commands of the Stavka into the field and to coordinate the activities of Fronts during strategic operations. It was his administrative skills which brought him to the attention of such as Chief Stavka Representative Zhukov, and ensured his ultimate rise to the highest posts in the land.

The wartime Stavka was a small command team of 6–7 men under the leadership of Stalin. Its value in providing strong centralized and united military-political leadership in time of crisis was such that it remained the model for the Soviet High Command in war.

Mazurov was cold and stiff when his housekeeper finally insisted that he come inside, flapping about him like a worried hen. Shooing him in the direction of a hot bath and warm clothes, she shot anxious glances at her employer. The old boy looked ill, she thought, and wondered what news the young men could have brought to him.

Wars to end all wars left altered those they did not kill. For Mazurov the idea of another great conflict was unthinkable. The might of the Soviet military machine and the sacrifices made by the people to make it possible were to ensure that there would be no war, since no one would dream of attacking so well-defended a nation.

Aleksandr Borodin had prepared a report for the eyes of only five men: President Yanov, a man as determined as Peter the Great to keep his nation in the front rank of powers; his defence minister Delyusin, who thought likewise; Kobulov, head of the KGB; Ogarkov, their best general; and Zossima, the Orthodox Patriarch, head of the Church. The keepers of the Russian soul.

Mazurov recognized the five-man group for what it was. It was a command team, a Stavka. Such a thing did not exist in peacetime. His country was planning war.

THE CATHEDRAL CHURCH OF ST PETER AND ST PAUL, MOUNT SAINT ALBAN

A small group stood at the great crossing where the north and south transepts met the nave, reduced to their proper proportions by the magnificence of the building which had been constructed, as were all the great Gothic cathedrals, for the glory of the Lord. In the morning it would be filled with the majestic thunder of the organ and the singing of choirs and 3,000 honoured visitors from all over the globe. Light would blaze through more than 200 stained-glass windows and a dead chieftain would be awarded the rituals due him. It was in the tradition. President McKinley had been present at the dedication of the Cross of Peace there in 1898; nine years later Theodore Roosevelt came when they laid the cornerstone; President Wilson slept there, and the funeral service for Eisenhower was held there. On the morrow, it would be the turn of President Hawkins.

For now the windows were dark. The cathedral was quiet and the rows of carefully-placed chairs empty, awaiting the occupants who slept in their hotels throughout the capital. Mae Hawkins stood in her widow's black, and the canon in his red cassock before her. At her back was Kuusinen, with a priest at his side. The canon's eyes kept flicking to the glorious vestments of the small, dark priest, wondering to what neo-Popish idolatrous sect he belonged. As a professional, he recognized that they were the vestments of the Eucharist,

97

directly descended and developed from the Lord's own dress in the upper room, but *what* descent and development! He wore a fabulous silver chasuble, beneath which peeped shimmering white surplice, amyss and alb. He also wore a stole, and over the chasuble a gloriously-patterned cope. In his hand he held a decent black bag, but one that the canon gloomily suspected held a thurible. The canon was an Episcopalian, and no Methodist or Presbyterian, but he had rarely seen anything so high-church. Behind this glorious creature, Reisch and two secret servicemen in their dark suits faded into insignificance.

'This is most irregular,' he murmured, in the complaining tones of a man who has lost an argument. 'They will be closing the coffin soon, and moving it.'

As Governor's wife and as First Lady, Mae Hawkins had been famed for her ability to get things done. Silver-haired, a grandmother, her soft Southern voice could cut the unwary off at the knees.

'Reverend,' she said, 'Dr Kuusinen was one of my late husband's most devoted servants. He wishes to pay his last respects to him here in the house of God in the company of his own priest, and it is my wish that he do so. In times long ago, if a man of my husband's rank died then he might easily have had to accompany him on his journey – as indeed, as priest or druid, so might you. Please show us to my husband's place of rest.'

The coffin, seven feet of ornate ash and brass that was to require six of the nation's strongest soldiers, sailors and airmen to carry it, lay not yet in the interior of the cathedral but below in the Bethlehem Chapel at crypt level. The canon led them through the cathedral. Ribbed vaulting soared, columns dwarfed them, arch and clerestory looked down upon them.

'We shall wait outside,' Mae Hawkins said, and it would be so. Ed Reisch provided a chair, then saw to the closing of the door behind Kuusinen and the priest. The two secret-servicemen took up their positions. From inside the chapel came the clear sound of a trained voice, beginning the sung Mass. Soon their nostrils began to tickle faintly as incense seeped through into the outside air. The disapproval of the canon deepened into gloom.

Inside the chapel, Kuusinen and Dr Vernon Fineberg stood over the open coffin. Gothic, dark, awe-inspiring, the brooding chapel reminded Kuusinen of the transience and insignificance of mere mortals, as it was supposed to do. On the altar the compact Sony tapedeck provided a true rendering of the service for the dead. Beside it was Fineberg's black case, a jar of incense and the spoon. In Kuusinen's hand was the thurible, the incense burning in its boat, and as he gently swung it, its pungent fumes escaped through the elaborate scrollwork of its sides.

'The robes worked real well,' he murmured. 'No one even looked at your face.'

'I'm a Jew,' muttered Fineberg, pulling on a green gown over the front of his fabulous vestments. 'I'm sure this is sacrilegious.'

'I'm a senior member of the administration,' said Kuusinen very quietly. 'I'm not supposed to be doing this either.'

With quick, practised movements Fineberg pulled on his thin rubber gloves. He had spread a green towel over the front of the dead man's trousers to form a small table. On it he had placed a small roll of his tools and two plastic containers.

Under the embalmer's art, the late President had acquired the solidity and dignity of a statue. Fineberg's deft fingers undoing the buttons of his fine shirt exposed the reality beneath.

Professor Cameron had made the pathologist's traditional incision from throat to pubis. Fineberg swiftly cut his sutures and opened up the dead President like a gutted fish. Inside were all his organs, removed for examination and replaced. Kuusinen ground his teeth with dislike as Fineberg searched expertly through the offal. It took him no more than a minute or two to find

99

what he wanted and place some lumps of what to Kussinen was only unidentifiable debris into his plastic containers. With that done, he took a large curved needle and heavy suture and made the body whole once more.

He took off his gown and gloves, rolled up his tools, collected sample boxes and towel and placed all in his bag. Then he buttoned the shirt back up. The air was thick with incense. Kuusinen's agitation had presented itself physically in the swinging of the thurible. It was as well; it masked any smell of decomposition.

On the tape, the priest sang the last prayer for the soul of the dead man. Kuusinen softly switched off the machine as his voice faded away, and placed it inside the bag for Fineberg, taking care to secure the locks.

'Well done,' he said sincerely. He paused as he passed by the President. 'I'm sorry,' he said, and bowed his head.

They went out, smoke still trailing faintly from the thurible in Fineberg's hand. Outside, the limousines were waiting.

Kuusinen paused again within the nave. In the morning it would blaze with light. High above him – lit by the moon, and so made even more terrible than it was in the daytime – was LeCompte's Noah window. Seeing him look, the canon paused as well.

'LeCompte depicts the evil on earth before the flood as dreadful violence,' he explained.

Kuusinen could see the two soldiers in the act of slaughtering each other and the deep pile of skulls.

'It is not the usual depiction of the story of Noah,' the canon went on, 'but it tells us what the story of Noah is all about – God's anger and hostility towards Man's violence.'

Outside, Kuusinen paused while Mae Hawkins climbed into her limousine. 'Thank you,' he said quietly. 'Thank you very much.'

'I granted your request on one condition,' the widow said grimly and precisely. The glass connecting window between her and the driver was closed, and their words were private. 'If my husband was assassinated. You have agreed.'

'Yes.'

'So say it.'

'Those responsible.'

'Yes.'

'I'll have them killed.'

'Do it,' she ordered. The limousine hissed away and Kuusinen stood looking back at the cathedral. In the evening, sunlight flooded through the magnificent and huge rose window in the west front, filling the interior with shafts of colour from its prisms, bringing both glory to the day and, as it dimmed, the promise of the dawn.

The great window was dark. Kuusinen climbed into his car, overcome with foreboding.

SEE CUBED EYE —C^{3}I
– INTELLIGENCE

ZHUKOVKA-2

At almost the same time the following day, the Chaika came rolling up the path through the pines and birches to park beneath the balcony overlooking the river. This time, three of them got out: Yuri and Otari, and his cousin Alexei Mazurov, on leave from his tank unit. He was in the élite Rogachev Guards.

Mazurov rose from his chair on the balcony and embraced the young Lieutenant, bending over the little tank man. To keep their tanks small, the Soviets selected crews for size.

'Have you been helping these rascals?' he asked.

'I am not selfish,' Otari said. 'I am happy to share my pleasures.'

'I have some leave. It's good to be in Moscow again. We're out in a hell-hole in Yakutia,' said Alexei.

'Enjoy yourself. Come to see me again before you return.' He turned to Yuri.

'You succeeded?' he murmured. Yuri nodded triumphantly and passed him a folded wad of tractor-feed paper.

'You did not read it?'

'I did as you asked.'

'It is best that way. What you do not know cannot hurt you. And Alexei?' He glanced down to the end of the balcony, where the other two were leaning over the rail.

'He is a soldier, like Otari. He does not ask questions. He has had fun with Otari and the woman. Galina is making some food for us tonight, I think afterwards they would like to celebrate.'

'You are good boys, all of you. Otari! Go to Rai, take some bottles of the Polish vodka.'

105

With them gone, Mazurov called for tea in his tall glass and, opening the file, became the sixth man privy to the secrets of Operation Lightning – *Zarnitsa*.

Given its contents, the document had a very dry title: *The Future of Sino-Soviet Relations.*

Borodin began with a brief review of the state of play within the Soviet Union. He noted that *uskoreniye, perestroika* and *glasnost* had both raised expectations of butter and jeans and aroused nationalisms within the bosoms of the non-Russian peoples of the empire. Historically the USSR had weighted the military slice of the cake heavily against both citizens' expectations and economic growth. Borodin noted soberly that Great Britain had once been the undisputed industrial leader of the world, but within 100 years a 1 per cent lag in productivity growth had turned her into one other country foreigners could not find on the map.

The point of all the reforms begun by Gorbachev, and continued by Yanov – the point of the Peace Treaty itself – was in order to make the system work better, in order for the Soviet Union to survive as a great power in the turbulent and high-technology century ahead. Which meant economic growth ... and efficiency. The days of achieving high growth rates simply by throwing vast amounts of personnel, raw materials and energy into the cauldron were long gone. High technology meant sophistication.

Borodin turned to the People's Republic of China. She was, he admitted, the poorest of all the major powers and the least well-placed strategically. Yet he found that her leadership had evolved a grand strategy that was far more coherent, forward-looking and long-term than anything to be found in Washington, Tokyo, Western Europe ... or Moscow.

The reforms and self-improvement embodied in Deng Xiaoping's 'four modernizations' had not only been most successful, but had survived under his successor, his fellow veteran of the Long March, Chiang Shikai. Borodin compared the transformation in the PRC's fortunes with

106

Colbert's France, the early stages of Frederick the Great's reign, or Japan in the post-Meiji Restoration decades. Borodin pointed to the massacre in Tiananmen Square as evidence that the Chinese leadership would not allow their *étatiste* determination to achieve the national goals as quickly and smoothly as possible to be deflected by anything. Even to the extent of partnership with her ancient enemy, Japan. The Japanese were providing the Chinese with the management methods, techniques and training she needed to propel herself to greatness – the very things that the Soviet Union so desperately needed herself.

China was a rare thing: a nation with a great past *and* a great future.

Maybe.

'Ever since the collaboration between the Japanese and Chinese manifested itself three years ago, it has worried me,' wrote Borodin. 'Historically they are enemies, and have little in common. The Japanese may have borrowed their method of writing from China so many years ago, but took none of her culture. The Japanese live in time, the Chinese in space. And they loathe each other.

'So why collaborate? Strange bedfellows can be found in history, of course. Did we not ourselves collaborate secretly with our enemy, Germany, after the War of 1914–18? Did we not, indeed, sign a non-aggression pact with Adolf Hitler himself? It was, after all, greatly in our interests to do so, and our leader Josef Stalin did everything in his power to make it work. What were the benefits to both sides? Hitler received from Stalin the materials he needed for his war economy – a million tons of grain, a million tons of oil and aircraft fuel, iron ore, manganese and cotton. And we in turn received the things we needed – aero-engines, naval blueprints, torpedoes, mines, munitions.

'When I saw that the Japanese with their powerful and advanced industrial economy were collaborating with the Chinese, I asked myself whether or not history might

107

be repeating itself. After all, what has been the attitude of the Orient towards we Slavs, throughout history?

'The attitude of the Chinese – whether that of Genghis Khan, Mao Zedong or Chiang Shikai – has remained one of immutable hostility to we Russians. When they have been able to do so they have made us suffer, as we did under the yoke of the Tatar-Mongols. Were they able to today, their billion-plus population would surge over their borders into the USSR. Recall the words of Mao Zedong in 1963: "About a hundred years ago, the area to the east of Baikal became Soviet territory, and since then Vladivostok, Khabarovsk, Kamchatka and other areas have been Soviet territory. We have not yet presented our account for this list." Perhaps that time is due. The Japanese are no better. They too hate us. They too lay claim to parts of the Soviet Union. For a start, they want Sakhalin and the Kurile islands from Hokkaido to the Kamchatka peninsula. They would like much more as well, would they not? Things that we have which they must buy from the outside world – titanium, aluminium, beryllium and other strategic minerals. Our oil reserves are second only to the Persian Gulf. We produce more natural gas than the USA.'

It was getting cold and Mazurov got stiffly from his chair on the balcony and went inside. He made his way to the library where Rai had a fire burning in the grate. Putting the file down for a moment he stood in front of his books, musing anxiously. He recognized the power of Borodin's words. He was a Russian. Mazurov knew that his people were religious; whether served by ikons and priests, or the Lenin Rooms and political officers which had temporarily replaced them – servants of a religion that had little to do with morals but a great deal to do with hatred of foreigners. Especially a certain type. Although privilege separated him from the mass of the people they – and Yanov and Delyusin, Ogarkov and Kobulov too – all shared a common fear of the Orient, whether perceived as the 'yellow menace' or the 'red dragon'.

108

Mazurov reached up to his bookshelf and took down Andrei Bely's *St Petersburg*. Set on the eve of the Revolution of 1905, when far away the Japanese were slaughtering Russian soldiers in Manchuria and massacring her fleet at Tsuchima, the 'Orient' stood for the forces of destruction. Mazurov fingered the pages, lost in thought. Bely's fear of the Orient was so pathological that he would hide if he saw a slant-eyed face approaching on the street. Mazurov was educated, like the author, yet knew he shared his fears and prejudices along with all his countrymen. He sat down in his armchair by the fire to finish Borodin's report.

'Ever since the collaboration – secret, but known to us – between the Japanese and the Chinese came to my attention, I have had meetings with our intelligence officers concerning the subject, and have been kept abreast of all events by them. Last month we had the breakthrough we so desperately needed with the defection of Chen Tsung-jen. Tsung-jen, who served on the staff of General Secretary Chiang Shikai, brought with him a copy of a document simply called Plan 19. I was the first person to read Plan 19 (your copy is on the red tab in this package). Once I had done so I was able to interrogate Tsung-jen. I found that he was an opportunist who feared for his own fall should his boss Chiang Shikai be deposed, as he considered likely. Seeking to assure his future, and aware that *something* was afoot between the Japanese and his own government, he managed – as much by good fortune as skill – to obtain a copy of this document. Once I was sure that he had little else to offer, and aware of the crucial importance of the PRC leadership being unaware of our possession and knowledge of Plan 19, I requested the services of Department Eight of the KGB's Directorate S. With consummate skill, for which they should be commended, they arranged the return of the corpse of the traitor Tsung-jen to a remote part of a wood outside Beijing where he was known to walk. There, suitably rotten, it was found two weeks later. We may be reassured that the PRC leadership has no knowledge of our possession of Plan 19, and may make our own plans concerning them in safety.

Plan 19 itself is nearly sixty pages long, and I recommend that you read it once you have finished this action paper. In order that you may make a judgement on the justification for our own Plan *Zarnitsa* (blue tab in the package) I will summarize its intent here:

PLAN 19

The author, or authors, of Plan 19 note that:

1) Today, at this moment, the USSR possesses the most formidable military force in the world, almost certainly capable of taking on and defeating the forces of any other nation or conglomeration – e.g. NATO – in a conventional war of short duration.

2) Within five years this will change. Firstly because the Soviet military establishment is an institution under siege, challenged from every quarter including from within. The influence of the military in Soviet society is declining; the prestige formerly attached to military service has dropped dramatically, as the growing incidence of public harassment of its officers illustrates (2 officers murdered on the streets in 1988, 368 last year). This, combined with the growing force of nationalism, makes it certain that the USSR will move to some form of non-conscript, professional army. This army, being expensive, will of necessity be much smaller than its present size, possibly as small as one million men. *Quite certainly, for the Soviet military, things will get worse before they get better.*

The second factor influencing the effectiveness of the Soviet military is the imminent arrival of radically new conventional weaponry, based on the 'emerging technology' of the West, which it is believed – allied to new tactics – promises to make the kind of massive conventional forces of the USSR today completely obsolete. It was the fear that NATO would deploy such weapons, as much as anything else, which forced the Soviet leadership to the historic 'Peace Treaty' with President Hawkins and the USA.

3) In five years' time, the picture within the USSR threatens to be analogous to the period 1913–14, in terms of large numbers of national actors whose behaviour is not entirely predictable and who are operating within a rather fluid and essentially unreliable security system. In five years' time, the USSR will not be the formidable military force she is today.

4) With regard to the People's Republic of China, of the 'Four Modernizations' it was the military which was kept back on a short rein, well behind agriculture, industry and science. This has proved prescient. With regard to the re-armament of a nation, it is the *timing* that is important. For example, had Great Britain rearmed a year or two earlier than she did prior to the 1939–45 conflict with Germany, she would have faced the Luftwaffe with obsolete fighters and lost the Battle of Britain and the war. As it was, she possessed the most modern eight-gun fighters – Hurricane and Spitfire – and survived.

If the People's Republic of China were now to rearm with the radically new conventional weaponry, based upon the 'emerging technology' of the West, she could inflict total defeat upon the enfeebled and obsolete forces that the Soviet Union could field in five years' time.

Lenin makes it clear that victory in war goes to the side with the stronger economy.

Marx points out that: 'War puts nations to the test. Just as mummies crumble to dust the moment they are exposed to air, so war pronounces the sentence of death on those social institutions which have become ossified.'

The People's Republic of China has secretly allied with Japan, whose economy is much stronger than that of the Soviet Union. Japan is to secretly rearm China with the very latest weaponry; the process will be complete in five years' time. Under Plan 19 the Chinese military will fall upon the Soviet Union like a thunderbolt. No institu-

111

tions are as ossified as those of the USSR. In a lightning war, the Soviet Union will suffer total defeat, and cease to exist except as a prize to be divided up between the two victors. Japan and the PRC will have rid themselves of the Russian threat once and for all, and will have access to all the raw materials they require in their rise to global supremacy.

OPERATION ZARNITSA

In five years' time, all things being equal, the People's Republic of China and her ally Japan will be able to inflict devastating defeat upon us. That is in five years' time. We will have paid the price for massive security today by weakness tomorrow.

Massive security today. Our military forces are second to none in the world. The certainty exists – **today** – of being able to inflict a devastating defeat upon the Chinese in a lightning war. All factors are in our favour. The modernization of the People's Liberation Army (which includes the navy and air force) has hardly begun. They have none of the new weaponry they will have in five years' time. They have very little in terms of weaponry to compare with our forces. The leadership is in a state of flux, with Chiang Shikai in the middle of a power struggle with younger 'democratic' elements. He seems likely to lose the services of his most competent colleagues, including the nation's best general Zhao Teh and Prime Minister Hua Ziyang. There are still those within the PRC who cleave to the Soviet model of Communism, and once we have defeated the Chinese in battle we will have ample opportunity to install a government there whose efforts will not threaten us, but assist our own.

I leave the members of this *Stavka Verkhovnogo Glavnokomandovaniya* to decide – on the evidence of General Ogarkov's own report detailing the military planning for Operation *Zarnitsa* – the feasibility of such a lightning war. I myself have no doubts as to its efficacy

112

and guaranteed success.

I make only the following point. What we are being offered is a 'window of opportunity'. It will pass very quickly. We do not have five years. Take this window of opportunity, and the future of our great nation is assured. Pass aside, and our destiny is to become slaves of the descendants of Genghis Khan. The description of our fate in such an event I will leave to the words of that man himself, the Great and bloody Khan, when he came into our country so long ago:

Happiness lies in conquering one's enemies, in driving them in front of oneself, in taking their property, in savouring their despair, in outraging their wives and daughters.

Mazurov put the report down on his table and stood up. As he did so, the door opened and Nikolai Serov came in.

'My son told me that he had obtained the document you asked for, Operation *Zarnitsa*. I must see it.'

'Are you sure?' Mazurov asked softly. 'There are things it is better not to know.'

'I am the leader of our party,' Serov said seriously. 'One day I shall be leader of our country.'

'Very well,' said Mazurov. 'Here it is. It is, I fear, a document from the box of Pandora.'

Mazurov handed it to Serov, who quickly went to a chair to read it. As a young man Mazurov had paced about like a tiger when worried, until the solution to his problem came to him. Now the habit returned, and at a pace commensurate with his age he began walking up and down his library.

'*Zarnitsa*,' he muttered, and waved an angry finger as though Borodin was himself sitting in the chair he had vacated. 'Have you not heard them say: *Tishe yedesh, dalshe budesh* – You will go much further if you start slowly? The fascist Hitlerites believed in *Zarnitsa*, only they called it *blitzkrieg*. The meaning was the same, lightning war.'

113

Mazurov resumed his slow journey to and fro along the polished pinewood floor. The report was too attractive, it offered the solution to too many problems. Inherent within the concept of a great victory over the Chinese was the effect *within* the Soviet empire, the refurbishing of nationalism, the restoration of the position of the military, the buttressing of the power of the KGB, the consolidation of Yanov's power, the dampening of independent action by the subject races, the provision of goods, the maintenance of the massive subsidies of rent, food and power to the people by the exploitation of the Chinese.

Mazurov came out of his reverie to find Serov staring at him, the red folder closed on his lap.

'It is a proposal,' he said, 'not a battle plan. There is no reason to suppose that we are really going to do it.'

'On the contrary. There is *every* reason to suppose we are going to do it. Take the membership of the Stavka. Ogarkov is our best general: modern in thought, seasoned by combat in Afghanistan, brought in to do the fighting. His man Suvurov in the GRU is obtaining the world's best computer to handle his battle management, if your son is to be believed. Defence Minister Delyusin, the Red Army's own man, is known to be appalled at the decline in the status of the armed forces in the eyes of the citizens of the Soviet Union. Kobulov, head of the KGB, is a worried man since the signing of the Peace Treaty with the USA. The KGB is actually the impelling drive of the Communist Party whose servant it appears to be. Its overpowering concern is with 'enemies', which may be internal, external or both. The security of the state and the crushing of threats to it, whether real or imagined, has become the overriding task of the KGB. Take away the threat from the USA and where does it leave the KGB? By its very nature, it must find a new threat to be countered. I speak as one who knows: I was head of that organization, once. Borodin has presented it with the reason it must have for its existence. And then the tsar, President Yanov. Yanov is as obsessed with the

114

Great Power status of Russia as was Peter the Great, whom he so admires. Furthermore, he is politically indebted to the military and to the KGB, without whose support he cannot survive. And simply at an ordinary political level Yanov is old enough to remember that one of the principal reasons for Krushchev's fall from ultimate power was his inability to control the conflict with China. He will have found the prospect of undying fame as the man who defeated the ancient enemy and renewed the status of Russia as one of the world's Great Powers irresistible. Patriarch Zossima, who has emerged from Zagorsk like a modern-day Cardinal Richelieu. No, we may take it for certain that Operation *Zarnitsa*, Plan Lightning, has been under way for some time. You do not undertake great enterprises such as this at a moment's notice. Vast preparations are in hand. Note the very name – Lightning. It is meant to be very, very swift, to avoid the twin dangers that haunt the modern general and his political masters – the threat of the attack bogging down and being contained by the defence, perpetuating the war in a bloody stalemate like the war of 1914–18, or the more recent Iran-Iraq conflict. And the second danger, the threat of nuclear war. *Zarnitsa* is clearly meant to take out the limited nuclear weaponry of the PRC right at the beginning of the conflict. If the plan is to succeed, then Ogarkov must achieve complete strategic surprise. The opposing forces must be unprepared to face his attack. To this end Yanov, Delyusin and Kobulov will be expending enormous amounts of political and diplomatic capital to put him into this very advantageous – but essential – position. His fighting troops will be fired by the righteousness of their cause by their comrades-in-arms, the priests.'

The old man paused.

'That is another overriding reason why the Stavka will have accepted the plan. Do not forget, all its members are patriots. They are like you and me, they love *rodina*, our motherland.'

At the mention of the word, both men felt a stirring of

115

love. It was a reflex that never failed.

'For the sake of *rodina*, to save the motherland, they would do anything, as would we.'

'So will *Zarnitsa* work?'

'I do not think either *Zarnitsa* or Plan 19 will work in the manner intended by their advocates, if either are actually put into effect. None of these wonderful military plans – exotic, glittering with shiny nuts and bolts, polished levers and machined cogs and wheels – ever works as it is supposed to. Did the Schlieffen Plan bring lightning victory to the Germany of Kaiser Wilhelm? It did not. It brought four long years of war that brought down three great empires and beggared a fourth. Did Operation Barbarossa bring victory to the Reich that followed that of the ruined Kaiser? It did not; it brought about the total defeat and dismemberment of the nation that put it into effect.'

Mazurov went over to one of his shelves, and ran his finger along the books until he came to one he wanted. It was a slim volume, leather-bound, old. He riffled the pages until he found the right one.

'Here it is,' he muttered. 'And by one of them. Yes:

Crows and hawks peck for human guts.
Carry them in their beaks and hang them on the
    branches of withered trees.
Captains and soldiers are smeared on the bushes
    and grass;
The General schemed in vain.
Know therefore that the sword is a cursed thing
Which the wise man uses only if he must.'

Mazurov looked up from the volume.

'Li Po knew that twelve hundred years ago!' he said angrily. 'Wars are much easier to start than to stop.'

'But in three and a half years' time – this was written eighteen months ago – under Plan 19 we shall be defeated.'

116

'*Will we*? Will there be a war then? We have had five years. Technological surprise is transitory, we will have had five years to prepare our defences. Another three and a half years to tell the world *about* their Plan 19. Five years to organize our diplomacy so as to isolate our opponents. It can be done, we have done it in the past. It is not Plan 19 that worries me, it is Operation *Zarnitsa*. It is too attractive, offers the solution to too many problems. And the authors of Plan 19 are right about one thing. They quote Marx: "War puts nations to the test. Just as mummies crumble to dust the moment they are exposed to air, so war pronounces its sentence of death on those social institutions which have become ossified." It is *our* institutions which have become ossified. We need to cast them aside, to put new life – democratic life – into our system. *Zarnitsa* is war. We do not need it. Even if we win, we will lose. No, we must derail this thing they are planning. And to do that, we must discredit the man who planned it. We must destroy Borodin.'

'How?'

'On the airplane, Nikolai Kaganovich compared me with an explorer, a man who left caches of food behind on his journey so that should he come that way again in need he would survive by calling upon them. He was right, in a way. When I wielded power, where I could, I spared. It was not always possible. But where it was, I did. I have, still, favours owed.'

Mazurov pushed the volume back into its place and hurried as quickly as he could to the end of the long room, with Serov following him. A small door led off to a storage room where Mazurov had put some of the many mementoes of his long life. Here were albums of family photographs, boxes of old letters, various bureaucratic awards.

There were desks, cabinets and chests of drawers. Mazurov went to a desk and began opening its drawers, muttering to himself when he could not find what he wanted. He found photographs, yellow with age, and recognized himself in the tall, powerful young man in

117

partisan clothing with a PPSh sub-machine gun slung over his back.

'Ah,' he said with satisfaction. 'We are close.'

At the back of the drawer he found a tiny parcel, a fragment of ancient cloth wrapped around something that was heavy for its size. As he carefully undid it, a smooth brass and lead bullet slid into his hand. He took it out into the light and peered at it. Scratched upon its tip in the form of a signature was a set of initials.

'L.T.K.' breathed Mazurov. He held the bullet fast in his hand. 'Yes, this is the way.'

He went over to the telephone that rested on the table and, lifting the receiver, began to dial.

THE STATE DEPARTMENT, 35TH STREET, WASHINGTON DC

The video cassette, combined with other features of high technology embodied in a squat, three-quarter-ton cylinder that hung 22,175 miles over Borneo, had revolutionized the work of the intelligence analyst. Working late in his office, Cy Rogers received one by messenger. They came in at any time of day as part of the vast intelligence output of the National Security Agency, a small city of its own nestled in the woods between the capital and Baltimore.

Rogers' room was not hung with Chinese trappings to the same extent as that of Aleksandr Borodin, but his tools were the same – filing-cabinets, specialist journals, SIGINT, SITREPs, CRITICOMs, an IBM word-processor, a VCR and television. Rogers was a senior sinologist for the State Department. When he received the cassette he peered at its covering note, debated whether to leave it to the morning, found as always that his curiosity got the better of him and decided to see what was within.

Noting that it was an update to a previous cassette, he ran through his collection – cassettes that took up two shelves of his office – until he found its predecessor. He inserted it into the VCR and his television lit up with the familiar revolutionary symbols of the People's Republic of China State Television.

The picture on the screen showed a rather bleak platform set up outside one of Beijing's 1950s government buildings, built in the Soviet 'wedding-cake' architecture of the time. Sitting stony-faced on chairs arranged in two rows were a score of Chinese men. These were, the

119

commentator explained in Beijing Mandarin, the senior party officials of the day. This might have come as a surprise to the unwary viewer, who might not have recognized a number of them had it not been for the presence of much of the old party aristocracy in grubby singlets and underpants standing in an unhappy group to one side. One by one, they came forward to speak into a microphone and confess their faults. Former Prime Minister Hua Ziyang accepted responsibility for the 'racketeering' and 'profiteering' his liberalization had caused. Former General Zhao Teh took the blame for his troops' 'oppression' of the people. When they had finished they shuffled off to a waiting cattle-truck, to the delight of the partisan crowd.

Once they had gone a very old, leathery man sitting in the middle of the front row of chairs got up, and made a short speech in which he blamed those now rattling down one of Beijing's broad highways in a strong aura of *fen*, or pig ordure, for the fact that matters had slipped 'out of control'. As he announced 'consolidation' and 'progress towards democracy' faint, grim smiles appeared on the faces of some of the newer and younger members of the party aristocracy. The picture cut to a line of clanking wagons containing evidence that a group of heroic miners had met their coal-production target two months ahead of schedule, and Rogers ejected the cassette.

To the educated viewer, such as Rogers, or Borodin, the meaning behind the little charade was clear. Those who had nailed their colours to the mast of student democracy had made an unexpected comeback following the post-Tiananmen Square repression. Chairman and Party Secretary General Chiang Shifai – old, leathery, a survivor of the Long March and a survivor ever since – had saved his own position by throwing his compadres to the student wolves. The use of a cattle-truck and the staged public 'confessions' suggested that the new party leaders were former Red Guards who had not enjoyed their experience of being 'tempered' by life on a commune once 'the decade' was up, but who nevertheless recognized the recipe as one redolent with potential for humiliating the once-mighty. The old guard was out and the new where taking over their nice homes in Beijing's Zhong Nan Hai, were the new emperors of China lived next door to the palace of the old.

Rogers' new cassette proved this to be the case. A glaring television light illuminated a man sleeping on a plaited mat laid on the wooden boards that went to make up a bed in a commune. This was, the young commentator announced gleefully, former general and oppressor of the people Zhao Teh, now a member of one of the production teams at the Yangzhou commune. Rogers noticed with some wry amusement and not a little admiration that in circumstances of extreme humiliation Zhao Teh managed to preserve the maximum amount of face by not even acknowledging the existence of the intruding camera with its team and gloating commentator. As if this was how he always awoke, he rose, donned the sandals that rested on the beaten-earth floor below his simple bed and headed out of the wattle-and-mud hut. It was dark, with dawn on the horizon. Waiting outside in similar simple garb was another man. In case any viewer had forgotten who it was, the commentator reminded them joyfully that it was former premier Hua Ziyang, once notorious for his love of fine clothes, food, women and Western cars. Wearing identical stony expressions, the two men marched across the earth courtyard as the inescapable public loudspeakers began to blare out the day's diet of announcements, exhortations and hearty popular music. They halted beside a long, dirty tanker that had been parked on the edge of what the television lights indicated might be a vast field. Taking a bucket, Zhao Teh opened a big tap and began to collect what flowed out. The commentator hurriedly backed away. The tanker contained night-soil from the nearby town, which sold it to the commune. Working in silence, using buckets and hoes, Zhao Teh and Hua Ziyang began to spread it over the field.

TECHNOLOGY TRANSFER
ASSESSMENT CENTER, WASHINGTON

'Okay,' said Thrale. 'So the Air Force say they haven't lost any of their F-117As anywhere.'

'They categorically deny it,' Curtis agreed.

'Not that it means anything,' Thrale grunted, leaning back in his grey, government-issue swivel chair. 'The Air Force denied having anything resembling a Lockheed U-2 right up to the moment when the Soviets put bent parts of one, and Gary Powers, on show in Moscow. The F-117A is technically a Stealth strike fighter, but it has long been pointed out that its radar-transparent characteristics render it highly suitable for a variety of covert activities. The Sino-Soviet border is still one of the most strategically crucial zones in the world. At a guess, the F-117A that crashed did so while investigating and mapping the radar defences. Presumably, since it crashed near Fukhai on the Chinese side of the border, it was testing the Chinese defensive system. Fukhai's in the Lenzhan Military District. It's bleak as hell up there, just the great mines and the railway – and the defences; one of the logical routes for the Soviets to drive through into the PRC in case of war. Which leads us to the question: whose F-117A was it? If it belonged to the Air Force, then it is nothing particularly to do with you and me, and we may or may not wait to see Chiang Shikai and his crowd produce parts of it and its pilot in Beijing, depending on how much they wish to embarrass the USA. If it wasn't an Air Force jet, then we must assume it was Soviet.'

'Could they do that? Make an exact replica?'

'They've been doing it for years. When a few B-29 Flying Fortresses went off course and had to land in the USSR at the end of the Second World War, the Soviets sent the crews back but not the aircraft. Shortly afterwards they fielded *their* strategic bomber, the Tupolev TU-4. Just about identical to the B-29, down to size and location of rivets. The Russians are better at copying things than the Japanese. Boeing made a V/STOL aircraft called the YC-14 back in 1976.'

'V/STOL?'

'Sorry, Curtis. I forget you haven't been with us long. Vertical stroke short take-off and landing. Just fourteen months later the Soviets produced the An-72 *Coaler*. Now that was so identical to the YC-14 that if you'd painted it in Air Force colours no one would have known the difference. And they didn't do it through telepathy. Espionage. Technological espionage by Directorate T of the KGB and the army's own GRU ... who are the boys and girls we are here to counter.'

Thrale peered inside his mug. 'Get us some more coffee, son. This has gone cold.'

While Mayer rinsed the mug at the sink and filled it with more of the thick black coffee from the hot jug, Thrale continued.

'I remember when a few years back some fishermen off Rhode Island fouled their nets and hauled out a Soviet eavesdropping buoy. When we got a look inside it we found that within its little electronic brain it had a computer chip labelled "series 133". Only thing was, it looked awful like an *American* chip – a Texas Instruments Series 5400. Circuit-for-circuit, pin-for-pin, in fact. So much so that when we plugged a TI chip in the buoy it worked perfectly. It's the same with everything else they have, from trucks to transport the men to missiles to shoot down aircraft. The Soviet military is extremely effective anyway. Don't you believe that crap about them being crude and unimaginative; they can do a lot themselves, and when they need something from the West they get it. They don't make deodorant or Levi's jeans, but show them something designed to blow folk apart and it's rolling off a production line in Petropavlovsk before you can say *yohannye tyuremsshiki!*'

Curtis grinned. 'What's that mean?'

'An obscene Russian expression. Not for your young ears.'

'In our house the worst thing you could say was anything that contradicted what my mom said. We didn't get around to obscenity. But the Peace Treaty's signed. Why would the Soviets need stealth fighters?'

'Well, if the crash site at Fukhai *was* made by a F-117A, and if it *was* a Soviet copy, it would have been built before the treaty was signed. But even if it wasn't, the Soviets would do their damnedest to get hold of the portfolio of Stealth techniques simply to get parity. The F-117A was probably the star of the 'Desert Storm' war against Iraq. It was responsible for the surgical elimination of the Iraqi C^2 on 17 January. They poked out the Iraqi radar eyes, deafened their microwave communication links and gagged their primary control sites. The coalition forces had a loss rate of 0.35/1000 sorties, and it was in large measure thanks to the F-117As. If you can't *see* a Stealthy fighter or bomber with radar, then what that means is that it can come and bomb and shoot you for as long as it has fuel to put in its tanks and bombs and shells to load up with. It's a case of a jump in technology providing a war-winning edge, like the breech-loading needle gun did for the Prussians against the Austrian Minie muzzle-loader in 1866, or the Krupp crucible steel artillery against French bronze muzzle-loaders four years later. But an advantage in technology is always temporary, for the other side always works frantically to get parity. Which is probably what the Soviets have done here.'

Mayer went back into his office and Thrale picked up the KH-11's image of the crash-site near Fukhai. The scar was long, and shallow; it could almost have been a fair attempt at an emergency night-time landing. Two Chinese men were in the picture: one in a dark parka squatted at the side of the torn earth; the other in white overalls stood where the aircraft had come to rest, looking pensively back along the line of accident. There was something about the scene that nagged at Thrale, and he was still looking at it as Mayer emerged from his office to take his lunch break.

'How are we going to know if the Air Force have been telling us stories, or if the Soviets have got inside the Stealth programme and have a plant somewhere turning out F-117As like doughnuts?'

'Even the Soviets aren't going to turn out Stealth aircraft in great numbers, or in any hurry. The technology is so involved and so intricate – and *expensive* – that it's very labour-intensive. And very skilled labour at that, of the kind that's always in short supply. But how are we going to know if the Air Force has been economical with the truth, as can be their wont? Well, this is the CIA, son. In our time we have penetrated foreign countries with small armies. I'm sure we can get just one person to that crash-site. Parts of the damaged aircraft will still be there – little pieces not worth taking away. If we can get hold of a few and look at them, we'll know. Whether it's ours ... or theirs.'

THE CABINET ROOM,
THE WHITE HOUSE

Kuusinen rose with the others of the National Security Council as Tom Barnet swept from the room – tall, broad-shouldered, and with a confidence that belied the news his pollster and film-maker must have been giving him: that as far as the folk in Atlanta and St Louis were concerned, the jury was still out. He noticed that Ed Reisch, who normally stayed as close to the big boss as a sheepdog to its charge, was staying behind. As the room emptied, the Chief of Staff made his way to him.

'Lief,' Reisch murmured, 'I thought I'd give you the good news as soon as I heard.'

He looked around. All the players had left the room, and there were only the two white-coated stewards standing ready to clear the big mahogany table of its jugs, glasses, notepads and freshly-sharpened pencils.

'Would you mind waiting outside for a moment?' he asked politely. When the two had gone into the corridor he turned back to the Security Advisor.

'The results came through,' he said, his voice still low. 'Seems the little doctor got rather over-excited. President Hawkins died of pulmonary thrombosis, just as the old professor said.'

'He did?'

'Yeah. It's a hell of a relief.'

'Right,' said Kuusinen.

'Now we can get on with running the country.'

'Right.'

'Must go,' said Reisch. 'When I first arrived in this

town I found the secret of being successful – make more appointments than you can keep! I'll see you.'

Kuusinen watched the Chief of Staff hurry from the room and smiled cynically. 'You ever hear the expression: "Work smarter, not harder"?' he murmured.

The National Security Advisor was an anomaly in the political town – he *didn't* make more appointments than he could keep. It was a result of his training as an academic, when time for research was more precious than gold. He glanced at his watch, saw he had an hour and twenty minutes free and took his car to Washington General Hospital.

Forensic Medicine had a small wing of its own, up on the eighth. Filing cabinets had overflowed out into its corridors. Kuusinen edged past the receptionist's small kiosk, which was empty. A small VDU hummed on her desk and from behind a half-closed door came the splash of water and chink of china. A sign saying 'Professor of Forensic Medicine' jutted out from the wall above his head, and he quietly opened the door. To his left was a room littered with esoteric items of medical equipment on white tables, and ahead lay a small but well-fitted office. Behind a desk sat Vernon Fineberg, going through a sheaf of papers.

'Hi,' said Kuusinen. 'Don't get up, I was just passing.'

In his youth Kuusinen had been a poker player; it was how he financed his first degree.

'Congratulations, Professor.'

'Thank you,' said Fineberg.

'Cameron got put out to grass?'

'Right.'

'Case?'

'He's getting a job in Idaho. Said he didn't want to work under me.'

'You see, being friends with the mighty has its advantages.'

Fineberg had the grace to look embarrassed.

'I never expected anything like this.'

'Pity the results weren't more positive.'

127

'Depends what you mean. The President didn't die of a pulmonary embolism. The problem is that he's in his grave, and short of digging him up again I can't find out what *did* kill him.'

'The blood tests?'

'Normal. Quite a high level of nicotine.'

'Nicotine?'

'Right. He was a heavy smoker, wasn't he? You could see that by the state of his lungs – and his heart, come to that.'

'That's right,' Kuusinen agreed. 'Cheroots, that's what he liked.'

'High tar.'

Kuusinen got up from the low chair, his long limbs unfolding like a Go-bot toy.

'Just thought I'd drop by to say thanks,' he said, 'and congratulations.'

He turned at the door.

'It's okay?' Fineberg asked, waving a hand around his former professor's room, suddenly anxious. 'It's okay, isn't it?'

'If Mr Reisch set it up, then it's okay,' said Kuusinen.

He went down to his car, and as the driver took him back to the White House, thumbed the buttons on his car-phone.

'Extension 432,' he said. 'K.K.? Lief Kuusinen. You doing anything this evening?'

128

THE WARDMAN TOWER, 4200, CONNECTICUT AVENUE

Thrale was standing by the window, looking down at the lights of the cars crawling through Rock Creek Park, when Kuusinen emerged from his study.

'Sorry to have kept you,' he said. 'My wife's staying over with our younger daughter. She's just had a little girl and Aileen's helping her and Joe for a few days.'

'That's nice. My boy's married with one of each, over in Arizona. I don't get to see them as much as I should. I got the file on Komura made up for you. I have it here.'

'That's great, I appreciate you doing it so fast. I'll have you go over it for me in a minute ...' Kuusinen folded himself down on a sofa and fiddled with a glass ornament for a moment. 'That wasn't why I asked you over though ...'

He put the fossil down and looked up at Thrale, who had parked himself opposite.

'I have a problem, which I would like to ask you to solve. If you will. Or want to. Going back into the field is something you can grow out of ...'

'I always felt I got retired early,' Thrale said helpfully. 'I don't mind getting out; looking for Soviets stealing widgets doesn't take all my time.'

'I can set you up, give you whatever clout you need in terms of opening doors, but at the end of the day it'll be as it always was.'

'"If you succeed you'll get no thanks, and if you fail we never heard of you." That right?'

'That's it.'

'That's the way I worked all the time I was in the game. If you are offering me some kind of project suited to my expertise, I'll take it. I was always a covert political action specialist. In my time I can claim – among professionals, because the outside world only hears about the time we screw up – to have been successful at removing serious dangers to the security of my country. I have always thought that those who advocate banning covert political action crazy. The men at the top have to be results-oriented, don't they? They have to approach things from the problem end. They may decide it's too risky to do anything about the problem. But if the problem is so serious that something *has* to be done about it, then they have to consider the complete range of solutions available. It may be possible to solve the problem by easier and less risky means. We are the strongest nation in the world, but our strength is that of a lion or an elephant. What happens if we are attacked by bugs, or a swarm of bees? Then, because there is *no other way*, then you turn to the people like me. So if in your mind there is a problem that has no other solution, please tell me about it. I am free to help. The only thing I had booked was to go piss on Admiral Turner's grave, but that pleasurable task can be performed any time.'

Thrale smiled. 'Sorry. I don't make a habit of giving out stem-winders like that,' he said. 'I promise not to do it again.'

Kuusinen let the smile die from his face.

'My problem may be real, it may not. But if it is, then someone has committed an act of war against the USA. I'll explain. Shortly after President Hawkins was found dead, Ed Reisch was approached by the junior member of the medical team that performed the autopsy. He claimed that the senior pathologist was senile, and his assistant incompetent, and that the diagnosis of death – a pulmonary embolism – was incorrect. Ed brought me in on this, and by covert means we were able to have the junior doctor – Dr Fineberg – examine President Hawkins' body before burial. Now, the results were

130

inconclusive. The late President didn't die of a pulmonary embolism, just as Fineberg had said, but equally the blood tests showed no signs of any form of poisoning, which he had feared, as apparently he considered that the corpse wasn't sufficiently cyanosed-blue.'

'Okay,' said Thrale. 'So do we accept this? Clearly not.'

'No. There are enough things about it that make me want to have you dig further. The first is that Ed Reisch is very happy to accept the verdict. Even to the extent of telling me that the President *did* die of a pulmonary embolism. It's not that he sees himself as doing anything wrong, simply that this is a problem he really does not want, and as far as he's concerned the blood tests show that the President wasn't murdered. Ed is on a power trip, and he's a street-fighter; he'd sell his mother to win. Now he can get on with his overriding concern, which is getting *his* President – Barnet – re-elected. Two things stick out. Firstly, that Fineberg's senior colleague, one Dr Bartlett, died some six months ago *from identical causes.*'

'This Bartlett, was he sharp?'

'Very, according to Fineberg.'

'Okay. So if someone murdered the President, then they could have been killing two birds with one stone, if you'll excuse the expression. By killing Bartlett they could remove the man who would spot what had happened, try out whatever method of assassination they had devised, and see whether it would pass as natural causes to the senile old guy and his incompetent assistant.'

Kuusinen got up and went over to a tray. 'Exactly. Drink?'

'I'll have a Jack Daniel's on ice.'

Kuusinen's nose twitched and he reached in his pocket for his handkerchief, smothering his sneeze.

'Bless you!' said Thrale.

'Thank you. I get hay-fever at this time of year.'

'In Japan, if you sneeze once they say someone's speaking well of you. Twice, then ill of you. But three times, someone loves you!'

'And four times?' asked Kuusinen, still snuffling.

'Hell, then you must have a cold. But take heart, if you go out and a bird dumps on you it's good luck.'

Kuusinen smiled. 'I'll remember that.' He helped himself to Scotch and gave Thrale his glass. 'Your health. The blood tests: the second thing is that they *did* show a high level of nicotine.'

'The late President smoke?'

'Yes. Heavily.'

'Ah.'

'Until three months ago, that is. His doctor gave him the choice of giving up smoking or, in a few years, the use of his legs – because he'd have to cut them off due to incompetent circulation. The President chose to give up smoking.'

'Me, too. But nicotine's really addictive. My dear wife Keiko smoked, which is why she isn't with me today. She must have tried to give up a hundred times.'

'I knew Hawkins. I didn't necessarily like him but he was a man of iron will. If he wanted something done, he got it done. No one else could have got the Peace treaty with Russia through. If he had decided to give up smoking, then he gave up.'

'So where did the nicotine come from?'

'That's what I asked. So I went to my encyclopaedia and looked it up. Do you know what nicotine is classified as? In the correct dosage?'

'What?'

'Nerve gas,' Kuusinen said levelly, 'which is what Fineberg suspected when he saw that the corpse was not correctly cyanosed.'

'Right.' Thrale stood up, draining his glass. 'You want to have me assigned to the Office of the National Security Advisor? Make me a special spear-carrier of some sort. I won't need a big budget, but I'll want to invoke your name if necessary.'

'I'll have it done by the morning.'

'I'll leave Komura's file with you. It's interesting reading.'

'I'll look forward to it. Find out who murdered the President, K.K.'

'Yeah – and something even more important than that.'

'What's that?'

'Why.'

MOSKOVSKIY ZOOPARK

Men lay scattered over the park, casualties of a decided battle. From over Gruzinskaya the hoots and growls and whoops of the creatures in the zoo came floating on the air, and the men moaned and groaned in symbiotic sympathy. It was Sunday morning, and the city's drunks were processing the vodka from their systems. It was a ritualized business. They stumbled along the streets and from the metros with the gait of somnambulists, to lay themselves thankfully on the grass. As the anaesthesia wore away, to leave a throbbing head and lead-filled eyes, they would drag themselves up once again, to head for the steam-baths where amid crumbling Tsarist icons – and with the aid of a few bottles of beer – the flagellation of *vaniki* birch twigs and the contrast of suffocating steam and the chilled cold tub the job would be complete. Gorbachev's campaigns against alcoholism had run into the sand.

The three party-goers, Yuri, Otari and Alexei lay stretched out like dead men. Slowly a new sound penetrated their numbed senses amid the cacophony. It was a sharp, shrill, angry sound.

'YuriOtariAlexei! YuriOtariAlexei! *Skahryehyeh!* Hurry up!'

It came from the south of the park, from the *Barrikadnaya* metro. It was Yuri's fiancée, Galina, ordering them to identify themselves. The three had collapsed near the Presnya River pond, and Yuri reluctantly raised a painful arm.

'*Vot,*' he croaked. '*Vot.*'

Galina was slim, green-eyed and angry at having her

Sunday morning disrupted.

'Telephone call for you, Otari. Your base. They want you to call them back.'

Under the prodding of her shoe and the lash of her tongue, they stumbled across the park and into the metro station. Its cathedral-like interior was a freeze-frame of revolutionary activity. They slid 5 kopek coins into the turnstiles and boarded for Tusino.

Yuri was fortunate in that his position at Moscow State entitled him to an apartment out of the ordinary. The vast apartment blocks were the same, the materials fabricated *en masse* for buildings everywhere, so that one in Pyatigorsk was the same as one in Balashikha. He had a four-room flat in a nineteenth-century apartment house – once elegant and magisterial, now dark and somewhat dirty. Heavy Russian furniture contrasted vigorously with the few items of bleached-pine Finnish which he had acquired through *blat* under Galina's pushing. Slowly but surely, she was transforming it. Her hands were tinged with white where she had been filling in a jagged crack in the ceiling while Yuri lay suffering the effects of his debauch in the park, and the 'phone rang.

Otari called his headquarters in Kirovograd. He was given orders to cut short his leave and return.

'To the baths,' he muttered. 'We are in no condition to serve the motherland like this. I will shoot myself in the foot, Alexei will drive his tank into a ditch and Yuri's computer will talk to him and he will not understand what it is saying.'

The three prepared to leave and Galina uncovered the pot of filler. As she did so, the 'phone rang again.

'I'm a *shabashnik*,' she joked, her good humour now restored. 'Someone's calling me to paint their front room. For you,' she said, handing the receiver to Yuri.

'Professor Serov,' he said, in as firm a voice as he could muster.

'This is General Ogarkov,' said the voice. It was a jovial voice, one pleased with what it was doing and certain of

135

its power to do so. 'I've had you transferred from the University. I've made you a Colonel, in charge of my Advanced Computer Projects Division. Report to GHQ tomorrow.'

'THE SKUNK WORKS',
BURBANK, CALIFORNIA

The Lockheed Advanced Development Projects office had always been home to the best scientific and technical brains in America. In 1943 they had included refugees from Europe who had found new employment under a man called Kelly Johnson. In time Johnson would become legendary as the aeronautical genius responsible for such fabulous vehicles as the SR-71 Blackbird and U-2 spyplanes. In the middle of the war, however, his collection of talent was busy designing the P-80 Shooting Star jet fighter in circus tents pitched on some ground next to a plastics factory in Burbank. The pungent odour reminded them of the foul-smelling 'Skunk Works' in Al Capp's 'Li'l Abner' comic strip and a legend was born.

More than half a century later the facility bore no resemblance to its humble origins. The big white buildings had seen the birth and construction of aircraft that were always the most advanced of their day, whether high-flying and supersonic like the SR-71, or low-flying, sub-sonic and Stealthy like the F-117A strike fighter. With Northrop, constructor of the B-2 Stealth bomber, Lockheed was the leading exponent of Stealth technology, the art of making an aircraft invisible to hostile detection systems.

At the end of the working day the cars began streaming out, causing a temporary tailback along San Fernando as everyone headed for home. As the flow diminished, Harold Templer drove his green Pontiac carefully out from the gates. To the south-west lay the sprawl of Hollywood, Beverly Hills and Santa Monica, but Templer headed at a steady fifty miles an hour in the other direction, towards the San Gabriel mountains where he lived. It was the only part of his persona that was out of stereotype. Small, unprepossessing, dusty and mousy, Templer should have had a small and unprepossessing apartment in somewhere like Pasadena or Temple City. Instead he had a comfortable split-level up in the mountains, well out of the smog and seemingly better than he might have been expected to afford. Harold Templer was an archivist, a librarian. Advanced projects like the F-117A, or the Trans-Atmospheric Vehicle, or TAV – thought to be equally capable of flying to New York to Los Angeles in twelve minutes, or bombing anywhere on earth within thirty – required access to very advanced documents, papers, theses, books. Some of this knowledge was stored, bound, on shelves. Some of it was stored, encoded, in electronic circuits within the CRAY computers buried underground. Harold Templer was a modern librarian, equally at home in tending to the spine of a volume before re-shelving among its million-or-more companions, or extracting a scientific document for appraisal from the electronic databank.

He left the palms and boulevards behind as he climbed up into the mountains. The air became crisp and clean. In the trunk of the Pontiac he had two brown bags of shopping – his weekend supplies that he had purchased during his lunch hour.

His house was secluded, set in the pines. In the summer the haze and smog sat below like an evil pool, but in the clear air he could see the great city below. The tyres of his car scrunched abruptly on the dirt as he pressed on the brake pedal in involuntary reflex.

A red Ford Thunderbird was parked outside his house. His heart beat a little faster, a new glitter of interest animated his prawn-like eyes and he put his foot back on the gas and parked close by.

He went straight in. Two striking young women were lounging on the sofa in his open-plan living room. One reached out a squid-like arm and gracefully pressed the switch to go on the CD player. They were oriental women, beautiful, sloe-eyed. He would not have been able to tell them apart, only they wore short light kimonos, one pure white and one blood-red.

The red one jumped to her feet in a swirl of long black hair and Harold caught a tantalizing glimpse of contrasting snow-white panties. On the CD player the Everly brothers launched into song and the girl went along.

'*It's Saturday night, just got paid –*' she chuckled. 'Hi, Harold, it's pay day.'

'Well, *all right*,' he grinned happily. 'I wasn't expecting anyone.'

'I'm Yin, this is Yan,' she said, indicating her companion, who was dancing a little jig next to her as the Everlys continued to rip it up from long ago.

'Yin and Yang,' he gurgled. 'I get it.'

Yin picked up a ready tumbler from the table – Canadian Club whisky and coke, his favourite party drink. The girls had their own long dark glasses a-clink with ice, and they all drank.

'Say, uh, you got your tickets?'

'Sure, Harold. Here you are.' She passed over two printed forms and he scanned them. Dated that morning, they were blood tests, certifying that the two women were not HIV positive.

'Now listen, Harold,' she said, taking the forms back. 'We're going to party tonight, but in the morning we'll all be gone.'

'Yeah?' he said doubtfully.

'You remember they said to you that one day you might have to leave? Well, you know they made the fighter aircraft from the plans you got.'

'No one told me about that, and I didn't ask.'

'They put it into production. They lost one. Unfortunately the Americans know about it. We have picked up the signals from their intelligence and defence establishments. They are on to it, sooner or later someone will turn up to see you.'

'Yeah.'

'Walker got life, Harold. His buddy Whitworth got 365 years. He isn't *ever* coming out. The Americans are taking this kind of espionage seriously.'

'Will I be looked after?'

By the sofa, Yan giggled throatily. 'Harold, you're gonna simply fuck yourself to death.'

'*Okay, then,*' he said grinning.

'You'll have to write a note to cover yourself. Address it to Elliott Reynolds, your boss. We'll mail it in the morning. Here's paper and pen.'

Yan was dancing by the light and it shone through the flimsy white kimono. Templer took a gulp of his drink and, while she dictated, Yin replenished it. He was stiff with excitement, his heart thudding in his chest.

'Dear Elliott. I just can't take it any more. I got to go. Please look after everything, and forgive me. Harold.'

The two girls kissed him as he lay on the sheets. Yan's teeth scraped him, her tongue wriggled. Yin bent over him, he took her in his mouth and gasped with joy.

Changing, with his face buried between her thighs he could watch along her body as Yan sucked and caressed her nipples, and he was aroused again.

They showered and, slippery with soap, the two lithe bodies drained him completely. Dry, lying back on the bed and intoxicated with liquor and pleasure he felt a light, massaging hand.

'Girls,' he moaned happily, 'I couldn't get it hard again if my life depended on it.'

Yan laughed. 'You need one of our special pills.'

'What's that?'

'Love-pill. You'll feel like you did when we started.'

'Hey ...'

He found two white pills in his hand and a fresh glass. He had washed them down before he knew it, and lay back on the bed. The two girls quietly got dressed from the bag they had brought with them. They buttoned their shirts and brushed their hair and put away their kimonos and underwear.

On the bed, life left Harold Templer like a dimmer switch being turned off.

They washed up their glasses and put them away. They had been filled with coke and ice, so the two were sober. The Thunderbird came to life, the lights illuminated the path down the pines.

'It is good to die,' said Yin, behind the wheel.

'Duty is weightier than a mountain, while death is lighter than a feather.'

They drove down the mountain towards Los Angeles, content.

THE WARDMAN TOWER

With his wife away, Kuusinen went to the refrigerator to fix himself some supper. He took cold cuts of beef, mayonnaise, lettuce, tomatoes and horseradish and made some rye sandwiches. Then he carried the plate and a napkin to his high-backed reading chair and opened the file that Thrale had left. Biting into his supper, he began to read.

KOMURA BUSSAN

First, a little piece of history.

In 660 A.D. the Emperor Jimmu built a palace in his capital city, decreed laws governing his people and promised to 'extend the line of the Imperial descendants and foster rightmindedness ... Thereafter, the Capital may be extended so as to embrace all of the six cardinal points [of the compass] and the eight cords may be covered so as to form a roof.'

This remarkable ambition, which may be called a polity, since it becomes visible throughout Japanese history, is called *hakko ichiu*, meaning all eight corners of the world under one imperial roof, or rule of all the world.

Komura Bussan is a very old, very big company. The word *bussan* means 'products', and in its time Komura has produced almost everything and sold to almost everyone. The skies above Japan's cities have in their time been darkened by smoke from Komura factories and mills. The rivers and seas have been polluted by the effluent from Komura mines, pulp-mills and refineries.

142

Steel from Komura foundries has made ships which in their turn have carried Komura products to the ends of the earth.

Komura has owned forests, fisheries, plantations from as far north as Hokkaido to as far south as Kyushu. Komura banks, insurance and commercial houses have been the biggest in Japan. In the days of empire, Komura operated the most lucrative concessions in the colonies. She was the most important backer of the South Manchurian Railway; she paid for armies of mercenaries for the acquisition of China. Her political and military intelligence network, which spanned the globe, was more extensive and better organized than that of the government. That government was often partly controlled by Komura, who owned and paid for one of the major political pre-war parties. Komura used her power to suppress reform movements, imprison or execute opponents, smash unions and secure total immunity for her own – who included cabinet ministers, generals, newspaper editors, police bosses and the leaders of terrorist societies, all of whom were bought and paid for.

The *zaibatsu* or family-owned financial cliques of pre-war Japan were immensely wealthy. The four biggest owned over a quarter of the corporate assets of the nation. But biggest of all was Komura – greater than Mitsui, greater than Mitsubishi, greater than Nomura. Her empire spread over every significant sector of industry, finance and commerce. It was controlled by the Komura holding company, which ruled its businesses in the same manner as the shoguns of Tokugawa had ruled the lords of feudal Japan. And at the head of all was the Komura clan. They were like – but more powerful than – the European houses of Rothschild and Krupp, and as closely bound up with the fortunes of empire. The house of Komura thrived and expanded in time of revolution, rebellion and international warfare. Without Komura the Meiji revolution of 1868 which founded modern Japan would not have taken place. Without Komura Japan would not have had an empire. In 1942, Komura Bussan

143

was the greatest single beneficiary of that empire. Three years later the acquisition of the empire brought Japan to total defeat. In 1946 the major *zaibatsu* found themselves abolished and their assets confiscated.

Today, Komura Bussan is the biggest company in Japan. It is the biggest company in the world. This is the doing of Komura Tadaji, the direct descendant of the firm's founder, Komura Saburozaemon.

There is a parallel between the founding of the house of Mitsui and that of Komura, which is that they were both founded by *samurai* who voluntarily gave up their warrior status to become merchants. Saburozaemon lived in Edo – what is now Tokyo – in the years that followed Tokugawa Ieyasu's victory at the battle of Sekigahara in 1600. This battle was the culmination of centuries of anarchy and war in Japan, and marked the beginning of centralized rule – the Tokugawa Shogunate that lasted from 1603 to 1868 – as Ieyasu took 40,000 heads at Sekigahara including that of Ishida Mitsunari, leader of the forces that opposed him. Mitsunari was offered some fruit on his way to the traditional execution grounds of the Kyoto dry river-bed, which he refused, saying it would be bad for his digestion. When it was suggested that as he was about to lose his head he need not worry about his digestion he said, 'Don't you believe it. You never know how things may turn out.' With regard to Japanese history in general, this may be considered a most reasonable view to take.

In Edo in the years that followed, Saburozaemon watched as Ieyasu successfully established his central government under the Shogunate, and came to the extremely intelligent conclusion that in a pacified country the role of – his – warrior class would inevitably wane, and that of the – then – depised *chonin*, or merchants – held to be only one social rung above the *eta*, or outcasts (who were not considered to be human beings at all) – would rise. He saw that under orderly rule agriculture, industry and trade would thrive, and that despite social rules to the contrary those who

144

engaged successfully in commerce would rise in power and influence.

In 1616 Ieyasu's rule of Japan was assured, when he overcame his last enemies and executed the last surviving member of their house: an eight-year-old boy. Assured that his world would now be as he had divined, Saburozaemon then took the unprecedented step of exchanging his samurai's swords for the *soroban* – the abacus of a tradesman – and in so doing changed the history of Japan and of the world.

Ieyasu died shortly after his triumph in 1616. The man who brought the anarchy of centuries to an end and established a central military government which was to last for two and a half centuries was a brilliant military commander who displayed almost faultless judgement of men and unshakable patience throughout his life. His words on the subject are worth quoting; like the polity of *hakko ichiu*, they recur:

> The strong manly ones in life are those who understand the meaning of the word Patience. Patience means restraining one's inclinations. There are seven emotions – joy, anger, anxiety, love, grief, fear and hate – and if a man does not give way to these he can be called patient. I am not as strong as I might be, but I have long known and practised patience. *And if my descendants wish to be as I am ... they must study patience.*

Saburozaemon opened a small brewery selling sake and soy sauce in 1621, and the dynasty he founded thrived. The most flourishing market in Japan was in Edo, whose people were renowned as spendthrifts, and the disciplined and personally-austere Komuras set about separating fools from their money with a will.

They had an extraordinary aptitude for commerce, and in the years that followed originated such practices as sales for cash at fixed prices, direct and indirect advertising, market research, chain stores and double-

145

entry book-keeping. From the flow of money from their trade they branched out into finance and became money-changers – predecessors to the bankers they later became.

Their success brought them little love. Their social status can be judged by the early eighteenth-century saying: 'The commonest things in Edo are merchants, Inari shrines and dog turds.' To survive, a merchant had to be cringingly obsequious to his superiors, mercilessly competitive with his equals and pitilessly grasping in all dealings with people more helpless than himself. In this world the Komuras were more successful than any, and acquired the traits that brought them to greatness. As they grew in power the necessity to grovel to anyone grew less and less, but the crushing of opposition and exploitation of those below them grew in scale and in sophistication.

The world that they were living in, however, was one isolated from the rest of the world and the many changes that were taking place within it – the Renaissance was in full flood in Europe at this time. Hidetada, Ieyasu's son, put into effect a rigorous programme of persecution against the Christians within the country, correctly recognizing that acknowledgement of a transcendental authority was a direct threat to his own, and by 1637 it was decreed that Japan be isolated from the rest of the world. No Japanese might leave, under pain of death, and any who did leave would be executed upon their return.

The rest of the world found this misogynistic attitude hard to understand. A deputation arrived from Macao in 1640, bearing gifts. The Japanese response was to execute all on board except thirteen who had to watch, burn the ship and send the survivors home. 'Think no more of us; just as we were no longer in the world,' said the official in charge.

Faced with so churlish an attitude, the rest of the world decided to do just that, and for nearly another two and a half centuries busied themselves with their own

146

affairs, leaving the Japanese to themselves.

Another great nation was denied both Renaissance and Reformation, with similar effects. Russia adopted the Greek Orthodox faith under the Grand Prince Vladimir almost a millenium ago. This and the Mongol invasion cut her off from Catholic Europe as surely as the Japanese sealing themselves away. The result has been the same in both cases – a feeling of intense exclusivity and a hatred of foreigners that can amount to paranoid xenophobia.

The house of Komura thrived during the centuries of the Shogunate and, what was more, emerged from its fall with its powers enhanced. The reason the Shogunate fell was that once again the outside world was becoming interested in Japan.

American sailors were shipwrecked there in the 1820s, and most executed under the policy of *uchi harai* – shell and repel, expel the barbarians. In time, the Americans became resentful and sent emissaries. The most successful of these was Commodore Perry, and his black ships, who succeeded in negotiating a trade agreement through *force majeure*. The Americans were followed in quick succession by the Russians, the British, the Dutch and the French. The years of isolation were bringing in a harvest of bitter fruit; the Japanese – cut off from the revolutionary discoveries in astronomy and the natural sciences, from the experimental method itself, from modern Western technology – were in no position to oppose the new visitors. In 1857 the shogun assented to intercourse with America, 'continuous from that point for ever.'

Japan had become a part of a world about which the Japanese knew virtually nothing. What they did know was that it was a desperately dangerous one for people in their position to be in, as the fate of China, India, Indochina, the East Indies, the Malay Peninsula and the Philippines at the hands of the Western powers clearly showed.

What was the Japanese response to this situation?

147

Masayoshi Hatta, chief councillor and foreign adviser to the shogun, expressed it most clearly in a memorial to his head in 1858:

> In establishing relations with foreign countries, the object should always be kept in view of laying the foundation for securing hegemony over all nations. The national resources should be developed in military preparations vigorously carried out. When our power and national standing have come to be recognized we should take the lead ... declare our protection over harmless but powerful nations .... Our national prestige and position thus assured, the nations of the world will come to look up to our Emperor as the Great Ruler of all the nations, and they will come to follow our policy and submit to our judgement....

HAKKO ICHIU!

The process of modernization – of learning from the West – began apace. The Imperial Japanese Navy was founded in 1855 under Dutch and later British tutelage. Schools were opened in Edo, where young samurai began to study foreign languages and learn the secrets of engineering, physics, chemistry and other technologies and sciences from foreigners hired to do the teaching. Others were sent abroad to look, do and learn.

The intrusion of the foreigners after 1857 brought about great loss of prestige for the shogunate, and undermined its authority to the extent that ten years later it fell. The *bakumatsu* – the twilight of the shogunate – released the forces that were to modernize Japan. Among them were the merchants who had so gathered wealth and power under its rule, and chief among these were the Komuras. Displaying the political intelligence shown by their ancestor, Saburozaemon, the Komuras allied with and bank-rolled a number of very able young men from the western clans of Satsuma, Choshu, Tosa and Hizen. In 1866 these men led an

148

armed movement to restore the power of the Emperor, which the shogunate was unable to suppress, thus sealing its own fate. In 1867 the Emperor Komei – the main obstacle to the opening of the country to foreign intercourse – died, officially of smallpox but in reality of poison administered by Prince Iwakura, close ally of the Komuras.

It was fitting that the Komuras should have entered in such a manner the new age in which they were to play such a part.

The new attitude of the Japanese towards the West was summed up by the young Emperor Meiji himself, in his Charter Oath:

Knowledge shall be sought for all over the world and thus shall be strengthened the foundations of the imperial polity.

Or, *hakko ichiu!*

The foreigners came and taught, they managed, and as the Japanese learned they quietly sent them home; and as the foreigners went home, so returned the Japanese who had been sent aboard to learn their skills.

The slogan of the times was *fukoku kyohei*, meaning 'a rich country, with a strong army'. With such a policy in motion the popular cry for other Western imports like democracy and people's rights seemed to the oligarchs who ran Japan to be frivolous. Grimly, they concentrated their attention on building the economy and their armed forces. But who was to run that modern industrial economy, and who was to equip that strong army? The oligarchy turned to those private businessmen who seemed to have the best chance of success – to their friends, the Mitsuis, the Mitsubishis and the Komuras. Thus it was that the *zaibatsu* were formed.

The fortunes of Japan, and of the *zaibatsu*, prospered as the twentieth century arrived. The military proved its ability by decimating the Chinese in the last years of the nineteenth. The hostile attitude of most Western powers in limiting the Japanese gains from that war allied all sections of Japan's leadership and brought about a new

149

and for the rest of the world baleful policy – *Nippon shugi*: Japanism. They set about surrounding themselves with protective territory and the means to total self-sufficiency – Empire. Alliance with England, the greatest power of the day, was followed by victory in the Russo-Japanese War of 1904–5. A prize of this war proved to be Korea, which Imperial Japan absorbed. Now the Empire had Taiwan, Korea, Sakhalin, the Ryukyus, the Bonins and the Kuriles.

Hakko ichiu!

The Great War of 1914–18 which proved so ruinous to the European nations who fought it was an unmixed blessing to Japan, who acquired more empire in the form of the Shantung Province, the Marshalls, Marianas and Carolines, and a vast boost to her economy as the Western allies commissioned ships and armaments from her rapidly growing industrial sector.

The years from 1900 to 1918 were truly 'golden' for Japan. Under the Emperor Meiji, and guided by the *Genro*, the old men who had led the restoration, the nation had risen in accordance with the Yamato race's view of its place in the world. There seemed little reason to fear the future. The liberal-minded men in politics benefited from their association with the victorious democracies in Europe, most especially Great Britain, and the military was falling out of favour – especially with the defeat of Germany and the ill-considered Japanese military moves in Siberia following the Russian revolution. A fresh wind of radical thoughts – socialism, communism, even – was blowing through thinking society. The police referred to it as 'dangerous thoughts'.

The war boom collapsed in 1921, bringing about much unrest. Many small men suffered, but the *zaibatsu* did not. The politicians and the rich men of the *zaibatsu* were becoming identified in the eyes of the public. When Great Britain failed to renew the alliance with Japan in 1921–2, under pressure from America, the liberals were discredited. The 1920s became known as the era of '*Ero, Guro, Nansensu*' – eroticism, grotesquerie and nonsense.

150

All that came to an end in 1927, when a financial slump put hordes of small businesses under, to the benefit of the *zaibatsu. That* was followed by the depression of 1929, which brought ruin to the farmers; it became common practice for them to sell their daughters into prostitution to survive. The junior officers in the army came from those farms; when they saw what was happening they went back to their units, their anger burning like coals.

The Japanese were ill-served by history when it came to coping with the events that followed. Having sealed themselves off from the world in the second quarter of the seventeenth century, they completely failed to absorb any notion of individual moral responsibility – those gifts of Christian and Judaic tradition. Furthermore, as a method of self-protection they had evolved a tradition of *sodan,* or group consultation, which meant that no one person ever stood up for a cause or accepted responsibility. In feudal times to do so – and be proved wrong – meant *seppuku.*

Furthermore, when the Japanese were forced to emerge from their isolation, and emerged blinking warily into their new and dangerous world, what did they see; what lessons did they learn? They found a world which Bismarck described as *realpolitik,* of blood and iron, of rampant imperialism justified by racist theories of social Darwinism. They witnessed an unrestrained arms race, and the most brutal war in history fought without quarter. They saw the cult of power through violence and learned, through Lenin, that it *worked.*

And they learned something else, along with their acquisition of science and technology. They learned that the behaviour of the Europeans – who ruled the world, and carved up as much of it as they could for themselves – however frightful or atrocious, was always justified by reference to some set of beliefs, whether it be a British stewardship of backward races or the inevitable triumph of Communism. So observing that life was hard

151

and earnest, and that this world they had been forced into – and within which they wished to be first among equals – was a hard, competitive one, they set about forging their own set of ideologies. They invented a state religion and a ruling morality. These they called *Shinto* and *bushido*. *Shinto* they chose because it was a wholly Japanese element in the many-stranded religious culture of Japan and therefore entirely suitable to be married to the pursuit of *hakko ichiu*. Emperor worship was established, especially in the armed forces, and in the 1920s the military began teaching their national code of ethics, *kokumin dotoku*, to the children in the schools. *Shinto* became the religion of expansionist nationalism, and was deliberately married to a reworked and militarized version of the way of the *samurai*, *bushido*. During the 1920s the military, who were becoming a law unto themselves, popularized it as a code of military honour identified with the most extreme nationalism and militarism. They were led by the 'knights of *bushido*', the very equivalent of Lenin's 'vanguard elites' and Hitler's Blackshirts. They were said to embody the 'totality of the moral instincts of the Japanese race'. In the 1930s their leaders took control of the army and, in effect, of the nation.

It was no accident that the knights of *bushido* had their European equivalents, for during the 1930s there was a European or American parallel for every political event and movement in Japan. This wave of the future was the cosmopolitan and very fashionable trend known as fascism.

It involved murder and assassination. In America, an assassin's bullet narrowly missed President Franklin D. Roosevelt but killed the Mayor of Chicago, Anton Cermak. In Tokyo a young man walked up to Komura Yunosuke, the head of Komura Bussan, as he arrived for work, and emptied a revolver into his body. The young man was a member of the Blood Pledge Corps and fired by the ideals of Kita Ikki, the father of Japanese fascism. It has to be said that Komura Yunosuke contributed to his own death. At the height of the depression, in which Komura Bussan did not share – grinding as it did the faces of its workers and subsidiaries – he wrote in a magazine article: 'As you walk along the road, it is not your intention to crush ants. However, although you are not walking in order to crush the ants, you do end up doing just that. Our problem is the same. We walk down the road fairly and squarely, but our bodies and feet are large, and it naturally comes about that we trample down the small fellows.'

As Yunosuke was penning these profound thoughts, the young member of the Blood Pledge Corps had a thirteen-year-old sister who spent her days on her back or on her knees in an Osaka brothel, and little brothers who went to school with empty lunch-boxes. He went to his blood-brothers, who knew as he did that there was no construction without destruction, and they provided him with a pistol and obtained for him a job as a taxi-driver. Thus equipped he was able to follow Komura's car and, on the morning in question, to be waiting as the industrial boss arrived. With the oppressor's blood gushing over the pavement, with his body twitching at his feet, he felt overwhelming content. He stood, and waited for the police to take him away.

Yunosuke was succeeded by his nephew, Kisaburo, a travelled man. Shortly before his uncle was made to lie on a Tokyo street and leak his life away, he had been to Europe. As one of the wealthiest industrialists in Japan he was able to make the right connections and meet interesting people, people who thought much as he did himself. He met John Foster Dulles, and heard how Mussolini had been brought to power by the financial élite of Italy with the aid of a hundred-million-dollar loan from J.P. Morgan of New York. He saw how Adolf Hitler was aided by the steel and munitions trusts. In England he mixed with the Cliveden set and met William S. Knudsen, the President of General Motors, who told him that Hitler's Germany was 'the miracle of the twentieth century'. Charles Lindbergh told him that Nazism was 'the wave of the future'. He was introduced to Moral Rearmament, where he met Henry Ford and William Randolph Hearst and, in Germany, Heinrich Himmler and Rudolf Hess. He found the company and sentiments congenial and realized that fascism – while attractive to the middle class to which it held out glittering inducements, and even seductive to the proletariat with its promise of 'national socialism' and opportunities of subgroups like Jews, gypsies, homosexuals and communists to oppress – was *really* the ideology of the monopolists, of the super-rich. *They* were the ones who had the most to gain from foreign expansion, preparations for war and the suppression of domestic dissent.

He returned to Japan convinced of fascism's efficacy, and shortly afterwards became head of Komura, the biggest *zaibatsu* in the land. Like his predecessors before him, like the very founder of his house, Saburozaemon, he had very sensitive political antennae, however. He realized that if Komura was to obtain the maximum benefit from the new · order of things she would have to get into bed with the military, many of whose leaders were imbued with Kita Ikki's fanatical anticapitalist – but imperialist – views. It could be done. The Kwantung Army needed millions of yen to finance its expansion in Manchuria and into China.

But it was necessary to do more. A further gesture was necessary. A gesture of blood. Komura Kisaburo offered up his son, Komura Tadaji, to be one of them.

The telephone rang and in the Wardman Tower Kuusinen put down the file next to his empty plate and went to answer it.

'*Hakko ichiu*,' he muttered.

THE PENTAGON

It was a little after noon and Susie Farr was getting ready to go home after a full day's work. For her it had begun ten hours earlier. She was editor of one of the best-read papers in Washington, one you couldn't buy on the news-stand, couldn't take out a subscription for. A sixteen-page digest called the *Current News*, its arrival on your desk gave you a certain measure of your standing in the military and defence communities. Its readers knew it as the 'Early Bird'.

Farr enjoyed her job despite, even because of, the strange hours. At one-thirty a.m. it was a fifteen-minute ride on cruise control down the expressway from her Springfield home to the vast military headquarters by the Arlington Cemetery on the Potomac, where she was one of the very first of the building's 23,000 occupants to arrive. She sipped a cup of coffee on the way and mentally geared up for the four hours of high-pressure editing with her five-member team. The Early Bird was sixteen *Time*-magazine-sized pages of the hottest Pentagon-oriented news of the day, taken from nine major daily newspapers and the overnight take from two wire services and the largest television networks. It was a cut-and-paste operation that highlighted senior Pentagon pronouncements and the speeches of the Defense Secretary of the day, but also provided room for the dissidents within the defence community to get exposure of Pentagon waste, leak details of cost over-runs and weapons systems in trouble and provide coverage of military incidents abroad that their perpetrators would rather keep concealed. It was a very democratic paper.

Weekly and monthly Susie Farr and her team would produce longer supplements in which the net was spread to include over sixty newspapers from coast to coast and three hundred magazines. It was one of these supplements that she was now finishing before going home to do her shopping, prepare the evening meal, put her feet up to a soap for half an hour and collect her eldest grand-daughter from school. She was looking for something to fill a last half-column, and found it on page 23 of the *Los Angeles Times*. Among the scientific community that produced the exotic hardware for the military, there had recently been something like a spate of early deaths from stress-related diseases such as heart attacks and strokes; there had even been a few suicides. Farr suspected that it was something of a media-induced trend, not unlike the way in which it would suddenly seem as though aircraft were constantly falling out of the sky, only for that to be forgotten a week later when instead the water one drank was apparently filled with toxic chemicals.

However, the half-column on page 23 was the right size, and a topic of the day, so she put it in. A librarian working for the 'black' – secret – Lockheed Advanced Projects Office in Burbank California had been found dead at his home with a suicide note and a bottle of pills beside him. Two of them were in his bloodstream, dissolved in half a bottle of liquor.

Farr photocopied the article and stuck it in. The copy was now ready to go off to the Air Force printers, and the supplement would join the next day's edition of the Early Bird. The Defense Secretary would get first look at it on his ride in from home to work shortly after six a.m. After the rest of the top hierarchy got their copies, the full print run of 6,000 would be despatched around noon. The Technology Transfer section got a copy; they had to pass it around. K.K. Thrale usually got a look at it when he was getting ready to go home.

KANAZAWA, HONSHU, 1936

The dawn wind from the Japan Sea came over the frozen snow like a razor. In the half-light, figures emerged from the holes where they had bivouacked. They had not slept for three days, but under the sergeant's command the young voices barked as one.

'Whether I float as a corpse under the waters, or sink beneath the grasses of the mountainside, I willingly die for the Emperor.'

Lieutenant Komura Tadaji, fresh out of the *Shikwan Gakko* military academy, watched with approval as Sergeant Takahashi organized bayonet training. Close combat was the best way to fight. Komura stepped forward to address them.

'Always attack,' he urged. 'Never think of defence. Under the falling blade there is a river of hell. Jump into it and you might float. Let the enemy cut your skin, you cut his flesh. Let the enemy cut your flesh, you cut his bones.'

The young men in the platoon all grunted with approval at his words, all except Cadet Kenji who was still coughing. It had started on the second day of the manoeuvre. The wretched soldier was shivering as he dressed himself in the padded apron and gloves of bayonet training. Komura looked at him disapprovingly as he stood erect, a proper officer, and tapped the hilt of his samurai battle sword. The twin killing swords had been reintroduced into the army as a part of the *seishin kyoiku* spiritual training that was transforming the nation. Komura was an object of envy to his contemporaries as his *daisho* pair were historic treasures from the

157

Togugawa shogunate. Less fortunate men had to make do with new ones from the smithy in the Yasukuni Shrine, the Shinto shrine of heroes across from the Imperial Palace, for which they would give half a year's pay.

The sound of an engine penetrated the wind blowing past his ears and, turning, he saw Major Iwane's Nissan half-track grind to a halt on the snow.

'Komura! Come here, there's someone I want you to meet.'

'Carry on the training, sergeant,' Komura instructed Takahashi. As he walked over to the vehicle he heard the shrieks as the first two cadets began pounding each other with the long, rifle-sized padded sticks.

He climbed into the cab, holding his *katana* carefully to avoid damage to the scabbard.

'Lieutenant Komura, this Major Yonai.' Iwane's foxy face broke into a sly smile. 'You may have heard of him.'

Komura bowed as far as he could inside the cab and hissed respectfully.

'To be sure,' he said, 'but ...'

Yonai was everything one would have expected from a hero: tall, light-skinned, handsome, with full and almost purple lips framing white teeth.

'But what am I doing here?' he smiled. 'I am here because I have served my sentence.'

'He got twenty days,' Iwane interjected admiringly. 'Served in an Osaka geisha house.'

Komura gave an approving chuckle. 'A fitting reward for a perfect act.'

'Not perfect,' Yonai barked. 'I am a fencing instructor. I failed to despatch Minister Taku with one blow. For that, I am bitterly ashamed. But for the rest....'

'He was disloyal to our national policy, our *kokutai*. He deserved to die.'

'He knew it,' chimed in Iwane. 'They found a poem he had penned: "Praise be to men who may attempt my life, if their motive is to die for their country."'

'How, sir, did you manage to get close enough to the traitor Taku?' Komura enquired. 'It was known that he

158

had been threatened with death for his views, that he took precautions.'

'I cultivated him from afar. I indicated secret support for his views. All the time I remembered the words of the *hagakure*: "Walk with a real man a hundred yards and he will tell you at least seven lies." I told more than seven lies to Taku, and the time came when I was able to enter his office. There my sword danced in my hand and the traitor was dead. Now the old men and the cowards who would block our natural rise to the leadership of Asia and the world are no longer in charge,' said Yonai. 'Now we are in charge. We need to cleanse Asia, remove the white man. In China, we need to take away the suffering of the people there. We will be in charge.'

Outside in the snow the cadets rushed madly at each other, their screams of fury penetrating the glass.

'War is the highest ideal of humanity, the father of culture and the mother of creation,' murmured Yonai. 'We shall be moving soon. It was felt that you, because of your family, should be there. Under military rule there will be many opportunities for robust and hustling Japanese businessmen, go-getters, to invade these territories under our protecting wings, to double and treble Japanese exports. You in the army, your family in business, you symbolize our partnership.'

'I shall be proud,' Komura assured him.

Yonai tapped his nose. 'We of the Yamato race, we, being pure, are peculiarly sensitive to the smell of decay – however well screened it may appear. When we sense a lack of firmness, we strike! When we smell decomposition, we savage! Out there, out there, Komura, we sense it. We sniff the breeze and out there, where we are going, we smell something bad.'

Yonai looked out of the cab, where frost was creeping up the window, and his face wrinkled in disapproval.

'I smell something bad closer to home,' he said. Komura looked anxiously out. Crawling on the snow, seemingly unable to rise, was one of his cadets. He thrust open the door.

159

'*Sergeant Takahashi!*' he screamed.

The sergeant's entire body stiffened and he bellowed at the fallen figure. It was Cadet Kenji, who struggled to his feet. Takahashi lashed out with his heavy boots on to Kenji's shins. The boy's face winced with pain and the three officers in the half-track grunted with contempt. Takahashi smashed his fist into his face and the slight figure flew backwards on to the snow. The sergeant seized a Type 92 heavy machine gun, which he strapped over the cadet's shoulders. Buckling under the weight of the weapon, lashed by the sergeant's tongue and fists, Kenji began to half-stagger and half-run around the perimeter of the bivouack area. Yonai grunted once more, but this time with approval.

'A soldier always has a reserve of strength to serve the Emperor,' he said. 'Very well, Komura. When you get back to barracks you will find orders cut to join the 96th Guards. You will be going to Tientsin.'

It was snowing again. A figure appeared, weaving and staggering; it was Cadet Kenji. He came to a stop, his eyes rolled up in his head and blood suddenly gushed from his mouth. The body fell without resistance on to the ice, and dark blood began to seep along the slope. All – officers, non-commissioned officer and cadets – stood around the corpse, staring down at it in disapproval.

'Take this as an example of a soldier unfit to serve the Emperor,' Komura said.

He bent, and taking a pocket knife cut a lock of hair and took a nail paring to send to the boy's parents, together with the note which would inform them that their son had died a hero's death for the Emperor. It was all that they would have to remember their child by.

The blood had congealed into ice. In the spring it would melt and fertilize the green grass beneath. This would not be its first taste of human life. The cadets were training on the site of an old battlefield. Here, Oda Nobunaga had sat on his battle stool and viewed heads, one after the next, washed and drained, on spiked boards.

160

To prove their fitness to serve the Emperor the platoon ran at double time all the way back to the barracks, carrying equipment and the corpse. They poured kerosene over the body of Cadet Kenji and burned him behind the kitchens, where they disposed of the refuse.

161

HUAI RO KHI, THAILAND, 1943

The operating table was made from bamboo, it made a waist-high platform over which a mosquito net was hung to keep off the blowflies. Two tents stood nearby. One was the convalescent ward where men recovered from their operation, or far more often died, at which point they were carried over to the second, holding tent or morgue, to await transportation over to the hill where the fires burned night and day, consuming the dead.

Outside the tent of the living Major Ross, the British Medical Officer, was boiling a few surgical instruments in a pot. Thrale came across from the other side of the camp carrying a small saw; he handed it to Ross, who put in with the other tools. Thrale was thinner than he had been, but still distinctive in his American flying clothes, which had not yet begun to rot.

'How's the dysentery?' Ross asked as they waited.

'Better. Not so much blood.'

'M&B 693. That's what you're taking. Sulphonamides are the original "magic bullet". If this place was a real hospital I'd be using them on just about everyone. As it is, we have so little they're only for really essential personnel like you and me. If I could give them to Jones in there, his chances of making it would improve dramatically.'

Thrale gestured to the hut. 'He still wants to go through with it?'

'They all do. They know it's down to about one in ten, but they take it. The will to live can be pretty strong.'

'Yes, I know.'

'If I don't operate it's death for certain,' Ross said with a small, sad smile. 'If I do, it's death almost for certain. But they'll go for the option with some hope. Okay, these are sterile.'

Thrale was looking about. 'Where're the guards? They're usually about here thicker than the flies when we do this. It's better than going to the theatre for them.'

'The Engineers are gone. We have a new set of masters. Give them time.'

'Yeah.'

Three men carried a fourth from the tent and laid him as carefully as they could upon the crude operating table. All were malnourished; those standing showed the signs of beri-beri, exhibiting swollen stomachs and oedematous legs. The man on the table showed the reason for his presence there – a bare, necrosed shinbone protruding from the little that the huge tropical ulcer had left of his calf.

The orderly at his head slipped a wad of cloth into the patient's mouth for him to bite upon. The ether had run out a long time ago. Ross hefted the saw in his hand.

When it was done, Ross put a dressing of par-boiled banana leaves over the stump and the orderlies carried the man back inside the tent, to lie on his blanket on the bamboo floor. Ross gave the saw back to Thrale.

'Thanks for getting it. Without that, it would be even more mediaeval than it is.'

Blood had spattered his hands and he used the back of his wrist to wipe sweat out of his eyes.

'When I think with what care I was trained at Tommy's! Now all is speed, so that he doesn't die on the table from shock.' He shook his head wearily. 'Thanks again, K.K.'

Ross went inside to attend to his patients and Thrale washed the saw before heading back across the camp from whence he had come. There seemed to be something different about his surroundings and he paused, warily, like an animal sensing the air. He realized what it

163

was. The screams of the guards: *'Baka Yaro!', 'Kora!', 'Speedo!'*; the sounds of cudgels hitting flesh and bone, the whistle of the wire whips and the moaning of the prisoners – all had gone. The air was quiet.

It seemed a good omen and the pilot resumed his progress across the camp. At the kitchen hut he returned the butcher's saw to the cook.

'It's clean?' the man demanded and roared with laughter. It was his favourite joke. Thrale assured him it was, bowed as he left.

Outside the guard-room where the working parties assembled in the mornings he saw the senior British officer, Lt-Colonel Harris, talking to a young Japanese officer. Harris waved at him, and he went over.

'Thrale, this is Lieutenant Tanaka. The Engineers have now moved on as you know, and he and his men are our new guards. It is rather an unusual event to find him here. He and my son knew each other in Paris before the war when they were studying there.'

Tanaka turned to Thrale. He was a small man about Thrale's height, and of the same age.

'The Colonel and I were exchanging memories of a happier time,' he said politely in good English. He bowed. 'It will be good to work with people who understand each other,' he said formally.

When he had gone Thrale walked with Harris towards his hut.

'I think this calls for a celebration,' he murmured. He fished in the pocket of his mildewed jacket and took out a screw of black tobacco and a page of thin printed paper which he carefully tore in half.

'Some Sikh's Beard, Thrale?'

'Thank you, Colonel.'

The Englishman passed over one half of the paper and both men dextrously rolled thin cigarettes.

'I'm afraid the Lord's book makes the best cigarette paper,' said Harris. He peered at the print before sealing it with spittle. 'Exodus 33.3. "A stiff-necked people." How appropriate! I always try to read what I am about to

164

desecrate. It makes it seem a little less blasphemous.'

The closest source of fire was the pyre where the dead were burning. Thrale went over and returned with a short, glowing piece of bamboo. Both men lit and inhaled with joy. In the conditions of the camp tobacco had an allure second to none. Not only did it cut down on hunger but it provided comfort and solace. Non-smokers had been known to take up the habit for the pleasure it would bring.

'Saito and his Engineers were a stiff-necked people. Now things may be different.... You know how the Nips all take their cue from whoever is charge. Saito was a brutal man and his men were all goons. Now we have a chance....'

Harris took a long pull at his cigarette and held the smoke in his lungs. When he spoke he did so through a thin jet of tobacco.

'This place is undoubtedly one of the ante-rooms of Hell, Thrale. Since I have been here I have not allowed myself to hope that I might leave it alive. Or any of us. But now I think we might ... do just that.'

In his bed, unable to control his screaming as he awoke from the past, Thrale buried his head in the pillows until he gained control of himself once more. Slippery with evil-smelling sweat, he got up and went into the shower. It was four in the morning, but he was afraid to go back to sleep for demons awaited him there.

He went through to his kitchen to brew coffee. The image produced by the KH-11's camera of the men standing about the crash-site at Fukhai had been nagging at him like an uncomfortable tooth, and he had slipped it into his briefcase and brought it home with him. Now, as the water dripped though the filter, he took it out and stared at it once again.

The fearful events of his dreams had taken him back into the past, and though now awake some portion of his mind stayed there. As he looked into the image that the

165

CRAY computers of the National Photographic Interpretation Center had produced from the KH-11's digital information, he knew that he too had been there. He too had stood where his P-38 Lightning fighter had come to rest at the end of a gouge of torn earth; had returned to the site and stood reflectively, staring back down the way he had come, now calm – reliving the last desperate moments of frantic control movements, hands shaking as they gripped stick and throttles, kneecaps trembling with ague as feet rattled on rudder bars, all to kiss the ground in the best manner possible, to live and not to die.

The young man in white was staring back down the way that *his* fighter had come. He and Thrale had been there together, separated by half a century. He was the pilot of the F-117A.

When Major Hank Caid, late of the USAF, aviation analyst at NPIC, arrived for work at the Interpretation Center's big warehouse-style block near the old Navy Yard, he found Thrale waiting for him.

'Hi, Hank,' said the old fighter pilot. 'I want you to do something for me.'

NANKING, CHINA, DECEMBER 1937

The fighting was over, and those victorious moved into the city. The aircraft that had destroyed its buildings were back at the air bases, the field guns of the army silent on the edge of the Yangtze.

Komura's platoon occupied a house which had miraculously escaped damage. A fire was lit, and pans put on to cook *meshi*. They had fought their way up the Shanghai-Nanking rail-line, pushing back the Chinese forces since early November. This was the first time they had been able to rest. They picked shady corners around the courtyard, took off heavy helmets and caps, wiped their faces and the stubble on their heads with silk scarves, took off their canvas and rubber boots and began cleaning their weapons, handling them as if they had been born with them. The air filled with the low, pleasant murmur of their voices as they conversed. Komura was filled with pride as he watched his *butai*; they were perfect fighting animals.

Outside a car door slammed. He looked out and saw Yonai picking his way across the shell-rubble in the street, carrying a wrapping cloth in one hand, sporting new Lieutenant-Colonel's badges on his shoulders. As he came in Komura sprang to attention. Like Yonai, he was dirty, and smelled from weeks of day and night fighting, an odour that was in one's very skin – compounded of sweat, stale urine, explosive and other men's blood.

'Congratulations, Colonel,' he beamed.

Yonai smiled back and, reaching in his pocket, took out brand-new badges – collar and shoulder badges –

167

resplendent in red, yellow, silver and gold, tossing them on the table.

'Congratulations yourself, *Captain*,' he said. 'There's nothing like a good war for promotion.'

Komura picked up his new badges of rank, filled with pride. Yonai opened his cloth and handed over a parcel wrapped in green paper.

'The mail came up the line,' he said. 'This came for you.'

Komura opened the comfort package. He unwrapped the contents carefully, wrapped as they were in coloured crepe paper, placed in small, crafted wood boxes, protected by layers of patterned cotton.

'It's from my parents,' he said proudly. Yonai nodded with approval.

Komura opened the letter that accompanied the parcel and skimmed it briefly.

'My father sends his thanks. He says Komura Bussan trade with China and Manchuoko has more than doubled. In Shanghai, we have control of the cotton and silk mills.'

Yonai nodded again. 'Bureaucrat, politician, banker, businessman, all work together and benefit from the army's glorious deeds.'

Komura folded the letter. 'I will read it later,' he explained, putting it inside his jacket. He took out a copy of *Manga*, his favourite humorous magazine, and put it aside to read when he had time.

His parents had sent him a new headband and some new silk scarves from the Mitsukoshi Department store. There was some *momme*, sweet soybean paste and some lacquered boxes of *chagashi* tea sweets.

Komura sighed with pleasure. 'My mother makes these herself,' he said. 'Will you join me?'

He called to the kitchen for some *sencha* leaf tea.

As it came steaming in army mugs there was a howl of triumph from the rubble of the house opposite. Emerging into the daylight, prodded by the bayonet of Corporal Nanjo – the platoon's best seeker, and finder of things

168

left hidden – were an old man and a young woman. At the sight of them the men of the *butai* chuckled with pleasure.

The young Chinese girl they stripped in the courtyard, so that all might see and enjoy what they were to have, and then they dragged her inside, Corporal Nanjo making clear his right to be the first. She began to scream.

Komura offered Yonai one of the boxes of sweets.

'I apologize that we have no proper teacups,' he said. 'Try the *kikugoromo*, it is delicious.'

Yonai bit into the round, delicately-patterned sweet and exclaimed with pleasure. 'You can smell the chrysanthemum,' he said.

The old man stood in the courtyard, fearfully listening to the screams of his grand-daughter. He was balding, with a pigtail down his neck. Near toothless, he showed a single front tusk as he grimaced, bare feet shuffling on the beaten earth, pulling his dirty shirt closer around him.

'We've fought hard,' remarked Yonai, helping himself to some *higashi*. 'It's been agreed the troops can have the city as a reward for fighting so well for the Emperor.'

They poured petrol over the head of the old Chinaman and applied a match. He screamed even louder than his grand-daughter. They offered him a pan of water with which to put out the flames. It was boiling. He flung it over his head and screamed as the flames hissed out. More petrol from the can, another match, more water. Much, much laughter and excitement.

They were still laughing and chattering, and calling for whichever of them was enjoying the young girl to hurry up, some time after he had died.

'The people are pleased,' said Yonai. 'There was a great parade in Tokyo last night – half a million, with lanterns. Now it's time to think about kicking the white men out of Asia.'

'We're beginning,' said Komura. 'When I was in Tientsin we always stopped the British at the checkpoints.' He tapped his nose. 'I smell decay. We used to humiliate them. Strip them – the women especially. It's good for

169

the men to know they aren't white gods. We, the Yamato race, are first among peoples.'

'The Navy sank some American and British ships on the Yangtze two days ago. That toad Hirota at the Foreign Ministry's grovelling to them about it. It won't be long now before we do it in earnest – get rid of the whites and then destroy the Communist Russians.'

Yonai tossed back the rest of his tea and stood up.

'But before that, there is work to be done. We're not leaving these bastards here for Chiang Kai-shek to enlist when our backs are turned. You'll need heavier weapons than rifles. I've arranged for you to borrow two heavy machine guns and some light machine guns. Go and get set up by the city wall and they'll bring you them in batches. Chinese burial squads will take them away after you've done. You can tell the men they have free rein here. They can take what they want, do what they want.'

The troops were getting ready under the sharp eye of Sergeant Sugiyama, buttoning their flies, putting on both belts and wrapping puttees. The exhausted moaning from the room where the young girl had been destroyed was suddenly broken by a hideous gurgling shriek. It died away and the last man emerged, wiping clean his bayonet before fixing it to his rifle.

They moved out. From the ruins across the road a young boy stared at them, his face a mask of horror. Komura took out his type 14 pistol and shot him dead. The troops broke into spontaneous applause at his marksmanship. The shot had been a difficult one and the target small.

They formed up and moved out and Corporal Nanjo began to sing. He sang the new song they all liked, it was white, and bright, and red; cherry blossoms on the slopes of pure white Mount Fuji, the red plum blossoms in winter; the crimson camellias and sparkling chrysan-themums. They sang about purity and radiance, and felt themselves uplifted.

They marched down to the city walls, where the first five hundred Chinese civilians were waiting.

170

SHIBUYA UDAGAWA-CHO, TOKYO

Stanislas Yerokhin was the spirit of *glasnost*. To the Japanese – who had got used to Russians as malodorous, sweating buffoons in hideous suits made from felt carpet underlay – the sight of this slim, handsome young man with his razor-cut hair and Hugo Boss suits was a breath of pure clean air from the vast, brooding evil empire. Stan, as he told his new friends to call him, was proof that Gorbachev's reforms would work. He was the Japanese stringer for *Technology Internationale*, a Leningrad-based magazine born from *perestroika*, and further proof that the new regime wanted to sell more to the outside world than MiG fighters, *babushka* dolls and revolution.

He stunned the scientists and businessmen whom he made it his business to know once he had come to Tokyo, working from his spacious three-bedroomed apartment in smart Shibuya Udagawa-cho. While they were uncertain whether Gorbachev was some kind of political *poseur* or a future candidate for the Gulag, Stan – breezily calling his mentor 'Gorby' – declared his revolution unstoppable. His opening line in the early days was to ask his companion what he thought they'd do with all the secret policemen now. He could usually entice them into asking how such a person could be recognized, which gave him the opportunity to beam with delight and say: 'They always go in threes. One to read, one to write and the third to keep an eye on the two intellectuals!' It was quite heady stuff in the early days.

He rapidly made a good name for himself. They liked him not only because he was good company but also for the fact that he had a Master's degree in chemical engineering himself, so all were on broadly common ground. He worked hard to produce his copy, and they found his plea for information – 'because if I don't they'll send me back to Irkutsk' – irresistible. He was generous with money to commission articles of interest to his readers and, once he was accepted within the high-technology community, also with introductions to other people of interest outside Japan. Gum-chewing, hyperactive, he was no *moujik*'s son as he worked the telephone from early on, then bounded out into Tokyo to meet and entertain, in hotel coffee shops and *yakitoriyas*, and finally back in his expensive apartment.

He remained in Tokyo long enough for people to almost forget he was Russian, for while the Berlin Wall fell and the satellite nations started agitating for democracy he never went home. Tokyo was home, he'd say, and he had friends to prove it. One such was Konoe Masaaki, a talented young computer engineer working for Komura Industries. Konoe was of the team harnessed to the *Coral Spear* supercomputer programme, and very discreetly had provided Stan with enough snippets to whet the appetites of his readers as to the nature of the cutting edge of Japanese high technology. The journalist had repaid him with an introduction to a Californian Silicon Valley firm, a meeting which had blossomed into a lucrative weekend consultancy for the engineer.

They met at least once a month, usually in the Russian's apartment with its collection of *ukiyoe* prints, where they ate *sushi* and drank Johnnie Walker Black Label. When Konoe arrived from work one Friday evening, following the call from his friend, he expected the usual wise-cracking, bubbling figure and was saddened and alarmed to see that his friend was clearly very worried. Yerokhin poured them both hefty Scotches.

'Masaaki,' he asked, without preamble. 'Are you still

working with SilTeck? The American firm I introduced you to?'

'Why yes,' Konoe said, puzzled. 'I do work for them every month.'

Yerokhin slumped on to the sofa and thrust his fingers through his blond hair. 'I was afraid of that. I have been told something terrible. SilTeck is owned by the KGB; you've been working for the Russian Secret Police.'

Konoe's wheat-coloured skin went a most peculiar and sickly hue. 'No ...' he muttered. 'No ... I will resign. Today.'

'Yes, yes,' said Yerokhin. 'You must, of course.'

Konoe took a big swallow of whisky to restore his nerves. 'I would be ruined,' he exclaimed as the real horror of it became clear. 'My family, my boy's chance of reaching Todai. All, all would be ruined.'

'Yes, yes,' agreed Yerokhin again. 'Ruin, ruin ... you would all become *burakumin*, to be sure.'

The use of such a word was too much for Konoe. Stiff-legged, he staggered to the bathroom. Had he been less preoccupied with bringing up his whisky he would have been horrified to see the chill satisfaction in his friend's eyes. But when he came back into the room Stan was once again all concern.

'*Burakumin....* outcasts ...' Konoe muttered in horror, as well he might. All decent Japanese felt the same about those of the ritually unclean, the murky sediment of Japanese society, the descendants of butchers and gravediggers, itinerants, gangsters' coolies, those who were not brought up in conversation.

'I can't believe these prehistoric types are still about,' Stan said sadly, shaking his head. 'They're some awful relic of the Cold War ... I feel like some early man, busy inventing fire or something, and seeing one of those great dinosaurs lumbering uselessly over the horizon.'

'Yes, yes,' muttered Konoe. The whisky burned as it went down his already upset oesophagus. 'It is too much that they should do this to honest working people like us.'

'Yes, yes,' Stan murmured softly in sympathy. 'But when the *Tyrannosaurus Rex* crashed over by the caveman and in a manner of speaking suggested he share his lunch, I don't guess the caveman countered with arguments as to the dinosaur's inevitable approaching demise. He passed over his plate of *sushi*, right?'

Konoe peered at Stan through his glasses, which were trying to mist up. 'What do you mean?' he asked in alarm.

'It's like the old joke, Masaaki. You know, what do you call an ape with a machine-gun?'

'Sir,' Konoe whispered.

'What do you say to the KGB, who can ruin you and your family totally, tomorrow, when they ask for a little favour?'

'What do they want?' Konoe asked miserably.

'Just a detailed printout of the physical specification of the supercomputer, *Coral Spear*. Dimensions, weights, parts.'

'What good will that do them? The secret of *Coral Spear*'s power does not lie in its macro-structure. It is like wanting to know how big a tank is without knowing what it is made of.'

'*I* know that. *You* know that. But you have no idea how primitive these people are, Masaaki. They're like a bunch of aboriginals who see a jet airplane and build one themselves out of rocks to worship it. They just aren't a part of this century at all. It's some fool of a bureaucrat in the Lubyanka who wants to pass on a file to his superiors, saying: "See, now we can build our own supercomputer."'

'They won't.'

'That's it,' Stan beamed. 'So it really won't do any harm if we go along with them. You see, it's my ass on the chopping block too. If I don't come up with something they'll call me home and put me on the political staff at *Pravda*.'

Konoe smiled weakly.

'You can do it,' encouraged Stan. 'You have the senior-

174

ity to extract that kind of information. And then you're home free.'

'Okay,' agreed Konoe. He rose unsteadily to his feet. 'I do it.'

Two days later they met in a busy bar across the road from Ueno Park, a 'pencil building' no more than fifteen feet wide and eight storeys high, eight identical stories of Chinese Ming architecture, black-tiled roofs and red-lacquered balconies packed with *saraarimen* consuming Sapporo and Scotch. Konoe arrived with a brown envelope wrapped in a newspaper; he did not touch the whisky the Russian had ordered.

'I do not wish to cause offence,' he said unhappily, 'but I feel we should not meet again.'

'Of course,' Stan murmured. 'I understand.'

As Konoe got up to leave, the man who had been his friend stood as well. He thrust a small envelope across the table.

'Take it,' he urged, pressing it into his hand. 'I can't undo what's done, but take it.'

Stanislas Yerokhin took his envelope and went straight home, where after a swift examination he resealed it and made a short telephone call. Within the hour it was at the heavy eleven-storey Soviet Embassy across town. A little while after that it was in a white minibus heading for the airport.

The Soviets had two avenues open when it came to the acquisition of the high technology their military required. Out in the open worked the well-trained and educated men and women who lobbied the Japanese business and political circles in the same manner as their counterparts in the USA. They were referred to as the clean trade mission people, and concerned themselves with legitimate trade agreements. Their achievements could be great, as when they acquired one of the biggest dry docks in the world, supposedly for the repair of fishing vessels. It was duly delivered to Vladivostok, where the *Minsk* was moved into it. The *Minsk* was an aircraft carrier.

175

When the Japanese balked at selling certain processes or machines, the problem could be handled differently. It could, for example, be turned over to the no less well-trained and educated Scientific and Technological officers of Line X, of Directorate T of the KGB. Line X was the field element of the Directorate, and its S&T specialists by their nature worked clandestinely. Their job was to steal what was required. The headquarters of Line X in Japan was within the KGB's residency that took up the top two floors of the Embassy. From there the Line X agents had links to their comrades elsewhere in Japan. Some were based within the trade mission, some in the Aeroflot offices, some at TASS, some sent in as tourists. The activities of the talented men and women of Line X gave the lie to the belief that Communism was necessarily inefficient. When twice a month the diplomatic couriers arrived from Moscow to escort the diplomatic mail home, they rode from the Embassy to the airport in a white minibus filled with boxes from floor to roof. Weighing as much as a ton, these were samples, technological finds and plans, just two weeks' worth of swag from Line X. The men and women of Directorate T were very proud of themselves, so much so that they gloried and strutted in the publicity they acquired in the West, fast becoming paranoid about the theft of its high technology.

Stanislas Yerokhin did not belong to the KGB, which he regarded with contempt and dislike. Yerokhin was a soldier; he had made his long way from the *Komsomol* through *Spetsnaz* to the *Aquarium* itself, that grim organization which took care of its own in life and in death. All who joined left through the chimney of its crematorium. With honours, in a fringed wooden coffin, if they had served it well and died of natural causes. Strapped to a stretcher, alive, if they ever made the mistake of betraying it. Yerokhin belonged to the GRU, the *Glavnoye Razvedyvatel'noye Upravleniye*, the Main Intelligence Directorate of the General Staff of the Red Army.

The GRU was secret, even within the Soviet Union.

Everyone knew the KGB. Few knew that the KGB's main enemy was not the CIA but the GRU. The GRU also had two floors of the embassy, as far removed from their competitors as possible, in the basement. There their officers worked in packs; it was no accident that their own name for themselves was wolfhounds.

The competition was fierce, for in the Russian manner the many were made to support the few. To be among the few you had to be ruthlessly successful. Those who were were called Vikings. The best of them did not work from the Embassy at all but from elegant apartments in places like Mayfair or Georgetown. Or Shibuya Udagawa-Cho.

A week after the brown envelope left for Moscow there was a light tap on the fire-escape door at Stan's apartment. He had been alerted by telephone and was waiting to let his visitor in. It was Vladimir Livenko, the GRU resident or 'Navigator'.

He embraced Stan. 'I bring official congratulations, Lieutenant-Colonel Yerokhin,' he said, announcing his promotion.

Taking a small, flat box from his jacket pocket – as Stanislas Yerokhin stood rigidly, proudly to attention – Livenko pinned through the soft cotton of his Studio Ferre shirt the order of Hero of the Soviet Union.

The KGB was to have no part in the magnificent victory the Red Army was about to win. And was it not the victors who set the terms? In the long war between the KGB and the Red Army, there might be a final victor. After the victory.

THE WARDMAN TOWER, 4200 CONNECTICUT AVENUE, WASHINGTON

The Wardman Tower was old, by the standards of the city. It had turn-of-the-century architecture, and plumbing to match. In its days of glory Mrs Eisenhower had lived there, along with Chief Justice Earl Warren and General Lawton, while in the lobby a string quartet played light opera. George Bush, Spiro Agnew and the CIA's original political operative Miles Copeland had lived there too. Its acquisition by Sheraton Hotels reduced its exclusivity for those who cared about such things, but National Security Advisor Kuusinen – a historian by training who gained intellectual pleasure from being in old places, simply from the company of the ghosts whose lives had been lived there – snapped up a lease as soon as it became available, and had himself installed within the week.

In the morning as dawn was breaking he enjoyed the view from the highest point in Washington, looking down over the Rock Creek Park towards the city itself; at night, the sparkling lights beneath.

His government Lincoln dropped him off, he rode the elevator to the sixth floor, and when he went in his private telephone was ringing. His wife was away, visiting their elder daughter, and the suite was empty.

'Hallo?'

'Mr Kuusinen. I'm glad to find you at home.'

The voice was Russian, a Muscovite. Kuusinen had

178

spoken Russian as a second language when he was six.

'Yes?' he said warily.

'My name is Mazurov, Viktor Mazurov. I am a captain with Aeroflot.'

'May I ask how you got this number, Mr Mazurov? It is meant to be private,' Kuusinen said mildly.

'My father gave it to me,' the voice said softly.

'Yes,' said Kuusinen.

'May I come to see you? I have a message for you from my father ... and a gift.'

'Come now. I'll leave word that I'm expecting you.'

'I'm in the lobby of the Sheraton. I'll be only a minute.'

Mazurov's son was as good as his word.

'You look like your father,' said Kuusinen, 'although it is very many years since I was with him.'

They went in. Kuusinen favoured the elegant furniture from the land of his birth, so both host and guest were at home, for in Moscow it was the chosen trappings of the *vlasti* of whom Viktor Mazurov was one.

'First,' said the middle-aged pilot, 'the gift.'

He took a small envelope from his jacket pocket and gave it to Kuusinen. It was heavy for its size, and on opening it an old but unfired lead and brass cartridge fell into his hand.

'Do you know what it is?'

'Of course.' Kuusinen turned it to look at the tip. Scratched into the lead, once shining bright but now dark with age, were a set of initials.

'What would your father like in exchange for this gift?' he asked levelly.

'He would like you to do something for him – something he cannot do himself. In Moscow, there is a man called Aleksandr Borodin. He lives in Alexei Tolstoy street and he is the foremost expert on the People's Republic of China within the Soviet Union.'

'Go on.'

'My father wishes this man to be ruined.'

'In what way?'

'He is very expert. His predictions as to events within

179

the PRC, as to the attitudes and policies of that country's leaders have much more often been right than wrong. My father would like to have ... "evidence" ... that this has not been due simply to professional skill but to the fact that Borodin is, and has been for years, a Chinese agent within the USSR.'

'And I can do this?'

'Yes. You are a powerful and influential man. You know who to tap to do this.'

'I am a powerful and influential man: I can give you back this gift and tell you to return home.'

'You are alive,' said the Russian. 'The bullet is in your hand, not in what would remain of your head, in Karelia.'

'Nor my father,' murmured Kuusinen. 'Those are his initials, scratched there.'

'My father says that the past is always with you, it never goes away.'

'He is right. Very well. When I have what your father requires, how shall I pass it to him?'

'We stay at the Marriot, downtown. Leave the bullet in an envelope for me there. When I find it I will return and collect the evidence.'

'How will your father put it into effect?'

'My father was head of *Komitet Gosudarstvennoy Bezopasnosti*, the Committee for State Security.'

'I know what the KGB is called, Mr Mazurov,' Kuusinen said mildly, 'and I know the heads of the Russian secret police from Dzerzhinskiy through your father to Kobulov, under whatever title.'

'So when my father was head of the KGB,' his son continued, unabashed, 'he ensured, by one means or another, that there were certain officers whose promotion and continued good fortune were dependent upon his good will. That good fortune still remains dependent upon his good will. He will have no problem in presenting your evidence as part of a counter-intelligence investigation that – starting within the USA – uncovered evidence of a traitor high in the ranks of our own government, a traitor who is revealed as the foremost sinologist – Aleksandr Borodin.'

'Very well. I will have it done.'

The Russian bowed. 'My father thanks you. And he says, if you will, to do it sooner rather than later. This is something that will not wait.'

'What is it that Borodin has done, I wonder?' mused Kuusinen. 'I was under the impression that your father had miraculously metamorphosed into some kind of avuncular political wise man, friend of sapling political parties and lame dogs.'

'I am just a messenger, sir. I take orders and transmit them.'

'Sooner rather than later, then.'

With the Russian gone, Kuusinen was as good as his word. He picked up the phone and dialled; when he got no reply he checked his telephone book and pressed the buttons again.

'Hallo, K.K.? You're in your car. Are you nearby? Would you like to stop by on your way home? Yes? See you soon, then.'

Thrale was at the Wardman Tower within thirty minutes.

'I was on my way from McLean,' he said. 'That's where Dr Bartlett's widow still lives. Do you want me to tell you how far I've got, or do you want to talk to me first?'

'You go ahead,' Kuusinen told him. The suite was quiet, his wife still away helping her daughter to cope with a new baby.

'Okay. The similarities between the two deaths, Bartlett and the late President. Both happened at night, both men died in their bathrooms, both in circumstances that the ailing Professor Cameron diagnosed as pulmonary embolism. I asked both Mrs Bartlett and Mrs Hawkins whether it was common for their husbands to get up in the night, and both ladies said it was the rule. The President had a slightly weak bladder following a prostate operation some time ago, and Dr Bartlett liked to drink several glasses of mineral water before going to bed,

181

which always had the effect of getting him up again in the middle of the night.

'Now. It is just possible that an assassin managed to get inside Bartlett's house, waited in his bathroom for him to get up, shot him with some kind of KGB/CIA type gas gun and then made good his escape. Possible, but unlikely, since apparently he was very security-minded and the house well equipped with devices.'

Kuusinen fixed two drinks and brought them over to the bleached pine sofas across the glass coffee table.

'Thanks,' said Thrale. 'An assassin within the White House becomes even less likely. Whoever did this did not set about it in order to gamble; in which case it had to be real certainty. Similarities. Both bathrooms ensuite with the master bedrooms, both equipped with non-opening windows, air-conditioned. Air-conditioned. Apart from the door the only access to both rooms was through the air-conditioning duct. Now, I don't know how you'd get a nerve gas to your victim through a duct, but as Sherlock Holmes said, if you have eliminated all the other possibilities then that must be it.

'Mrs Hawkins wouldn't know anything about the air-conditioning in the White House, but I thought Mrs Bartlett might. I asked her if she'd had anything at all done to hers – she had a big unit serving the whole house. When I prodded her a bit she remembered that not long after her husband's death someone had come by, an air-conditioning technician, to fix something in the unit. He said it was a replacement of some part within it, done free under the manufacturer's instructions as it was a faulty design. She was grieving at the time, and didn't take much notice. She said he was a nice, polite young man, some kind of Asian – Chinese maybe, or from Hawaii or the Philippines, she thought. He did his stuff very efficiently and went away.'

Thrale took a pull at his bourbon. 'I called Westinghouse and they say there's nothing wrong with that model, and never has been.'

'Ahhh ...' breathed Kuusinen.

182

'Now, if anyone got at the air-conditioning in the White House he'd have to be a member of the Public Service Bureau. So I went along there and had a look through their files, found three Asian-looking technicians there. When I borrowed the photographs and showed them to Mrs Bartlett, she identified this one.'

Thrale opened his briefcase and pulled out the PSB folder. It showed a pleasant-faced young man, oriental, neat, well-groomed.

'Lin Pao. Lives on his own over in Chinatown.'

'What're you going to do?'

'Wait until he goes to work tomorrow, have a look around his rooms. Then go from there.'

'Okay,' said Kuusinen. 'Take care.'

'You know it.'

'You look better. Are you sleeping?'

'Work seems to be agreeing with me.'

'The ghosts gone away?'

'For the time being,' Thrale said fatalistically. 'They'll be back. They always come back.'

'Want to do something else for me, special assistant?'

'What?'

'You ever use disinformation to ruin anyone?'

'Sure. We ruined a number of left-wing politicians in Japan during the occupation. That was when we were getting worried about the red threat and the Korean War. That's why the Liberal Party ran the place from then on; that's why Komura got so powerful. We did it, you know. If we're complaining about what the Japs are doing now we ought to remember that we did it, we put the same bunch that fought the war against us back into power in the first place.'

'I need to ruin someone.'

'Yes?' Thrale said warily.

'A Russian. Aleksandr Borodin.'

'I know Borodin. The sinologist. Lives on Alexei Tolstogo like a Yansheng Duke. If he wasn't so good at his job, you'd say he was a nut.'

'It has to appear that Borodin is so good because he is

183

actually a Chinese agent.'

'Sure ...' Thrale said softly. 'Okay, then. I won't ask why. You and I always read from the same sheet of music on these things.'

'Thank you.'

'Where do I start?'

'With one of *our* sinologists – guy over at State, Cy Rogers. He owes me. Start with him. When we know what evidence we want, we can start putting hard pieces together.'

'I'll call him in the morning.'

'Good. I read your file on Komura. Can we deal with him?'

'Not unless he wants to. He lives out at the Komura mansion. The politicians come to *him*.'

'He really is as powerful as you say?'

'Isn't the President of the USA one of the two most powerful men on earth? But Barnet's a lame duck. Yanov's got troubles of his own. *Komura* understood what the young officers of the Kwantung Army understood in the 1930s, that the heart of the Japanese system of power is hollow. Occupy it and the system obeys you. Japan is the most powerful economy in the world, and Komura is the most powerful man in it.'

'So what do we do?'

'Do? That's above my pay grade. But he's an old man, like me. I'd say you hope he dies before he does something nasty to you.'

SEE CUBED EYE — C^3I
— CONTROL

ADAMSTOWN, MARYLAND

Betty's Place was strategically situated to net the thirsty and hungry streaming back from the nation's capital to their Maryland homes at night. It did not attract trash; these were respectable folk. Clean and softly-lit, with college girls in cowgirl dress waiting table, it featured live music at the weekend; in the week the patrons made do with music from a genuine Wurlitzer, or watched the big television over the bar.

Thrale had stopped off there for years; since the death of his wife he had taken to eating his evening meal as well. His house was empty and filled with memories, and the bar created an illusion of companionship. It was also only a short ride home when the time came.

His neighbour at the long wood and brass bar was Ryan Murphy, a big, red-haired man with his own construction company who liked to stop off for one Bud before going home. The two men arrived almost simultaneously. Out of habit they peered up at the screen, which was in the middle of changing programmes.

Barnet was on the screen. He wore a dark double-breasted suit and a striped military tie. The silvering at his temples only served to add *gravitas* to his appearance. Behind him at his leather and oak desk were the potent symbols of his authority – the Presidential flag and the flag of the United States of America. He was in the Oval Office, the illuminated Rose Garden visible through the open drapes.

Murphy grunted. 'Say, Charley, where's the football?'

'President's on the tube,' shrugged the bartender. 'All channels.'

The big Irishman grimaced in resignation, but dutifully

187

sat back to listen to what his President had to say.

'My fellow Americans. After I came home from church on Sunday, and before we had our meal, I had a little free time. I was in the library and I found some old books I had not read since I was at college. In one of them I found a character called Mrs Doasyouwouldbe-doneby. Do as you would be done by. And you know, that set me thinking.

'Do as you would be done by. That's the American way. We face the world four-square. We're not under-hand, and we don't expect other folk in the world to be underhand with us. What you see is what you get. Isn't it? Since the end of the Second World War the world has seen unprecedented prosperity and, well, I think we Americans can take a little bit of the credit for that. We've allowed anyone who wanted to to trade with us, the way we've traded with them. In fact, we've allowed people to trade with us who didn't allow us to trade with them. But that's the American way. We understood that after the devastation of war people had to rebuild their economies, and we helped them to do it with grants of aid and ideas that were far from insubstantial. We helped put on to their feet the very peoples who had waged war upon us in the first place. Because it's the American way. We do as we would be done by.'

Barnet's handsome face creased into a set that was both sad yet stern.

'But there are folks out there who don't think that way, and who have taken advantage of our open natures to make deep inroads into our own fine economy. They rig their own market so that we may not compete freely with them. They use unfair commercial practices to drive honest American firms out of business, and when they have waxed fat on the proceeds they come into our country seeking to buy up good American enterprises with the money they have cheated out of us.'

A Massachusetts card table was set at the President's right hand, on it it kept photographs of his family. He gestured to them.

188

'It's been worrying me for some time. There are good people out there hurting, and it's not their fault. Yet I wasn't sure what to do. So I did what I always do when troubled in mind, I talked to my family. When I was through, my youngest boy looked me in the eye and he said to me: "Dad, you know what to do. You talk to the Congressmen and Senators and they'll help you, because they're Americans first and party second. But I'll help you myself." And he got up from the dinner table and went out.

'He wasn't gone too long. I was working on some papers and he came in and asked if I had a moment free, since he wanted to give me something. He took a badge from his pocket and placed it on the table. It was off his automobile. He had worked hard to buy it; it took him a while. I have the badge here.'

Barnet reached in his suit pocket and tossed a twisted roundel of aluminium on to the leather top of the desk. The Honda logo was clearly visible to the camera.

'He put it in the crusher. He's got a new one, an American one. He gave me a grin as he left, he said: "It's back to working nights after college, Dad." And he's told me he's going to do the same with all the other things, the television, the hi-fi. He's going to buy American.'

On the screen, Barnet spread his hands to his nation in enquiry.

'Me? What am I going to do? Well, I've already done something. I went and talked to the Congressmen and the Senators, and they're passing a bill. The Do As You Would Be Done By Bill. The Fair's Fair Bill. Honest folk who want to trade with us and let us trade with them have nothing to fear. Others do. Unfair competition, unfair practices, the unfair subversion of our society stops here.'

Barnet tapped the desk in front of him significantly.

'Here. Where the buck stops. And now. It's time now for a new chapter, a new start.'

The picture faded and, beside Thrale, Murphy slammed his beer can to the bartop.

189

'Damn if he ain't right! Charley, hand me the phone!'

Murphy stabbed out the numbers with a finger like a tie-rod.

'Hank? Glad you still in the office. You got Chevy pick-ups on your lot? Okay. Put three by for me. I'll take them in the morning.

'That you, Tom? I want you to get your ass down to your plant, because I'm coming by. This heap of Japanese junk I been riding in is going to get turned into aluminium to hold American beer for Americans to drink.

'Shelagh? Get the old Ford out of the garage, come meet me at Tom Bailey's crusher. Just do as I say, woman.'

Murphy thrust the telephone back into its cradle and stood up tall and fired by his mission. He grinned savagely at Thrale.

'Got to go,' he said. 'Got a date. Say, K.K., what d'*you* drive?'

'1970 Cadillac Fleetwood,' Thrale said unemotionally.

'Well *allright*!' Murphy turned grinning to the other similarly-fired patrons. 'You wouldn't get old K.K. driving Japanese, would you? Man, he used to kill those little yellow bug-fuckers for a living!'

Thrale left the bar early. He slid behind the big wheel, fired up the huge V-8.

'Oh, Lord,' he said quietly.

THE OVAL OFFICE, THE WHITE HOUSE

The White House Office of Communications cameras and their crews had gone back across the road to the EOB. Barnet still sat behind his ornate desk, now in shirtsleeves, a cup of cold coffee in front of him. Time to be on your own was rare and to be valued, he had discovered. The burble of the telephone cut in on what he had left before going to bed. It was Ed Reisch from his adjoining office.

'It's Tony Jacobs,' he said.

Barnet picked up his receiver. 'This is the President.'

'Tony Jacobs, Mr President. That was one of the best performances by a politician on the tube I have seen,' he said sincerely. 'The visual as you tossed the bent Honda badge on the desk was brilliant.'

The director – a lean, nervous boy whose thirty-second messages had picked up awards and sold beer, deodorant and politicians to the public with equal success – had had Barnet practise the action over and over until perfect.

'You seem to have found the hottest button around. Radical chic is going to be driving an old muscle-car while waiting for your new one from Detroit. And playing your American hi-fi. And watching your American tube. It'll do wonders for the economy.'

There was a pause.

'When we met after your inauguration I said that unless you had access to some hot button I did not know about, then through circumstances not of your

191

own making you would lose the election. Without doubt you have found that button, and it is yours to keep. If you'll have me, I'd like to come on board.'

SINGAPORE, FEBRUARY 1942

They had come all the way down the peninsula, slipping through the rubber plantations, fighting in the dark, pushing the enemy back, back, back. Until they were here ... at the island at the end, where the reality came home, that 30,000 of them were attempting to defeat 100,000 of the enemy, now inside the defences of that island. A fortress. The greatest symbol of the enemy's might in his Empire in the far east. The officers seated and squatting around the sand-table were fired by *bushido*, but were also seasoned professionals who knew that when assaulting defensive positions, let alone fortresses, the odds were supposed to be in *your* favour, not the enemy's.

'We have command of the air,' said Yonai.

'Brigadier, the aircraft are short of petrol,' put in the Colonel who had come from Yamashita's staff.

'Our artillery can fire at will. We are in range.'

'We are short of shells.'

'Our troops are second to none. The fighting spirit of the soldiers of the Emperor will crush all.'

'Assuredly,' the Colonel said hurriedly. 'But they are also down to one hundred rounds per man. Without artillery, without constant bombing, without ammunition, even the soldiers of the Emperor will find it difficult. It will be done, of course, but it has to succeed, for our reserves are not sufficient to allow much more than one more week's fighting.'

There was a silence while all stared balefully at the sand model of the island.

'May I make a suggestion?' asked Komura.

193

'Please do,' Yonai answered politely. 'Colonel, this is Major Komura, our intelligence officer.'

'If I may give you my assessment of the enemy, I can then pass on some intelligence I have received and make a suggestion. At the beginning of the century, did we not see the British as strong? As virile, as male. They held the greatest Empire on earth, they behaved as men. We were pleased to make our alliance with them. But since then it is we who have become the man – and the British and the Americans, they have become soft, they are indecisive. Feminine. For example, when our soldiers of the Manchurian Army moved into Mukden in 1931 the British and Americans made threats and complaints, but did not back them up with action. They were feminine. It was we who were masculine. Nothing has changed.'

Komura took a flimsy piece of paper from his jacket.

'I have here some intelligence from inside the fortress. The British are shipping out their own. Running. Leaving behind the Chinese, Malays, Tamils. A few days ago a ship filled with naval technicians, army nursing sisters and senior harbour officials left secretly. Now I am told that others are making secret plans to leave – most of the staff of the public works department, an admiral and the head of their air force. The general commanding the Australian troops.'

The officers all were watching Komura intently.

'They are feminine. Afraid. Ready to run. I believe that with the limited supplies we have left we can make a final push that will secure us the island. But, let us make sure.'

Komura put his intelligence report back in his pocket.

'We have been here before. When we were taking Hong Kong. After we had captured the city, I found signals from their leader, Winston Churchill, in the Government House, clearly ordering them to fight to the last man. On Christmas Day, our forces entered the hospital of St Stephen, where they bayoneted the patients and most of the staff. The bodies they threw in a pile outside. They captured many of the nurses, and

194

these they kept in a room. Some they took out and fucked on the pile of bodies. There were plenty, so from time to time some were bayoneted. They screamed, of course, as women will.'

There was silence in the little room, just the intermittent rattle of machine-gun fire not far away.

'From my interrogations after the British surrendered it is clear to me that by our actions in the hospital we weakened the British will to fight on. They were ordered by their commander – their emperor – to fight to the last man. They disobeyed, and surrendered, because they were as women are, and cowardly. No Japanese soldier would do that.

'Once again, my intelligence reports indicate that Churchill has ordered his commanders here to fight to the last man. They will not do it. They are short of water. So are we. They are short of ammunition. So are we. They are short of spirit. We are not. It will require but a small gesture to make them surrender once we attack.'

Komura leaned over the sand table, and indicated with a slim bamboo stick.

'Here. The military hospital in Alexandra. An attack in force. Take care of them the way we did in Hong Kong. I believe it will work.'

They paraded the British general through the streets in his underpants, remarking to each other just how much like an old, frightened woman he looked. They put his soldiers in the jail while they tried to think what to do with them all. So that the Chinese, Malays and Tamils understood the Imperial way, they executed groups of them and stuck their heads on poles, in threes, on the street corners.

Then they moved on, in search of more victories.
Hakko ichiu.

195

ZHUKOVKA-2, MOSCOW

Vyacheslav Mazurov had taken to not going to bed in his old age. Instead, well-wrapped in pyjamas, cashmere dressing-gown and wool slippers – all spoils of a past visit to represent his country at the UN – he preferred to sleep in front of the fire in his library. There he reclined in blissful comfort in a magical American chair which adjusted itself wholly to his whim at the touch of an electrical button, producing footstool, spreading arms and leaning its back at will. His library looked out over the clearing in the birches and maples outside, where the lane that led from the highway ended. Beyond was the slow-flowing Moskva River. A light sleeper, Mazurov would sometimes rise in the night to peer out over his rural domain, lit by the stars and moon, and return to his chair where he would lie refreshed before dropping off to sleep again. He was often awake again in the hour before dawn, a habit that was a relic from his past.

It was thus that he saw and heard the KGB coming to take him away for execution.

The glare of the Chaika lights splashed over the walls; there was the tattoo of slamming doors. The boots that crashed on his wooden steps were heavy, the gloved hands pounding on his front door like hams. They were doing it in the old style; it was the way of Mazurov's youth.

He heard the frightened footsteps of Rai, his housekeeper, going across the hall, and he operated the button of his chair, which pulled itself in and became upright once again. He switched on the light by the table to show where he was and sat waiting.

The door to the library burst open, slamming back against the shelves on the wall. A huge figure advanced, in the hallway Rai wailed, and the doorway filled with goons. A hand shook out a newspaper and thrust it in front of his face.

'You're famous,' sneered the voice. 'You made the papers.'

Mazurov brushed the paper aside with one hand.

'I do not read the news until after breakfast,' he said coldly.

The man dropped the paper to the floor and put his hands on the arms of Mazurov's chair, thrusting his huge, beefy face up close to the old man. Stale sweat billowed out from the folds of his stained raincoat; he spoke with the putrid breath of old vodka.

'You're coming with us,' he said. 'It's your turn now.'

'Gorkov, you are a decaying piece of a pig's anus. You stink.' Mazurov's voice cracked like a whip. 'Stand away from me. Stand there, while I inform you of some immutable truths.'

Uncertainly, the big man shifted away from Mazurov. He had forgotten that this old man was not like the others – the ones he had tormented, abused and killed in a long career of service to his party.

'From what vodka-sodden pit did they drag you, I wonder?' Mazurov mused. 'I guessed that he would send one of your ilk. It would appeal to what passes for the little man's sense of humour. I know you, Gorkov. I know you better than whichever sow it was that gave birth to you. I know you because I have your file. Not just your official file, but your real file. The one I had made for me. It's all there. The things you did.'

'I have only ever followed orders,' Gorkov said uncertainly.

'We did not accept that from the Hitlerites, and the Westerners will not accept it from you if I show them your file. And did not your orders tell you to but arrest and send to the Gulag the Simenov family? Where was the order that told you to rape the daughter before you

197

did so? I see why you did it; no decent Russian woman would lie with such as you voluntarily, and you doubtless reasoned that a man had to have relief somehow. And what of the Orlovs, who wished to emigrate to Israel? Did you not bleed them of their money with false promises of aid in their quest? And when it was gone, did you not betray them and did they not die in the camps?'

'If you knew these things then, why do they matter now?' asked Gorkov. 'What has changed?'

'The world has changed. *That* was the reality of Communism, that was how it worked. While we preached the world revolution we could treat our own in that way. But Communism is a dead letter. To support ourselves we have gone cap in hand to the West for money, for the technology Communism cannot invent. In the West, they are not used to governments and their employees behaving in this way. Men and women who work for their television channels would love to make programmes about it for their viewers. If I feel like it, I shall donate your file to them as a suitable place to start.'

Mazurov stared up at Gorkov like a rattlesnake.

'There are still camps. Not as of old, but still up there are suitable places of punishment. For spattering our motherland with filth before the eyes of the Westerners, I think they would very happily send you there for a few years of treatment.'

'But ... it is you that is to be taken away, not me ... how can you do this ...'

'I do it because I use my brain, an organ you do not possess. Now go! Go back to the little man and tell him just why you have not brought me before him in manacles, as you were instructed. You may as well, for I shall. Then tell him I will see him too. He is to come here. Not before noon, I think.'

'You cannot address the President like this.'

'I can. I do. Now take your foul presence from me. I never wish to see it again.'

As the lights of the cars vanished down the lane Rai stood trembling where the men had been. She wiped the tears of terror from her face.

'Rai,' Mazurov said benignly, 'our sleep has been disturbed. It is not yet dawn. I shall breakfast at eight as usual. I am indebted to the Westerners today. I shall eat like they do. Coffee, toast, scrambled eggs, jam. But for now, a little rest after our interruption.'

When his housekeeper had gone, Mazurov picked up the paper that had fallen on the floor. It was the *Washington Post*. A picture filled the page. A man stood at the head of an open grave, where Russian soldiers were throwing in the bodies. The man directing them was young, it was an old photograph. Half a century later, Mazurov stared at his past.

SHINJUKU, TOKYO

The trains on the Yamanote Line were nearly a quarter of a mile long, crammed tight, shipping out the millions who every morning came into Tokyo to work. They arrived and departed every two to three minutes during the evening rush hour, and were as full as they could become.

Stanislas Yerokhin stood by the ticket gate for Nakano on the Chuo Railway Line as the immaculate, expressionless, almost odourless crowds of people flooded off the Yamanote trains. He knew he did not have long to wait; the little computer engineer was as reliable as his machines.

He picked Konoe Masaaki out of the crowds like a sportsman picking out his target in a flock of fast-flying pigeons, and intercepted him before he could go through the gates.

'Masaaki,' he said, and the engineer looked at him in horror.

'I have to see you,' the Russian said urgently. 'Something has happened.'

Konoe looked longingly through the gate, where only twenty minutes away stood his little stucco-fronted wooden house with its Mediterranean-blue roof tiles, his wife and two children, in a good part of the town where the road wound through the houses like a little, friendly alley. But Yerokhin had a hold of his elbow.

'It won't wait,' he insisted.

They went to a bar, where they slipped into a small booth.

'Masaaki,' Yerokhin said sadly, 'our balls are in the

wringer, old friend. Last night I was contacted by someone in the KGB. The same man who wanted the drawings of the *Coral Spear* computer.'

'But I gave you what he wanted!' Konoe yelped fearfully, and then put a hand over his mouth, thinking that other people might hear.

'You did, you did,' Yerokhin agreed miserably. 'But you know how it is; they always want more.'

'Well, I won't do it!' the little man said bravely. 'No more!'

The Russian sighed and reached inside his jacket.

'He gave me these,' he said.

The photographs showed the interior of the 'pencil building' bar where Konoe had handed over the envelope containing drawings of the Komura supercomputer. Although it had been dark, the photographs were clear, taken through an image-intensifying lens. They showed Yerokhin picking up the envelope, they showed him thrusting a small one with money into Konoe's hand.

'They'll say I'm a KGB agent. *I'll* get shipped back and you ... you they will hang.'

'You *are* a KGB agent,' Konoe said bravely.

Yerokhin sighed. 'I'm not, you know,' he said truthfully. 'But anyway, is it important? The important thing for little people like us is to avoid being crushed by the unfeeling and uncaring mighty. They do not, after all, want you to do much.'

'What do they want?' whispered Konoe. He wiped his glasses, which were beginning to mist up. Yerokhin glanced across to a nearby table. Another European got up, bringing the beer he had been nursing, and slid in opposite them in the booth. He was round-faced, with enquiring eyes, and had hands with long, sensitive fingers.

'Masaaki, meet a fellow-colleague, Yuri Serov. He knows about computers, the same as you. He would like to have a look at *Coral Spear*. To play with it for a while. We'd like you to get him to it and leave him there. Overnight, on his own.'

201

RABAUL, SOUTH PACIFIC, APRIL 1943

The nurse came out of the room and went down the corridor carrying her tray. Komura slipped through the *fusuma* paper door and slid it shut behind him. The room was lit by a simple lantern of split bamboo and oiled paper, one of its four faces displaying an ideogram of bold brushwork. On the table by the bed a single white iris bloomed from a bed of washed stones.

The man in the bed was very, very thin, and his pale skin the deep yellow of jaundice. Under the wrap of his *yukata* Komura could see a body stitched like patchwork. The eyes snapped open; he was as alert as a dragon.

'Komura.'

'Brigadier.'

Komura bowed respectfully and Yonai inclined his head.

'What are you doing here?'

'My boss, General Hori, stopped off to see Admiral Yamamoto on his way to Truk. They told me you were here.'

'You are kind to come and relieve me of a little time spent waiting for this feeble body to recover.'

'Not so feeble ... I have a little piece of intelligence, gleaned from the Americans.'

'Ah?' Yonai pushed himself a little more upright, looking interested.

'At Guadalcanal, the first week of February, as the Navy was taking off our troops. There was a battalion

202

there, fighting a rearguard action to assist in the evacu-
ation, to cover for its fellow-soldiers getting on to the
ships. It fought so hard the Americans thought that it
was fresh – reinforcements sent in – that they could
expect a renewed attack by our forces.'

Yonai's sunken eyes gleamed.

'It was the Yano Battalion,' Komura said.

Breath hissed from Yonai's chest, filled with pride.

'We came in with the 38th Division in October. By
February there were so few of us left that I, a Brigadier,
commanded a battalion. And they thought we were fresh
troops ...'

'I thought that you would like to know. Our withdrawal
from Guadalcanal was one of the most successful in
history. And much credit goes to you.'

Yonai turned his face away. 'Withdrawal ... retreat ...
these are not words to be associated with the Japanese
Imperial Army.'

'It was not your fault.'

'There were no supplies ...' whispered Yonai. 'No food
... my troops spent their days foraging; we lived on rats
and insects, and bitter roots. One day a submarine
arrived, it brought seeds for us to sow "victory gardens".
Seeds were not what we needed. Where were the
convoys? Where were the supplies?'

'The Americans sank them,' Komura said softly.

'*Sank them.*' Yonai stared angrily at Komura. 'We won
the battle of Midway in order that the Americans sink
our supply ships?'

'Warships,' said Komura. 'Only warships could survive.
Sometimes. And we lost the battle of Midway.'

Yonai's face was like stone.

'Why do you tell me these lies?'

Komura looked down at his hands, clasped between
his knees.

'I'm an intelligence officer. When I was an infantry
officer I believed what I was told. As an intelligence
officer, for me to serve the Emperor, I have to know the
truth. Not what we tell the hundred million at home, but

203

the truth. And we lost the battle of Midway. Just as we lost Guadalcanal. We had "victory disease". The admirals didn't tell Tojo about Midway until a month later. The hundred million aren't going to be told.'

'How can the Americans sink our ships? If we send warships to supply our soldiers?'

'Have you heard of Commander Sanematsu? Of the Navy General Staff?'

Yonai's brow wrinkled. 'Yes ... he praises America, isn't that right? He's in love with their materialism. I'd like him in my Brigade; he wouldn't last long.'

'He was stationed in Washington when we attacked Pearl Harbor. He was repatriated in an exchange of diplomats. I was able to talk to him a little while ago. The USA is the greatest industrial nation in the world. Her productive capacity is ten times ours.'

'The Americans are women,' Yonai said contemptuously. 'No nation on earth can match the fighting ability of our soldiers.'

'No nation on earth,' agreed Komura. 'And no nation on earth can match the Americans in production of war material. Last June their government signed a contract with a shipbuilder – Henry Kaiser – on their west coast, to build escort aircraft carriers. Two weeks ago the wife of President Roosevelt went to the yard in Oregon to launch the first one. It's called the USS *Casablanca*. It carries thirty aircraft – as many as one of our light carriers. They built it in nine months, but that's down to three, now. They laid the keel of number two hundred and ninety-one last week. Do you want to know what happened to the warships sent to supply you? Sunk. *At night.*'

'It is well-known that the Americans, like women, dislike the night. Our forces are far superior.'

'True. The Americans tracked our warships with radar. They directed their gunfire with radar, and they launched their torpedoes with radar. Our mighty fighter, the Zero, is being beaten by new American aircraft – the P-38, the F-6U. My boss went to see Admiral Yamamoto

204

last November – when you were fighting at Guadalcanal. They are old bridge partners, they talk freely. The Admiral said: "The real battle now is a competition between Japanese discipline and American scientific technology."'

'Exactly. The fighting spirit of our soldiers can defeat all odds. The hundred million advance as a single bullet.'

'Our discipline made one thousand men advance into the mouths of the guns at Guadalcanal. They all died. Because the Americans have new *men*, too. Admiral Halsey is not an old woman. He tells his men to "kill Japs, kill Japs, kill more Japs" – and they do. "Howling Mad" Smith's Marines don't take prisoners. We are everywhere on the retreat.'

'It will take the Americans for ever to fight their way down the Solomons. By which time we will have won the war in China, and there will be no reason for the war to continue.'

'Ahh ... but the war in China was supposed to be won in a month. That was four years ago ... and what if they *don't* fight their way down the Solomons?'

'They must.'

'What if they take one island, then go around? Encircle, let our troops starve to death while they attack another further along? "Leapfrogging", they call it.'

'It will still take them for ever.'

'They will be bombing our homeland soon.'

'With what?' Yonai jeered. 'So Doolittle's terror fliers managed a token raid. It did no damage.'

'B-san is coming,' Komura said softly.

'And who is B-san?'

'B-san is their new bomber. The B-29. I talked to some engineers at Mitsubishi, once I heard the news that Boeing had a new four-engined bomber under construction. *They* have plans for a bomber that could bomb the West Coast from the Kuriles. They have plans, the Americans have the aircraft. In a year, they'll be here.'

'The *Kempe Tai* is looking for people like you,' Yonai said coldly.

205

'They should look for Admiral Yamamoto. He and my boss had drinks last night. He says the war is lost.'

Yonai managed to sit upright despite his wounds, so angry was he.

'Yamamoto shall be shot,' he spat out.

'He has been,' said Komura. 'American fighters ambushed him today. He went on a long trip to tour the advanced bases. They found him and shot him down.'

'Chance.'

'It was a special, élite unit. They *knew*.'

'How can they know?'

'What if they have cracked our codes?'

Yonai sank back in his bed. 'They cannot even understand Japanese, let alone crack our codes.' he said contemptuously.

'Perhaps their technology can. Perhaps they know everything we do.'

Komura stood up. 'I am sorry to have taken your time.'

Yonai did not reply.

Komura paused by the door. 'The hundred million advance as a ball of flame,' he said. 'Of course we will win.'

ZHUKOVKA-2, MOSCOW

The soft buzz outside told Mazurov that the car which had arrived was not Russian, but from the West. A glance through his window showed Nikolai Serov hurrying from his smart white Volkswagen, and within a few moments he was with him in the library. Gripped tightly in one hand was a copy of the *Washington Post*.

'Have you seen?' he said fearfully. 'I came out ... I was not sure if you would still be here.'

Mazurov held up a hand reassuringly. 'Calm yourself. Yanov sent goons, but they have been repelled. I await the arrival of their master.'

'Yanov is coming here?'

'I sent for him,' Mazurov said simply.

'Sent ... sent ... oh....' Serov muttered, frantic with anxiety.

'Nikolai, I can defend us. Yanov will not destroy us as he thinks.'

'I came to see if you were gone, to warn you, but now that you know ... listen. I called Nick Galloway, the American. The correspondent for *US News & World Report*. He's over at the Gorki. Now I know they haven't taken you, I'll go and see him.'

As quickly as he had come, hyperactive with worry, Serov had bounded out of the library. He was scurrying through the larches and birch trees to his car before the realization of what he had said hit Mazurov. The old man got out of his chair and went as quickly as he could to the window.

'Nikolai!' The sound of his voice was drowned by the whirring of the little car's starter motor, and then earth spurted from the front tyres as Serov pressed the pedal.

He drove quickly along the leafy lane that led to Mazurov's dacha, before pausing by the gate where he joined the road that led to the Uspenskoe highway, his car very white against the green foliage. A mile down the way, where the ground rose again after falling into a gentle valley, two vast tank transporters – complete with loads of a T-72 tank each – stood parked where the road widened. As Serov turned towards Moscow, they began to move.

Serov was hitting seventy-five miles an hour as he came to the base of the valley and began to climb the gentle slope. The transporters were grinding towards him, their enormous diesel engines bellowing at full throttle. As he skimmed over the road towards the leading one – as his bonnet was almost passing the massive front of the first one as it travelled the other way – the second, pressed close up against its partner's tail, pulled out with a speed that belied its size. The transporter was seventy-six feet long from its girder front bumper to the folded ramps behind the 48-ton main battle-tank on its deck. Nikolai Serov travelled the entire distance with all four of the wheels of his Golf locked, slowing down from over seventy miles per hour to under forty.

The tank transporter smacked the little car off the road as though kicking a football. Crumpled, shattered, unrecognizable, its wreckage rolled down the hill, coming to rest in a hollow in the ground near some alders.

Gorkov found the politician crawling for the cover of the bushes, like a maimed animal. Both legs were broken and blood streamed from cuts on his head and arms, but he lived – his faith in the construction of his little car justified. Tucked away in his coat, Gorkov had the billy club he had hoped to use when he had his little fun with Mazurov.

Blind with blood, Serov could smell the freshly-torn earth, the pleasing scent of the grass under his hands as he dragged himself towards shelter. A shadow he could not see fell over him, and a stench of sweat and rotting vodka enveloped him.

The club swung murderously in Gorkov's hand and Serov's head smacked into the ground. Gorkov bent, beating until the groaning was finished.

'Bastard,' he belched. 'Yanqui-loving bastard!'

OKINAWA, MARCH 1945

'*Shido minzoku, Yamato minzoku*.' Yonai's voice caressed the crowd that filled the arena. 'We are the Yamato race, the leading race of the world.'

His audience, men, women and children, listened rapt.

The general was gaunt, but his face was filled with life. Over his shoulders, partly covering his many decorations, he had a pure white *hachimaki.*

'Ours is a shining history. We protect 2,600 years of greatness, a history of shimmering glory that began when the Emperor Jimmu founded our state. This war we have been fighting was forced upon us. *Teki*, the enemy selfishly desired world conquest and made war unavoidable. Ours is a moral cause, in which we have sought a new world order, to enable all nations and races to assume their proper place in the world and all peoples to be at peace in their own sphere. Who better to rearrange the world to this peaceful end than we, *shido minzoku*, the leading race in that world?'

Yonai held up his hand, palm foremost.

'*Sekishin*,' he said. 'We have red hearts.'

As he spoke he traced the two ideographs on his upheld palm and all knew that, separate, they meant 'true heart, faithful mind'. A soft hum of approval and agreement ran through the crowd. Redness and the intimation of blood brought vague, pleasing and deep feelings of purity and sincerity.

'We alone are divinely descended. Ours is a consanguineous unity, for in all our veins runs the imperial blood; we are all kinsmen descended from a common ancestor, Ameratsu, the Sun Goddess herself. She left

210

her descendants to reign over this country for ever and ever. This is only true of Japan, and nothing similar may be found in foreign lands. That is why it is called the divine country.

'Alone in the world, only Japan has never been conquered. We stand, one nation and one people, like a mighty rock in the turbulent waters of history. Is this not proof that our country does not exist only for itself, but rather for the two billion people of the world? Ours is a heavy responsibility, for duty is as weighty as a mountain. Ours is the task to be the model, the pattern, the standard for the world. Our destiny is to lead the whole world along the path of virtue.'

The people were quiet as they waited for Yonai to continue. He stood on the podium, tall and thin. He made a minute adjustment to the *hachimaki* around his shoulders. Behind him was a huge scarlet and white flag, the rising sun.

'In the past, we have strayed. The inherent character of the people has been one of a pure, cloudless and contrite heart, but thoughts of the individual and the self – the thoughts of the West – have led to the corruption of the true spirit and the clouding of knowledge. Thoughts of the individual and the self create a heart that is filthy and impure.

'This Greater East Asia War in which we fight is a purifying exorcism, a cleansing ablution. Only a holy war like this can create a brightness that leaves no corner untouched. Our war is like the power of the sun, purifying us; it is not white but faint red, tinged with the pinkness of blood; it is the colour of life itself. This very warmth and purity we have has made the cherry blossom the symbol of the Yamato spirit.'

Yonai paused again. From a vase in front of him he took a small, elegant branch, swept with fresh purple leaves and tight white blossom.

'We are companion cherry blossoms. We flower in the garden of our country. Just as the blossom here will calmly scatter, we too are ready to fall for our country.

211

Gyokusai. The jewel smashed. In dying, we will become even more pure. The blood of our dying will be our water of *misogi*, our Shinto rite of purification.'

Yonai raised his hand, pointing at the shimmering white and scarlet flag behind him.

'Out there, evil things are coming. Monsters and demons trailing darkness in their wake seek to extinguish the clean brightness of our sun, seek to sully the pure unclouded heart of the Yamato people.'

Once again Yonai raised his hand, tracing out the ideograms.

'America,' he said, and his finger drew the ideogram, adding the radical so that all could read that it meant 'bestiality'.

'*Kedamono, yaju.* Brutes and wild beasts, wearing masks of humanity. Impure, thinking of sex, comforts and conquest. They ride on black, red and brown men. They believe that power determines all, and desire to destroy our divine state of Japan simply to gratify their insatiable carnal desires. When they take any of our brave soldiers prisoner, wounded in the fighting, they kill them by driving tanks over them. They wrap them in barbed wire and throw them in rivers. The sacred bones of our war dead they use as playthings. You have all seen the picture of the American woman with the skull of a brave soldier on her table, sent to her by her boyfriend. You know the President of America was sent a letter opener – made from the arm-bone of a Japanese hero. Their marines wear necklaces of the teeth of our soldiers, they pickle their ears in jars. Desecration of our sacred dead is worse than cannibalism.'

In the audience, hearing of such terrible things, some were crying, silently wiping away the tears that slid down their cheeks.

'The men and women of Saipan knew that contact with *kichuku* and *kaibutsu*, with devils and monsters would pollute their pure hearts. When the time came, rather than fall into the hands of demons they took their own lives, and those of their children. On the high cliffs,

they performed *misogi* and fell to their deaths. *Gyokusai.*
The jewel smashed.'

More were weeping, and shaking their heads in agreement. They knew how the fifty thousand military and civilians had perished to the last soul.

'The decisive battle approaches. Ultimate victory for us is certain if *ichioku*, if the hundred million all embrace the spirit of Yamato. *Yamato damashii.*'

'*Yamato damashii.*' People in the crowd took up the cry.

'The heroes of Saipan showed the way. "Human bullets" destroyed the demons and achieved purification. Our soldier heroes strapped explosives to their bodies and ran into the enemy. Now we have the Special Attack Forces, the *Tokkotai.* In the air, our young men are like fire-arrow deities as they sink the warships of the devils with their aircraft. They have the spirit of the Divine Wind, the *kamikaze.*

'But we do not have to have an aircraft to have the kamikaze spirit. Soldiers bearing satchel charges are throwing themselves under tanks. Soldiers in small boats sail to the ships out here at night and, climbing aboard, achieve purification with their swords. One-man submarines are sinking their ships.'

Yonai took his *hachimaki* from his shoulders and slowly wrapped it around his head.

'We all can have the spirit of the Divine Wind. Ultimate victory will be ours. Reflect on the alternative. Last week the American devils sent B-san over Tokyo. The city still burns. They have set our country alight, two hundred thousand are dying in the ruins. B-san will come again and again. The Americans are monsters; better to die than fall into the hands of demons and devils.'

Yonai held up his hands to calm the people for a moment.

'*Ichioku Tokko.* The hundred million as a Special Attack Force.'

'*Ichioku Tokko.*'

'*Ichioku gyokusai.* The shattering of the hundred

213

million like a beautiful jewel.'

'*Ichioku gyokusai.*'

'Every man, woman and child of the Yamato race. *Ichioku gyokusai.* We make the ultimate sacrifice, and attain ultimate purity.'

'*Ichioku gyokusai. Ichioku gyokusai.*'

Weeping with joy, his white and scarlet *hachimaki* wrapped around his head, at the back of the arena Komura chanted his pledge.

'*Gyokusai,*' he howled. '*Gyokusai.*'

ZHUKOVKA-2

Mazurov was in his library when Yanov came. He arrived in a five-car motorcade at the hour of his choosing, late in the afternoon. It was his normal time of going home from the Kremlin to his own magnificent dacha nearby, set in its own walled grounds. The timing gave his visit a convincing appearance of normalcy. The General Secretary was dropping by to see an old comrade, to exchange views. But there were no aides in Yanov's party, only security men. A chill KGB captain from the 8th Directorate made his way up the steps, where the waiting Rai let him in. He silently looked about the library before going back outside, then Yanov left his shining Zil and came into the house alone.

Mazurov was sitting at the end of the long table that ran along the room, at the place where he ate. On the tablecloth were the newspaper Gorkov had brought with him and a slim file in a blue folder.

Yanov came in, and sat down opposite Mazurov.

'You are a cultured man,' he said, indicating the shelves of books in different languages lining the walls. 'Yet one who has done most uncultured things. I knew that you would be familiar with the British composers Gilbert and Sullivan, and their Mikado who believed that the punishment should fit the crime. It seemed appropriate to send a former KGB goon to arrest the former head of the KGB in the old fashion. Yet the goon returned defeated by words. So I have come myself.'

Yanov pointed a smooth, manicured hand at the cars outside.

'There is a car out there for you. It waits to take you

215

to your cell in Dzerzhinsky Square.'

'Then let us go together. For if I face a trial, then so will you.'

Yanov raised his eyebrows derisively.

'I? *I* am not a mass-murderer.'

He reached out and turned the folded newspaper flat on the table. The young Mazurov stood at the head of the long gouge in the earth, at the point where the bulldozer had stopped. The hole it had made was being filled with the dead.

'Karelia. 1945. Six thousand murdered ... by you.'

'It is true,' agreed Mazurov. 'I do not deny it. If I had refused to obey the commands of the man who sent me, then mine would have been the first of those bodies in the trench. Josef Djugashvili, who called himself Stalin, the Man of Steel, made all those who directly served him participate in his crimes. Where I could, I spared. I allowed men and women to go free if it was possible. Where I could, I allowed those who might escape to be alerted. It was not, as you see, always possible. But I reasoned, perhaps falsely, that it was better for such things to be done by me – who might temper them with some mercy – than by some higher grade of brutality, some beast like Gorkov whom you sent to arrest me here. *But it was not always possible*. When the gaze of the man with the broad back was upon you, you had to pick up the butcher's knife and emerge drenched in gore, if that was what he willed.'

Mazurov gestured at the *Washington Post*. 'In Karelia, at the end of the bloodiest war in history, that was what he wanted.'

'Which is why there is now a cell, a trial and a firing-squad waiting for you,' Yanov said coldly.

'I do not think so,' said Mazurov. 'We are all children of our time, are we not? I a creature from dark days of horror, a man encrusted with the blood of those long since dead at my hand. But you, you must be as the Western public perceives you, must you not? A child of the Twenty-Second Party Congress. You embody *glasnost* and *perestroika*, do you not? Did you not agree the terms of the Peace Treaty with the late President Hawkins? To the Western public, which is as we both know gullible, trusting and naive in these matters, you appear as some combination of flower-child and knight in shining armour. Imbued with transcendental beliefs, you seek to create world peace and create democracy for the peoples of the USSR. Those right-wingers who quote from your private speeches and point to your continuing and firm belief in the primacy of Leninist thought and of the Communist Party over those peoples are ignored.'

Mazurov paused and took a sip of cold tea from his glass. Fighting for one's life made the mouth dry.

'If there are some differences between the way the Western public perceives you and reality, then may there not be others? You must surely be as much a child of your time as I was of mine. What are your generation of leaders like? Your route to power was by becoming party boss of the Ukraine. You held the job for nine years before coming to Moscow and entering national politics. What sort of a man were you? What did the shining armour in which the Western public has you encased conceal?

'Nothing nice. Your politics were the politics of Huey Long. You too were Kingfish. You extorted money and favours from all those in a position to require your good-will. You lived in the style of a prince; you still do, of course. You were venal and corrupt at a level the Western public, unused to the exploitation of people by their rulers in an undemocratic society, cannot compre-hend. However, it does not end there. You used your position of power to prey upon the weak. You ensured a constant flow of pretty young secretaries through your office, whose sole function was to satisfy your sexual wants. These were many, were they not? You suffer from satyriasis, that disease which afflicts many in what the Americans call the fast track of politics. It was never a problem for me, I must say, steeped in gore though I

217

may be. In your abuse of these young girls, in your thrusting of yourself into their bodies, many became pregnant. On the route out of your life – a happy road, we must assume – you ensured that they called by at the abortionist to be relieved of that which grew within them.'

Mazurov paused again to drink tea. 'They were all young, these girls, were they not? Is that not one of the other symptoms of your disease, that those upon whom you prey must be young? Children, almost.

'Olga Khudenko was a child.'

Across the table Yanov's eyes narrowed, but he remained silent.

'Olga Khudenko was fourteen years old and the daughter of a couple who were secret, devout and practising Christians. She was by all accounts a truly beautiful child. You used the threat of the family's ruin to gain access to her new-formed body. Like some of the other unfortunates you abused, she became pregnant. Like them, she was taken on your orders to the abortionist. But unlike the others, she died. When you heard this news you had the parents arrested, charged and tried and shipped to the camps. Like that. We both know how simply it can be done, if you have the power. What was more, they both died there. Both. Separately.'

Mazurov leaned back in his chair and smiled like a shark opening its jaws.

'So you see, the generation gap is not so wide after all. You are a murderer just as I am. The blood will no more wash off your skin than it will from mine.'

Yanov's round face was coated with a thin, slippery sheen of sweat.

'It is all in the file there on the table. You may have it if you wish. I have other copies; I have some here, and I have sent others out of the country. They are in the West. If anything happens to me or to mine, then they will be published in the Western newspapers, broadcast on their television. Your fall from grace will be catastrophic. Such revelations as to the true face of our society may well cause a backlash over there, one which could lead to a cessation of the most valuable and pleasing aid which is propping up our ailing economy. In which case you can join me in front of that firing-squad. For everyone will want the man who is to blame to pay.'

Yanov got to his feet like an ill man. 'Very well,' he said. 'It shall be as you say.'

Mazurov waved a hand at the *Washington Post.* 'Issue the usual denials. Accuse them of fabrication and attempts by Cold-War warriors to undermine the new friendship of the American and Soviet peoples. You know the sort of thing.'

Yanov walked stiffly to the door. He is not used to having it done to him, thought Mazurov. But he will quickly recover; his kind do. He will not forget, however. So we are safe.

'An inspired stroke,' said Mazurov, picking up the paper.

'What?'

'Using the Western media to make your attack upon me.'

'I? I did not do that. I planned to denounce you at the Party Congress.'

Mazurov's face tightened.

'You did not ... then who did? And why?'

TOKYO, FEBRUARY 1946

Lying in his hospital bed in the camp with the rest of the military, Komura had heard two GIs discussing their impressions of the capital after 4,870 US heavy bombers had visited it.

'Hell,' said one. 'Stand on a soap box, see the whole town.'

As he trudged across the muddy ash in his Imperial army uniform, the only clothes he possessed, he reflected that that at least was no longer true. As far as the eye could see, hovels made from anything that would keep the rain out had sprouted from the cinder fields. Rusty metal, pieces of wood, string. The capital of Japan was a gigantic slum.

He paused in the gathering dark, his wrapping cloth slung over his shoulder. He was close, but in the absence of street signs accurate navigation was difficult. A group of dirty, hungry children stood watching him.

'You know where Kodama-san is?' he called.

'*Gunso*,' they jeered. 'Military. *Gunso.*'

They threw dirt at him.

A piece of corrugated iron nailed to some wood screeched as it was pushed open.

'Komura Tadaji,' called a voice, and he went gratefully inside the one-roomed hut. A kind of bed was arranged by one wall of tin; there was a table, some matting on the earth floor and a few utensils by a little stove. Some cans of water. By the standards of the time, a most desirable residence.

'*Banto*,' said Komura, bowing, and the old man did the same. Komura brushed some mud from his uniform.

220

'I shall have to find new clothing,' he said. 'We are not popular now.'

Silently the *banto*'s wife went to a corner of the hut. Hanging from a nail, protected from damp by a piece of valuable plastic, was a pre-war Western-style business suit.

'Here it is,' she said. 'It was your father's.'

Komura bowed in gratitude. In his turn he opened his cloth, and took out a paper sack filled with rice and a handful of vegetables.

'You were lucky to get here safely,' observed the *banto*. 'The streets are dangerous. The proud starve. Those less proud are armed, and steal.'

While his wife began to boil water the two men, the heir to the house of Komura and his manager, talked.

'I have not wasted my time,' Komura said. 'Because in the Great East Asia War I was in intelligence, I have been of value to the Americans and they to me. But first, tell me what has happened to our house.'

'All our stock is frozen. None of us is allowed to take more than 500 *yen* from our bank accounts. SCAP believes that the *zaibatsu* at the very least directly financed the war machine, and is moving to break us into fragments. While they will find it difficult to navigate within our business world, given time I have little doubt that they will be able to succeed.'

'Maybe,' said Komura. 'Maybe not. As I said, I have not wasted my time. SCAP is not a monolith; it has two sides. One is "liberal" – the "New Dealers" – and is pushing for the democratic "reforms". Within SCAP that's the Government section, GS, headed by General Whitney. But there is another side. In America, for many we are no longer the villains we were just recently. You must understand, the Americans have no sense of history. They have forgotten. Now they have a new enemy – "global communism". They fear the USSR, and Mao Tse-Tung in China. To counter the new foe, they need allies. General Willoughby is MacArthur's chief of military intelligence. He's head of the G-2, the Counter-

221

Intelligence Corps. Do you know what the Supreme Commander, SCAP calls him? "My lovable fascist." It's not a slip of the tongue, the man's a long-time admirer of Mussolini, says he's going to go work for General Franco when he retires. General Willoughby *likes* us. He doesn't understand that here Marxist terminology is simply the way the intellectuals talk. He doesn't understand that the trades unions have to profess to be socialist, at the very least, in order to be taken seriously. To him, Socialism's a way station on the line direct to full-blooded Communism. He's recruiting agents from the old right. He opposes the liberals, is infiltrating the Socialist and Democratic parties. If we can just last out, we may get through. We lie on kindling and lick gall for a few years, practice *enryo*. But first, we will need money.'

Komura opened his cloth. Inside lay some round, flat tins.

'What is that?'

'Film. Movies. *Gone With The Wind*.'

'Film?' Kodama said doubtfully.

'I know a young *yakuza* in Kyoto, a young gangster anxious to profit from these years. He's got a warehouse there for me. I'm going to turn it into a cinema.'

'In our time we have rolled steel, made ships and aircraft, woven cloth, dug mines, harvested plantations, owned forests and fisheries, run newspapers and pulp mills, made dyes and explosives and shells, but never has the house of Komura owned a cinema,' Kodama said gravely. 'I congratulate you.'

'*Sen ri no michi mo ho ippo yori hajimeru*. A journey of a thousand miles still begins step by step.'

The interior of the shack was becoming filled with the scent of cooking food. It was the smell of life, of hope.

'The house of Komura will have all that it had in the days of its might. And then it will have more,' Komura promised. 'But we begin step by step. First, the cinema. To make the money. To buy the power. To reclaim our own.'

KOMURA RESEARCH,
YOKOHAMA

Kantaro Itagaki had been born Kitsuju Hattori. In 1945 he completed his military training and was posted to join the Japanese Army in Manchuria. He arrived at his unit, stationed to the east of the Great Khinghan Mountains, just in time to meet the Soviet 6th Guards Tank Army coming the other way. As Japanese military intelligence considered it impossible for armoured forces to cross the desert to the west, let alone the mountains, his unit was weak and quite unable to withstand the armoured thunderbolt that fell upon it. It fell back in disarray, where a few days later it encountered General Kazartsev coming from the other direction with a whole corps of 14,000 men, together with 1,092 guns and 198 tanks. The few that survived this indulged themselves in the un-Japanese habit of surrender. Itagaki, born Hattori, was one of them. His captors stripped him of everything he owned, pulled out his gold teeth with a pair of pliers they kept in the toolbox of their T-38 and passed him along to other men, where in the usual manner of things he was worse treated the further he went from the front line. He ended up in a camp in Siberia, where they rearranged his thoughts for him.

Not only were these men very expert and experienced at their job, but in Itagaki and his compatriots they had peculiarly malleable material. But at home the *Tokko*, or Thought Police – equally as experienced and skilful as their Soviet opposite numbers – had practically one hundred per cent success with left-wingers unfortunate enough to fall into their hands. Within a few months of very painful brainwashing they emerged more imperial than the Emperor, and set about hunting down their former ideological colleagues.

Itagaki and his friends became more Communist than Lenin and Trotsky. With the promotion of liberal values by the New Dealers in Japan post-1945, their Soviet captors put the gold back in their teeth and sent most of them home to 'participate' in the exciting new world that was emerging over there. Highly-trained and ideologically-motivated, they proved superb militants. With the outbreak of the Korean War, the Americans decided they had had enough of progress in Japan and all the militants were rounded up and re-educated once again by the Thought Police, who had their old jobs back under new names.

Itagaki, born Hattori, was still in the USSR. The Soviets, who never did anything without both belt *and* braces, infiltrated him into Japan in 1952 under his new name, where he joined Komura Research, then a very fledgling computer company. It was the Soviet hope that as a mole within, he would be able to provide them with technological information.

Their timing was out. Itagaki duly rose through the ranks of seniority, and by the time that Komura Research was developing their fifth-generation supercomputer *Coral Spear* was so far removed and out of touch with theoretical research that he would not have known what the machine was if he had been shown it – which he was not. However, what he could and did do was provide his controllers with the codes and programmes of everyday matters within the running of Komura Research. Things as innocuous as the management of the electrical supply to the great complex, operated by central computer, and the delivery system in and out, once again handled by computer.

It was to the central computer that Yuri Serov went once the building was empty and quiet. He was in Konoe Masaaki's office, and used his console. Using the codes which he had been given, he was able to reprogramme the handling of the electrical supply. When a large white Nissan van arrived at the outer gate, the gate-guard received confirmation from the central computer that it was expected. He allowed it in.

The men who emerged from the van were commanded by Otari Yhetsov. They were *Spetsnaz* soldiers, who had arrived from Stockholm, Oslo and Copenhagen within the previous few days in the guise of Scandinavian tourists. Inside the building they moved swiftly. The internal security had been neutralized by Yuri Serov, and they were able to drive their fork-lift truck all the way to the great room where the supercomputer operated.

It was not particularly impressive, although quite elegantly constructed. In a gleaming red and black cabinet, the mainframe was contained in sixteen vertical columns arranged in a 310° arc. It occupied fourteen square feet of the highly polished, tiled floor-space, and was 42 inches tall. It was inert, since Yuri had shut it down and disconnected it from its power supplies, and drained off its coolant. The troops carefully manoeuvred their truck into place and lifted it up. *Coral Spear* weighed just under one ton. They drove back to their truck, and returned. Under Yuri's direction they then proceeded to pick up and take away the accessories of the fabulous machine; its foreground processor and five background processors, its maintenance control console, its magnetic disk subsystems and disk drives, daisy-chained on to a single controller, its tape controller and magnetic tape subsystems, its front-end interfaces, fibre-optic links and HSX high-speed external communications channel. They took its disk arrays and the many workstations and neural processors within the room, together with its compilers and libraries. By the time they had finished the van was full. They drove out through the gates with it sitting two inches lower on its suspension than it had when it had come in.

At 2 a.m. the six-lane highway still had traffic on it, but it was at least flowing. They moved with the great, polluted bay on their left hand, heading west. All around them the lights of the vast megalopolis diffused into the smog, turning it a hideous bronze.

In the front of the van, Otari looked around him as they went carefully on their way.

'Hell must be like this,' he said.

IRO-ZAKI

It was a myth that the Japanese people were a uniformly conscientious people, totally dedicated to the work ethic. Shimada Osani and Fumio Nikawa of the Iro-Zaki traffic police would have disputed this. It was not that they would not have been happy to work through their night-shift, it was simply that along the little coast road that ran around the peninsula there was very little traffic in the daytime and practically none at night. So come about three in the morning they parked their Honda patrol car behind some trees, where they could keep an eye out, and took it in turns to nap.

It was patrolman Osani who was awake and in the driving seat when the big white Nissan van went slowly by. His eyes were fully accustomed to the dark, and what he saw astonished him.

'*Gaijin*,' he grunted. He kicked patrolman Nikawa, who wakened in alarm, and pointed at the vanishing lights. '*Gaijin*. Foreigners.'

He hastily started his engine and pulled out on to the road, his light flashing. He was amazed to see the van put on speed and turn off down a side road which he knew led only to the sea itself. He switched on his siren, earnestly desiring these intruding foreigners to halt and be examined. One of the rear doors of the van opened as they hurtled down the little tree-lined lane, and a hand threw out a clutch of black nuts.

As his car went over them the steering blew apart in his hands and, without control, they spun around – shortening their vehicle at both ends as it bounced off the tree-trunks.

Patrolman Osani left patrolman Nikawa struggling to free himself from his seatbelt in the dark wreck and, suffused purple with rage, ran down the road after the vanful of foreigners.

He arrived at the water's edge in time to see no van but a vast, howling hovercraft vanishing into the night. Its three giant turbofans covered him with sand and spray as it accelerated to sixty knots over the choppy ocean. He was quite close to it; when they took him to the Shizuoka military base he was able to identify it as an Assault Hovercraft of the Pomornik Class of the Soviet Navy, 350 tons, and 57 metres in length. By then, however, it was back in the USSR, as was its cargo.

ADAMSTOWN, MARYLAND

Thrale had kept most of the equipment he had used in his working career, thinking not unreasonably that one never knew when it might come in handy. While waiting for Cy Rogers to arrive at work he took an AT&T workman's overall from the closet in the room where he had stored everything, and an electrician's toolbag which he opened on his work-bench. Humming quietly he fingered through a drawer – finding laid out such innocuous items as a box of sugar cubes, some ballpoint pens, a selection of light switches, a three-way adaptor, a hand-held calculator and an ordinary electric plug.

He made his choice and put the adaptor, plug and a rocker light switch into the bag. He added a pair of surgical gloves to the tools already there, also a can of shaving foam. From another closet he took a blue and white cardboard box. Going to the garage, he loaded first the bags and overall and then the box into the trunk of his car. He was smartly dressed in a blue pinstripe suit, white shirt and striped tie, with polished black shoes. The night before he had put a dark rinse through his hair, and now looked – like any President of the USA – ten years younger than he was.

He started the Cadillac and, as was his habit, let the engine idle for a few minutes while it and the oil warmed before selecting drive. He lived in the development on the Tuscarora Creek which had been built a few years before to attract some of the growing number of well-paid workers commuting into the capital or one of the many ancillary government organizations in or outside the beltway.

229

He took the Mountville road over the rolling farmland, heading into Adamstown. As he paused to cross the old B. & O. railroad line he saw the town's oldest resident, Walker Smith, coming the other way in his 1955 Dodge pick-up. He waved and the old man responded with a smile. Going through the old part of town on to the Adamstown road, he passed the only auto dealer in town, Charlie Wyatt, who ran Carroll Autos, dealing exclusively in used American station wagons, pick-ups and muscle cars. For a moment Thrale thought that there had been a big auto wreck. The place was beseiged with excited people and in the middle of it all – flushed, happy and rich, jumping like a Mexican bean, his hands full of title documents and money – was Charlie Wyatt. It took Thrale a few moments to negotiate the happy throng of patriotic citizens, but as the bellow of V-8 engines faded as he went out of town past the Carroll Manor Elementary School, he picked up his carphone and dialled.

'State Department. Can I help you?'

'Extension 211, please.'

'Rogers.'

'Hello, Cy, this is K.K. Thrale, special assistant to Lief Kuusinen. He asked me to give you a call.'

'Oh, sure, K.K. What is it I can do for you?'

'I guess I should say first that he said to say this is a non-conversation.'

'Uhuh,' said Rogers warily.

'Lief wondered if you'd be free to give me a little of your time if I came around to see you.'

'Why, sure. Let me see, now. I'm leaving early today to make a long weekend of it, going over to Baltimore to see my wife's parents. How about next week? Say Tuesday, eleven o'clock?'

'That'll be fine.'

'You want to give me an idea of what you'd like to discuss, so I can get the relevant material together?'

'Sure. It's about one of your opposite numbers: Alexander Borodin.'

'Oh, Borodin. Now there's a guy.'

'He's good, right?'

'The best,' Rogers said simply. 'I'll see you Tuesday then.'

'See you then,' agreed Thrale, and put the phone back in its cradle. At the junction he turned left on to 85, heading for Urbana and route 80 into Washington.

The radio transmission from Thrale's carphone was picked up by a small grey microwave antenna in a field a few miles away. It occupied a microwave repeater site, was owned by American Telephone & Telegraph, and formed part of the broadband microwave net of electronic communication by which – when the domestic and international satellites owned by such as Western union, RCA, COMSAT, as well as AT&T were included – handled practically all forms of distanced communication, from telephone calls and telexes to complex computer data transfers and electronic mail.

Voice communication by telephone had for a while been electronically converted to digital signals, something that made greater use of the efficiency of the computers that ran the whole affair. It also made it easier for suitably commanded computers to eavesdrop on what people were saying. It was no accident that the National Security Agency not that far from Adamstown, out half-way between Washington and Baltimore, had a computer capacity that was measured not in square feet or metres but in acreage, since the Agency's main reason for being was to stick its nose into everyone else's business.

In order to do that, the Agency had the use of more computers, microwave dishes, antennae and satellites of varying descriptions than any other organization on earth. The days when such equipment was an American or Soviet monopoly were long gone, however, as Europeans, Chinese and Japanese companies and governments all got in on the act, and the cold space around the earth began to resemble Connecticut Avenue at five-thirty in the afternoon as satellites and spacecraft orbited at various altitudes or hung parked above strategic sites.

One such – a squat one-and-a-half-ton cylinder – hung motionless some 22,500 miles over a bleak part of the Indian Ocean. It was a communications satellite with a capacity of some fifty-five thousand long-distance circuits. Owned, designed and built by Komura Industries, it had been blasted into orbit atop a Chinese Long March II rocket. Had an American or European telecommunications engineer been allowed to look at it, he would have commented that it appeared to be too large for its task, and the rates for putting every pound of electronics into orbit being so high would have moved to the correct conclusion that it was designed to do something other than transmit phone calls from London to Delhi, or New York to Tokyo, which was why its makers had sent it to work aboard a Chinese missile rather than an Atlas. The Chinese knew that it was an eavesdropping satellite, a gatherer of SIGINT, signals intelligence, but since they were allowed access to that intelligence they were not about to reveal its secrets to anyone.

In a quiet, white room in Tokyo a computer called its operator's attention to something it had been commanded to listen for. Simultaneously, it transcribed the conversation from which it had found its trigger. In the time it took to do this, it identified the telephone numbers of the person called, and the caller. It noted that the caller had been speaking from a carphone, and gave his name and licence plate as well as make and colour of car. It provided the names, work addresses and home addresses of both men.

Hamaguchi Kijuro took the sheet of paper from the laser printer and went over to his waiting supervisor.

CHINATOWN, WASHINGTON

Thrale parked his car in a multi-storey near the Greyhound terminal and walked the short distance into Chinatown, crossing the heavy traffic on 9th with care. The refurbishment and face-lifting that was going on over and around the Judiciary Square was creeping towards the enclave of Chinese businesses and restaurants, and the hammer of pneumatic drills was in his ears as he turned into the small street off I Street. There was a little over an hour to go before the technician left to begin his shift with the Public Services Bureau. Thrale walked under the ideograms and dragons, the blue and white cardboard box clasped under his arm.

Lin Pao lived on the second floor, above a Chinese grocery. With his oriental appearance, Thrale attracted no attention whatever as he negotiated the stalls and went up the worn wooden staircase. The house smelled of *h'ui* and *lo-han chai.* He knocked on Lin Pao's faded red door. A young man, very neat and clean and with freshly-washed black hair, opened it, dressed in white shirt and blue trousers. His feet were bare.

Thrale beamed at him. 'Mr Pao?' he said. Placing the box on the floor, he reached inside his coat pocket.

He was aware of the young man assessing the appearance of this well-dressed and affable stranger at his door.

'Yes?'

Thrale produced his card, which he showed to Pao.

'Kenneth Chan, from the Climate Control Manufacturer's Association.'

'Ahh.'

233

'Every year, sir, we ask organizations that service our products to pass on to us recommendations for their best employees. This year your name was given to us by the Public Services Bureau, Mr Pao. I am delighted to be able to inform you that you have won one of our highest awards as one of our Technicians of the Year.'

Beaming even more widely, Thrale reached out and pumped the young man's hand.

'May I?' he said, gesturing slightly towards the inside of the room.

'Please. Please come in, Mr Chan.'

Lin Pao lived in one large room with a small bathroom and kitchenette. A futon was neatly placed against one wall behind a screen, and there were two armchairs and a small table at which to eat. Whatever belongings he had were clearly kept in the fitted cupboards along one wall. There was a telephone and an old television set.

Thrale opened his briefcase and took out a handsome engraved plaque.

'Lin Pao,' he read reverentially. 'Climate Control Manufacturer's Association Technician of the Year. Sir, I congratulate you.'

He handed the handsome award over to the young man, who looked at it seeming pleased.

'Now, our recognition goes somewhat further than that. Yes, sir.'

Thrale tugged open the box and pulled out a brand-new package of electronic wizardry. Pulling away the styrofoam and plastic wrapping, he revealed it as a multi-functional entertainment centre.

'May I?' he asked, holding up the plug.

'Yes, of course. The plug is here, Mr. Chan.'

Thrale put the power to it and expertly tapping the controls revealed it in all its glory.

'Stereo-radio, tape deck and compact disc flat-screen colour television with seven-inch screen. Here a VCR. Remote control here. All fully guaranteed for five years.'

Lin Pao's eyes gleamed. He was young, he liked technological toys.

'Mr Chan, you are too kind ...' he murmured.

Thrale held up his hand. 'Don't thank me,' he said avuncularly. 'Thank yourself. It's purely because of your efforts that you have won this award. Now, sir, if you'll excuse me it's back to the office for me, and I'll let you enjoy this wonderful piece of equipment.'

Thrale bowed himself out and went back down the stairs. Moving swiftly, he returned to the Cadillac in the multi-storey where he took his bag from the trunk and sat in the back. He took out a small television monitor, which he plugged into its purpose-built socket, and connected to it a joystick of the kind used in computer games. The television screen came to life to reveal the happy, absorbed features of Lin Pao.

Thrale sat watching. After a few minutes the young man glanced at his watch and reached out to switch the television off. It made no difference to Thrale's picture as the television camera within the entertainment centre that he had given to Pao remained connected to the mains as long as it was plugged in. Four inches square by one-and-a-half inches deep, it was buried within the electronics that ran the stereo, radio, VCR and television. It peered out through a fish-eye lens, connected to it by a thin bundle of fibre-optic filaments. The fish-eye was concealed behind plastic that from the outside was dark and opaque, but from within was clear.

Lin Pao went to his bathroom, and the fish-eye moved to follow him under the instructions of Thrale's joystick. Pao brushed his hair and came out, taking a small lunch-box with him. He paused and opened his cupboard, looked inside for a moment, then shut it again. He went out through the door, locking it twice behind him.

While watching his monitor, Thrale had changed out of his business clothes and into the workman's AT&T coverall. He pulled on a Dodgers baseball cap, took his work-bag and went down to the street. He was in time to see, at a distance, Lin Pao boarding his bus to work.

Once again, no one took any notice of him as he went up the stairs. Nearly half a century earlier, as a member

235

of the Counter Intelligence Corps, he had been taught how to defeat a lock's defences by a man who had found the knowledge of such things necessary to further his business interests. Hank Travis had been released from the Alabama State Penitentiary with half his term served in order to help his uncle's employees. Thrale had the locks open with a speed and skill that would have won approval from the old burglar, had he still been alive, and slipped inside.

He went first to the telephone, which was an ordinary white Bell push-button model. It took him a few seconds to take its cover off to reveal the electronic innards. From his bag he took a little striped box with the markings of its manufacturer, Fox Electronics. Opening it and shaking the contents into his hand, he obtained a tiny piece of circuitry no bigger than the end of his little fingernail. Two bare wires protruded from it, and these he connected to the circuit board inside the telephone where they blended with the other components. He put the phone back together again, and returned it to its cradle.

Lin Pao had a simple lamp standing on a table near where he ate, and taking the plug he had brought with him Thrale substituted it for the original. The entertainment centre that he had given to Pao was plugged into an adaptor along with the young man's own old set, and again Thrale substituted his own for the original.

His primary tasks done, he went to the cupboard that he had observed Lin Pao open before leaving for work. Inside some jackets and pairs of trousers hung, and a few pairs of simple shoes lay neatly on the floor. There was a tool-box and a pile of magazines. Looking quickly through them, Thrale found that Lin Pao had a taste for violent comics, fast cars and bondage. Trussed women lay on the pages like so many pieces of meat on a butcher's slab. He grimaced slightly.

At the back of the cupboard was a brightly-coloured package. Taking it out, he saw that it advertised as its contents a Galactic Battle Cruiser, complete with Laser

Death Ray Weapons, All-Terrain Capability and Command Center. A garish picture of the tracked monster slashing its outer-space competitor machines with white laser swords sprawled across the packaging. Intrigued, Thrale opened the box and took out the war toy.

It was well made, better constructed than its advertising would have led a vendor to believe. Although its hull was brightly-coloured plastic, the mechanism of its tracks and the turret of its main armament – a long barrel similar to that of a tank – were precision built. It was heavier than it should have been.

Thrale quickly turned it upside down and undid the four Allen screws that fastened the hull to the base. It was powered by two Ni-Cad batteries. Thrale was familiar with the type; he knew of their advantages of long life and output in powering surveillance devices. The batteries ran the electric motors. The components, the gears, were of industrial quality.

The turret contained what looked like a miniature 3 mm zoom lens, a gun-barrel and a tiny laser designator, and was mounted at the very front of the fighting vehicle. The gun-barrel was connected by tube to a small bottle of compressed gas; the lens to a television camera hardly an inch square by fibre-optic cable. All to the micro-circuitry of a small computer.

As soon as he realized the level of sophistication of the machine he slipped the hull back on; then putting the toy beside the phone, he took a small modular pack from his tool-box. Connecting it to the phone line, he switched it on and watched as it automatically swept the spectrum of frequency bands from 20 kilohertz to 2000 megahertz. Just as he was satisfied that his Fox lost transmitter would indeed remain lost he suddenly stiffened, watching the display in alarm.

'Shit,' he said shortly. He quickly disconnected his spectrum analyser and put it into the bag. As he did so, the door burst open and Lin Pao was on him.

The forty years that separated the two men had

237

slowed Thrale's reflexes but taught him the value of thinking ahead. Lin Pao covered the distance from the door in a fraction of a second, but as they crashed to the floor Thrale had his hand still inside his bag. As Pao's hands seized his throat he hit him with the can of shaving foam and the top came off; as the grip tightened and he heard his breath rattle in his throat and cease, and his world become dark, Thrale held the can to his assailant's face and pressed the trigger.

Lin Pao screamed. His hands clawed at his face and Thrale heaved air into his lungs. Then the young man was on his feet, frantically wiping at his eyes. Thrale crawled towards him, pushing himself up, but before he could administer another dose Lin Pao had grabbed the Galactic war toy Thrale had found and – with tears spouting from his eyes – ran out of the door. Thrale went after him, picking up the small television as he did so. Pao was staggering down the stairs, bouncing from wall to banister, and Thrale hurled the television at his back. The impact threw him into the street and through the stall outside in a frantic mêlée of dead ducks, monosodium glutamate and imploding glass.

By the time Thrale had got to the street Pao was running towards I Street, moving as best he could, blood spattering the sidewalk from one leg, but still gripping the toy fighting vehicle. Thrale pushed aside an old woman who was screeching in Cantonese from the wreckage of the stall and set off in pursuit. Because Lin Pao was making much slower progress than he might, Thrale began to catch up. His quarry turned on I and ran along to the torrent of traffic pouring down 9th Street. Thrale was almost upon him as they arrived at the great thoroughfare.

Lin Pao halted not for a moment. There was a howl of rubber and the shattering bang of metal and glass as two cars collided, and then a third, and Thrale – who wanted to live – was still on the sidewalk as Lin Pao was running up the middle of the highway.

A Mack truck hauling freight was coming. Thrale heard

the bellow of its horn as the driver pulled on the air.

Lin Pao's feet seemed to go from under him as he made a shuffling dive, holding the war-toy out in front of his face like a ball-player going for the line.

Thrale turned quickly, walking away up the street, his heart pounding, sweat streaming from him, the screaming of the people on the sidewalks in his ears, wondering why the very air held the stench of the slaughterhouse, and where the blood and ordure that coated them had come from.

THE WARDMAN TOWER

'The truck was an eighteen-wheeler hauling machine parts from Detroit; nine of those wheels went over it and it is now just so many tiny pieces of plastic, glass and wire, so I'll have to tell you what it was and how I think it worked,' said Thrale.

'Go ahead,' invited Kuusinen. He glanced across at the television, where some men from the fire department were hosing down part of a street. Then the picture changed to the black girl in the studio and he thumbed the remote control.

'It was very well made; presented as being a sophisticated child's toy – the kind of radio-controlled thing kids play with. Good thinking; if someone had stopped Lin Pao and asked what it was, he could say he'd bought it for his nephew's birthday. Lin Pao was a trained air-conditioning technician working for the Public Services Bureau, so he had every right to be working on the air-conditioning in the White House. No one would question him, in his overall and with his pass.

'It's my guess that he introduced the Galactic Battle Cruiser into the ventilation system through some inspection panel or other fairly close to the President's family quarters – perhaps during some routine work on the Queen's Bedroom, or the Lincoln Bedroom maybe, both of which are not far away. Once introduced, it is my supposition that using its tracks it made its way through the ventilation tunnels until it arrived at the grille in the President's bathroom.'

'Well, how the hell would it do that? You mean that Lin Pao guided it, by radio control?'

'No, I mean that it made its own way there. When I opened it, it had inside it a considerable amount of circuitry. A small computer. Lin Pao would have had access to the plans of the ventilation system, and would have written a programme which he then introduced into the machine's computer, just as a modern fighter or bomber pilot plans a route on a computer and then loads it into the on-board computer of his aircraft. The analogy is a good one. A fighting aircraft is meant to kill people. This machine, crawling quietly towards its target within the pipes of the White House, was designed to kill someone: President Hawkins. It was an automated assassin. Once it arrived at its destination, it would park itself and switch off all except housekeeping functions to save energy. Its clock would wake it up in the night, and it would wait for the light to go on. At this point it would be looking through the grille with its television camera.'

'What if it had been Mrs Hawkins?'

'Then it would have sat and waited. You see, it *knew* what the President looked like. It would wait until someone appeared who matched the image it had been given when it was programmed. Now, the President *did* arrive. We assume that he relieved himself and then stood in front of the hand basin – below the grille where the machine was waiting – to wash before going back to bed. The machine identified him as its target. It assessed the range and painted the area to which it should fire using its on-board laser. It aimed its gun-barrel and fired a jet of nicotine concentrate gas into the President's nose. He inhaled and was dead within seconds, falling to the floor and grazing himself on the basin as he did so – classical signs of a man dying from a pulmonary embolism.'

'All right,' said Kuusinen. He had the air of a man very much hoping that at some time in the future he would not be explaining himself to a Senate committee. 'So tell me why, while I was eating lunch, they were washing what was left of Lin Pao into the city drains.'

241

'I went to see him before he left for work, and succeeded in introducing a Trojan Horse into his apartment: an entertainment centre within which was a miniaturized television camera. WIth it I was able to see that there were no burglar alarms within his room which Lin Pao might have armed before he left. He believed that he had won the entertainment centre as a prize for being a good worker ... which he was. His supervisor told me that he was a first-rate employee, hard-working, and a stickler for having his job done correctly. Lin Pao was pleased to get the prize.

'Once he had gone off to work, I returned and let myself in ... by picking his locks. Once in, I proceeded to bug his room. First off I placed what is known as a "lost transmitter" within his phone. It is very small and so designed to blend in with its background, appearing to be part of the interior of the telephone and thus be missed by a physical search. Once in place it would transmit what it heard – either a phone call or conversation within the room down the phone line. Once I got home, I planned to contact it via *my* phone and have it send me whatever it heard, all of which I would record on my reel-to-reel tape-recorder in my workshop.'

Thrale paused. 'You got a drink, Lief? It's a long time since people tried to kill me in the course of my work.'

'Sure. Yes, sure.'

'Then as back-up, since you rarely use but one bug I replaced a plug and an adaptor with duplicates of my own, which were of course transmitters. Now before Lin Pao left, through my little camera I saw him look inside his cupboard, so when *I* was there I looked inside his cupboard. The only unusual thing I found – apart from his taste in literature – was the Galactic Battle Cruiser. I was intrigued because it seemed too well made to be a toy, so I opened it and found inside all the features I have told you about.'

'But how did Lin Pao come back and find you in there? Did he forget something, do you think, and have to return for it?'

242

'No. He came back because he was alerted to my presence.'

'How?'

'Before I was getting ready to leave, I checked my lost transmitter to make certain that it couldn't be found. To do this I used what is known as a spectrum analyser, which is something that sweeps entire frequency bands in the same manner that a field-strength meter searches for radiation. It's a clever piece of stuff, miniaturized, and contains things like IF amplifiers, crystal filters, AM/FM detectors, signal level indicator circuits and so forth. What's more, it does it all automatically. Now, I was having my analyser check out my bug when I noticed that *someone else at the other end of the phone was checking me out.* It was lucky, my analyser just happened to be checking the same thing as the thing at the other end and I noticed. What had happened was that when I originally installed the bugs someone at the other end of the phone knew what I was doing, and via some radio bleep told Lin Pao about it. He probably had a pager that would print out messages. When I started checking out my lost transmitter, whatever was at the other end checked again to see what I was up to. And luckily for me, I just saw it. Which gave me a fraction of a second to grab hold of my ammonia can before Lin Pao came in to kill me.'

'So who was monitoring Lin Pao's line to keep it free?'

'Not who, what? What can do something twenty-four hours a day without tiring, seven days a week? A machine. A computer.'

'So you sprayed Lin Pao with ammonia and he ran away, still carrying his automated assassin, all the way to 25th where he got hit by a truck. I suppose he couldn't see, with that stuff in his eyes.'

'No,' Thrale said quietly. 'I think he could see.'

Kuusinen looked at Thrale strangely. 'So who's at the back of all this? Constructing the machine can't have been easy. Owning a computer that guards your home from afar is not the sort of thing most people have. So

243

who was Lin Pao working for? And while we're at it, why did he still have the machine? Why not throw it in the Potomac?'

'Maybe they wanted to use it again.'

'Why?'

'Ah. That's what I haven't got. Why. Why kill President Hawkins? I don't know. But I do know who.'

'Yes?'

'Lin Pao passed for Chinese, the way that some Germans or some Frenchmen might pass for English. Or vice-versa. He *could* have been Chinese, but he wasn't. He was an excellent employee, who took exceptional pride in his work. Rare at that level, I would say. He liked violent comics and pornographic magazines of the S/M type. Bondage. Typical of a certain type. His one concern, once he had failed to kill me, was that I should not capture his assassination machine intact. When he ran away from me towards 25th, it was not an accident. He ran into the road and caused an accident – some cars collided – but he dodged out of the way. When he ran up the middle of 25th he was looking for something and he found it: an eighteen-wheel Mack truck. He got the Galactic Battle Cruiser smack under its left front tyre, and the next eight followed suit.'

'They ran over him, too.'

'That's right. That's when I was quite sure who he was, where he came from. It was straight out of the *Hagakure*. I can quote it for you: "In a fifty-fifty life or death crisis, simply settle it by choosing immediate death. There is nothing complicated about it. Just brace yourself and proceed ... One who chooses to go on living having failed in one's mission will be despised as a coward and a bungler ... in order to be a perfect *samurai*, it is necessary to prepare oneself for death morning and evening, day in and day out." Lin Pao took his choice without questioning it, for he was *samurai*. Not Chinese, Japanese.'

244

GEORGETOWN, WASHINGTON

Ala's soft hands turned Reisch's own in his.

'You have little calluses on your palms,' he said gently.

'That's your Shelby muscle car,' said Reisch. 'See what you've done to me. I'm getting arms like Arnie Schwarzenegger. But look what it's done! God, but we've turned it around. Have you seen the President's ratings? He's extending the list of firms prohibited from foreign take-over – that's an extension of the late eighties bill prohibiting the Japanese from taking over US semiconductor firms. The Japs are going to have to disgorge a whole lot of what they've been taking, and since the yen's taken such a beating we're going to be paying them back with Monopoly money.'

Ala grinned. 'That's naughty.'

'Nobody gives a toss what we do to the Japs as long as it's along the lines of giving them the shaft. Anyhow, now we're riding high we can think about who to take on board as Veep. With an eye to the election.'

Ala turned the television to PBS in anticipation of MacNeil/Lehrer, which Reisch liked to watch, and fixed them drinks.

'Who are you thinking of?'

'We can take our pick now. Unlike last week, when the politically ambitious ducked down alleyways when they saw us coming.'

'Not a young man, and not too good-looking. You don't want to detract from Barnet. A seasoned pro. Silver hair, experience in government. The image will look good. The brilliant young President – get some echoes of JFK in there – and his solid, workhorse running-mate.'

245

'Yeah. That's the way I was thinking.'

'Can I suggest something?' Ala said, slipping on to the sofa beside him.

'Darling, I rely on you.'

'Not a hawk. Now the world's safe for peace, isn't it? The Peace Treaty's signed, now the Cold War's over, and we can get on with enjoying the goodies – which, thanks to the President, the economy's going to provide.'

'Someone with a track record in the disarmament field?'

'Right. It'll reinforce Barnet's commitment to peace. The ass-kicking side of America's happy beating up on the Japs. They don't want to spend quadzillions on aircraft carriers and bombers and all any more. Go for someone who was always opposed to it.'

'Hell, you're talking about Marshall Telford. The man's a Quaker. His son wasn't, and he died in Vietnam. He sees war as the invention of the Earl of Hell. Solid, incorruptible, an able administrator, all the rest of it.'

'I know who you mean. Visually, he's perfect.'

'Just so long as we never have to fight anyone. Telford would resign.'

'Who's left, apart from the Colombian drug barons? Telford's totally anti-drug. I'm sure he'd let us napalm *them*,' Ala said, grinning.

On the tube, whooping Georgian rednecks were burning down a Mazda car dealership. Members of the Sheriff's Department seemed to be helping them.

Success always made Reisch hard.

'Let's do it,' he said, his voice thickening with desire.

They slithered on the sofa like a strange two-backed beast in the act of devouring itself. Reisch squinted past his lover's testicles as MacNeil/Lehrer came on. BARNET. EIGHT MORE YEARS, was the headline, and he noticed the lack of any query.

His climax was perfect.

ADAMSTOWN, MARYLAND

Thrale was coming up the New Design Road – straight as a die all the way to the Potomac – when the phone in the Cadillac burped.

'Thrale.'

'K.K.! It's Takashi!'

'Takashi,' Thrale said warmly. 'Where are you?'

'In town. I'm here with Trade Minister Saito, for the talks with Secretary of State MacGregor.'

'I hope you aren't out on the street. There's some folk out there who're taking all this America-first stuff further than they should.'

'Hell, no.' Takashi still spoke like an American, Thrale noticed. 'I'm in a Thunderbird, actually. I called earlier but couldn't get a hold of you, so I thought I'd drive out and see if maybe you were at home. Where are you?'

'Almost in Adamstown,' Thrale said, turning into Mountville Road.

'Ah, then I'm not far behind you. I'm on 28. Do you have time to have a drink with an old colleague?'

'You bet. I've had a long day. My house, I think. Not a bar.'

'I think that is best.'

'Keep your windows rolled up.'

Takashi laughed as he cut off his phone.

Thrale had parked the Cadillac in his garage and opened up his house by the time the blue Thunderbird rolled up into his front yard. Tsunoi Takashi got out, beaming. He wore a well-cut dark suit and a large lapel badge that said: DON'T PUT ME IN THE CRUSHER. I LIVE HERE. He was about ten years younger than Thrale, with

247

greying hair and marked lines running from his nose to the corners of his mouth.

Thrale laughed when he saw the badge.

'It work?' he asked.

Takashi shrugged, grinning. 'No one's tried. I guess I can pass for *nisei*. I speak like you all do.'

'Yeah, you learned real fast.'

A long time ago, Takashi had been Thrale's Japanese assistant in the Counter Intelligence Corps. Their relationship was one peculiarly Japanese, and known as *oyabun-kobun*, or 'boss-follower'. It was one of the powerful bonds holding Japanese society together. Takashi owed his position in the Japanese Secret Service to Thrale's influence, and the *on*, or debt of gratitude, was one that could never be completely repaid but determined the relationship for ever.

They went inside, to Thrale's living room.

'Whisky?' asked Thrale, who knew Takashi's tastes. He went through to the kitchen and came back with two cold cans of Coors and some olives and biscuits on saucers. These were joined by a bottle of Jack Daniel's and two small shot glasses.

'*Kampai*.'

'*Kampai*,' said Thrale. 'How long are you in town?'

Takashi's cheerful demeanour vanished.

'Not long, I'd say. Trade Minister Saito was the one who made that remark that became famous a couple of years back. It was when there was beginning to be a lot of talk about our trade surpluses. He was asked how the rest of the world was supposed to fit in with it, and replied that America could become Japan's larder and Europe her boutique. Saito has a misplaced sense of humour, because the person who asked the question was now-Secretary of State MacGregor. He didn't find it amusing then and for him the joke hasn't improved with age. And now he can do something about it.'

Takashi sighed, and took a long pull of his beer.

'MacGregor's a *rikutsuppoi*, a reason-freak. He doesn't seem to understand *tatemae* and *honne* at all.'

248

'On the contrary,' Thrale said gently. 'Only he sees the difference between *tatemae*, what you *say* you're doing, and *honne*, what you're *really* up to, as simply bare-faced lying.'

'Aren't contradictions simply two sides of the truth? You Americans are always looking for consistency. It isn't so.'

'And the Red Queen could believe as many as six impossible things before breakfast. She could have lived in Japan.'

Takashi smiled, and put down his beer. 'I think I'll be going home with Saito the day after tomorrow. So I'll say goodbye now. I brought you a present, if you will accept it.'

Takashi pulled back his sleeve and unstrapped his watch. It had a wide black strap like a diver's watch, and a large, flat black face. He sat next to Thrale to show it to him. The upper part of one strap had small push-button controls and a slim, blunt pin with which to operate them. Takashi expertly pressed them and the screen came to life.

'It's a watch – see? Also a calculator. But now watch.'

The screen lit up in full colour, and on its two-inch square Thrale found himself watching a baseball match.

'Satellite reception,' Takashi said proudly. 'Fifty-six channels. Which gives you the opportunity to do this....'

He swiftly tapped a series of numbers and a few seconds later the telephone rang. Thrale looked at it in disbelief.

'It's a telephone too?'

Takashi terminated the call and the telephone stopped ringing.

'Via satellite. You can call anywhere in the world. With it on your wrist you just speak. I called you with it from the car.'

'Well, damn,' said Thrale, who had a weakness for exotic technology. He strapped it on, and it was surprisingly light.

'You will wear it?'

249

'Of course. Say, who makes it?'

'Oh, it's Komura Electronics' new baby. It isn't on sale yet. I got it through a friend. Now, I must go.'

'You sure?'

'We're having a conference in an hour.'

Thrale went out and saw him to his car.

'They killed an American serviceman in Shinjuku today, K.K.,' Takashi said suddenly. 'A crowd beat him to death and left him in the street.'

He looked out over the rolling Maryland countryside.

'It's never going to be the same again. It was better when the world did not think they understood us.'

Thrale watched the lights of the Thunderbird go away down the road.

'Who started it?' he murmured.

SEE CUBED EYE — C³I
— COMMUNICATIONS

FAR EAST MILITARY DISTRICT HEADQUARTERS, VLADIVOSTOK

The Trans-Siberian Rail Road arrived in Vladivostok in 1903 and brought Leonid Bruyevich with it. It was a frontier port, as far from the capital of the Empire as it was possible to get, and a place for men like Bruyevich to thrive. It grew rapidly in the years that followed, and the young merchant was able to build a fine mansion set in its own gardens behind a tall, strong brick wall. He married, and raised his children there.

Revolution and war came to Vladivostok. In 1917 the Russians left and the Japanese, Americans, British, French and Italians used it for their war effort. Leonid Bruyevich stayed and accommodated them all, becoming richer in the process. In 1920 they all left, except for the Japanese, and he worked with them too. Two years later *they* left, and Trotsky's Red Army finally arrived to incorporate the Far Eastern Republic into the Soviet Union. Leonid Bruyevich, as willing to adapt as a chameleon, came out of his mansion to make his accommodation with the new rulers of the city.

They shot him. They shot him and his family because it was clearly wrong that some men had big houses while others did not. Those who did it – and who had as their mission the extermination of the entire bourgeoisie, first within the Soviet Union and then the rest of the world – were the Cheka, Lenin's secret police. As the mansion from whose well-tended garden they were

253

removing the bodies of its occupants was large and strongly-constructed, they took it for their headquarters.

The mansion had a number of occupants after that. The NKVD had it in the 1930s, and after the Great Patriotic War various army groups used it as their headquarters. In the end, it became the headquarters of the Far East Military District itself. The handsome building was not much changed, although the fine french windows which had led out to the gardens had long been bricked up, and the grottoes and arbours where roses bloomed and fountains played replaced by the rough grey concrete of machine-gun casemates.

The real differences concerned what had been done *underneath*. The mansion itself was but the small part of the iceberg above water. Below ground was the command point itself, built deep, protected by thousands of tons of concrete and steel. Here was both working and living accommodation, a communications centre, a well-equipped hospital, two restaurants, stores of all kinds and everything necessary for men and women to live and work totally isolated from the outside world. Provided they did not go mad while they did so, they could live for up to two years down there while they fought, at a distance, a war above.

The command point also contained a briefing room, known as the cabin. It was so called because it felt like one, the sort you would find on a luxury liner. When the security systems which kept safe what was said inside were switched on, the floor, walls and ceiling vibrated very slightly, throbbing like a powerful ship thrusting its way through the ocean. The cabin walls were very thick, and hidden behind the layers of insulation were the jammers. The deafening noise they produced was muted to a soft swish by the time it reached the inside of the cabin, just like the sea rushing past the hull.

The inside of the cabin was brilliant white, and the fully-fitted carpet was grey. It contained one long table and six chairs, all made of transparent plastic.

Yuri Serov faced General Ogarkov across the table. For

254

ultimate secrecy both men wore transparent helmets connected by clear plastic tubes. Neither thought such overkill strange; they were both Russian.

'You have to know what I'm going to tell you because the computer will have to know. And you will have to give it all the information it needs. It's going to know as much as I, my general staff and all our files, records and sources know.'

Ogarkov's voice boomed strangely inside the plastic helmet. Yuri Serov found himself beginning to sweat.

'All things being equal, in about three and a half years' time the People's Liberation Army of China will roll across the border over there. It will be equipped with extraordinary weapons that will render those of the Red Army obsolete. The destruction of our forces will be so total that our leadership will sue for peace under any terms well before the Chinese arrive in Moscow.

'The weaponry will have been supplied to the Chinese by their – unlikely – allies, the Japanese. The two victors will then tear off whatever parts of the USSR they require. The Soviet Union will have ceased to exist, of course. We proud Russians will have become no more than the serfs of a new Mongol despotism.'

Ogarkov slammed a fist like a cabbage on to the plastic table, and it groaned under the impact.

'But it's not going to happen! Things *aren't* equal because *today* our motherland has the Red Army to protect it. In three and a half years' time the boot will have been on the other foot and it is *we* who will carve up China as we will – yes, Japan too, and remove the oriental threat for ever. For as we speak, using *maskirovka* – deception, camouflage, hiding – at all levels from the actions of the state to those of the individual soldier, we are preparing a blow that will fall upon the Chinese like a thunderbolt. The operation is called *Zarnitsa*, and lightning it will be. We will inflict total defeat upon the Chinese within two weeks. Your computer will handle the battlefield management, communications, command and control – the BMC-cubed, and also the

Intelligence of the C^3I. You know what that entails? The See Two – C^2 – functions are the monitoring of enemy troop strengths and resources, and of our own troop strengths and resources; the planning and replanning of electronic warfare scenarios; assessing warning signals and evaluating attack damage; monitoring specific combat situations; choosing from among operational options and facilitating their execution; assessing and controlling remaining military capabilities; reconstituting and redirecting forces; negotiating with the enemy and terminating conflict.

'The two sets of systems that make C^2 function are the communications systems – that's what makes C^2 into C^3 – that ensure that forces and intelligence sources are connected, and the information-gathering and -processing systems, the I in C^3I.'

'For the past five years I have been special adviser to the Red Army on simply this.'

'That's why I have you here. But, *yedinonachaliye*, I am responsible for all. I have to be sure. If this thing breaks down at the heart of the BMC^3 system and fucks up some part of the battle, then to be sure I will have you shot. But if enough damage is caused to the war, then they will have *me* shot too. Now, can you get the computer up and running for this?'

'When is *Zarnitsa*?'

'The last week in July.'

'I will do it,' Serov said, steadfastly.

'Very good,' Ogarkov pulled off the humid helmet and dumped it on the table. 'You will have to stay here until all is done. Now you know too much.'

He pushed back the chair and pressed the command to switch off the cabin.

'You have this *Coral Spear* put together?' he demanded.

'Yes, I am going to run it this morning.'

'We will rename the machine, now that it is ours. It shall be called *Red Banner*. It is appropriate: it is in the Red Army now, like all who are to save our homeland.'

He bent down to put his face close by Serov's. 'Don't forget that. The Red Army will save Russia, and will take back her rightful place. No snivelling civilians will kill my men on the streets after *Zarnitsa*. All will owe what they have to us. Not the KGB, not Yanov. To *us*. The KGB weren't even involved in obtaining this computer of yours. It was GRU! And all you hear from the KGB is how wonderful their Directorate T is. How many tons of Western technology they steal a day. Bah! Directorate T are a bunch of tossers who wouldn't know one side of a cap-badge from the other. Our boys in the GRU have come up the real way. *Through the army*. We are the ones who got the computer, we are the ones who will win the war. *Operatsiya "Zarnitsa".*'

Ogarkov grunted with pleasure at the thought. 'The computer, then. Take me to see it. By the way, I was sorry about your father.'

'Yes,' Serov said sadly. 'My loss, and our country's.'

Ogarkov thought that Nikolai Serov had been a dangerous lunatic who was much better off dead, but since he was – and had provided the Red Army with a son of genius – he allowed it to pass.

The two men – the tall, wide-shouldered general with gold epaulettes on his shoulders and broad stripes down his trousers, and the small, enquiring engineer in his sports coat and flannels – came out of the cabin, and Serov took Ogarkov to the big room which had been allotted to him. At the door he put his hand into the cipher lock and pressed the buttons in sequence.

The computer was once more as it had been where it was born, in Yokohama.

'It's not very impressive, is it?' grunted Ogarkov.

'No coloured lights or bells,' Serov said sharply. 'If that's what you mean. But I think you'll find what it does quite impressive enough.'

Ogarkov looked at Serov in amusement. 'I wasn't criticizing your baby,' he said. 'Explain to me how it works, and then switch it on. If you're ready.'

'We are,' Serov said stiffly.

'It is, clearly, very advanced,' he said. 'You can tell that from its size. The cabinet is physically very small – look at it. Yet it's the most powerful mainframe in existence. Liquid coolant circulates across the circuit boards. Physical memory in the order of several tera-bytes, cpu with a clock cycle measured in pico-seconds. Disks again are physically very small, they consist of large arrays of high-density platters. I assume that files are spread across the platters so that one read instruction invokes all the disk heads to operate in parallel and down load all the information at once. I assume that transfer rates to and from disk are in the order of thousands of mega-bytes per second. If they are, then Red Banner will sit at the heart of our BMC^3 system with ease. It will receive inputs from our array of sensors – satellites, radar, sonar, HUMINT and so forth – form a coherent picture of what is out there, examine the status of our own forces and disseminate our response to the various battle groups, command centres and anyone else with a need to know. And do it very, very fast. We should be able to gut the enemy command-and-control cycle.'

He moved about the large spotlessly clean room, pointing out items of the architecture.

'Communications, by fibre-optic media. Eliminates susceptibility to jamming interference. Speeds over these links, in the order of tera-bytes per second. Over here, some separate machines. I'm not entirely sure what they do, yet. For a start, they work through photonics, not electronics, and they are intelligent. They're neural network processors.'

'What's the significance of that?' asked Ogarkov.

'Neural network processors simulate the neural inter-action of human brain cells. Neural computing is funda-mentally different from the conventional von Neumann approach to algorithmic computing. Its advantage is that neural networks can operate with contradictory and imprecise data. Furthermore, they are not rigid. Expose them to real-world data, and they learn. In effect, they discover the rules for themselves. And like human

258

beings, the more they do, the smarter they get.'

'Very well, then,' said Ogarkov. 'So let's see how smart it is.'

Yuri sat at the console, looking like a choirmaster about to have his organ strike up the first few bars of a hymn. His fingers moved expertly over the keyboard and a few small lights glowed.

'All right, then,' he murmured. 'Now let's see . . .'

'*Ohayo gozai-mass*,' said a voice. Serov stared in disbelief, the colour draining from his face. The voice was coming from the machine.

'What the hell?' said Ogarkov, his heavy boots smacking on the tiles as he came forward to look at the computer.

'*E? Nan dess ka?*' it said, sounding politely enquiring.

'The fucking thing's *talking*, Serov,' said Ogarkov.

'*Chot-to!*' Red Banner, *née* Coral Spear, said to itself. It sounded pleased. It cleared its throat while the two men goggled at it. 'Ah-hum. *Dobrahyee ootrah*.'

'*The fucking thing speaks Russian.*'

'Ah,' Red Banner said happily. 'I thought I was right. *Dobrahyee ootrah*. Good morning, sir. To whom am I speaking, may I ask?'

ADAMSTOWN, MARYLAND

Now that he was widowed, Thrale was in the habit of leaving his house early and going to his office. His home, once so happy, had become little more than a shell, and the disciplines of work the hawsers to keep him sane. By training and age he was naturally a man of routine, and once established he rose, got himself ready for the day and left in his old Cadillac at the same hour every day. At that time of year it was still dark, with dawn lightening the far sky.

The road on which he lived was a winding, hedged lane off which lived professional people, comfortable in their split-level ramblers. Nearly all, like Thrale, were a part of the vast, government-connected machine that provided employment for much of the Washington citizenry, both within and without the Beltway.

Thrale's nature had been forged a long time before, by the necessities of staying alive as a young man while simultaneously exerting all his skill to kill other young men. It was the need to ensure that engine oils and parts reached working temperatures, to avoid the lethal horrors of cold, thick lubricant within a variable-pitch propellor, of the surge of full-throttle power sending the pressure of cold oil past the red line, emptying the contents of an engine through the split line a few seconds after take-off which half a century later had Thrale sitting patiently in his Cadillac as the engine ticked over and the water temperature gauge slowly came off its stop.

Thrale's garage abutted on to his house and was possessed of a slight slope, enabling him to allow the car to roll backwards into the fresh air while he warmed the engine through. Now he was ready, he closed the door by radio signal from his seat. It would have been little more effort to get out and do it, but he told himself that it saved him from getting wet when it was raining. It did, but the truth was that Thrale liked gadgets.

In drive the big limousine, one of the last of the great gas-guzzlers with its 400-plus cubic-inch engine, rolled effortlessly out of his driveway and down the lane. Dawn had arrived early with the clear day; Thrale drove on dipped headlights that soon he would be able to extinguish.

Other habits which he had brought with him from a war almost half a century earlier included an instinctive awareness of events all around him. In a fighter, that meant above and below, to the front and back, to each side. In his car, he was conscious of his environment all around him on the road.

In his mirror, something moved behind him. He lost it as he travelled on in the dim light. It had almost seemed as though, as he had passed, someone had stood up coming out of the hedgerow.

At nineteen years of age Thrale had been able to extract more information about the future from a glimpse of a far-off, flying speck or a group of twisting contrails than a man had any right to. His had been a sixth sense given only to a few, the handful of aces who did most of the killing. He belonged with Ira Jones and Erich Hartmann, Nishizawa and Bong, Finucane and Richtofen. Like them, he saw more than other men.

Without realizing he was doing it, he slowed his car, and his hand shifted his gear-lever from drive to low. He leaned forward in his seat, his head darting to and fro, twisting, assessing the threat. His left hand pressed his window command and it rolled down. Nose and ears sensed the air.

The people who lived down the road did so because it was countryside. They might have to work in the city, but they could live out in the fresh air.

It wasn't fresh. It carried a tang of the city, something smoky, some partly-burned hydrocarbon. A diesel engine. There was a deep rumble on the breeze, the hiss of great tyres on the asphalt. Through the twisting hedges, did not something flicker faintly?

Thrale floored his gas-pedal and the warmed-through engine boomed with sudden power. His tyres howled as they attempted to absorb the sudden torque going through them. The nose of the great car rose high as it accelerated and Thrale spun the wheel hard to the left.

The truck burst upon him. Unlit, vast, leviathan, it towered above the Cadillac. The bellow of its huge engine at full power engulfed him.

Its own engine roaring, the Cadillac crashed through the hedge with the full impact of its two and a half tons. The truck had vanished. Coming through the hedge, earth flew high as the car spun out of control on the wet grass. A wide pond received it and the front of the car sank deep into its rim.

The water came in like a fire-hose and Thrale struggled to free his seat-belt. He pushed the heavy door away from him and fell into the pond. In the dim light he felt grass under his fingers and scrabbled frantically up the bank, gasping for breath.

Steam, fresh earth and oil were on the air. In the half light he saw two figures moving through the gap he had torn in the hedge. They were dark, lithe, they moved quickly and silently.

Thrale hurled himself backwards into the pond. He went under, like a scuba diver. Hampered by his clothes, he struggled towards the other side. With his breath running out he came to the surface. The lights of the house were on. With water in his eyes he peered desperately across the pond. Past the wreck of the Cadillac something vanished into the dark.

Floundering, he splashed his way to the far bank, where he became caught among the water plants. A voice was calling his name, strong hands pulled him out, helped him inside.

262

Thrale dripped pond-water on to the floor of the Meades' kitchen. Lee Meade was a big man from the South, a computer man who tended the acres of them over at the National Security Agency on the way to Baltimore, off the Parkway. His neighbours had a little gentle fun with him and his pond, which he claimed was ornamental. They said he kept catfish in it to remind him of home.

'Sorry about the pond, Lee.'

'It don't matter about the damned pond, K.K. But how the hell you get in it?'

His wife appeared with a blanket and fussed him to get his soaked clothes off. Thrale began doing so.

'A truck, Lee. A damned great truck. Came right at me. Sure thought I was a dead man.'

'It hit you?'

'No, I went through your hedge.'

'I heard the impact. It got me up. I looked out to see what had happened. I saw you do some kind of backward leap into the pond.'

'Guess I wasn't thinking straight ... I thought there was someone there trying to kill me.'

Katie Meade came in and began scooping up the clothes as Thrale wrapped the blanket around him, suddenly cold.

'Ain't you got more sense than to stand there quizzing poor Mr Thrale like this?' she snapped. 'You know he ain't been well since his wife passed on. Go call for the doctor now.'

Thrale heard the rattle of cups and crockery, the rumble of a kettle starting to boil. He went to the window and looked out. In the dawn light nothing moved. The road outside was empty.

OGAWAKEN, SHIMBASHI, JUNE 1951

The restaurant simply buzzed. Even Komura, who probably dined in the fabulously expensive steak-house more often than most, had not seen it so busy since he started dispensing hospitality to the great and powerful five years before. The steak and *tempura, sushi* and *fugu*, the parties at the great Komura villa in Kyoto, the beer and whisky in the bars of Ginza and Akasaka, the purchase of stature within the financial and political community, Japanese-style, had destroyed his lean physique and he was sleek. That, too, brought respect.

His dinner-guest was already seated. To those who had known him in the days of his power, Major-General Yonai presented a bizarre spectacle. On his head he wore a Dodger's baseball cap, on his back a satin Giant's jacket. He had on a check shirt and chinos that were too short, exposing yellow socks above two-tone loafers. He would have been well-dressed in Boise, Idaho. On the table in front of him was a large tumbler, half-empty, where an iceberg was disintegrating in a brown sea. He beamed.

'It's good to see you again,' said Komura, sitting down.

'I'd have come before, but I wasn't free,' said Yonai. 'But from the look of you, you've been here for some time.'

Komura smoothed the fine white cotton of his shirt over his stomach.

'I'm a bit bigger than I was,' he admitted.

Yonai burped as he leaned forward, and a haze of fine whisky drifted across the table.

264

'That's good stuff,' he said, tapping the glass. He looked at Komura conspiratorially. 'I've seen more Class "A" war criminals in here tonight than were with me in the camp.'

'De-purged,' Komura said succinctly.

A pretty kimono-clad waitress came to take their order, and they decided on 16-ounce T-bones, baked potatoes and salad.

'It's the American way,' grinned Yonai. He ordered another giant Wild Turkey, and Komura Hennessey brandy.

'Look over there,' said Yonai, peering across the discreetly lit room. 'Isn't that Odachi Hirokichi? The last time I saw him he was being led off in handcuffs.'

'He's vice-minister at MITI.'

'He was the Naimusho police bureau chief,' said Yonai. 'That's why they locked him up.'

The former general squinted about the room, picking out people he knew.

'There's Niwa Keikichi.'

'Minister of Home Affairs.'

'Okuno Shigeo.'

'Leader of the Japanese Democratic Anti-Communist League.'

'What? In 1939 he was boss of the Black Dragon Blood Corps.'

'Same thing,' said Komura.

'Nadao Bumbei. He was the *yakuza* boss in Aichi.'

'Still is. Also special assistant to the minister of home affairs.'

'Who is?'

'Furui Kingo.'

'Who was a *Tokko* section chief in Tokyo. And who uses Bumbei for what?'

'Busting heads. Breaking up union meetings, beating up socialists.'

'And *there* is Okazaki Seisuke. Now what is *he* doing out of his cell at Sugamo Prison?'

'*He* is minister of education,' said Komura.

265

Yonai suddenly looked bewildered. He shook his head. 'Do the Americans know about all this?' he asked quietly.

'They're *responsible*.'

'Okazaki Seisuke was procurator-general. He ran the Special Higher Police – you know, the Thought Police. The education of our nation's children is in capable hands, all right ... and you say that Americans know about this?'

'They've forgotten,' Komura said gently.

'Forgotten? How can they? It was yesterday.'

'They have no historical memory; they have new things on their minds. Tell me, who did you see today?'

'A General Harris.'

'What did he want to know?'

'Whether I stood four-square – whatever that means – for democracy and the American Way.'

'You said yes.'

'Of course.'

'Anything else?'

'Whether I was appalled by and opposed to the global conspiracy of godless Communism. Whether I would fight it to my dying breath. I said that I was and I would.'

Komura chuckled. 'Walk with a real man a hundred yards and he will tell you at least seven lies.'

'I would have,' Yonai said modestly. 'But he only gave me time for three or four.'

'He give you a job?'

'I am vice-chairman of the Un-Japanese Activities Committee. Apparently we are to take after some Senator McCarthy in the USA. I think our real task is to bust opponents of the LDP. "Conform, or be re-educated." Well, we know how to do that.'

'Well, today *I* saw John Foster Dulles. He's come from President Truman, to sound us out about the forthcoming peace treaty. While you were in prison we had the "red purge" last year, got rid of all progressives, busted the leftish unions, crushed the Communist Party.'

'As far as Komura Bussan is concerned, we have emerged almost intact. I have been allowed all my

266

former top-echelon *zaibatsu* managers back. The Americans' loss of memory has not extended to forgetting that Komura Bussan was our country's biggest munitions manufacturer during the Great East Asia War. Komura Bank is once again the biggest.'

'You should have seen us,' Komura said dreamily. 'Most of the heavyweights Dulles saw were rehabilitated bosses from the pre-war and wartime Empire. Men who ran Manchurian Heavy Industries and Nissan Chemical. Nomura Kichisaburo was there, *he* was ambassador to America at Pearl Harbor. Hatoyama Ichiro, who purged the student bodies and the professors. And some of us younger men, leaders of the *zaikai* – we don't call it *zaibatsu* any more.

'The Americans have lost China to the reds. They're fighting in Korea. They want us to rearm for their war effort. So to establish a bargaining position, we in effect asked for the moon. We asked for ample supplies of food, raw materials, fuel, and most of all for the technology to catch up with the West. We asked for the restoration of economic and political independence, membership in world organizations and military protection to be paid for by the USA. There were some of us there who were worried, I can tell you. We thought that Dulles might throw us out for being so damned insolent.'

'What happened?' Yonai asked softly.

'We got it all, and then more,' said Komura disbelievingly. 'We would have been content with half, less than that, even....'

Yonai looked around the buzzing room. The waitress arrived with their fresh drinks.

'It could be 1941,' said Yonai. 'It's as though we never lost. *Nothing's changed.*'

Komura raised high his tumbler. A huge smile split his face.

'Cheers, as the Americans say.'

'Cheers.'

'Or as we Japanese say, *hakko ichiu!*'

'*Hakko ichiu!*'

267

THE STATE DEPARTMENT, 35TH STREET

It had to be said, Cy Rogers was enjoying himself. Paradoxically, it would have been far more difficult for Borodin to do to him what he was in the process of doing to Borodin. Rogers had three degrees concerned with the people of China past present and future, the most senior of them being a doctorate. He spoke and read Mandarin and Cantonese fluently and could conduct a good conversation in a number of the many other dialects. However, he had spent a total of about nine months in the country, on various grudging visits. Borodin had lived there for years in the very heyday of Sino-Soviet camaraderie. He knew the bastards in a way Rogers could never hope to emulate, for all his academic ability.

That gave Rogers a rich vein to mine, along with the fact that Borodin had managed to retain contacts within the PRC even after the rift between the two countries. That was clear from the accuracy of his assessments, which occasionally had the eerie quality of a seer's. Borodin was more than an analyst; he was in some ways a spymaster, with his own network.

It was for all these reasons that Borodin would have found it more difficult to fabricate a convincing case against Rogers than the American was in the process of doing to him. But the real reason that Rogers would be able to make the mud stick lay in the inbuilt paranoia of Soviet or Chinese bureaucratic dictatorship. When you dealt with a state founded upon a virulent secular religion, it was easy to convince people there that within their number were witches.

Rogers was able to make use of the records of US intelligence going back into the Second World War. A trained academic, he could move swiftly and surely through the forests of files and papers from the OSS, CIC and CIA. He visited the National Security Agency, where 14 vertical columns of CRAY-2 mainframe set in a 300-degree arc helped him reach effortlessly back into the electronic past. The National Photographic Interpretation Center provided him with images shot at distances of 100 yards and 150 miles, through a 300 mm Zeiss and a two-position zoom set in front of a six-and-a-half feet 'rubber' primary mirror in a KH-11.

He was at his desk, collating his material, when his secretary came in.

'You're due for your meeting over at Langley,' she reminded him.

'Thanks, Molly,' he said absently. Rising, he looked down at the image that had come in that morning. A young Borodin guffawed with an only middle-aged Chiang Shikai.

'You see, the s.o.b. *knows* them,' he said. He put the photograph in the file and reached for his coat. 'It's one of the reasons he's better than me. But not the only one.'

He went out, leaving his efficient middle-aged secretary shaking her head at the obsessions of the academic.

Rogers took the lift down into the car park underground where his Chevrolet waited among all the others. The park was a vast, rambling affair guaranteed to get anyone lost who was not familiar with its ramifications. Rogers had a slot in a corner in an annexe.

As he approached, he heard a sudden slap of flesh on flesh and the whimper of a female protest. A slim woman in a red dress was pressed up against the side of a car. Menacing her, with his back to Rogers, was a young man of her own height. He held up a threatening hand.

'The fuckin' money, bitch,' he heard him snarl.

Rogers was six feet and a half tall and had played

tackle at college. He broke into a run.

'Hey, you!' he shouted. 'You get away.'

The young man in his brown leather jacket broke like a jack-rabbit and scampered away down the subterranean lane. He vanished among the cars. The woman came out of the corner where she had been pushed, smiling gratefully with relief. She was young, in her mid-twenties, very pretty, and oriental.

'Thank you very much ... I don't know how that happened ...'

'Are you all right?' he asked protectively. 'This is awful, getting mugged in the State car park.'

'Yes, yes ...' The young woman was rummaging in her bag. 'Where is it? I must look such a fright.'

Women, Rogers thought fondly. Worried about their looks even after nearly being mugged.

Searing pain lanced through his stomach and he fell like a chopped pine. He hit the side of the car and grabbed on to the mirror. The young woman hit him again in the neck and Rogers saw the shining blade bloody in her hand. He fell heavily on the asphalt floor. As he died, uncomprehending, he looked up at the young woman, and the young man who had returned. Two beautiful, oriental faces looked down at him. They seemed to approve. It was strange. Blood gushed from the two fearsome wounds inflicted on him.

The young woman carefully removed Rogers' wallet, sliding it into her bag out of sight. Her companion took off her leather cap, shaking out her long black hair, and became a woman again. They walked quickly along the lane towards the lifts and the killer wiped the hand which had done the deed clean of some specks of blood with a moist tissue, which she folded neatly and put in its plastic wrapping in her bag.

They put on their passes, rose up into the building and left into the streets of Washington.

270

ADAMSTOWN, MARYLAND

Thrale recovered sufficiently from the shock of his accident to regain control over his environment, countermanding suggestions that a doctor come to the house, and had Lee Meade drop him at home when he headed off to the basement of the National Security Agency and its acres of computers. He put his pond-drenched clothing into the washing-machine and himself into the shower, and began the morning again.

Having called the office to let Curtis know he wouldn't be in, he spent his time organizing the removal of his Cadillac from the pond by the local wrecker and its transport to the dealer for repair. He hired a two-door Ford and arranged for gardeners to go in and replant the Meades' hedge and yard.

Then he went home, where he sat on his sofa, the temporary glow and vigour imparted by the boost of adrenalin into his system entirely used up. Once the presence of death had been as familiar and common to him as a cold in the head, but that had been a very long time before. Now he was old, and used to peaceful routines. He poured himself a large Jack Daniel's and sat nursing it. When it was finished he lay on his sofa to rest, and slept.

He was awakened by the telephone's bell.

'Thrale here.'

'Uncle K!' The young voice bubbled down the line, washing over his bruised mind like mountain water. 'It's your niece, Masako.'

It took Thrale a moment to fit the description to the person for Masako was not really his niece at all but an

271

honorary one, the niece of his partner Hasegawa Nobi. He remembered her – a small, pretty girl one year older than her sister, Kiyoko. It was over fifteen years since Thrale had been in Japan. I won't know her from Eve, he thought.

'Masako, what a pleasure to hear you. Are you in town?'

There had been no delay on the line to indicate a very long-distance call.

'Yes. Kiyoko is with me. We have come on holiday.' She paused. 'Uncle, we wish to say how very sad we are that Aunt Keiko is no longer with us.'

'Yes.' Thrale was waiting for the pain that came every time he had to remember his wife's death to lessen, but it was always the same. 'Yes.'

'Uncle, we have a promise to keep. Before we left Japan, our mother told us that we must come to see you and cook you a proper Japanese meal. Without his wife to keep him in order, she said, he will have fallen into bad habits. He will be eating hamburgers and fries in a bar.'

Thrale laughed ruefully. 'Yeah. There's some truth in that, I guess.'

'We are only in Washington until tomorrow. Then we go on to Boston, to see where they threw the tea in the harbour.'

'The tea party.'

The young voice giggled. 'We are having a very nice time. To travel abroad is wonderful. But it means that we could only see you tonight. May we come and cook for you? We have found some good Japanese shops where we can buy everything we need.'

There was a part of Thrale that was wholly Japanese, he knew. A part that remained unchanged, however long he lived in America and thought himself American. It was a part kept content while his wife had been alive. A sudden longing to see two good Japanese girls broke over him.

'I would love it,' he said honestly. 'But what may I do

272

in return? What shall I buy?'

'You may buy nothing,' she admonished. 'But our mother sends a request. She remembers your calligraphy; she asks if you would copy something for her.'

'It's been a little while, but I've still got my brushes. I'd be real glad to do that for your mama; I remember her well. But say, listen. If you two are going to cook for me, I must also cook for you. When you do your shopping, bring flour. I'm not a real chef, but *soba* I can do.'

Masako giggled. 'But I love soba! We can all make lots of noise; it will be fun.'

'Come soon,' urged Thrale. 'It will be good to see you.'

As he put down the phone Thrale realized that he meant it. He was a part Japanese, part American. While his wife Keiko had been alive the two parts had been in balance, the yin and yang of his life were in harmony. Her death had taken that away from him; that Japanese part of him needed to be fed.

He put his empty tumbler in the dishwasher and went off to brush the taste of Jack Daniel's from his teeth and shower away the sweat of his uneasy rest. He dressed in a white *yukata* – it was the first time he had worn the clothing in a long time. He got out ink, brushes and paper from his desk, and sat practising ideograms. The bell rang soon afterwards. Two young women stood on the porch, their small Volkswagen parked discreetly behind some bushes in his yard. Smiling, all three bowed formally and Thrale surrendered to the delicious pleasure of allowing himself to be guided by the myriad customs and rituals of the other half of his race, travelling like a boat on a certain stream.

Masako, the elder, and her sister Kiyoko were dressed in jeans and coloured cotton tops, like any American girls their age. They were carrying bags, some of which they deposited in the kitchen, and Thrale showed them to the guest bedroom which had its own bathroom ensuite. When they emerged shortly afterwards both had changed their dress. Masako wore a snow-white kimono, Kiyoko one of scarlet. The girls had exchanged obis, so

273

that Masako's waist was encircled by a blazing red river of silk, Kiyoko's by shimmering white. They had put their shining black hair up, and had decorated their work with a chrysanthemum blossom each. Thrale bowed, and sucked in his breath in admiration.

'We have a gift from our mother,' said Kiyoko, and held out a polished wooden box. When Thrale laid it on the table in his living room and opened it, he found wrapped in scarlet and white tissue two bottles: a blue and white *choko* drinking cup and a *tokkuri* bottle. The cup was of delicate porcelain, the bottle – made for holding one *go* of sake – made of glazed blue pottery.

'Our mother remembers you as a sake-*tsu*,' explained Masako. 'So far from home, she felt the sake for a connoisseur would be hard to find.'

Thrale took the wrapping from the bottles.

'Hibikinada *ginjo-zukuri*,' he said reverently. 'Your mother is most knowledgeable.'

The girls smiled happily.

'I think,' said Thrale, 'that I should repay your mother while my eye and hand are as sure in reality as I will feel them to be after a *go* or two. What would she like me to write?'

'She remembers seeing you copy from the *Heike Mori-gatari*.'

Thrale smiled. 'What a chronicle! Such heroics. I loved it. Yes, I know the passage your mother remembers. I have my materials ready on the desk. But tell me, with this trouble between our countries, you have not run into any problems?'

They giggled. 'We speak good English. We tell everyone we are from Hawaii.'

Thrale sat down. Behind in the eating room he heard the girls working quietly. The brush-strokes flowed over the heavy paper, painting it with jet asymmetry.

The girls came in. Masako sighed with admiration. 'Yea, the proud are but for a moment, like an evening dream in springtime. The mighty are destroyed at the last, they are but as the dust before the wind.'

274

She presented him with the sake *choko*, now filled with *ginjo-zukuri*.

'*Kampai*,' the two girls murmured.

'*Kampai*,' said Thrale. He lifted the cup to his lips and savoured the richness of the special drink. 'It is as though I had never been gone,' he said.

Kiyoko was admiring the calligraphy. 'Where did you learn to do this so well?' she asked.

'I was ill as a boy; for nearly two years I was not at school. My grandmother, who was Japanese, used to teach me. All kinds of things, not just how to write.'

'The *Heike*. Perhaps that is where you first learned to be a *samurai*.'

'Maybe.'

'You were a great warrior.'

'That was a long time ago,' smiled Thrale. 'Now I am just an old man, very happy to see two young friends from home. Now, before the sake affects my abilities further I must make *sugo*. Have you both found what you need in the kitchen?'

'Oh, yes. It is most properly equipped.'

'Keiko would have it no other way,' Thrale said simply.

In the kitchen he seasoned the Edo buckwheat flour with salt and mixed in hot water, quickly kneading it into a ball. Using a long, slim, wooden menrui rod, he flattened the ball into an even thickness and rolled it out. Then with the rod he lifted the sheet of dough to fold it.

His knife was a chef's knife – oblong, its handle formed from a cut made in the metal below the upper edge. Thrale handled it dextrously to slice the thin grey-brown noodles from the folded sheets of dough. When it was done, he stepped back, and the two girls bent over the tray.

'You are a *sugo*-master,' Masuko said admiringly. 'See, the waves have formed.'

The thin noodles of the fresh *sugo* had curved, making a pattern of waves.

'I used to do a whole lot – *udon, hiyamugi, tamago somen*. If I made *soba* at one time it had to be *cha-soba*

275

because I liked the green colour. But in the end plain *soba* is hard to beat. You sit there and slush and gulp like Kosan Yanigiya doing his *rakugo* act and have a real good time.'

Kiyoko stood by his elbow bearing a small red lacquer tray holding his refilled *choko*.

'Excuse us for not drinking with you yet,' she murmured. 'We are unused to such sake as this.'

'*Kampai.*'

From an insulated bag Masuko had taken chilled fillets of fresh fish which she arranged on a plate. She had a bowl of rice and a small one of *wasabi*, the horseradish that gave it spice. Using swift and precise strokes of her knife, she cut and sliced, then scooped up a double fingerful of rice, adding a little *wasabi*. Her slim fingers danced, performing the seventeen steps of making *nigiri-zushi* so swiftly and deftly that the *sushi* seemed to develop in her hand like an expanding flower.

Thrale drank sake and exclaimed with admiration.

'See,' he said to Kiyoko. 'All the grains of rice face the same way.'

Masako arranged the *nigiri-zushi* on a round, glazed pottery dish in a *hiramori* style. *Shiso* leaf and pickled ginger provided contrast. When it was complete it was a palette of colour.

When she had finished, and her work had been duly admired, Masako opened a bottle of Toyojo *junmai-shu* sake. The West intruded on the Yamato festival briefly in the form of the Screwpull, which grasped and removed the cork in one simple movement.

'Here,' she said to Kiyoko. 'You will need this for your part.'

The two girls smiled deadpan at each other. Thrale sensed that there was more to this than simply drinking sake. He took a sip of his own and raised an eyebrow.

'Which is?'

'A simple fish dish,' Kiyoko said demurely.

'But with sake?'

'To drink first. As *hirezake.*'

'*Ataru to, ipatsu de shinu,*' said Thrale seriously. 'If you get hit, one bullet's enough.'

Hirezake was a drink served as an aperitif to the main dish of fish, and was made from pouring warm sake over the toasted *fugu* fins. *Fugu* was said to have a number of qualities, the most prized being its supposed aphrodisiac effect. Those who felt such stirrings after dining on *fugu-sashi* were probably confusing the effects of adrenalin on their desires rather than any raised levels of oestrogen or testosterone, for *fugu* had one quality over which there was no disagreement.

'"Last night, *fugu* with a friend. Today I helped carry his coffin,"' Kiyoko quoted in her turn. 'Someone wrote that poem five hundred years ago. But do not worry, I am a *fugu-tsu*. I am licensed by *Koseisho*.'

Few meals required a licence to prepare. *Fugu* did. *Fugu* could kill the unwary gourmet, for the ovaries and liver of the fish contained tetrotodoxin. Colourless, odourless and without antidote, there was enough in an adult fish to kill more than thirty of those consuming its own dead body.

Thrale and Masako watched with a certain *frisson* as Kiyoko prepared the rather ugly blowfish.

'*Tora-fugu,*' Masako said approvingly. 'Tiger-fish.'

Thrale nodded in agreement. Tiger-fugu was by far the best. They both held their breath and then exhaled with relief as Kiyoko sliced with the sureness of a surgeon, removing the *kimo* intact. With the innards gone, she cut the *fugu* into thin, almost transparent strips of *fugusashi*. From the speed at which she worked, Thrale could see that she was indeed *fugu-tsu*.

Warmed from within by the effects of the sake he was drinking, Thrale mused on the fascination of the fish for the Japanese. We like it, he thought, because of its power of death. We enjoy the sensation of Russian roulette. As Masako refilled his *choko*, and in turn replenished the *tokkuri* bottle, he realized that he had thought of himself as one of them.

The dish was complete. The ugly blowfish was trans-

277

formed into a white chrysanthemum of a thousand petals. The fins rested aside, ready to be toasted. The girls took the food through into the eating room and when they summoned him he followed, having placed a pan on the stove to boil for *sugo*. The room smelled of fresh reeds from the new *tatami* matting. The *sushi* and *fugusashi* were like palettes of colours. Chopsticks and the dishes chosen, the flowers and leaves on the low table were in harmony. In the middle of the table a small white gladioli stem grew from a blue ceramic bowl filled with smooth white pebbles. A mile down the road someone is eating hamburger and fries to the thudding of an electric guitar, thought Thrale happily, and sat down.

Their short chopsticks darted to and fro, capturing choice items from the *nigiri-zyuchi* and transferring them to their bowls. Polished and patterned, the sticks were symptomatic of a nervous people aware of time, very different from the long, contemplative sticks of their neighbouring Chinese. It was said that the Japanese version had evolved during the centuries of incessant warfare, when a man sitting down to eat did not know whether within minutes he might not be reaching for one of the two swords at his waist rather than a morsel of food.

Having prepared his senses by brushing hands and face with his ice-cold *oshibori* hand towel, Thrale nibbled on perfect *sushi*. As well as *ebi* – boiled pink shrimp, *uni, agakai and tako*, sea urchin roe, ark shell and octopus – Masako had prepared *chu-toro*, made from the half-marbled side of tuna.

Thrale selected one from his bowl, using his fingers, as one should, and turning it over dipped the seafood side lightly into the bowl of soy sauce. He took a bite, and savoured the different textures within his mouth. He took a sip of sake, refreshed his mouth with a pinch of pickled ginger and continued, this time with shrimp, delicate and pale pink as the dawn.

The two girls were drinking sake as well by this time:

278

amakuchi sake, a rather sweeter and lighter drink as befitted their age and sex. As host, Thrale poured for them from their *tokkuri*, and as they must they did the same for him. It occurred to him that by the end of the meal he would have drunk quite a lot of sake, as indeed as a *tsu* it was expected that he would. There would probably be a terrific hangover in the morning. He did not care. He had come home for an evening. Tomorrow he would be back in the USA.

Quietly excusing herself, Kiyoko left the room to go into the kitchen. A few minutes later she reappeared, bearing a small black lacquer tray on which rested three glasses. Bowing once at the entrance to the room, she came in and presented them with the *hirezake*.

'There is a slight numbness on the tongue, is there not?' murmured Masako.

'Also the lips,' said Thrale. 'But it wears away.'

They placed the empty glasses down and reached for their chopsticks once again. The *hirezake* was capable of a slight anaesthetic effect, as the fins from which it was made contained a very small amount of the poison for which *fugu* was famous. Tetrodoxin was akin to curare, and being both colourless and odourless there was no way for the chef to know whether his skills of preparation had fallen below the standard required of them until the diners informed him. Amateur anglers were notorious for slaying both their guests and themselves by ill-advised forays into *fugu* cuisine. The first symptoms were lack of control over the chopsticks as the motor nervous system came under attack. Dry-mouthed and unfocusing, the unfortunate gourmet then fell face-forward into the remains of his executioner, there to expire shortly afterwards from the effects of respiratory collapse.

The *fugu* was sliced perfectly, and the flesh of the fish as fresh as any connoisseur could ask. Kiyoko's preparation had included the sauce, which was made from soy sauce, bitter orange *sudachi*, chopped spring onion, *daikon* radish and red pepper. For aficionados, the *fugu*-

279

sashi would normally be followed by another dish, a one-pot stew, and then by a form of rice porridge, once again flavoured by the remains of the *fugu*. It was the latter dishes that the amateur anglers sometimes allowed to get cold.

When the beautiful chrysanthemum of sliced fish had been reduced to strewn petals, Thrale rose, excusing himself, to put the *soba* on the boil. Their meal was something of an *alfresco* affair, and his noodles took the place of the more traditional dishes following the *fugu-sashi*. *Soba* was served better done than *al-dente* spaghetti.

As he came back into the room, the chopsticks fell from Masako's hand with a clatter.

Kiyoko and Thrale stared at her in horror. Her jaw sagged and she stared unseeing. Thrale's mouth was suddenly very dry.

Then suddenly she returned to life, pealing with laughter at the horror-struck expressions on their faces.

'April fool!' she laughed. Kiyoko threw a napkin at her in relief. It was the traditional joke played on the chefs at a *fugu* parlour.

It did not stop the heart beating a little faster, thought Thrale. They all refilled their *chokos* and drank to calm their nerves.

Soba, they all agreed, was fun. It was the noisiest meal you could eat. While all other food should be consumed quietly, it was obligatory to slurp and smack and gulp when attacking *menrui* of any sort. Thrale served it with a Kanto bonito and soy dipping sauce, and the three attacked it with vigour. The girls made more noise than he did.

Peace returned to the room when they were finished. Thrale sat unmoving, his senses bathed in the glorious effects of very good food and rich sake. It was more than that; there was the company. He was going home ...

He was afflicted by a power sense of déjà vu. He had been here before, feasting and happy, in the company of pretty young women, going home.

280

Kiyoko quietly gathered dishes. There were *tsukemono* pickles and *ocha* green tea yet to come.

Thrale knew where he was. He was in a single room – feasting, slaking his thirst and sating his hunger in the company of two half-naked whores. He was free. The camp was days behind him, he was going home.

RANGOON, 1943

They sat cross-legged on the floor, and had the floor as their table. The food was in the simple metal pans one of the girls had taken to the chop-house, and to Thrale the aroma of warm spices filling the room was as intoxicating as alcohol. That they had as well – bottles of beer with moisture frosting their sides, and others up to their necks in water in the sink. It was early evening, cherry-blossom pink clouds were chasing each other towards the horizon through the window.

The three clustered round the food, helping themselves to pieces of curried lamb and prawn, to dahl and rice in an atmosphere of genial good humour. They could have been friends of long standing, instead of birds of passage, but in times such as those you lived for the day and took whatever pleasures it offered with as much enthusiasm as you could. Thrale was in loose shorts and an open shirt, the two girls in *yukatas*. In the heat, they had left these half undone, allowing the air to circulate around their bodies. They were *geishas*, but the subtleties of the tea ceremony remained arcane ritual to them. They were farmers' daughters from Honshu. Life had always been hard for such as they. As Meiji rule blossomed into empire, grinding economic necessity had forced their families to sell them to the factories of the *zaibatsu*, the giant combines like Mitsui and Komura, or to the tea houses. In either case they became little more than slaves. These two were pretty; the Imperial government had proved a willing master and had shipped them out where the troops were. They were 'comfort girls'.

All desires returned with a full stomach. Thrale leaned

282

against the wall with one of the girls on each side of him. He allowed his hands to slide down inside the open necks of their light gowns cupping smooth and firm, slightly slippery breasts in each hand. He found the sensation exceptionally pleasing. Their hands slid up his thighs inside his shorts and met.

The light for the room was a simple candle. While the girls slept on the *futon* Thrale dressed himself in the uniform of an officer of the Imperial Japanese Army. He had washed the shirt free of Tanaka's blood. In the docks there was a Swedish tramp steamer due to cross the Bay of Bengal. On the other side was India.

The girls lay twined, more certain of finding comfort in each other's arms than in the company of brutal soldiery. Thrale peeled a couple of notes from Komura's wonderful wad of money and left them on their abandoned *yukatas*, lying pooled on the floor.

He went out of the door, out into the streets of Rangoon, on his way to freedom.

Thrale came out of his reverie. The two girls were quiet on the other side of the table, watching him.

'You were a long way away,' said Masako.

'A long time ago,' said Thrale. 'And a long way.'

'*Kampai*,' said Kiyoko, refilling his *choko*. He reciprocated, but Masako held up her hand.

'*Tejaku shimasu*,' she said, smiling. 'I am driving.'

The last cups of sake were sending Thrale into oblivion, he knew. Now he was tired. He had a sense of something very large, huge and dark rushing towards him.

'Someone tried to kill me today,' he said slowly.

They stared gravely at him.

'A great truck, travelling at speed ... they came for me in the pond, thinking to drown me.'

Green tea was before him. Celadon green *gyokuro*.

'Everything has been the finest,' he said.

'You are *samurai*,' Kiyoko told him. 'The cherry is a

283

king among flowers, as the *samurai* is a king among men. But the blossom's life is short, as is the *samurai's*. You are that rare thing, an old *samurai*. We salute you.'

The two girls bowed formally. Thrale's head was nodding; he did not have long to go. They helped him to his feet with gentle hands. They smelled sweet, their bodies were soft against him as they held him up.

'The driver of the truck was strapped in,' he said. He was slurring his words, but in the manner of the very drunk he had a window of absolute lucidity. He stumbled as they went down the corridor to his adjoining garage.

'Full harness,' he said. 'Like a fighter pilot.'

They opened the door to the garage.

'There were two afterwards. Young ... young women ... fast.'

'That's right, Mr Thrale,' Masako murmured.

They helped him on to the front seat of the hired Ford and laid him down. They started the engine. Before they closed the garage door behind them, they looked back at the car. Thrale lay across the front seat, and did not move.

As the fumes from the engine began filling the garage the two Japanese women moved away, not wishing to sully themselves, and shut the connecting door firmly.

Lying across the front seats of the Ford, Thrale opened his eyes. Rage at having been so easily taken in kept him conscious against the effects of the alcohol filling his veins. He was angry with himself just as he had been when – as a smooth-cheeked nineteen-year-old executioner – he had allowed some other young killer a temporary advantage.

He held the vision of one such, captured in his mind's camera. Kiyoko, expertly guiding her speeding truck, as safely strapped in as a fighter pilot, making a curving attack on the Cadillac in the lane. Surprise – what was it, respect? – as Thrale made the limousine jump out of the way like a jackrabbit.

284

The fumes entered the car – evil, choking. He had been breathing deeply, quickly as if running a great distance, and his face stung as the carbon dioxide left his blood. When he smelled its lethal relation, the carbon monoxide of the exhaust fumes, he drew one last long breath and held it.

He waited. The interior of the garage was dark, lit only by the light coming through the window. He lay as he had been left, across the seat, his eyes almost closed. He waited perhaps two minutes, with the blood beginning to roar in his ears and the breath in his chest demanding to be released, and then the interior of the garage was flooded with light. Peeping through his lashes he saw Masako quickly put her head around the door, a wadded kitchen cloth over her mouth. He lay very still. The door closed.

It was what he would have done himself in their position, he reasoned. A last check just in case there was a drunken, half-dead old man staggering about in there, only requiring a simple helping hand to leave this world for the next.

He moved. He opened the door as quietly as he could, his lips beginning to draw back over his teeth with the effort of holding his breath, the toxic fumes stinging his eyes. On the wall hung a yellow tank of air. Thrale had liked to go scuba-diving on holiday, while his wife sat enjoying the view above the waves. He grasped the tank, taking it from its hook, and carried it back into the car. The effort of doing so silently, battling against the unco-ordinating effects of all the liquor he had drunk, was immense.

The breath rushed from his lungs. He bit the soft mouthpiece and turned the handle. Magical sweet air flowed from the tank. He lay down once again on the seat.

The alcohol was seeping steadily into his blood. He took the keys from the steering lock of the car and sawed at a finger to keep oblivion at bay. Blood dripped on to the floor.

The air ran out and he was sucking against rubber. He weaved, staggering and bouncing off the car and the wall. The door opened for him and he pushed through, remembering to close it.

His house was empty. The remains of a meal for one lay on the table in his eating room. When he took the phone on his desk from its rest, the line was hollow. He knew enough to put it back. Spread out was his thick sheet of paper, covered with the black brush strokes of his calligraphy.

'The mighty are destroyed at the last, they are but as the dust before the wind.'

Thrale fell across the desk and ink spilled over it. It stained his white *yukata* as he slid helplessly to the floor and lay still.

LOCKHEED SPECIAL PROJECTS
OFFICE, BURBANK, CALIFORNIA

Elliott Reynolds lived as Harold Templer should have done – responsibly, safely and faithfully. He had a three-bedroomed house with neatly-tended front and back yards in a solid residential area a short drive from the Lockheed Special Projects Office. His two children went to the local school, where they got good grades. He and his wife were elders of their church. When Thrale came into his office in the SPO library, he looked at him as though he had brought a particularly unpleasant smell with him.

Thrale had. He wanted to know about Harold Templer, one-time employee of the company in the department of which Reynolds was head, of whom all that was left in the world was ashes and a bad memory.

'I arranged Mr Templer's affairs, yes. He had no immediate family that the company knew of. Two cousins in Sacramento are the beneficiaries of the estate.'

'Is that estate substantial?'

'Not abnormally so ... only the house, which is larger and more expensive than one would have expected. Apparently he benefited from the will of an aunt, and moved shortly afterwards.'

'When was that?'

'Some four years ago?'

'Did you notice if the move seemed to make any difference to the way he was?'

'No,' Reynolds said shortly.

'Mountain air, that kind of thing?'

287

'No.'

'You handled his affairs. Was that company policy?'

'I had company approval, yes. But he left a note. In it he requested that I do so.'

'Do you have it?'

'Not the original, no. The Sheriff's Department took that. I believe we have a copy in his file, however.'

'May I see it?'

'I suppose so,' Reynolds said ungraciously. 'I'll have to go and get it.'

He went out of the room and Thrale peered out of the window at the modern white buildings of the complex. Struck by the lack of windows in parts of them, he wondered what exotic aerial machinery was being constructed within now that the F-117s were gone. He retained good feelings for the company's products; almost all his victories as a fighter ace had been in the cockpit of his P-38 Lightning.

Reynolds came back with a photocopy of a smaller piece of paper. Possession of it seemed to have increased his disapproval of the dead man, and by implication of Thrale.

'Thank you.'

Thrale read it.

'It's short and to the point. "Dear Elliott, I just can't take it any more. I got to go. Please look after everything and forgive me. Harold." But the question is – is that a suicide note?'

'Of course.'

'Not necessarily. "I got to go." "Forgive me." You can put a different interpretation on that.'

'I don't think so.'

'Mr Reynolds, I do take it you know what technological espionage is, and what we do?'

'Certainly. You are concerned with the prevention of the transfer of high technology from this country to hostile foreign powers.'

'Exactly. We have very good reason to believe that a most major leak of Stealth technology has occurred, and that it has done so from this company. It occurs to *me* that this note might not be from the hand of a man about to commit suicide, but from a man preparing to run from retribution.'

Reynolds sighed with exasperation. 'Templer is *dead*, Mr Thrale. That's how far he ran.'

'But did he fall or was he pushed? Maybe *he* thought he was getting ready to run. Maybe those who dictated the note to him were those he thought were getting ready to help him to do so.'

'There was no indication of coercion. Templer drank a lot of alcohol, took a shower, wrote a suicide note and took two barbiturate tablets. The combination of the liquor and the drug was well sufficient to suppress his breathing responses within a few minutes. He died by his own hand; the pathologist and coroner said so.'

'If I may say so, you seem mightily sure that he died by his own hand.'

'I am,' Reynolds said certainly. 'There is no doubt in my mind about it.'

'Why?'

The librarian was quiet, although he looked troubled.

'There's obviously something about his death that you aren't telling me.'

'Very well. The company felt that in the absence of any close relative, I should abide by the dead man's wishes and settle his affairs. There were no legal objections and although the taking of life by one's own hand is directly contrary to Our Lord's teachings, I agreed to do so. His affairs were quite orderly: there were no outstanding debts and the house was paid for. I arranged for his car to be sold. A charity accepted his clothes. A furniture store with a second-hand outlet paid a fair sum for the contents of the house and agreed to send a truck to pick them up. Before they did so, I made sure that all drawers and so forth were empty of contents.'

The chief librarian paused and an expression of extreme distaste came over his face.

289

'It was as well that I did so, Mr Thrale. You see, what you have been saying is – and what had troubled me – where is the missing piece? The coroner said that he took his own life while the balance of his mind was disturbed, but *why* was it disturbed?'

'What I found in an album in a locked drawer of his desk answered my query. Harold Templer was a man as deeply steeped in sin as anyone I have ever known. Page upon page of that album was filled with the most obscene photographs. Of him ... and women. Engaged in the most depraved acts.'

'One at a time? Or more than one. Women, I mean.'

'He was always with two,' Reynolds said in a choked voice.

Templer was a sandwich merchant, thought Thrale, but did not say so to the librarian.

'The same ones?'

'No. A great variety.'

'Young gals? Attractive?'

'I did not study them in detail,' Reynolds snapped.

'But they weren't old, or malformed?'

'No.'

'I don't want to sound cynical but to a lot of guys access to batches of good-looking and immoral women would be something very much worth staying alive for, not ending it all.'

'I assumed that he had contracted some terminal infection of his body to match that of his soul. I had his remains cremated, needless to say.'

'Yeah, Mr Reynolds. I assure you that my questions have an investigative quality. I am not asking you to act as a voyeur for me. The photographs of Templer and the women – did they seem always to be in the same place? The same room?'

'Well, yes. A bedroom.'

'His?'

'It could have been.'

'From the same angle?'

'Well ... yes, I suppose so. Looking down, but from the side.'

290

'Has the house been sold?'

'It is for sale, but no one has yet come forward with an offer.'

'You got a key?'

'Yes.'

'Mind if we ride out there?'

The room was bare but the sun had left the ghost of the bed's headboard on the wall.

'Okay. Now if we take the bed as being like this – from where were the photographs taken?'

'Over here ...'

'Yeah. Yeah. I think I see it.'

Thrale found the ladder and vanished into the loft, where Reynolds could hear him creeping carefully over the joists. He paused, and a minute later there was the faint whirring of an electric motor. Thrale came back down the ladder.

'There's a Nikon up there with an electrically-operated timer. It's set up to take a shot every couple of minutes once it's told to start. If you traced it, you'd find a switch where Templer gave it the order to go. Clandestinely. Once his fun was about to begin.'

Thrale held up a yellow roll of film.

'Thirty-six shots. All exposed. Do you get me?'

Reynolds slowly nodded.

'He never had the chance to develop them. Did he have facilities for that here?'

'Yes. A dark-room.'

'Yeah. You wouldn't be sending that kind of thing through your local friendly store, now would you? Nor will we. Do you have a lab, back at the plant that I can use?'

Reynolds moved away as Thrale laid out the glossy prints on the desk in order, as though seeking to avoid contamination.

'Busy gals ...' murmured Thrale, 'and athletic. Well, looky here. I think we may have got lucky. What's this one here got in her hand? Sure looks like a little bottle of pills.'

He laid down the last picture and Reynolds peered at it, puzzled.

Templer lay naked on the bed; his body was darkening. The two young women were dressed, about to leave the room. They were in the act of bowing.

'What are they doing?'

'Paying respects to the dead.'

Thrale ran his eyes along the sequence of photographs. The two girls were magnificent young animals, he thought, their bodies sleek and pulsing with life.

'I never thought to see them without their clothes on,' he murmured.

Reynolds looked horrified. 'You *know* them?'

'I met them once. Pretty gals, aren't they?'

'I don't care to comment on the physical attributes of whores.'

'They aren't whores, Mr Reynolds,' Thrale said gently. 'They are *kaishaku, samurai* executioners.'

ZHELTYYE VODY, UKRAINE

Corporal Drozdhov they called the Eel. He was cipher clerk of the 35th group of the 277th independent reconnaissance battalion of the *Spetsnaz*. Everyone in the group had a nickname, and it was he who had come up with the one for their commander, Lieutenant Otari Yhetsov. The choice of pet name for the officer was crucial, for while they would obey whoever was in command of them – for they were soldiers of the Red Army – respect was an entirely different thing. Their previous commander had not come up to their standards, and they promptly and accurately called him the Useless Extra. How they laughed when his parachute failed to open on the hundred-metre drop that began the exercise! All soldiers in the *Spetsnaz* packed their own parachutes and signed them, from the general down, so that if they failed to open they would know whose fault it was. So they shovelled the culprit into a bag, wiping the tears from their eyes, and left it while they went on their planned mission to destroy the communications centre of the 7th Guards Tank Army, manned by its bespectacled, overweight signals troops and telephone operators, men and women simply eaten up by idleness and lechery. Of course, being an exercise, they couldn't do what they would have in wartime, which was convert the lot into dog-meat, but there was a certain fun to be had in hearing the wailing and carrying-on as the whip-tough troops drove them naked into the snow-filled woods.

That exercise lasted twenty-four days. The remnants of the 35th group 'died' to a man, out of ammunition, fighting with their giant *Spetsnaz* knives, with shovels, with fists, their backs to the sheer wall of a ravine. All except the Eel, who escaped across a river filled with breaking ice-floes, and who walked back into the battalion barracks four days later – thin as a skeleton, wearing a warm wool coat with a *karakul* collar that he had stolen. For that feat he was promoted to corporal, and awarded fifteen days' leave by the Army and his nickname by his mates. His 'dead' comrades received the Army's approval, because that was what *Spetsnaz* sabotage forces were there for, to cause destruction among the enemy until they died. On that understanding its soldiers were credited with eighteen months' service for each year served and were paid half as much again as other soldiers, together with awards for parachute jumps and for every day of exercises. They were paid ten per cent extra for each foreign language they could learn, and twenty per cent for each oriental language. There was method in this, as in everything the Red Army did. It was taken for granted that any of them could swiftly extract information from anyone unfortunate enough to fall into their hands, *but what if you couldn't understand what the bastard was screaming about?*

They got all that and, of course, the faded blue beret that set them apart from all the other trash in the Army. Which was why the choice of nickname for the commander mattered.

When the Useless Extra was shipped back to his wife four feet shorter than when he had been alive, the 35th got Lieutenant Otari Yhetsov. The eleven other men in the group regarded him with grave suspicion. He was an aristocrat, a grandson of a very powerful man. He liked to wear Western clothes, had his own apartment in a good part of Moscow, and also a car. Reading his decorations, they admitted that he had been in Afghanisan but probably, they said to themselves, one of those bastards in the rear areas who ate all the food meant for the fighting soldiers, and cut their fresh uniforms to appear like them while brave men were serving the Soviet Union at the sharp end in rags. They called him 35-I, his group number, while they waited to make up their minds.

Two weeks after Lieutenant Yhetsov took command, they were dropped from one hundred metres at night in the biggest exercise of the year. All the gas canisters exploded on cue and opened their parachutes for them, and within a minute of landing they were moving out on their fox-skin-covered skis. Three weeks later the 5th Guards Tank Army was practically paralysed and unable to fight, so busy was it trying to catch those who disrupted it behind its own lines. When the exercise was over, the 35th marched back to barracks, twenty pounds a man lighter than when they had gone out in the An-22.

The Eel called Otari Rhino.

In time he and the other members of the 35th almost came to love the lieutenant. They loved him because although they were to a man tough nuts from the harder parts of Kishinev, Kaluga or Kovrov, men born with calluses on their knuckles and dirt under their finger-nails, and he a pampered offspring of the *nomenklatura*, he thought exactly like them.

The troops of the *Spetsnaz* risked their lives every day, peace or war, and every day were able to observe others on the edge of death, as they were themselves. This gave them a flint-like judgement of human nature, which they saw as vicious and incorrigible. Since this was so, they divided everyone up into the good and the bad. The good were those who did not hide the animal within them. The bad were those who tried to appear good. Indeed, the worst of all were those who believed that they *were* good. Were not the great crimes in history performed by men who thought they were acting from the best of motives?

Furthermore, since everyone only had the capacity to be good up to a certain point, when life got difficult the good ones would become bad – which could be bad for you if you had to be with them. Much better, therefore, to associate with those you knew to be animals anyway. Men like Lieutenant Otari Yhetsov. The Lieutenant liked vodka. So did they. If they saw a good-looking woman in the street, breasts and buttocks bouncing like firm melons, they would rape her with eyes and mind. So did the Lieutenant. If it was war they'd do it for real, if they had a minute or two to spare, and they'd all have to wait for the Lieutenant to take first turn.

And the Lieutenant liked power. He was ambitious, and aimed to make Colonel-General. Good luck to him! And good luck to them, for a rising star always pulled his own team with him, and he always chose from those who had come from nothing and who only then had him to thank. So yes, good luck to you, Lieutenant Rhino. We're with you, all the way.

It was the Eel who realized just how much the Lieutenant liked power, just as he liked the female sex and Polish vodka. He realized that the day they were given a 'puppet' to practise with.

'Puppets' were important because what the *Spetsnaz* had to do was important. In wartime, what would happen if a group of *Spetsnaz* tasked with killing another group of enemy soldiers – in their sleep, maybe – hesitated? Got sudden feelings of compassion? Charity? Humanity?

It would be terrible. They might fail in their task. Be wiped out themselves. Wreck the operation upon which their task had depended and cause the deaths of thousands of its soldiers.

Which was why from time to time they were given a 'puppet' to practise on. A 'puppet' was actually a man. To practise, to rid themselves of any of the unwelcome and unnecessary feelings towards their fellow human beings, they were allowed to fight this man, to hit him as much and as hard as they liked. And the difference between this kind of fight and a training match with an instructor was that while they could punish the 'puppet' as much as they wished, they might not break his bones or kill him. However, the 'puppet' was under no such restrictions. How could he be, when he was already sentenced to die?

Men sentenced to death in the Soviet Union were not

necessarily killed immediately. There were a number of tasks they could perform to be of more benefit to the state than fertilizer. They worked in the VPK – the armaments industry, in GCh service, fitting and servicing warheads. They mined uranium. The idea of using highly-paid personnel to build nuclear power stations in the Western manner would have caused those in charge of electrical supply within the Soviet Union to guffaw mightily. Use prisoners. And when Chernobyl melted down, use them to clear it up!

The other people who had a use for prisoners condemned to death – very tough, very brutal prisoners – was the *Spetsnaz*. They used them to fight against, to bring themselves to peak performance.

It was when the Eel saw the Lieutenant fighting with one of the 'puppets' in the training centre that he realized how much his officer liked power. There was no sadism involved; the Lieutenant did not get pleasure from inflicting the pain that he did; he got pleasure from the exercise of might and merciless power.

It was in his blood, of course, the men of the 35th commented to each other out of Otari's hearing. Was his grandfather not Vyacheslav Mazurov, once head of the *Komitet Gosudarstvennoy Bezopasnosti*? And were not all heads of the KGB only barely distinguishable from each other in volume of blood spilled and number of gore-spattered corpses they left in their trail?

It was the Eel who noticed. The problem was that the state wasn't sentencing enough people to death. There were only about three thousand a year to go round, and about half of those – the weak, old, sick, especially dangerous or just the ones who knew too much – were shot, incinerated or hanged immediately. And unfortunately, there were lots of people who wanted the ones left. The *Spetsnaz* were in line with everyone else, and they only got a few and had to make them last a long time. And they got worn out, like old carpets, from all the beating.

They were given fresh supplies. Tough, violent young

297

men with an animal rage burning within them, not yet snuffed out by the brutal fists and feet of the *Spetsnaz* soldiers.

After a week, they all agreed, they hadn't been in such fighting trim for a long while.

To the Eel, it meant only one thing. They were going to be used. Out there, in the real world. And he even knew where. For after training, and before the good food they were given for supper, they put on their red shorts and white singlets and went out and practised their basketball skills against their cousins in the 27th group. They were going to Beijing, the capital of the People's Republic of China, as part of a goodwill mission.

THE WARDMAN TOWER

'You know the old saying about happenstance, coincidence and enemy action?' asked Thrale. 'Well, take a look at this.'

He had a file, which he put on the sofa next to him and opened.

'Let's begin with the day we had lunch together at the Met. You were called back to the White House because the pathologist, Dr Fineberg, had gone to see Ed Reisch to tell him that he did not think the late President had died of natural causes.'

'Right,' said Kuusinen. The suite was quiet once again; his daughter – very pretty, very young – was finding the support of her mother in looking after his granddaughter hard to give up. The refrigerator had been supplied with cold cuts, salad and beer.

'After you left I went back to my office, where my assistant showed me this overhead that had just come in.'

Thrale reached in his file and took out the image, shot from one hundred and fifty miles up, as crisp and clear as a society wedding.

'Taken by accident over Fukhai, near the Sino-Soviet border, by a KH-11 satellite. They were having housekeeping problems with it and when they'd got it sorted out ran some shots to check it was all in order. One of which was this.'

'Airplane crash?'

'Right. The wreck's gone, but the boys at NPIC ran the image through their CRAYs and came up with a *possibility* that it had been caused by a F-117A, the Stealthy

299

strike fighter. Only the Air Force categorically deny having lost any of theirs.'

'Which leaves technological espionage. Someone's stolen the plans and built their own. It's happened before.'

'Sure. The Russians have a track record of doing it that goes back to Peter the Great. It would certainly fit. They fear the arrival of technologically highly advanced weaponry which would render their own military forces obsolete, and are certainly doing their best to keep up by theft. But. But ... There was something about the image that bothered me. I had one of my bad dreams with the ghosts a little while later, and rather than go back to bed I sat up and had some coffee. I was looking at the image and realized that I myself had been there.'

He reached out a finger and tapped the man standing looking back along the scar.

'I've done that. After putting a bird down in bad circumstances. *He's the pilot.*'

Kuusinen nodded. 'Right. That's a kind of flight suit he's wearing, I'd say.'

'It is. Most unusual, being white. I went over to NPIC, where I know a guy called Hank Caid – used to be in the Air Force himself. I asked him to run it through the computers to give me face-on shots of him and the other man. The information's all digital, and they can do very clever things with it. He did so, and produced this.'

Thrale pulled two more images from his file.

'This is the other, middle-aged man. It's difficult to judge, because he has his hand partly over his face. But could he be this man?'

Kuusinen compared photographs. 'Could be, yes. Who is he?'

'He's Wakatsuki Shigeru. Chief of the design bureau, Komura Aircraft Company,' Thrale said levelly.

There was silence for a few moments. 'Okay,' said Kuusinen. 'I don't like the sound of all this and I have a feeling it gets worse. What about the pilot?'

'What's that? The decoration on the front of his flight suit?'

'A flower?'

'A chrysanthemum?'

'Yes.'

'It looks to me like it has sixteen petals,' Thrale said casually.

'And the significance of that?' Kuusinen asked sharply.

'The imperial symbol. Pre-August 1945.'

'Who is he?'

'Lieutenant-Colonel Nozaka. A Japanese fighter commander.'

'I knew I was not going to like this. What else?'

'Let us now move to Lin Pao, who died like a samurai, destroying the evidence linking him to the assassination of President Hawkins in the process.'

'But *why* assassinate Hawkins?' Kuusinen mused.

'I don't know. But that evening I received a call from a very old friend of mine who works for the Japanese Secret Service. Used to work for me in the Counter Intelligence Corps. He was over here with Trade Minister Saito for their very unsuccessful and very brief talks with MacGregor. He came by my house, both sad and resentful about the recent American moves *vis-à-vis* Japan. Saying that it would be a long time before we met again, given current trends, he gave me an expensive and exotic present. It was a watch, calculator, television and telephone all combined. Very advanced piece of kit. He said it was made by Komura Electronics, but was not yet on sale.

'I wore it when I went to see Cy Rogers,' he said casually, 'to discuss your project for ruining Aleksandr Borodin.'

'Do you have it?' Kuusinen asked curiously.

'I'll come to that. The following Friday I got up early to go to work as usual. As I was driving down the lane I sensed something not right ... like I used to as a fighter pilot. A few of us had it, and shot down the aircraft; most didn't, and didn't. The Air Force guys call it situational awareness now. Anyhow, fortunately for me I still have it, and I was able to get out of the way when a very large dump-truck came hurtling out of the dawn light at me. I put my Cadillac through a hedge into my neighbour's pond. Shook me up a bit, and I spent the day at home – organizing for the damage to be fixed, and resting.

'In the late afternoon I got a call from two very charming and lovely young Japanese girls, who claimed quite plausibly to be my late wife's nieces. They asked if they might come over and cook a meal for me, as they had been requested to do so by their mother on their trip to America. I was pleased to accept, to be honest; since Keiko died I've missed that side of me ... Anyhow, they came over and we had a perfectly splendid evening. Ate well and drank a lot of *sake*. Before I got drunk, at their request I did some calligraphy. They knew that it was my *kakushi-gei*, my hidden talent. In Japan everyone has at least a little *kakushi-gei*, which they can pull out when called upon at a party, dinner, wedding or whatever. It's a useful social talent. It might be dancing, singing, doing imitations. Mine's calligraphy. So I did some for them – they even knew what they wanted. They wanted a passage from the great samurai chronicle, the *Heike Monogatari*. They said their mother had asked for it as she remembered I used to do it when I was in Japan. And I did. Done in ideograms, it looks very beautiful. In English it goes: "Yea, the proud ones are but for a moment, like an evening dream in springtime. The mighty are destroyed at the last, they are but as the dust before the wind." It commemorates the death of the *samurai* hero, a lonely, solitary figure who dies bravely but tragically battling against overwhelming odds.

'Okay. We had, let me say, a wonderful evening. The girls were great company, we cooked very good food, drank superb *sake*. I got as drunk as I was expected to and the girls kindly helped me off to lie down asleep ... across the front seat of my car, in my garage. Where they started the engine and shut the door behind them.'

'Oh, Jesus,' whispered Kuusinen.

'The fighter-pilot thing, the being aware of mortal danger, somehow saved me again. I managed to drag

302

one of my scuba-diving bottles from the wall and go lie back down on the seat. I breathed on that air until it ran out, and by the time I staggered back into my house the girls were gone. Inside, before I passed out I found a table laid for *one* and the copy of my calligraphy laid out on my desk. And the telephone, when I picked it up, was hollow.'

Kussinen got up and fetched some cold Red Stripe from the refrigerator, and they drank from the cans.

'My reconstruction of it the next day, through a truly shocking hangover and the most filthy taste in my mouth was this: The girls attempted to kill me in the early morning with the dump-truck, but failed. In the afternoon, having adapted their plans, they called me to set up the supper, and once I had rung off left their telephone connected to cut me off from the outside world. Just prior to that call, they had murdered Cy Rogers in the State Building car park. They came to me for the evening, and as far as they were concerned killed me too. They cleared the room where we had eaten, set it up as though for one, laid my calligraphy on the desk and took the watch/television that was also a telephone with them. Because it was a bug.'

'Your old partner did to you what you did to Lin Pao. You didn't suspect?'

'Never. Takashi is in the position of owing me a debt, an *on*, which in fact cannot be repaid. It is inconceivable that he would do that to me.'

'He did,' Kuusinen said dryly.

'Yes. And the girls arranged things to look as though I had committed suicide. Which, hangovers being peculiar things, made a connection with a snippet I read in the *Early Bird* about a librarian in the Lockheed Specific Projects Office in Burbank committing suicide. *That's* where they made the F-117A.

'I went out there. It transpired that the dead man had been some kind of sexual athlete, and had kept a photographic record of his marathons with the pairs of girls involved. This caused me to think, and in his house I

303

found a hidden camera with an exposed roll of film still within it. I developed it and found these.'

He spread some photographs on the table.

'Remember to take these with you, K.K.' Kuusinen observed. 'My wife'll think I've been going down to the stud shop.'

'There's the bottle of barbiturate pills. There, they're paying their respects to the dead. *They* are the girls who claimed to be the nieces of my late wife.'

'An unbroken Japanese connection.'

'Right ... Takashi planted the bug on me because, somehow, he knew I was going to discuss something about Aleksandr Borodin with Cy Rogers. Cy is dead as a result, and I very nearly joined him. You'd better tell me why you want him ruined.'

'*I* don't. A man called Vyacheslav Mazurov does.'

'I know Mazurov. One-time head of the KGB. Why are you doing his bidding? You're the National Security Advisor.'

'I have done his bidding,' Kuusinen said levelly, 'because I owe him my life. During the Second World War my father was a partisan leader in Karelia. Aged ten, I was a guerrilla fighter. The Russification of Karelia at the end of the war was very bloody, and Mazurov was in charge of it. Mazurov is a strange man. Where he could, he would let someone go, save a life rather than take it. He saved the lives of my mother and father and mine. On the understanding that we would leave Finland and go to America. He had my father scratch his initials on the bullet that would have taken our lives. It was that bullet which accompanied the request that I provide him with evidence to ruin Borodin. I should, without a doubt, have sent it back. I did not. Now I have a death to live with.'

'I'd have done the same,' said Thrale.

'It doesn't make it easier.'

'Now you know what I mean about the ghosts. They come back to take revenge....'

Thrale stood up, looking out over Washington from the open window.

304

'There's something huge ... and hideous, out there in the fog. I wish I could see it. All this ... and the America, Love It or Leave It stuff going on.'

'That's Ed Reisch. I told you, he's on a power trip, he has Potomac fever worse than anybody. He's a street fighter and he's using the device of unscrupulous politicians everywhere – rampant chauvinist patriotism allied to a minority group brought out for everyone to beat up on. Hitler used the Jews. Idi Amin the Asians. Ed Reisch's got the Japs. The really sad thing about it all is that it works, at least in the short term. It'll get Barnet re-elected, for sure.'

'Reisch lives over in Georgetown, doesn't he?'

'Down by the P Street bridge.'

'I know where.'

Thrale stood thinking. 'I'm going to have to go back there, Lief.'

'Go where?'

'Japan. Since I'm supposed to be dead, I can go in quietly under another identity. Find out what's going on.'

'You need passports, anything like that?'

'I got all that. I'll need access to the CIA station. You'd better tell him, Top Secret Umbra, that I'm coming.'

'Okay.'

It was a warm summer evening and Thrale suddenly shivered, wrapping his arms around himself as though to keep out the cold.

'Someone walk on your grave?'

'Sins of the past cast a long shadow ... "By the pricking of my thumbs, something wicked this way comes".'

Thrale spotted the Shelby Cobra in Reisch's driveway. He parked across the street, and a little while later Reisch came out. With him was Ala, his soft black hair tied back in a ponytail. Thrale took his Nikon and got a shot of them through the 180 mm zoom lens.

305

THE WARDMAN TOWER

The Russian came no further into the suite than the small hallway behind the door. From inside came the happy noises of a baby bathing, and the laughter of mother and grandmother.

'I received the bullet,' said the airline pilot.

'Mr Mazurov,' said Kuusinen, 'once I put your father's request into motion attacks were made upon the two men involved. One died, the other barely survived. Someone knew what we were doing and reacted very quickly, very positively to put a stop to it. I would suggest to your father that it might be worth reconsidering his desire to ruin Aleksandr Borodin. He would seem to have powerful protectors.'

'I am sorry for the harm done to your men. It is my father's wish that you proceed no further. My father has just recently retired from public life; he is to spend the rest of his days quietly, in his dacha.'

Mazurov's son held out the old bullet.

'Here,' he said. 'It is yours now.'

FAR EAST MILITARY DISTRICT HEADQUARTERS, VLADIVOSTOK

Lieutenant-General Alexander Ogarkov blinked at the afternoon sun which was sinking in the sky. He was very, very tired. The doors to the powerful lift that had brought him to the surface closed with a hiss and he went out into the glorious summer sunshine, to the car that was waiting for him.

He did not look like a general, sitting slumped in the back as it headed out of the city. He wore a grey overall, with the neck open so that his blue and white striped paratrooper's vest was visible, and had a dusty blue, faded beret on his head. It is as well I am not driving this car, he thought. I would probably crash it.

It was ever so. The preparations for war were so vast that those responsible for them were completely exhausted even before it started.

Ogarkov had the cure. He had known it since he was a little boy, told to him by his grandfather. His grandfather had died aged over ninety with a smooth face and all his own teeth, because he knew the cure.

The car drove out into the pine forest and Ogarkov had the driver stop and bid him wait. He strode into the forest, joyously inhaling the scent of resin and pine, his boots scrunching over the deep carpet of needles. In a clearing he found what he wanted. There it was, and there they were. An anthill filled with busy big, brown ants. Wood ants.

Ogarkov stripped off his clothes and jumped into the hill as though into a pool of icy water. The ants swarmed over his body in fury; he felt their rage as they bit into his flesh. If he stayed long enough they would eat him alive, but only a minute was required. No elixir could do this job, for the ants bit where it was important, just as an acupuncturist knew where to stick his needles in the correct places.

Ogarkov leaped from the hill like a stag and, bellowing with pain and joy, rushed about the clearing brushing the ants from him. Then he dressed once again.

'Thank you, comrades,' he roared. 'Thank you for your attentions.'

He went back to the car at a jog-trot, his entire body on fire. The weariness had left him. He was ready.

So was the war.

YELANSKOYE, YAKUTIA A.S.S.R.

Strangers were taking over the Rogachev Guards Motor Rifle Division. They arrived in trucks, wearing the correct uniforms, and disembarked within the vast storehouses of the 14th Army. There the soldiers of the Rogachev Guards were waiting, and when the strangers had got out they got in. They felt a certain disgust that such flabby, rear-area types should ever put on the uniform of the Guards, but were pleased to be leaving Yelanskoye wherever they were going. The mortification of the entire Division at being posted to such a place following their withdrawal from the NATO front line after the signing of the 'Peace Treaty' had been acute. Next to a punishment posting to the sand, loam and stone of the Caspian deserts, a dump like Yelanskoye was the worst.

Lieutenant Alexei Mazurov felt a lightening of his heart as the big trucks rolled out, leaving the giant main battle tanks, the armoured personnel carriers, trucks, artillery, anti-aircraft and anti-tank batteries, sapping equipment, chemical warfare units, repair sections and support behind in the immense park. After leave in Moscow, the return to Yelanskoye had been hard.

The trucks took them to Yakutsk, to the rail junction. Trains and trains. Barbed-wire fences. Vast, ugly storehouses that the trains vanished into and re-emerged from. Inside one of which the Rogachev Guards climbed down from their trucks ... and stared at the next stage of their transport in disbelief. *Coal trucks.*

They were truly huge, you could have driven a tank-transporter into them. Coal was visible, filling their tops. They had small, concealed doors in their sides and the

309

Division embarked. Inside, although windowless, the trucks were comfortably appointed with bunks and washroom. It was evening, and hot food and drink were aboard. The train, over a mile long, began to clank south.

It was dark when they disembarked and they went down a tunnel into the ground, leaving the trucks in a huge rail siding. There was a glimpse of the lights and smoke-stacks of a vast building, and then they were marching down the broad, well-lit tunnel – Lieutenant Mazurov at the head of his company, the first company of the battalion. Their guide was a lieutenant unfamiliar to him.

Brand-new T-80M tanks stood formed up in front of them. Their tracks were thick and unworn, their camouflage paint fresh, the reactive armour unscarred. Mazurov could see that there were 31 in all, the entire battalion complement. There was a 2-S-6 tracked armoured gun-missile anti-aircraft system and an SA-9 surface-to-air missile platoon on its wheeled vehicle. Behind his battalion Mazurov could see the combat support vehicles of the division with Luna-M missiles, the *Gvozdika* 2S1 122mm howitzers, the BM-22 *Uragan* multiple rocket launchers, PRP-3 mobile reconnaissance vehicles of the *razvedchiki*, the scout troops, abristle with sensors, and their RKhMs, for moving into chemically-contaminated areas, the engineers, NBC defence, signals, combat engineers and support stretching into the glare of the neon lighting in the vast underground park.

'This is your company,' said the lieutenant. 'Get rucksacks, greatcoats, overalls, pistols and helmets from the quartermaster over there and store them in your tanks. We'll be fuelling and arming. Your quarters are over there, but don't get too used to them. We're moving out in the morning.'

'Where is this?' asked Mazurov.

The young man grinned. 'Up there,' he pointed at the ceiling, 'is the Shimanavsk power station. Over there,'

310

and he pointed to his left, 'five hundred miles away, is Vladivostok. Behind me is the Amur River.'

He pointed straight ahead of him, up the wide, smooth tunnel that led outside.

'Over *there*, five miles away, is the People's Republic of China.'

KABUKI-CHO, EAST SHINJUKU, TOKYO

Chuck Imamura received his education in 1945. He should have gone to college in Eugene, Oregon. Instead he went to a number of devastated islands in the Pacific where amid the reek of explosive and burning flesh he interrogated the few of his own kind still alive. Imamura was *nisei*, first-generation American Japanese. During the course of his short but intensive indoctrination into war, he had hung around with the Marines who were doing the fighting and killing long enough to pick up a few tips – almost half a century later he still remembered enough to stay away from the windows of Thrale's little apartment. It was afternoon, the *sakariba* pleasure-quarter had hardly woken up. The neon lay inert in the tubes, the loudspeakers that competed fiercely for business – peepshows, adult toys, cop-a-feel parlours – were quiet. Across the alley a little girl sat with her granny on a stool and munched noodles provided by her from a bowl. It was cluttered down there – old plant-pots, styrofoam boxes, bicycles and buckets. The little girl's mother was sweeping, preparing her tiny bar for trade; it gleamed like a hat-box, and was not much larger.

'We're too old for this shit, Thrale,' grumbled Imamura. 'Old guys like us, we done paid our dues, shouldn't have to get out in the field like this.'

'Yeah, I know.' Thrale took two cans of Sapporo from the tiny refrigerator on which he had stored his futon. He tossed one to Imamura.

'The white boys can't go out,' Imamura said, pulling

the tab. 'They go out and some crowd'll beat them to death. So all the troops're confined to base, and the spooks are crouching inside the Embassy. Which means if they want to know what's going on, they have to use guys like us. You'll pass, you look more like a Jap than an American. Can always tell'm you're the son of a G.I. who's aged pretty bad.'

Imamura took a swig of beer and chuckled. Then he seemed to recall something and reached inside his jacket pocket to pull out a brown envelope.

'I forgot; this arrived for you. They asked me to give it to you.'

Thrale opened it. There were some sheets of type-written paper and a note from Cy Rogers' secretary saying that she had found them when ordering his papers, together with a memo linking them to Thrale. She had sent them to the office of the National Security Advisor, who had sent them on.

'Anything important?'

Thrale put them back in the envelope, intending to look at them later.

'Just a message from a dead man.'

'So why are you here, K.K.?'

'Remember the late President – Hawkins?'

'Sure. Died of a heart attack, something like that.'

'Someone killed him.'

'No shit?'

'Someone Japanese.'

'Ahh ...' Imamura said gloomily.

'You're not surprised?'

'Well, sure, I *am*, but I'm not ...'

'How's that?'

'We must be the easiest people in the world to get whipped up about foreign folk. Hating them, I mean ... Us and the Russians, maybe. And there's been this terrific wave of anti-Americanism. You should watch TV. They keep showing films like *Minami Jujisei* with that goddam mushroom cloud, and *Dai Nippon Teikoku* with the US soldiers playing football with Japanese skulls.

313

Chushingura's on every other afternoon. I swear, Thrale, anyone who can sit through that is demented. The papers are full of editorials saying how the outside world, led by America, is against Japan and always has been. There's a lot of *higaisha ishiki* about, the ordinary people are being encouraged to see themselves as victims.'

'What about within the system itself? What's Komura up to?'

'Ah, well.' Imamura looked slightly sideways at Thrale. 'Well, we do have a source in there ... and we don't like what we hear. What the people are thinking about the US is nothing to what Komura's lot are thinking.'

'This source? One of them?'

'No ... a ... relative. Of one of them. The small group that has control of the system.'

'It's hollow,' said Thrale. 'The boys in the Manchurian Army knew that, that's why they could do what they did.'

He looked out down the alley. A sign flickered into garish red, white and green life and like a virus it infected the others. A loudspeaker scratched.

'*Irasshai, irasshai*! Welcome, welcome.'

'This whipping up on the Yanks,' he said. 'Started after Barnet made his little speech about cleaning up the environment by putting your Honda in the crusher, I guess.'

'No ...' Imamura said slowly. 'Not if you were looking. It started before that.'

The homely air of the alley had vanished. The little girl and her granny were gone into the twilight. Kabuki-cho was ready for pleasure and vice.

'Right,' said Thrale. 'That's what I thought.'

BEE EM SEE CUBED —BMC^3
– BATTLEFIELD

ZHONG NAN HAI, BEIJING

The entrance to the park was half a mile west of the Tiananmen Gate, along Chang An Boulevard. It was marked by a red screen with golden calligraphy, the red flag and two military guards at all times of day; for around the two lovely lakes which gave it its name were the most important Party committees and the houses of the highest-ranking Party members. These men were understandably anxious to keep their luxurious lifestyle from the eyes of the proletariat, and very few people were allowed in under the red screen, golden calligraphy and red flag. The men of the 35th group of the 277th independent reconnaissance battalion of the *Spetsnaz* thought it unlikely that they would be granted admission if they knocked at the gates at 2.a.m., so they swam in from Beihai Park, where the lake went under Wenjin Lu. Underneath the surface of the water a hole had been cut in the brick wall which kept the ornamental ducks in and people such as they out, so it was little problem.

The 35th would not be attending the semi-final basketball match against their fraternal comrades of the PLA's Beijing Third Garrison Division at the Worker's Stadium on the east side of town in the morning, nor would they be cheered on by the members of the 28th, 33rd, 46th and 51st, for they came too. There were sixty men, and they slid out of the water like crocodiles on each side of the Zhongai Lake. They were dressed in black. As each came on to dry land they substituted velcro-sealed trainers for the rubber flippers, taken from a plastic bag, where their P-8 silenced pistols and ammunition had also been protected.

317

The unit was under the command of Otari Yhetsov of the 35th, newly promoted Captain. He took over the thirty men on the west side of the lake. A light flashed from the opposite shore: Lieutenant Orlov's group was ready. They moved swiftly in groups of two, seeking out the bungalows in the park with the assurance of bees heading for flowers.

A light webbing harness held all they needed for this particular task. Huge *Spetsnaz* knives with spare blades, a short curved crowbar, extra magazines for the P-8 pistol. It was meant to be done quietly. If things did get out of hand, they had a large number of Chilean GM 78-F7 grenades. The plastic bodies of these grenades were fitted with coils of pre-notched steel wire which when blown apart created a lethal zone up to twenty-five metres in radius ... Certainly enough to kill everyone in a room. Special forces liked, and were allowed, a cosmo-politan choice of tools for their tasks. As well as the grenades most carried a Kalashnikov AKSU automatic rifle fitted with PBS silencer and flame suppressor, aimed by the NSP-3 night gunsight.

Otari was accompanied by Corporal Kryshinin of the 35th, like himself a veteran of Afghanistan, an *Afganets*. A big man, he was known as Genghis Khan. Everyone had a nickname.

They approached the bungalow from the rear, coming up from the lake through an ornamental garden which had been laid out by Zhou En Lai when he lived there. They inserted the slim, sharp-clawed ends of their crow-bars into the jamb of the kitchen door and heaved in unison. The door fell out and they laid it on the ground. Both men took their pistols and giant knives from their webbing and moved quickly and silently through the kitchen into the hall.

Water flushed and a thin bar of light under a door behind them opened out in a column that illuminated the hall. A beautiful young woman in a short nightshirt stared at them in horror and opened her mouth to scream. There was a short, explosive hiss from the knife in Otari's hand, which jumped back as the spring propelled the heavy blade across the hall. It caught the woman in the throat and knocked her back into the lavatory. She lay on the floor, her fingers scrabbling in bewilderment at the piece of horror behind her tongue.

The bedroom was to the right. The door was half-open, the covers pulled back where the now-dying woman had got out of bed. Kryshinin held the sleeping man down, muffling his cries of waking terror as Otari injected him with a one-shot syringe. The officer had hands like bunches of bananas; he tossed the drugged Chinese over his shoulder like a man carrying an empty sack and they went back out, jog-trotting through the park to the gate that led to West Chang An Boulevard.

The others of the unit were assembling. They brought with them the smell of propellant and the metallic tang of blood, and Otari knew that they had been successful in taking out the Chinese higher command authority within the park.

'Chiang Shikai wasn't there,' the Cossack, Orlov, grumbled.

'We get the rest?'

'Every one,' the lieutenant assured him.

They opened the gate. Troops in PLA uniforms were moving on Chang An. They had it sealed off with barbed-wire and spiked metal barricades from the Great Hall of the People to the Nationalities Cultural Palace on Xidan Street. The *Spetsnaz* soldiers peered from the gate, looking east.

Something swooped over Tiananmen Square. Two of the PLA troops were holding a hooked ladder. Lined with flagpoles, and planted with young poplars and willows, Chang An was a vast eight-lane artery laid straight as a die east and west, following the sacred geomancy of the mediaeval Chinese where force fields radiated from the emperor's inner palace to the farthest ends of the empire.

The Sukhoi Su-24C came past the Tiananmen Gate that led into the emperor's forbidden city at forty feet and one hundred and twenty knots, its wings fully spread, and the pilot planted it on the centreline. An orange parachute blossomed.

Otari was standing opposite the Telegraph Building with his captive over his shoulder as the big attack aircraft rolled up, turning under the guidance of one of the PLA-dressed soldiers. The pilot's canopy was up, and as he halted – the aircraft's nose bobbing briefly – the two waiting men went forward with Otari following them and hooked the ladder over the cockpit rim. He climbed smoothly up with his cargo and heaved the unconscious Chinese into the empty weapon systems operator seat to the right of the pilot. He strapped him in the way he had been shown, then he and the pilot exchanged a brief, powerful hand-grip and he was back down the ladder, pulling it away as the canopy descended once more. He ran to the shelter of the side of the street as the twin Lyulka turbojets bellowed at full power. The boulevard was filled with heat as the Sukhoi accelerated. The nose rose and it rode on torches of shimmering fire, climbing out over the square, turning north.

The troops were ready. Sixty soldiers had taken part in the operation within Zhong Nan Hai and two more groups of twelve had secured Chang An. As the crackle of the afterburning jet engines faded they heard the softer whine of turbines. The An-72 STOL transport touched down on the boulevard as softly as a ballerina. The high-set turbofans blew over the slotted flaps hanging down from the wings, giving great lift. As the low-pressure tyres contacted the tarmac, the thrust reversers erected and the little fat transport rolled to the speed of a trot, turning round by the Telegraph building where the troops were formed up. Its beavertail rear door was down and they jogged inside in formation.

Sealing it up, the pilot gave the two Lotarev turbofans the fuel and they accelerated back the way they had come. The Antonov lifted off, tucking in its fat tyres and climbing out over the very yellow tiles of the forbidden city. Inside, the troops were already exchanging their black aquatic suits and light webbing for the full conventional equipment of the *Spetsnaz* parachute soldier. *Rodina*, their Motherland, still had use for them. The bureaucrats and officials of the Cultural Exchange they left behind in Beijing. Their task, the part they had unwittingly played in providing Lieutenant-General Ogarkov with the most precious of gifts an operational commander could receive – strategic surprise – was over. They could remain in Beijing, for the Chinese to shoot in the morning.

The eighty-four soldiers crammed into the AN-72 dressed methodically; they had fifty minutes to prepare themselves. The transport was low over the ground having left Beijing, and heading east for the Bo Hai Sea at 450 mph. They wore linen underwear and thick string vests, designed to keep the other natural residents of the *Spetsnaz* troops' favourite habitat – the marshes and woods – at bay. The mosquitoes' sharp proboscis found nothing but air to suck on. Over that, triple-stitched tunic and trousers. On the feet, very thick wool socks worn under soft, strong ox-hide jump boots. On the head, a fitted cotton helmet that exposed only eyes, nose and mouth during the jump. Over everything, the thick, light, warm anorak that dropped to mid thigh, light grey like last year's grass or dirty snow.

Like all infantry, the *Spetsnaz* soldier was a beast of burden. His backpack carried water-purifying tablets, 2,765 grammes of high-calorie food, matches that would light underwater, dry spirit tablets, medical supplies, towel, toothbrush, razor, soap, needle and cotton, fish-hook and line, mess-tin and spoon, compass and maps, wire saws and folding spades.

All these did not weight too much. What *did* was the AKMS automatic rifle with 300 rounds, pistol, fighting knife, grenades, RPG-22 grenade-launchers, laser designators, passive night vision equipment, plastic explosive and directional mines that all except officers and radio operators carried. In addition they would haul some part of the weaponry and supplies in the containers that dropped with the first three men of each group.

Being *Afganets*, a veteran, Otari allowed himself idiosyncrasies. His fighting knife he kept, together with the four spare blades, strapped to the left calf of his J-B. His Kalashnikov he abandoned. Above all else, Otari liked firepower. There was a limit to what foot-soldiers could haul with them, and if you could make one weapon do for a number of roles it helped. Otari's personal firearm was American, a Barrett light 50 automatic rifle. The name was a misnomer, for next to the McMillan M87, which it resembled, it was the largest shoulder-fired weapon available. It was .50-calibre and only marginally lighter than the 21lb of the McMillan. Otari would have had the bigger gun, but it wasn't semi-automatic. The Barrett fired eleven-round magazines which he had loaded with ball, for people; tracer to check his aim; armour-piercing, to open up hard targets like APCs, light tanks and bunkers; followed by incendiary to brew them up nicely, and armour-piercing incendiary for the best of both worlds – most useful on helicopters, turning them into interesting catherine-wheels of fire as they tumbled down. The .50-cal bullets the Barrett fired came from hand-made ammunition, for accuracy, and weighed over 40 grammes – more than four times the weight of a standard 7.62 mm round. They travelled at 900 metres per second, and had a destructive impact upon arrival second only to a 20 mm cannon shell. In addition to its role as artillery, the Barrett was so well constructed as to be a sniping rifle. Through the Zeiss variable-magnification scope, which cost as much as the rifle, Otari could put the reticule on a general standing outside his headquarters, let the post and cross-hairs settle on his chest and squeeze the trigger from 1300 metres out. A second and a half later the giant round would impact, turning the contents of the chest cavity to offal. Together, he and the gun were not simply a good shot with a well-made rifle, they were a complete weapons system.

He was not particularly fond of his issue pistol, the

P-8. As he believed in firepower, he had managed to obtain a very unusual weapon indeed. It was an Israel Military Industries Desert Eagle automatic. Empty, it weighed 1.7 kilogrammes and was chambered for the .44 Magnum cartridge. It was more a small artillery piece than a pistol and required both the expertise of an instructor and the strength of a gorilla to use it. Otari had both. On undercover duty as an Avtotransport lorry-driver he had spent a few weeks in England, familiarizing himself with the environment he would have operated in had the Soviet Union gone to war with NATO, and had taken time out to rent some Dirty Harry movies for his video. He fully shared the film detective's views on the desirability of weaponry that would take the head off an opponent with a single shot.

The An-72 dropped low as they came over the Bo Hai Sea, heading north-east over the Liaodong Wan. The troops were fully dressed except for the close-fitting cotton helmets which they put on last. Shaven skulls gleamed with sweat in the hold lighting.

It was a hundred-metre drop, so they would only be using a single parachute, opened with the assistance of a gas canister. Otari squinted out of the blister window past the NKPB-7 airdrop sight and saw the Yingkou coastline coming up, pale in the moonlight. They began forming up in columns, the heaviest men first, so that falling faster than their lighter comrades they would not descend upon their canopies and collapse them.

The An-72 was still low, following the path of the Yun Hee River. As Shenyang appeared, the pilot began to slow from his 400 knots. The beavertail door descended, gears and servos whirring, and all the troops were in line, five rows of men all waiting for the green light. One-hundred-metre drops were horrible, and nearly all eyes glinted with a hint of craziness.

'Coming up, boys,' called the *shturman*, the loadmaster by the long tongue of the door, his jacket flapping in the gale.

The troops all began squashing up into five solid units,

each man pressing up against the back of the man in front. When the *shturman* gave the signal those behind leaned on those in front and the whole bunch went out of the big door as one.

The An-72 had climbed to about one thousand feet, slowing to around 120 knots. As the target came into view the pilot came back to flight idle and let the nose drop, maintaining airspeed in his shallow dive. The small, fat transport swished over the defences like a glider.

The blue light flickered. The siren howled.

There was a ragged roar as everyone bellowed at once: 'We're off!'

Otari was fifth in line. The wind blasted his face, tipped him upside down, got inside his jacket. The parachute lines whipped across his face and snapped him the right way up. At one hundred feet he could see he was spot on target, descending into the neatly-tended forecourt of the building with its lawn and flower-beds. He hit the ground with a thump and the rough lines of the parachute scraped his face again. He shrugged out of the harness and pulled the Barrett from its case. The ugly, slab-sided building in front of him bristled with antennae of various kinds. He ran towards the doors under the big red star.

Genghis Khan and the Eel, Corporals Kryshinin and Drozdhov were ahead of him. When he crashed into the hallway the two guards who checked the passes of those permitted to go through lay dead in their blood on the floor. One looked sleepy, the other surprised at the nature of the credentials shown to him.

He ran down the corridor. In a small white room with communications gear two terrified Chinese soldiers stood by the wall.

'Open the door,' ordered Drozdhov, in Mandarin.

'*Bu dui*,' said the taller of the two, shaking his head. His companion stared at him and the three giant soldiers, like a rabbit in a snake's nest.

Kryshinin held the obdurate soldier against the wall

324

and sealed off his mouth with one hand like a ham. Drozdhov yanked down the blue trousers below the olive tunic and grabbed hold of the young man's genitals. Slender hands beat a frantic tattoo on his back.

The huge *Spetsnaz* knife was sharper than a butcher's.

A hideous gurgling seeped through Kryshinin's huge fingers. He let go and the soldier dropped to the floor, both hands clasped between his legs. Blood poured out across the floor.

Drozdhov held it up where the second young man could see.

'Open the door. *Qing*.' he said. 'Please.'

The soldier nodded violently. Drozdhov stopped him as he was about to bolt from the room.

'Calm yourself,' he said. 'Appear normal.'

They went down the corridor. There was a leather door and the soldier selected some numbers in the concealed code console. It slid open. Behind it was another door made of armour-plate. He pressed a bell and an eye peered through the thick glass viewing slit. The locks buzzed and the door opened.

The 35th were bringing in the incendiaries and plastic by the time Otari and the corporals had access to the big lift. They had wiped their knives and put them back. They carried their firearms and had grenades at the ready as they descended deep into the bunker.

The lift doors opened and Otari was first out. The corridor was deserted, dimly lit with night lights. To the left, the kitchens. Plenty of cooking oil there – that'd burn a treat. Give it a phosphorus lighter. To the right, the restaurant. Nice inflammable furnishings. Give it one too, Genghis.

They went up one floor. Here was the guts of it all, the rooms filled with communications equipment. A man dozed at his duty console. A knife-thrust sent him asleep for ever. Slap plastic here, boys.

Up another floor. Corridors of rooms. Quietly, now, boys. Toss a few phossies down each one.

At each floor they opened the lift doors, like firemen,

and at the top they sent the lift up a floor and opened that door too, to create a nice draught.

The ground shook under their feet as the plastic went off, and smoke began gushing from the lift well. Outside, there was firing and the crump of more plastic going off. As they moved out of the building a terrible noise came from below, up the well, the noise of a thousand cats and dogs being burned alive. People had been sleeping down there in the bunker.

Buildings were alight. An APC grumbled out of the smoke, its tracks squeaking. A burst of fire came from a tower and Otari loosed a burst from the Barrett up into it. There was a gout of brilliant white flame and it burned like a giant garden torch. When he turned they were heaving Kryshinin into the back of the captured APC.

There was a little over an hour before dawn. The unit moved out of the destroyed complex in the YW 531H armoured personnel carriers they had taken from their owners. On the road they could make 60 kilometres in an hour. By dawn the APCs would be stuffed away in the forests of the Jilin Hada Ling mountains, and the *Spetsnaz* troops back in their natural environment, where no one could find them.

The unit had taken only one casualty, Corporal Kryshinin; his round face was slick with sweat. He lay on the bottom of the APC as Otari cut away the blood-soaked leg of his trouser. Shattered bone gleamed through the blood and ripped red flesh. Otari reached for the little pocket on the sleeve of his tunic and took out a small disposable syringe.

'Here we go, Genghis. A little something to take the pain away while we bandage you up.'

'Is it bad?'

The needle slid in and Otari squeezed the plunger home.

'Flesh wound,' he said casually. 'Like you get shaving.'

The big man grinned.

They went out of the gates that told visitors they were arriving at the August 1 Shenyang Military Headquarters,

Command Centre for the entire Shenyang Military Region, which went north from that of Beijing to the long border with the USSR. In under an hour the armies of General Ogarkov were to pour over that border like an armoured tidal wave.

They would sleep in the Jilin Hada Ling mountains. In the day. *Spetsnaz* soldiers were like prostitutes, they worked at night. That night they would move at the tremendous, punishing pace of the *Spetsnaz*. Re-supply by parachute from the air. The war would be well-started by then and the Chinese reeling, vainly attempting to react to the force, weight and speed of the Soviet attack. With the Shenyang Command Centre out, they would be re-establishing some form of C^3I for what remained of the 5 armoured divisions, 23 infantry divisions and border troops under their control. Before dawn Otari's unit would strike again. He peered out through the firing port of the APC. The sky glowed cherry red. The pattern would continue – night march, re-supply, attack, escape, hide up and sleep, night march – until either the war was won or they ran out of troops to do it with.

Otari looked down in the crowded personnel carrier. Kryshinin had stopped breathing. The syringe in the little pocket of his sleeve was known as 'Blissful Death'. There was no provision for evacuating the wounded in *Spetsnaz* – only re-supply, so that they could go on doing their job. In order to survive in wartime they had to kill off their wounded themselves.

They would be lucky to get away with just one casualty tomorrow, in the dim hours before dawn.

Otari wondered how long the war would last.

KABUKI-CHO, EAST SHINJUKU

The air that filtered through into Thrale's little room was spiced with the scents of the night that had passed – coffee, whisky, MSG-enhanced curry, beer. The people had gone – the gangs of giggling girls in their tight flared pants, hobo coats and great earrings, the discos dead; the *saraariimen* in their dark business suits back home past Shibuya or Ikeburo, or to a capsule hotel full of whisky fumes, the bars tight shut; the touts and the whores, the *yakuza* and the jiggle girls. Kabuki-cho was closed for business; like a vampire it could not come out into the daylight.

Thrale got up, folded away his futon and washed himself while the kettle was boiling for tea. He let the kettle cool while he dressed in the protective coloration of a businessman. It was warm in the little room, and while he was doing up his striped tie he opened the window to the outside world. The water had cooled sufficiently to make the tea and he sank a *bancha* bag into his mug.

It infused, slowly turning the warm water yellow. Thrale stood watching it, aware that he felt uneasy. He went to the window. In the early morning Kabuki-cho had the silence most places had in the middle of the night. Tired feet, cold neon, weary bodies, rubbish and drunk heads. Putting an ear out he could hear the city humming, crackling with energy and excitement.

He moved quickly to his small Sony television and switched on. A small, excited figure in a too-large flak jacket was signing off. As the picture cut to an advertisement for washing-powder, it seemed to Thrale that he

328

had been delivering a report from Tiananmen Square in Beijing. He took the opportunity to rescue his bag from drowning and take a gulp before the picture returned to the studio.

They had what looked like a situation room. A middle-aged man dressed in full combat fatigues was waving a large pointer at a map liberally supplied with the large, swooping arrows associated with military campaigns. Thrale had seen him reading the news from behind his desk in his striped suit the previous evening, and was so taken aback by the transformation of the Shimbashi skyscraper newsroom into subterranean combat bunker that for a moment he missed the significance of the map.

'Son of a bitch,' he grunted, and sank back on to his tiny sofa. 'They've gone and done it.'

It took him only a few minutes to realize that all they had – most probably along with everyone else except the Red Army and the People's Liberation Army – was the knowledge that a few short hours previously the former had moved – in massive strength, with great speed, from three different locations and a standing start – into the territory defended by the latter, and was pounding it into dust.

He watched for a little while to see whether there were any updates on these unvarnished facts.

Someone knocked on the door and he went over to open it. Chuck Imamura stood outside. He was unshaven and his chin gleamed silver; he was dressed in a suit, but had no tie.

'Morning, Chuck,' said Thrale, surprised. Unasked, Imamura came through the door, and as he did so Thrale saw why. He was acting at the bidding of a black SIG automatic pistol at his back. The 9mm weapon was held in a small but rock-steady hand.

'I told you we was too old for this shit,' Imamura said wearily. He went in and sat down on the sofa and at the urging of the gun-barrel Thrale did the same. The two girls bowed politely, one at a time, shimmering black hair falling down like jet waterfalls.

329

'Hallo, Mr Thrale,' said the one dressed mainly in red.

'Hallo,' he said. 'Do I call you Kiyoko? And your friend Masako?'

'Why not?' they beamed.

'You know, Mr Thrale,' Masako said reprovingly, 'you should not be alive.'

She was dressed mainly in white. Her pistol did not move in her hand either.

'He is *samurai*,' said Kiyoko. 'A true *samurai* always overcomes great odds, and escapes death many times before he succumbs. Is that not so?'

'Komura has sent you,' said Thrale. 'What is it he wants? Are you to shoot me here, with those very good pistols you are holding?'

'Mr Thrale,' she said, aggrieved. 'You haven't been listening. We are talking about *samurai*.'

Beside Thrale Imamura stared at his hands, seemingly bored and disinterested. He looked at the nails of his cupped left hand, as if deciding whether they needed attention, and scratched his palm with his forefinger, making patterns.

'A *samurai* is not shot to death in a room over a bar in Golden Town,' Kiyoko said reprovingly. 'He is allowed to die well, gloriously even.'

'It is good to die,' said Masako. 'You will find death lighter than a feather.'

'And how shall I die?' asked Thrale. 'What has Komura Tadaji arranged for me?'

'Many years ago, Komura Tadaji decided to give his life for the Yamato race. He prepared himself to die in the manner of Prince Yamato of antiquity, the forerunner of all *samurai*. You are, I know, familiar with the legend. Prince Yamato was a wandering hero. On his many expeditions he defeated great chieftains and monsters. In the end he became infected with a fever caught from the touch of the great eight-headed serpent whose sword, Cloud Cluster, he wore.

'Before he died he saw his true love Iwato-hime for the last time, and his spirits were raised, changing him

330

as he embraced death into a white bird which flew away to the south.'

On the television the announcer was talking about Operational Manoeuvre Groups and Combined Arms Armies. It was clear that they could have been Persil and Brand X for all he knew about them. Imamura ignored him, still scratching his palm.

'Komura Tadaji was unable to give his life for his race,' said Kiyoko. 'By the time he was healed the war was over. He emerged to serve his people in a different manner. For in the *Hagakure* does it not say that while a true *samurai* prepares himself for death every day, the moment when he should make that choice, to take death, may only come once in his lifetime? The time for Komura Tadaji came, but passed. Because of you. So now, he offers you the moment to make your choice. Now is your time, as it was his. We will be your friends, your *kaishaku*. We will help you towards death.'

Thrale got up from the sofa, and picked up the jacket of the suit.

'All this way of the *samurai* stuff is a load of horse manure,' he said. 'Anything else to tell me before I go face the elements?'

'The quick way to die is to contact any of your kind. The white men. The Yanquis,' Masako answered. 'We're watching them. Emulate the great Prince Yamato, who was a solitary hero.'

'It's all garbage,' said Thrale. 'I'd better go then.'

He looked at the television, where the world was being changed. 'I suppose you coming today has something to do with that. Yes?'

Kiyoko beamed at her partner. 'You see? I told you Mr Thrale would know.'

Thrale paused at the *fusuma* door. The painted irises on it were chipped; it needed a new scheme.

'*Sayonara*, Chuck. Sorry about this.'

'Make that *au revoir*,' Imamura said dryly.

'Yeah.'

Thrale went down the stairs, but instead of emerging

331

through the little doorway into Flower Garden Street pushed his way past some piled and empty Johnny Walker boxes into a dirty back room behind the bar. The whole street was wooden. He heaved at a loose and partly rotten plank, and within a minute had a hole big enough to crawl through. As he scrabbled through into the corridor of the houses behind he heard a sharp report. A gunshot.

He came out into the lane. There was no one there, just dead neon signs and dustbins. Thrale moved quickly down the tiny street, no wider than a prostrate man, and into a bigger, still jagged thoroughfare filled with storeys of neon, bar buildings, love hotels, more neon, restaurants and *rakugo* parlours. A few people were moving about. He headed downhill, going west.

Through a gap where some buildings were being torn down to put up others in the perpetual manner of the city – where you could leave, come back ten years later and not know where you were – he saw the great skyscrapers of West Shinjuku. At night the quarter had a population of six – the priest of Kumano Shrine in the central park and his family – while on the other side of the station East throbbed, but in the day it was host to a quarter of a million office workers and they all came in through Shinjuku station.

Two and a half million people went through the station every day, on and off the labyrinth of private and public railway lines, into the shopping centres, eating at the restaurants, playing *pachinko* in the seedy amusement arcades. It was a city. Thrale dived into twenty thousand besuited people coming off the Yamanote loop, and vanished.

NEN JIANG RIVER, HELONGJIANG

The interior of the tank stank like a latrine from which some maniacs had loosed off box after box of 7.62 ammunition and round after round of 125mm shells of different descriptions. They had. The Rogachev Guards had caught the Second Regiment of the Sixth Tank Division in the act of getting out of their barracks, and had slaughtered them. The wreck of that regiment lay four hours behind. After the fighting Alexei Mazurov had felt he wanted to make water nearly every five minutes, but there was no stopping and everything had to be done in the tank. The old fighting vehicles produced a steady supply of shiny brass casings which the crew used as latrines, but the T-80's D-81TM gun used semi-consumable propellant casings that went down the barrel as white-hot smoke. The quartermaster knew it, and had issued plastic buckets.

The Guards were rolling down the river valley. Mazurov had his head out of the turret, and his driver Khrenov had his hatch-cover up. Only the gunner – the Asian, Khan – had to stay down in the awful stench of kerosene, propellant and excrement.

The air was clear, and even in summer cold up there. To the West was the vast range of the Da Hinggan mountains; to the East the Xiao Hinggan.

It was so deserted. Nothing moved except the Guards in their tanks, APCs, command vehicles, tractors, anti-aircraft gun and missile-carrying vehicles; the tank transporters, fuellers, trucks and ammunition carriers of the material support battalion. It did not seem right to Mazurov. It was war; the sky should have been filled with flame, the air with fragment and shell, the ground littered with burning wreckage and the bodies of the dead. The short, intense battle only minutes after they poured over the border had been war. Now they were driving down the valley floor at a steady 35 km per hour as though out for a Sunday stroll.

'All yellow and blue units. This is Arby. Hornets and ants in your area.'

Within the tank the crew could talk to each other. From without on the radio net came the voices of the other commanders in the company – from the other company commanders, the battalion major and the Colonel. And sometimes, Arby. They weren't quite sure who Arby was, other than that he had a very powerful transmitter that cut clean through any white noise and distant stations on the net, but in the short time they had been together, the tank men and Arby, the soldiers had come to love him. Arby was God: Arby knew what the enemy was doing, from somewhere high in the sky, and he told them. They loved him for it, him and his clear, crisp Frunze Academy accent. Arby was the sort of staff officer you dreamed about, he *knew.*

Now Arby's voice brought Alexei from his ruminations with a jolt. Hornets and ants. Tanks and infantry. But where? Mazurov craned his neck about. There was nothing, just this rolling, rather ridged valley floor with its rocks and dirty brown scrub. Over by the river some trees dipped their roots in the water. He looked behind even, through the dust being thrown up by the tracks. In the distance there were just some trucks of the rear services meandering about, looking for some cover in case Arby's warning signalled action. He turned back to the front.

From the corner of his eye he saw the turret of Yellow Two, next to him, come off and rise high in the air, tumbling over and over, seemingly as light as a football. Something black came skimming over the scrub, moving incredibly fast. The howl of a dying dog rushed past his left shoulder. A huge door slammed. He scrambled down

334

inside the turret, heaving the heavy steel hatch-cover shut.

'Oh, shit,' he whispered sincerely. 'Oh, shitshitshit. Gunner, traverse right.'

He pushed his face into the cowl of his optics, peering desperately through his periscope. Scrub. Rocks.

'Load hard core.'

The ammunition carousel under their seats whirred as the automatic loader sought out the anti-armour round required. Mazurov squeezed himself as far to the right as he could in the cramped turret, pulling his black cover-alls tight. The autoloader had a reputation for slamming the unwary into the breech along with the round, which Mazurov knew would spoil his entire day. The clanking ceased and the double smack of the projectile and propellant signalled the weapon ready.

'Hard core up,' said Khan, the *chuchmyek*, the Asian.

APFSDS, armour-piercing fin-stabilized discarding sabot was the tank-killer. The Western tankers called it sabot.

Scrub, rocks. Bushes. Trees.

Something moved.

'Target right, one thousand,' Mazurov called. He was surprised to hear his voice calm, unhurried. Below him Khan's horny hands gripped his firing console with the delicacy of an artist.

'Fire,' Mazurov ordered.

Khan's right thumb squeezed down and the huge machine shuddered as the gun fired. Mazurov watched the tracer flying across the scrub and flame suddenly lashed up out of the trees. Smoke gushed, thick and oily.

Mazurov kept his head crushed into his optics as the turret traversed, looking for targets.

There was an enormous jolt that seemed to lift the tank. Mazurov's teeth smacked into the periscope and blood ran down over his chin. The tank had stopped. With a jerk, it began to move again.

'Khrenov, you stupid fuck,' he yelled. 'Look where you're fucking going!'

'Wasn't me,' Khrenov said stolidly, heaving on his control levers with his great horny hands. 'Some bastard shot us.'

Mazurov's guts seemed to turn to chilled water. The terrific bang had been an incoming PTURS anti-tank missile striking the ERA explosive reactive armour and being destroyed inches from his head before it could penetrate the turret.

He peered out again down the tunnel of his periscope's vision. There was a lot of smoke drifting about. Yellow Five was yelling something, but it might have been in Khan's native dialect for all Mazurov could make sense of it.

Shit, where did that come from?

A T-62 came across their path. The gun belched smoke and flame and Yellow Five went suddenly silent. The Chinese MBT was so close it filled his optics.

'Gunner, target left, fire.'

'*Too close.*'

The big turret was beginning to turn their way.

'*Fire, damn you!*'

The optics filled up with blast effects. As the smoke cleared the tank was halted, a big scar on its turret. The 100mm gun began to move again.

'Down one and a half metres,' Mazurov ordered. 'Fire!'

When the flame and smoke cleared the Chinese tank was on fire. The commander came out of the turret ablaze and Khan hosed him with the co-axial machine gun.

'Driver, advance.'

The scream of the 1,000-horsepower turbine engine, the crunching of the tracks, the burned chemical of the guns being fired had an effect that was almost intoxicating. The turret traversed, looking for targets – crew and tank becoming one.

Khan howled like a wolf.

'*Infantry.*'

The camouflaged figures poured out of the ground. To the far right Blue Three jerked hard right, a track climbing high in the air. Anti-tank, at close range. Smoke gushed and the crew came scrambling out. The Chinese soldiers spitted them like chickens.

'Gunner, fire!'

The sabot screamed across the valley floor. Although an anti-tank round, its arrival among the infantry would be most unwelcome.

'Re-load HE.'

The high explosive was what you needed for the ants. They tumbled in the air and fell to the ground, tiny pieces of debris.

'Load hard core.'

The world stopped. The impact slammed Mazurov forward in his hard, narrow seat, and his nose crashed into the periscope. Blood sprayed.

The tank was at an angle, the mighty turbine mute. Frantically he swivelled his periscope. Infantry at two hundred metres.

'Gunner, traverse left. Co-ax fire.'

'*I can't,*' Khan screamed. '*The fucking fucker's fucked.*'

Mazurov desperately unfastened the hatch-cover and pushed himself up out of the turret. The smoke-laden air was sweet after the poison-filled interior of the tank. Wasps zipped about his head, cracking whips. Directly in front of him was the 12.7mm DShK anti-aircraft gun. He seized its grips with both hands and laid fire on the infantry coming at him.

There was the scream of a shell behind him and he instinctively crouched down in the turret, the heavy machine gun still pounding on his hands. But the noise went on and on. The wave of soldiers vanished in a wall of flame and over his shoulder screeched the Su-25K *Grach* responsible. It pulled up in a climbing turn, pursued by a vast cauldron of flame and smoke from the target area. Across the line of battle came another and another – ugly, venomous creatures fizzing and spitting flame. The valley boiled with fire, and the concussions of the rockets beat on their heads.

Mazurov, Khan and Khrenov scrambled out of the

337

wreck. A huge chunk of reactive armour was missing from the turret, and the right-hand track was blown clean away, together with most of the road wheels. They jumped down off the deck and began walking back the way they had come.

Vast and ugly, hunchbacked, a wave of *Gorbach* attack helicopters came clattering and shrieking overhead. Missiles hissed from their rails and the trees sprouted a new, oily black vegetation. The Su-25s were co-ordinating their attacks with the Mi-24s, swooping down from the clear blue sky like flying fish diving into dirty water. It was the classical ground attack manoeuvre, the one the Soviets called the 'wheel of death'. The wind of their passage, the beating of the helicopter blades whipped the scrub and trees into a sea of fire and smoke.

The BMP *Yozh* mechanized infantry combat vehicles of the motor rifle regiment came squeaking past Mazurov and his crew as they trudged to the rear. The gun-ports were abristle with Kalashnikov muzzles like a *yozh* – hedgehog – as the infantry within prepared to mop up the Chinese infantry out in the open.

A group already disposed of lay all about their path. Bits of human being hung in the scrub; a shell had done this. A soldier thrashed on the ground. The wailing he made penetrated Mazurov's gun-blast deafness and the noise of the battle. He stood over him and saw that pieces of teeth were mixed up with shards of bone in the gore that had been his face. Muscles moved amid the ruin as he shrieked, both hands between his legs, crushing his testicles to try to blot out the unendurable agony.

Mazurov pulled his Makarov pistol from its holster and shot him in the back of the head.

The fighting was moving up the valley as the Russians maintained the relentless pace of their advance. Walking in the tracks they had made coming up, they came across the big T-62 they had destroyed. The fire was out. The commander hung over the side of the deck, some flies already feasting on the sticky blood that soaked him. Where do the bastards come from, wondered Mazurov. Impelled by some dreadful curiosity, he peered in through the hole their sabot had blasted in the armour plate. Something horrid was coating the interior. Seated inside were two things the size of monkeys, wizened and charred like burned sausages. A hideous smell of incinerated pork assaulted his nostrils and he backed away. He slipped in a pool of liquid fat that had formed under the vehicle and a swarm of multi-coloured flies buzzed angrily in the air.

The noise of the battle was becoming less. There was the occasional roar as the ammunition in the burning tanks behind them cooked off. They encountered the Major in his BRDM-2U command vehicle. Riding with him was the priest, his inlaid box of oils and incense at his side, icons and holy soil from Nevsky's victory over the Swedes at his feet. What they were doing was blessed, the priest had told them it was holy work.

'Morning, Mazurov,' the Major called cheerfully. 'Unhorse you, did they? You'll find a new one over there.'

Behind him the support section was driving a brand-new T-80 off a transporter. The logic of building a tank with a gun-barrel good for only 120 rounds had been proved once more: the tank wore out before the gun did. The driver got out of it and Khrenov got in, Mazurov grabbed a bottle of water and took a swig. Khan climbed down into the new turret, Mazurov seated himself half-way out. He was exhausted, completely shattered. The wind was blowing from the battle and on the air came a hideous stench that caught in his throat – diesel and exhaust fumes, the garlic and onions of the explosives and the choking smoke of burning machines, burning bodies, the horror of fresh blood and entrails straight from the slaughterhouse. The most rigorous exercise was nothing like this. And he was on the side that was winning. The few roubles a day of a lieutenant's pay came cheap for murder.

'Driver, advance,' he ordered. The exhausts as big as funnels behind him belched smoke and the tracks squeaked. The great nose of their gun tracked left and right, up and down, as though savouring the foulness that blew its way. As they passed the Major's command vehicle the priest stood up in his seat and blessed them with the sign of the cross.

SPAIN DORI, SHIBUYA, TOKYO

The eyes were large and luminous; their owner was from Tohoku, where the women were famed for their beauty. They stared coldly at Thrale.

'You're wanted for murder,' she said.

'And you are the daughter of trade minister Saito, and you have been working for the CIA,' Thrale said equably. 'None of us are perfect. You going to let me in?'

'You forgot to say that I was Saito's *illegitimate* daughter. My mother was his mistress.'

'Illegitimate daughter, then. And a revolutionary. That's what Chuck Imamura told me.'

'How busy Mr Imamura was. Before you shot him dead.'

'Ah, yes ... But I didn't ... shoot him.'

'Who did?'

'Two young women, very beautiful, very imbued with *samurai* ethics. Female *samurai*. Executioners.'

'Who want to kill you. On behalf of whom?'

'A man called Komura. Komura Tadaji. You know him?'

'Ah, yes. When Mr Komura says to Saito, Come, he cometh. And when he says Go, he goeth. You had better come in.'

Outside people were coming out of Shibuya station and climbing up Spain Street on their way to the Parco fashion store. Thrale slipped inside the tiny cottage and Saito Fusako shut the door.

A French *chaise-longue* was along one wall of the little room and she sat on it. Outside in the tiny square a

341

Spanish fountain was playing underneath a Hawaiian palm tree, while two girls were making a call from a strange version of an old-fashioned English red phonebox. On the wall behind, a painted Romeo climbed up a *trompe l'oeil* creeper to kiss a swelling-bosomed blonde at her bedroom window.

'I like it here,' she said, making a statement. 'It's how Tokyo ought to be.'

'I like it too,' said Thrale. 'Adamstown ain't nothing like this.'

'So why did Mr Imamura tell you who and where I was?'

'The two women I told you about brought him to me. They had automatic pistols in their hands. They were fast, fit young women, and we old men. They were informing me how I was to die. While they did so, Chuck was writing ideograms on his palm; he told me where to go, who you were ... and he said you were a revolutionary.'

Fusako grinned a sudden savage smile, white teeth framed by purple lips.

'Not only a revolutionary, but the grand-daughter of a revolutionary,' she said proudly.

'It's in the blood, obviously. And where is your grandmother today?'

'Dead,' said Fusako. 'They hanged her. People like Komura. They took her out of her cell and hanged her from the neck until she was dead.'

'I'm sorry. What had she done?'

'Wrote a poem. But that was at the end, after she got out of prison the first time. Look, you want a beer, a coffee?'

'I think I'll have both,' said Thrale. 'It's been quite a morning.'

Fusako ran water and boiled a kettle in the little spotless kitchen looking over the square.

'It's Komura's fault,' she said, spooning ground coffee into a filter. 'And the Komuras in the past. They tell us and everyone else that we're unique, separate from everybody else.'

342

She poured on the boiling water and the room was filled with the wonderful smell of coffee.

'It's a lot of macho hogwash, Thrale. And all designed to keep the rest of us down here while there's a few bastards like Komura running things up there. Nothing's changed, you know. Everything is still run by the same people as have run it for over two hundred years. The Americans had the chance to change things in the occupation and they muffed it.'

'We did,' said Thrale. 'I know. I was here, busy muffing.'

'My grandmother wanted to change things. In the 1920s.'

'She'd have been a socialist? Like Sakai and Yamakawa?'

'She didn't have much to do with organized socialism. She was an anarchist to begin with,' Fusako said proudly. 'She was involved with the Koreans who wanted to gain independence from Japan; she knew Pak Yeol. They arrested her because of that. She was charged with conspiracy to assassinate the Emperor after the Great Earthquake, when they were looking for someone to blame. She got life imprisonment, but they let her out in 1934. Her husband was released too and they had a little girl: my mother.'

She poured coffee into Mickey Mouse mugs and took two *ko-bin* cans of Asahi from the fridge.

'If she was out, how'd she get hanged?'

'She wrote a poem. When the Pacific War started the government produced a lot of propaganda, all that rubbish about the Hundred Million – that was a lie for a start, there were only about seventy million – the Hundred Million advancing like a ball of flame. My grandparents had started a small underground newspaper to keep alive the flame of ... of just an alternative viewpoint to all that, and my grandmother wrote a poem. You want to read it? She had a younger brother, you see. It's on the wall there.'

Thrale got up and looked at the framed brushwork.

343

Oh, my younger brother, I weep for you,
Please do not die.
Did our parents hand you a sword,
and tell you to kill?
Did they raise you for twenty-four years,
telling you to kill and be killed?
This war we did not want,
did not ask for, is it any concern of yours?

Thrale nodded to himself. 'Yeah, you sure didn't say that kind of thing in 1942.'

'You sure didn't. You did, they took you away and put a hemp rope round your neck.'

'It's a long way from being the unborn grand-daughter of an anarchist to the illegitimate daughter of a politician.'

'When my mother grew up she did not want to earn the money to eat, go to school by selling papers on the street at night, the way her mother did. But she – her mother, I – we are all beautiful; we have "Ainu eyes". My mother became a geisha. And on the way became the mistress of a rising member of the LDP: Saito, who is my father. Although we don't get on. Not too well. You see, I'm a computer engineer. He got me in with Komura Research and I was allowed to train in America and England. For the New Generation Computer Technology programme. You know what happens to young people who go abroad and live, don't you? *Kikoku shijo*. When we come back we're different, we know that things aren't the way we've been told all that time. And they don't like it; they tell us we're unclean, contaminated, make us go to special schools to be re-educated as Japanese again.'

'And did it work?'

'Hell, no. I just wanted to change things. We could start by blowing up Tokyo University. That's where all the bastards like Komura get the stamp of approval from the system.'

'And work for the CIA.'

'I wanted to stop it happening again. But I haven't. You

344

saw the news this morning? Komura has something to do with it all.'

'I know,' said Thrale. He chased his coffee with beer.

'So what are we going to do with you, Mr Thrale? If you sit here too long your *samurai* girls will come and chop you up.'

'Me? It's Thursday. I'm going out to Chiba to play golf.'

PALACE OF CONGRESSES, THE KREMLIN

The great hall could hold 6,000 people. When the politicians weren't using it for their greater gatherings the public could seat themselves for the altogether more pleasurable and interesting function of watching the opera and ballet companies of the Bolshoi Theatre. This time, however, the politicians had a show that could rival culture for the interest of the Western journalists crowding the front rows.

It was rare for Foreign Minister Yegotov to receive such attention. He was in the mould of one of his predecessors, Gromyko, and his pronouncements tended to be as interesting. This time, however, all waited upon his word. He stood on the podium where Krushchev had denounced Stalin, where Yanov had meant to ruin Mazurov.

'Yesterday the forces of the Soviet Union entered the People's Republic of China in strength and are advancing on three fronts towards the capital Beijing. In the very first wave of our defensive attack our airborne and naval forces destroyed the nuclear capability of the aggressor People's Republic totally. This war will be of short duration, and will cease once the abnormal bandit government of the adventurist reactionary Chiang Shikai has been replaced by one acceptable to the peace-loving people of the Soviet Union. We in the Soviet Union cherish our comrades in the People's Republic, it is our desire that with our aid they overthrow the clique of

346

traitors around Chiang Shikai and return to the just cause.'

Henry Barber had been the London *Daily Telegraph*'s correspondent in Moscow for nearly ten years; it was the first time he had realized that Yegotov had a sense of humour. Contained within the coded language of the Foreign Minister's statement were some jokes to give any half-decent communese linguist a good belly-laugh. He especially liked the use of the word 'cherish' with regard to the people of the PRC. The word in its Marxist terminology had first been used by the Chinese themselves, under chairman Mao, when he urged the Red Guards to 'cherish' the people. The underlying message of Yegotov's speech was clear: for some reason the USSR had decided to attack the PRC, and once that difficult decision had been made had done so with the skill, secrecy and overwhelming force that epitomized Soviet diplomacy of this kind. Once the greatly superior forces of the Red Army had won the war, Chiang Shikai would be hanged from the neck until dead, a puppet government installed and the PRC would become a milch-cow for the USSR.

Barber stood up, tall and thin in his immaculate blue pin-stripe, and raised his hand. He felt confident of gaining Yegotov's attention: the two men were both conservatives, they understood each other.

'Foreign Minister, you describe your attack upon the People's Republic as defensive and General Secretary Chiang Shikai as an adventurist, thus implying that he is the aggressor in this war. Yet as I understand it the People's Republic has made no attack upon the USSR, only the other way about, and the forces of the PRC are as we speak in a deeply defensive posture, falling back on all fronts.'

Yegotov actually smiled. Some women were handing out blue files to the journalists.

'I am an honourable man. If you will wait a moment, Mr Barber, you will see that you have interpreted me incorrectly, and that what I say is so.'

The female government official gave Barber his file. Looking quickly inside, he saw that the document was entitled PLAN 19.

'The original of these copies came into our hands some eighteen months ago. You are all welcome to take them away with you and use them as you see fit. Plan 19 is a Chinese blueprint for an attack upon the USSR in approximately three and a half years' time, using technologically highly-advanced weaponry acquired in an alliance of running dogs from Japan.'

Barber was disappointed. For a moment he had thought they were going to do better than this.

'If you will permit me to say, Foreign Minister, the Soviet Union has a reputation for the dissemination of disinformation.' And he held up his file.

Yegotov beamed.

'You are a dishonourable and justice-hating man, Mr Barber,' he said amiably. 'Permit me to call to this podium someone who may change your mind.'

He sounds just like Perry Mason, Barber thought incredulously. His surprise gave way to astonishment when he saw who was making his way up the steps, moving cautiously like an elderly tortoise, as befitted his age.

'May I present the Defence Minister of the People's Republic of China, Hua Bai,' he said maliciously. 'Mr Barber?'

Barber cleared his throat. 'Defence Minister, is this true? Is this Plan 19 that we have been given authentic?'

'It is.' The voice sounded like crackling parchment. Hua Bai was old; like Chiang Shikai he had survived the Long March and, even more remarkably, the years that had followed. The old man was tough, he had retained his interest in young women into his eighties; he showed no signs that he had been kidnapped from his own bed by commandos, drugged and flown to Moscow above the speed of sound strapped into the seat of a Soviet fighter-bomber.

'But why?'

348

'We are a Great Power becoming greater, Mr Barber. The Soviet Union is a Great Power becoming weaker. These people here could never have permitted us to become greater than they, not while they had the power to halt the rise in our fortunes, and postpone the decline in theirs. It has ever been so. You are classically educated, are you not? "What made war inevitable was the growth of Athenian power, and the fear this caused in Sparta."'

'Thucydides. *History of the Pelopponesian War*,' said Barber. 'But, Defence Minister, they *have* attacked you before you could attack them. And they are winning.'

'Yes,' said Hua Bai and, his task done, went back down the steps.

MIDORI-IRO NO KI
GOLF COURSE, CHIBA

Chiba was far enough out so that you didn't have to play on the office roof. They'd got eighteen holes, a putting-green and the clubhouse into about four acres of rolling countryside. Thrale had a putter and was on his second round of the green.

He reflected that he was probably the only one having fun. Everyone smiled, but nobody was there to enjoy themselves. The businessmen, bureaucrats and politicians who passed by out to the first hole or back to the nineteenth were at work, expanding their *jinmyaku*.

Thrale tapped his ball and it rolled smoothly across the fine turf, cut with a nap like baize. Two middle-aged men had come out of the clubhouse, full of Sapporo and *bonhomie*; they were saying goodbye. One turned to go back into the clubhouse and the other came down the path past the little green to get to the car-park. Thrale held up his putter and beamed amiably.

'Takashi,' he called. 'Ready for our round?'

Tsunoi Takashi of the Japanese Secret Service stared in horror at Thrale, turning a sickly grey, the colour of old suet.

'I have your putter here,' Thrale said helpfully, and he came over on to the green on the wobbly legs of an infant.

'I'm *alive*, you bastard!' Thrale hissed savagely. He gripped Tsunoi's arm like a mole-wrench, preventing him from snapping into the kind of bow that would connect his head to his knees.

350

'Save the ceremony, I want results. Hit the damn ball and putt.'

'I did not *know*, K.K.,' Tsunoi pleaded. The putter shook in his hand like an aspen and he missed his ball. 'I was told to give you the television watch-phone. I did not know anyone would try to kill you.'

'Who gave it to you?'

'Komura's men.'

He swung again and the ball hurtled across the green.

'I have to get out of here,' Thrale said quietly. 'Off Japan. I am being hunted. They shot Chuck Imamura; I am supposed to have done it. I want to get out, by air if possible. *You* are going to get me off.'

'Yes.' Tsunoi was almost sobbing. 'I will.'

'You owe me,' Thrale said brutally. 'Even when this is done, you will owe me more than you can ever repay.'

'I know,' Tsunoi whispered. 'Call me tomorrow at my house. In the morning. I will arrange something.'

As Thrale walked away he heard a hideous bubbling and gargling and, looking back, saw Tsunoi throwing up beer and *tempura* into the ornamental water hazard.

As he came out of Shibuya station someone light and fragrant attached herself to his arm.

'Hi,' beamed Fusako, and began steering him.

'Just take a left, Thrale, and keep walking,' she murmured through her bright smile. 'We can't go back to my house. I went out to do some shopping, to get food, and when I was coming back down Spain Dori I looked ahead to my house, as you do. I was just in time to see someone moving inside the window: a woman dressed in red. It seemed to me it might be one of your killers.'

'It is,' said Thrale. 'Let's keep going. Give me the shopping-bag to carry.'

They went past a charcoal grill restaurant no more than fifteen feet wide, holding apart two slab-sided office buildings, and smelled the rich scent of *kobe* beef on the barbecue.

351

'I have a man getting me out,' Thrale murmured. 'By tomorrow we can be safe. We need somewhere anonymous, somewhere we can hole up until then.'

Fusako's eyes glittered. 'This is good; this is how my grandmother must have been.'

They were passing what had been a *meikyoku kissa*, a classical-music coffee-shop – thirty feet of fabulously foreign frontage where stained-glass windows hid chandeliers, spiral staircases and five stories of architectural kitsch bathed in Mozart pumped from high-fidelity speakers eight feet tall.

Fusako stopped.

'They don't serve coffee there any more,' she said. 'They found a better way to make money.'

Neon flashed, zipped, lit up one letter at a time, pulsated with arrows. The hotels were open for business. The streets were quiet, dark, deserted. Everyone was inside. Thrale and Fusako went through the classical pillars and into the lobby. Above them were six floors of pilastred balconies, mansard roofs, spires, turrets and cornices. Between two large plaster statues of naked ladies and under an enormous coat of arms was a large plexiglass panel with coloured photographs of the rooms, from the plainest to the most exotic. The Nakano Emperor love hotel was anxious that its esteemed clients should not want.

'What's your taste?' Fusako murmured. She giggled quietly. 'Shall we do it in a copy of Queen Elizabeth's coronation coach? How about this: a circular bed ten feet in diameter that vibrates, undulates and ascends into a mirrored hall complete with artificial moonlight. That take your fancy? They all have a full porn channel, of course, but can we interest you in our selection of S-M gear? Very popular, I assure you.'

'One with a shower and bath,' Thrale said quietly. 'I have spent the day being frightened, on and off, and I am sure I smell nasty. I would like to wash it off and soak.'

352

'Shame on you. Bringing a girl here just to have a bath.'

Fusako went over to the booth alongside, similar to the box office at a theatre only without the glass. Only the clerk's hands were visible; in a love hotel you left your identity outside. A key was passed over and they went up in a lift like the gondola of Phineas Fogg's balloon.

'It's a swimming-pool,' said Thrale, looking at the foaming white surface.

'It's a bath,' said Fusako, lying on the vast circular bed as equipped with gadgetry as the cockpit of a fighter jet.

'So here goes.'

Thrale let go and whizzed around the walls of the bathroom. From the shower, the only way into the water was via the slide. He vanished in a wall of white foam. Fusako cheered.

HUAI RHO KHI, THAILAND, SEPTEMBER 1943

Those who were left took bets on what the first trains to roll through on their way to Burma would hold. The railroad was almost finished.

Some thought troops. 'Tojo's starting a new front. Going into Russia from the bottom.'

Some thought bananas, the other way. 'The Nips are just down from the trees anyway.'

Most thought whores.

Lt-Colonel Harris did not care. The gossamer thread of luck which kept him alive had not snapped. With the railroad done, they would be back to Singapore, the few that remained. Changi Jail beckoned like Raffles Hotel.

There was a sudden, ominous barking from the guard huts; small men streamed into view, moving fast out across the camp. The hinged bayonets of their Type 44 carbines were out from their resting-places under the barrels and glittered. They were the private soldier's substitute for the officers' *samurai* swords, and in the blade-obsessed Imperial army were cared for lovingly.

Harris was used to the Nips being excitable. He had survived almost six months of their behaviour while others had not. It was when the first bayonet went into a prisoner shuffling with beri-beri, tearing him open like a paper sack, that he realized that the magic thread which bound him to life had snapped.

Harris even recognized the man who killed him. He was a young guard called Okasaki. Sweat slicked his entire face and neck, running into his tunic; he was

354

screaming incomprehensibly, froth running over his chin. A small part of the Colonel's brain even diagnosed what he was suffering from – *musekinin*: a form of fit or possession not unlike the Malay *amok*, and with similar effect, its victim wishing to kill and kill.

Harris was a fighting soldier. He had a piece of bamboo in his hand and half-parried the first thrust. Lack of vitamins, minerals and simple calories had rendered him slow and weak, however, and the next speared him through chest from front to back. He fell, and the bayonet followed him.

Still screaming, the guards went through the camp, killing all living things.

In the huge bed in the Nakano Emperor Hotel, Saito Fusako was torn from sleep by a hideous bubbling shriek. She snapped on the light to see Thrale far over on the other side trying to bury his face in the mattress, his nails scrabbling against the satin sheets. He screamed, and she had never heard such terror.

She scrambled over to him in her *yukata* and wrapped herself around him. He sobbed, and she stroked his soaking hair.

'It's all right,' she said, over and over again. 'It's all right.'

'They found Tanaka's body,' said Thrale. 'After I stabbed him I hid it in a ditch and took his uniform and the great wad of money he had. I took his place. He was away, he had connections at home, he had leave, maybe a new posting. I was his height, even looked a bit like him. I figured no one would miss him, and as for me – well, you got a few people who escaped. They died, usually. So many were dying anyway, the Nips wouldn't take much notice.

'I got away. I could speak Japanese, looked like one. Made it to Rangoon and got out on a ship. Made it to

355

India. I was a hero. Back in the camp they finished the railway, just about. And a dog dragged something out of a ditch at Thanbyuzayat. Tanaka was still just about recognizable. They got the news to Huai Ro Khi. The guards killed everyone.'

Thrale sat on the edge of the huge bed, his arms wrapped around him, and shivered with ague.

'Now they come back to see me, the battalions of the dead. All the men I killed.'

YANTONGSHAN, JILIN HADA LING

Corporal Artuzov grumbled a bit, but the others all said they had had to put up with his stories of going fishing, and if he claimed he knew so much about the water then he could be the one to paddle out into the lake and do it. So he put on the nasty clammy OP-1 suit, the 'slime suit' the general had sent along with the other supplies, and got in the little rubber boat, which the general too had sent; and using his oars without a splash – for an expert boatman he was, and many a fine perch eaten to prove it – went out in the long lake. The moon glittered on the water, the dam across the lake mouth glowed white in its light.

Breathing through his respirator and peering through the goggles of his mask, he opened the big 25-litre cans and emptied them into the reservoir, allowing them to sink to the bottom once their contents were in the water. Then he paddled quietly back to shore, where Sergeant Ivashutin decontaminated him and he was able to climb out of the horrid thing and put his fighting clothes on again.

The 35th and 51st groups were in the beautiful woods that surrounded the lake. They kept well away from Artuzov's dinghy, his suit and now the very water itself. Starting tomorrow, the people of Changchun, her soldiers and her airmen would be spending the next week crouched in or close to a latrine, and the men of the 35th and 51st had no wish to join them.

Otari divided or combined the groups in his command according to the tasks set them. For a major assault all participated. For raids, individual groups. The 35th and

357

51st had combined in an attack on the radar of the 29th Fighter Wing's defences, just in time for an Su-24 strike to come in and obliterate the 29th while its eyes were poked out. They had withdrawn into the Jilin Hada Ling, had poisoned the water supplies of the entire area in passing and were now forming up to move out.

The general was always generous to his boys when it came to supplies, and the soldiers were hung like Christmas trees with grenades, 50-round non-disintegrating ammunition belts for the PK general-purpose machine gun, mortar bombs, banana clips for their AKSUs, mines, RPG rockets and plastic, mortar tubes and base-plates.

'All right, boys,' said Otari. 'Jump about a bit.'

Everyone jumped up and down to make sure nothing made a noise, then they moved out.

Even the *Spetsnaz* could not march sixty kilometres in the four hours left to them, so they set up a road-block and manned it with Deriabin and Goglidze in PRC uniforms, who were Mongols from Ulan Ude and could pass for Chinese. They even spoke Mandarin with a Yue accent, as became a minority group from the sticks.

They netted a truck about half an hour after setting it up, despatched the driver and dumped the mailbags that filled the cab. The rest of the 35th and 51st emerged from the wood and began dumping the sacks and bales out of the back, so that they could get in. When they were finished they all stood and looked.

'Well,' said Ivashutin. 'What are we going to do with this?'

Squeezed into one corner, trembling with fear, was a small Chinese woman. She was dressed in the dark blue trousers, olive tunic and pink blouse of the Army Air Force. She was probably twenty, but looked about twelve.

'Better kill her,' said Orlov, the cossack. 'We need to get on.'

They all stood there, looking uncomfortable. It was not easy, killing a woman. It could be done, yes, in the fire of combat. When they put plastic on a bridge and sent the train two hundred feet into the ravine, you knew there were probably women aboard. But actually doing it to the little thing was not easy, no. It was like killing a pet animal. Not nice. No.

Corporal Artusov, the boatman, was moved by an unfamiliar emotion – pity. The young woman reminded him of his little sister at home, who he adored.

'Let's take her with us,' he grunted. 'She will do no harm.'

There was a general grumble of agreement.

'Just get in the fucking truck,' Otari snarled. 'This is not an outing for old women.'

They all piled in and pulled the covers tight about them. Deriabin and Goglidze occupying the cab.

'Here,' said Artusov to the girl, 'you sit next to me.'

She seemed to sense an ally and squeezed up close to the huge bulk of the soldier and his ordnance.

By dawn they were in position among the larches, silver birch and pine on the slopes of the valley, looking down at the straight road beneath.

It was regrettable, but a fact of life, that the aircraft of the Soviet air forces could not be in all places at once. When the Su-24s turned up at Kangbao Army Air Force Base in the afternoon of the first day of the war their cluster-bombs tore hell out of the hangars, storerooms, dormitories and latrines, even blew 155 craters per bomb in the very runways and taxiways, but did not damage the Shenjang J8 fighters of the 48th Fighter Squadron because their astute commander, Wing Commander Quan, had anticipated their coming and taken his valuable aircraft elsewhere.

He had brought them here ... to this valley.

The quiet of the dawn was broken by the rising whine of turbine engines. From well-concealed hides, the aircraft began to roll along improvised taxiways to the beginning of the runway. The delta-winged J8s were the best fighters the Chinese had. Capable of Mach 2, they had modern American-supplied avionics and were on a par with a MiG-23. It was one of the few Chinese aircraft capable of taking on its Soviet equivalent. The hardpoints under the wings of the aircraft moving out were hung with missiles.

Otari was close, no more than 350 metres away from the threshold of the road-cum-runway. He had festooned himself and his weapon with sacking and foliage to break up the characteristic human shape, and had spent almost an hour crawling carefully into position. He was looking down into the valley, the bipod of the Barrett firmly in the ground. Through the Zeiss he could see the scratches on the lead pilot's helmet, see his eyes moving as he manoeuvred his fighter into position. He could read his name: Wing Commander Quan was leading his squadron.

The Barrett was a huge weapon; the precision-built match-grade barrel was almost as long as some armies' rifles. You had to be a giant to carry it and have the strength of a lion to fire it. If you did so without fitting the recoil pad, it broke your collar-bone. It was a monster.

Quan lined up. His hand moved fully forward and on the air came the shriek of the twin Chengdu turbojets on afterburner. Otari led him a few inches and then squeezed the silky trigger twice. It was like being punched by a heavyweight boxer. The first armour-piercing round smashed a hole in the canopy; the ball that followed it blew off what was left of Quan's head.

The J8 continued to accelerate under full power, veering off to the left. It left the runway for the grass, lurching and bouncing, under no control. It struck the column of taxiing fighters half-way down its length and the fuel tanks exploded into a boiling sea of flame. One sharp-witted pilot ejected as the tumbling fireball came to envelop him, and shot high up into the valley.

Below him, the mortar rounds were beginning to explode and the RPGs setting the fighters alight. Otari killed the pilot of the lead aircraft and then began to work methodically, firing armour-piercing incendiary rounds into the engines and fuel tanks of the aircraft below. Missiles began cooking off from the burning fighters, weaving crazy patterns of white smoke as they raced about the valley unguided.

There was an enormous roar as the ammunition dump went up from a direct hit. A giant tongue of flame leaped up into the air; it engulfed the pilot coming down on his parachute, turning it to so much blazing nylon, and he vanished.

The pyre of smoke would be visible a hundred miles away. The soldiers hurried to get back to the truck, to get away from the scene as quickly as they could. Daylight was a bad time for vampires and *Spetsnaz* alike.

The young Air Force girl was still in the truck, tied up as they had left her.

They drove as long as they dared, then when they heard the thudding of the helicopter blades shoved the truck as deep in the undergrowth as they could and prepared to move out, getting back into the Jilin Hada Ling where they were safe. They went fast, each man treading in the footmarks of the one in front. Artusov was the last to get out. The girl was still in the truck.

'Kill her,' Orlov ordered over his shoulder.

'All right.' He untied the girl and pulled her out of the truck. The other men in the unit had vanished among the trees and scrub. He supposed that the knife would be best. Her neck was slim and delicate; he could snap it with just one of his enormous hands. She looked steadily at him, her slight back very straight.

'Go on,' he said wearily. 'Go on. Shoo! Go away.'

They were miles from anywhere. It would take her all day to get out of this, by which time they would be long gone and hidden up.

He flapped a tired hand. The problem with all the killing was that in the end you felt like a murderer. Sergey Artusov did not want to wake up from nightmares where he throttled, sliced to pieces or crushed the life from, a pretty little girl who reminded him of his sister.

'Go away,' he said, turning to follow his comrades. 'Run along.'

361

He pushed into the bush. There was a thud on the ground beside him and when he looked he saw one of his own grenades. Cursing his own sloppiness, he reached down to pick it up and attach it to his webbing again.

Sergey Artusov was very tired. There was something wrong with the grenade. He glanced over his shoulder. The young Chinese girl was lying flat on the ground with her hands over her head.

It had no pin. That was it.

After the flat bang of the explosion the girl scrambled to her feet and ran. She hid in some bushes and did not come out for a long time, until she was sure the soldiers were gone.

FAR EAST MILITARY DISTRICT
HEADQUARTERS, VLADIVOSTOK

Being an intelligence officer of the Second Department of the Staff was a dangerous job. If you were not careful, and if you did not handle it correctly, you could drown. Drown in the very reason for your being, which was information. The Second Department existed to provide the First Department – which handled battle planning and management – with what it needed to do so, which was accurate up-to-date information about the enemy.

This the Second Department had. It received both TECHINT and HUMINT, that was technical intelligence and human intelligence. The latter concerned the kind of spying that went back to Sun Tsu and beyond, the five types of agents – native, inside, doubled, expendable and living – who were the treasure of a sovereign. These traditional agents, who transmitted information by means as varied as Chang Yu's letter hidden in a ball of wax in a man's guts to microfilm hidden in a Mata-Hari's makeup, had been joined by the product of the late twentieth century, which was information gathered by machine: TECHINT.

Like the Americans with whom they had competed, the Soviets had a formidable intelligence-gathering capability. *Cosmos* and *Soyuz* satellites from Plesetsk provided overhead surveillance of any place on earth from bucket-dropped film or digital imagery. U-2 look-alike *Ram-M* reconnaissance aircraft could fly fifteen miles over people who could neither see nor hear them. Tu-142s – intelligence-gathering versions of Tupolev's old four-engined strategic bomber – prowled the borders of Europe, America, China and Japan soaking up communications signals, radar emissions and telemetry. In the oceans of the world Soviet trawlers, abristle with antennae from stem to stern, fished for more than *ryby*.

TECHINT itself was split up into many other INTs, from signals intelligence or SIGINT – which was itself divided into communications, electronic and telemetry intelligences, all with appropriate acronyms – to photographic intelligence or PHOTINT, and radar intelligence.

Every minute of every hour of every day, data rained into this immense gathering system. It was streamed and channelled and funnelled until it arrived as a never-ending torrent full in the face of whoever was responsible for it, gushing in through his senses and threatening to drown him.

The victims of the system responded by storing most of it that was routine and banking it without analysis, reserving their time and energies for things judged to be important and specially requested, or 'tasked'. In the case of the Second Department of the Staff within Ogarkov's headquarters, this meant handling the requests of the First Department, which was at that time up to its eyeballs in planning and managing the war. And the First Department was able to handle far more than it had in the past because it had the computing power to do so. It had Red Banner, or Arby.

Unlike the First Department, the Second did not care for Arby to whom they gave other, more derogatory names. Russian patterns of communication being based on personal contact within a close-knit cellular group, they regarded the increased power of the First Department with dislike. The First, of course, had adopted Arby as one of their own, which was why they had given him a human nickname, and Arby was more than willing to go along.

The Second felt that their role had degenerated into that of mere servitude. When they had time, they felt resentful.

There were ten men in the Department, in three groups under an analyst; Litovsev, a forecaster; Kuchumov and Pokryshin who handled troop movements. The three men were all Lieutenant-Colonels, with Litovsev the analyst in charge.

At his desk, Pokryshin hissed softly between his teeth. He went over what he had read again, then went quietly across to Litovsev.

'Look,' he said. Litovsev went carefully through the signals intelligence.

'Zhao Teh? He's on a commune in disgrace. Broken.'

'He's their best general. If he had still been in power the *Spetsnaz* would have taken him out the first night, with all the others. Chiang Shikai has put him back into command. He's raising the new big army around Beijing. *But look, we have an appointment for him.* Here, we know where he will be in two day's time.'

'Does the Red Baron next door want this?'

'The Yellow Bastard? No! It's not tasked.'

Litovsev grinned, for the first time in days.

'Then let's get a little credit for the Second. Enough of that number-chewing monstrosity next door. Give this direct to Kulikov in the Fifth Army. He has some funnies out there under his command. Some *Spetsnaz*. He'll know what to do with them ... and give us some credit for it.'

365

MISAKI, HONSHU

They were north of Sakata, and the folds of the land were green; between the valleys and ridges the paddies were watered by the fast-flowing rivers coming down from the steep mountains. The Toyota went over a wooden bridge, the tyres thudding rhythmically on the boards, and Thrale saw some men fishing, standing waist-deep in the water.

'It's not like the USA here,' said Tsunoi Takashi in the right-hand seat. 'We don't have airfields and flying schools in every other town. But there is a place here ... it's a kind of museum.'

They climbed up from the coast past some small farms and groves of cherry trees. There were pines, thin and spiky, and they left the tarmac on to a dirt road.

'There's quite a collection; when people want to make movies about the war they come here.'

They turned the corner and emerged into a flat valley bottom. Maples and pines climbed the sides and the floor was smooth, cut grass. Wood and corrugated metal hangars stood along one side and a windsock hung half-full, oscillating gently in the wind.

'It's an airstrip,' said Fusako. 'Look at the old aircraft.'

Tsunoi stopped outside a hangar and they got out.

Thrale stood looking at a large twin-engined aircraft in the hangar. It was military, its mottled camouflage paint said that.

'What is it?' Fusako enquired.

'We called it Betty. Its manufacturer called it the Mutsubishi Type 97. It caught fire rather easily, so after a while both us and the poor bastards who flew it called it the Flying Lighter. It's a bomber.'

'How do you know?'

'I shot down six of them.'

'Oh, I see. You were a pilot. In the Pacific War.' Fusako looked around at the airfield. 'So that's what we're doing here.'

'South Korea's just the other side of the Sea of Japan, due west,' said Tsunoi. 'You can land at Seoul.'

'In that? It had a crew of seven as I recall.'

'No, no. They have some other aircraft too, some American ones. Over here.'

'You say they ... I don't see anyone.'

'Only a handful of people work here,' said Tsunoi as they walked across the grass. 'I have ... arranged for you to have the loan of an aircraft, but it is best that no one sees you. So they have the day off.'

'They got a Zero there, I see.'

'Yes, many aircraft, fighters and bombers.'

'You shoot down those as well?' enquired Fusako.

'Some. I shot down Komura Tadaji in one, for a start. Stopped him from being a *kamikaze.*'

'A pity you didn't do a better job,' Fusako said acidly, 'or let him get on with it.'

'I did my best ... that Zero fly?'

'Yes, it has been restored to flying condition.'

Inside a hangar was an aircraft of different manufacture, smaller than the big bomber but similarly tailwheeled, painted white.

'Beech,' Thrale said immediately. 'Beech 19.'

'Can you fly it?'

'Guess I'll have to. I need to make a phone call, Takashi.'

'A phone call?'

'Yeah. Where is it?'

'In the office ... over there.'

Thrale went in where a little tin office was tacked on to the side of the hangar. It had the old familiar smells of oils and hydraulic fluid, rubber and gasoline. He stood staring at the elegant, trim Japanese fighter aircraft,

367

sitting nose-high, its three-bladed propeller in fine pitch. It was completely restored, from its markings of the Tainan *Kokutai* with the squadron's host of aces to the sun emblems on wings and fuselage.

Thrale turned and went into the office. By the door was a small certificate of liability insurance, and he stood looking at it for a while before picking up the telephone. There was a dialling code-book and he checked his group before pressing the buttons. The call took almost a minute to connect, then someone picked up the receiver at the other end.

'Savinkov,' said a voice like gravel.

'Sergey, this is K.K. Thrale.'

There was a long pause, then the voice spoke again.

'What do you want, K.K.?'

'A favour.'

Fusako was sitting outside the hangar looking at the white Beech 19 when he returned.

'Okay,' he said. 'I'm waiting for a guy to call me back. Where's Takashi?'

'He went for a walk round. Have you flown this aircraft?'

'No, never. But it's not unlike some of the aircraft I flew in the war. Same technology.'

'You have flown many aircraft?'

'No, not many. Stearman in basic training. P-40 Warhawk when the 49th were based in Darwin. P-38 Lightning before and after I was shot down. I flew an L-5 occasionally – that was a little liaison aircraft.'

'And now?'

Thrale smiled a humourless smile.

'I haven't flown an aircraft since 1945,' he said.

CHANGCHUN, HELONGJIANG

Liu Chen felt that his head was filled with many pieces of connected whizzing machinery – cogs, springs and ratchets. He was chairman of the Liaison Committee which communicated with the CCP Military Commission, Central Military Commission, Ministry of National Defence of the State Council and CPLA Headquarters. He had been at work since 5 a.m. putting the pieces back together with the men from Beijing. The losses following the Soviet assault were astonishing. Not one but three vast armies – armies *within* armies – had crashed over the border.

They were pulling back to Beijing. Let the Russians come. China was familiar with this kind of warfare; she had enticed the invaders forward before, only to envelop them at predetermined points within a mass of her fighters. Fighters she had in abundance, population she had. The Japanese had thought to defeat the Chinese in a month. They won victory after victory; it made no difference.

Enemy advances, we retreat.

Enemy stops, we harass.

Enemy withdraws, we attack.

The Chinese understood endless war; within the vastness of their land all lightning wars ran into the sand. Zhao Teh was putting together the new army to the south.

It was midnight, and Liu Chen drove home to pack what he needed before taking up his post in Beijing the next day. He parked his little Toyota outside his house – a small bungalow in the Changchun suburbs, quiet and respectable. In the dim light he stood looking at his

369

home, where his wife and children slept, unaware of the upheaval of the morning. Liu Chen wondered when he would see home again. He had survived the Great Leap Forward and the Cultural Revolution to get this far; now his little house would be the sty for rude Soviet soldiery, his lovingly-tended garden dug into pits for their ordure.

On the dark path, he sniffed. There was a bad smell on the air. Something feral, animal almost.

It engulfed him. Out of the dark monsters seized him; as he opened his mouth to scream a huge, evil-tasting cloth was stuffed into it.

He was in his own car. As they drove him away he caught a last despairing glimpse of his house where his wife and children were sleeping, waiting for him, then a massive hand shoved his head down into the vinyl upholstery.

They stank. Breathing stertorously through his nose, they smelled worse than anything. They smelled of decomposing blood and ordure and the pumping sweat of desperate physical exercise, and fear, all days old. The stench filled his little car like gas.

They were in a field outside town. He knew it. Over there Yi Ming grew his cotton; behind him, gleaming in the moonlight, was the river-bank where he had fished as a child. He was suspended in the air, he sat in a chair that swung gently. Why? What was happening?

Twisting about, he could see that he was suspended by a long vertical cable from a tall horizontal one some thirty feet above him, held up by poles. And something was coming. The beasts about him had lights; they glowed red and green in the dark; there was something hissing in the air, vast, monstrous. It came overhead and suddenly he was jerked backwards with a force he never knew existed – twisting, turning, blasted by the force of the gale.

And then it stopped. Hands had hold of him, they unstrapped him from his seat, held him as they pulled him forward. A great door closed behind him and the cold gale ceased. He was inside an aircraft.

He could hear the noise of the engines, but inside it

was quite quiet. They had two chairs in the metal hold; they strapped him to one, and a man came forward to sit in the other. He was young, intelligent and Russian. He spoke to Liu Chen in fluent Mandarin.

'Hallo,' he said. 'I'm Lev Shimanansky.'

Liu Chen's attention was taken by the man just behind the Russian, another terrifying Slav. He seemed to be preparing a tray, the kind Chen remembered as a boy when going to the dentist with his treadle-powered drill. Metal clinked. Things scraped.

Shimanansky sat himself down in the other chair.

'Now, let me ask you a few questions,' he said.

In the field where Li Ming grew his cotton the men of the 28th, 33rd, 35th, 40th, 51st, 73rd and 79th groups of the 277th battalion of *Spetsnaz* took down the poles and guy-wires that had suspended Liu Chen in the air, and hid them in the little river where he had fished as a child. Then some got into his Toyota and the rest into the Mazda, and they drove away.

They stuffed the two cars deep into the brush near Yitong and the eight men went back into the Jilin Hada Ling. They set up the beacon and on cue the parachute came down. Ammunition, explosives and food.

'Hey,' said the Eel. 'Look, they sent some vodka.'

'There *must* be only a few of us left,' the Cossack said cynically. 'They're looking after us.'

The enemy deployed helicopters in the day, together with dogs. There were ambushes, and traps set up by likely targets. They had accounted for another seventy-five men of the eighty-four who had left Chang An. The eight left had been ordered to a different task – the kidnap of the chairman of the Liaison Committee, Liu Chen, who at that very moment was at four hundred feet on his way to Vladivostok, spilling his guts in his anxiety to tell all he knew.

Drozdhov left the unpacking of the crate to Marchuk and Sergeant Ivashutin. He was the sole radio operator left in the unit. His P351-M radio set was burst-capable, and could transmit or receive long messages in less than a second. Earlier in the mission the group had used their directional receivers and transmitting aerials to identify an important communications centre and command post set up by the Shenyang command, and had used the radio to announce their discovery. The commanding officer of the 5th Army had been pleased; he congratulated them. The next time they listened in, the communications centre was silent.

That night Drozdhov was simply waiting to be told what to do. He looked at his chronometer and pressed a knob on the machine. It switched on and tuned itself automatically; it made a noise like bacon frying. A few little lights on the side of the machine went out and a length of photographic film emerged. Drozdhov swiftly wrote down the cipher groups and gave them to Otari, who was sitting with his back to a pine in the little clearing they had taken as temporary base. Troopers Stolyar, Polishchuk and Voronich were posed as lookouts.

Otari took his code-book from his breast pocket and began to decipher the message.

'What have they sent, Tarzan?' he murmured to Ivashutin, unpacking the supply crate.

It was the food they were interested in. They all knew the commander of the 5th Army would provide them with as much lethal ordnance as they could physically haul, but what about the *important* stuff?

'*Zakuski*,' the sergeant said wonderingly. 'Salted herring, salami, tongue, pickled cucumber, brown bread, red beet ...'

'Hell,' Orlov said sharply. 'You know what the Brits say: "The condemned man ate a hearty meal." Rhino, what is in the message? What is the mission?'

'Crack that vodka bottle and let's have a swig.'

He finished deciphering the message and took a pull. It was wonderful, the fire blotted out the weariness of his body that went through to the bone. He had lost twenty pounds in five days.

'Marchuk, take the bottle and give the boys a pull.'

The soldier took the Stolichnaya and slipped into the forest, as quiet as a mouse over the pine needles.

'They want us to assassinate the Field Marshal,' Otari said softly.

'Field Marshal? Who?'

'Zhao Teh.'

'Zhao Teh's shovelling shit on some communal farm,' said Orlov.

'Not any more; he's putting together an army.'

'Yeah,' Orlov said thoughtfully. 'That's what I'd do if I was Chiang Shikai. Who cares about ideological rectitude when it's your ass or theirs? Beria took my grandfather out of Kolyma in 1940. He was up there as a *katorzhniki*; the NKVD were killing him by the day when it was fifty below. The fascist Hitlerites came over the border and within three weeks they had him back in a general's uniform and gave him an armoured corps. So where is Zhao Teh?'

'The day after tomorrow he will be at the Fuxin Military Headquarters Command Centre.'

'Where we're to kill him?'

'That's it.'

'And after we have strolled past the guards and through the wire, nodded at the machine-gunners and asked the central security to let us in, shot the Field Marshal and waddled back out, what would they have us do next?'

'That's the wonderful part.' Otari gurgled happily, waving the piece of paper with the code groups on. 'They say we are free to make our own way back to our lines for being such good boys!'

The two men laughed. They laughed so much they had to muffle the noise in their sleeves and wipe the tears from their eyes.

When they were through they looked at each other and spoke as one: '*You shouldn't have joined if you can't take a fucking joke!*'

373

MISAKI AIRFIELD

Thrale's call came through that evening. He had spent some time reading the flight manual of the Beech, and sitting in the left-hand seat had familiarized himself with the cockpit. Fusako had driven into town and returned with the ingredients for *nabe*.

'Even revolutionaries must eat,' she said cheerfully. She set to, chopping and dicing the vegetables with a heavy oblong knife, tossing them into a heavy iron casserole she had bought. Thrale understood the therapeutic effect of being busy while waiting. Takashi had become very withdrawn and sat on a rock on the far side of the airfield, looking at a small stream that chuckled on its way to the sea.

'He is like a carp that struggles to be free but when caught lies still on the chopping-block,' Fusako said.

He did not eat with them, but when it became dark lay on a futon in the hangar. After his phone call Thrale went through there to find him.

'Takashi,' he said, 'I need a gun.'

'Yes. What kind of gun?'

'An automatic rifle of some kind. An M-16 would do. And ammunition.'

The faintest hint of his old self appeared on Tsunoi's face. 'This is Japan, not Texas. You know what happens to people who have such things here?' He pulled himself upright. 'But you are talking to the right man. I can find such a thing.'

He got up and went out to the Toyota. They saw the lights flickering as the car went down through the thin, spiky pines.

'Why a gun?' asked Fusako. Her large, luminous eyes were anxious.

'Tell me, how good are you?' asked Thrale, sidestepping the question. 'You worked for Komura on *Coral Spear*. Could you work on the guidance system of a rocket?'

'What sort of rocket?'

'An ICBM, say. A ballistic missile?'

'That's like asking a Grand Prix pilot if he could drive his son's pedal car. *Coral Spear* is cutting-edge of technology. *Coral Spear* can *think*. The guidance system of a rocket is clever and precise, but it's only a collection of microprocessors. I could work on one.'

'Then I have to know if you'll come with me in the morning. Or do you wish to stay here?'

'If I stay here, your mad *samurai* girls will find me. I don't think I would enjoy that. I'll come.'

'Thank you. And the gun? Don't all revolutionaries need guns? One of the most famous of them said that that was where power grew. Now, while Takashi is getting that we will look for some more mundane items. If you will find a set of small steps, I will search for some jerry-cans. This is an airfield, they'll have them somewhere.'

Thrale found a collection of brand-new oblong US military issue five-gallon cans in a storeroom. He took them out one by one and filled them with AvGas from the pump, then carried them to the Beech in the hangar. Fusako came up with a set of small alloy steps, shiny and silver.

'Perfect. And now a big funnel – to put into the wing-tanks while we stand on the steps and pour in the fuel from the cans.'

'It's full of fuel. You filled it.'

'Later. When we have used what's in the aircraft.'

She raised her eyebrows into arches. 'We have to refuel to get to Korea?'

'No, not to Korea.'

'Not to Korea. No. Well, then, I'd better get a funnel.'

375

She shook her head at him and he smiled. He made a quick calculation on the back of an envelope to get the centre of gravity within limits and then began carrying the cans of fuel into the Beech through the side door. The aircraft had nine passenger seats and he strapped the cans firmly into them, so that they did not move.

Fusako returned with a large square metal funnel.

'Here,' she said. 'Your funnel. Because not Korea.'

Tsunoi Takashi stood in the dawn light as Thrale manoeuvred the Beech to the end of the grass runway, the dew running off the wings and fuselage, the tyres painting the grass with their passage. He turned the aircraft to face down the valley. The radial engines throbbed harmoniously, rising and falling, the air condensing into whirling fog behind each propeller in turn as Thrale altered the pitch, putting hot oil through the governors.

The rudders, elevators and ailerons flapped and wriggled, doing callisthenics as he wrung the controls, checking for full smooth movement. The propellers ticked rhythmically, idling slowly enough to see them turning. Then the note of the exhausts rose as Thrale pressed for full power, and the propellers became clear, spinning arcs. The Beech began to roll over the grass, a wake of dew rising in the air behind it. The tail rose and the aircraft lifted clear of the ground. The spinning wheels braked and tucked themselves up under the wings.

Takashi watched it climb away in the milky blue sky like a white bird.

From the buildings behind him two figures emerged. Jet-black hair framed perfect oval faces. One wore mostly red, the other mostly white. They stood on either side of him.

'Come,' said Kiyoko gently. 'We will take you home.'

*

376

The hall of the temple was lit by tall candles. Before the altar was a red rug on which Tsunoi Takashi sat in his robes of ceremony. He allowed them to fall down from his shoulders – green and yellow and black, white and blue and purple. He tucked the sleeves carefully under his knees as he sat cross-legged, in order that he might only fall forward. From behind the altar came the two women dressed in red and white *jimbaori* war surcoats. Kiyoko had a single long *katana* fighting sword thrust through the white *obi* around her waist; she knelt down behind his left-hand side.

In front of Takashi was thick, fine paper, ink and a brush. He reached out and with a steady hand covered the page with flowing ideograms. When he had finished, he placed the brush back by the inkwell.

Masako came forward, bearing a tray. The short *waki-zashi* which was the partner to the fighting sword lay on it, wrapped in white paper.

'We are your *kaishaku*,' she said, bowing low.

Takashi raised his eyes for the first time.

'*Hanzai no kage ni onna ari*,' he said bitterly. 'There is a woman in the shadow of every crime.'

He took the short sword from the tray and unwrapped it, holding it up to his head. Then he placed it before him.

'To serve my lord I have had to betray a man to whom I owed honour,' he said in a clear voice. 'He will now be dead, as I was commanded to make sure. Therefore I shall follow him.'

He reached forward deliberately and took the short sword from its scabbard. He seemed to collect his thoughts for a few moments and then with a smooth action stabbed himself deep below the waist on the left side, drawing the blade across to the right. As blood gushed into the folds of his robes he gave the blade a half twist and completed the cut upwards, leaning forward and stretching out his head. For the first time an expression of pain passed across his face and Kiyoko, who had been watching him closely, sprang to her feet.

377

The blade was poised high in the air for one second. It glittered and hissed like silk as it swung.

Kiyoko wiped the blade clean and bowed reverently. Masako took the *wakizachi* from Takashi's hand. The swords were over four hundred years old; they were versed in death. She bowed, and from the end of the temple hall Komura Tadaji rose and came forward.

The old man was dressed in robes of ceremony. He paused by the body of the dead man and looked down to read what he had written.

As everything in the world is but a sham,
Death is the only sincerity.

He bowed and went slowly from the hall, leaving the executioners to attend to the corpse of Tsunoi Takashi.

FUXIN, LIAONING

'Now, Yang, old cousin,' Otari said pleasantly, 'as you can see we're large guys, so what have you got that we could get into?'

The little Chinese, small and beginning to go bald, was anxious to please.

'The only things I deliver that you could get into are the drums for cooking oil and the big canisters of orange juice.'

'Show me.'

They went out of the room and into the warehouse. The two sets of drums were roughly the same size; they looked maybe 200 litres, thought Otari, enough to hold a soldier and his fighting equipment. He rejected the oil, since it would be too difficult to clean out and any traces on their hands or weapons would hinder their effectiveness.

'We'll take the orange juice. They sure must like the stuff.'

'It is very popular,' Yang assured him.

There might be war, the Russians might be thundering down from the north, but people had to eat and places like the Military Command Centre had to be re-supplied.

Voronich was their mechanic. His big hands could mend the delicate insides of a radio set or fashion a bridge across a ravine from rope and branches with equal ease. Otari called him through.

'Tarzan, we'll need seven of these. Empty, clean, with air holes. Have whoever you need to help you.'

'Very good. Eel, Mozart, Rings, come.'

Otari went back into the office, where a very young

379

and pretty woman was nursing a small baby. She ignored the huge and smelly soldiers about her. Yang flicked one anxious and deeply loving glance at his tiny family before devoting his attentions to the one person who could save or take their lives. Yang'll be all right, Otari thought coldly. He'd die for those two.

'Do you usually do this on your own?'

'No, usually I have Ho Feng to help me, but he is ill.'

'Good.'

Otari turned to Marchuk and Stolyar, who like Orlov were lounging against the wall, simply saving their energies.

'The Cossack knows already,' he said, pointing to Orlov. 'The message came through last night. None of our missions in wartime can be considered exactly safe. The fact that there are just eight of us here says that. This one gives us less of a chance of picking up our pensions than most. Even if we can get back out, we'll have trouble getting away. Or we would have. They're sending a plane for us.'

Eyes gleamed. They were not Japanese, they could not do something for which death was the *certain* outcome. The chance of survival at the end was very, very precious.

Otari got out his map. 'Here, look, all of you. It's no more than a mile and a half from the Headquarters. This little road leads down into the wood here, and it opens out enough to get a light aircraft in and out again. That's where it'll meet us. Sixteen hundred. Yang, you may have to drive us there – you come here and look.'

The Chinese stared anxiously at the map and nodded quickly. He was a local boy.

'Your wife, show her too.'

Yang took the map. His wife glanced briefly at it and nodded.

'Has she got it?'

'She is from these parts, like me. We know the land.'

Otari went through to the warehouse where drums and boxes stood packed. He told the men there the news

380

and saw the same gleam of hope in their eyes. Ivashutin had finished the first drum. He showed Otari the concealed airholes and the lid.

'See,' he said. 'Once each man is inside he twists it like this, with the handle, and from outside it looks like a drum. He wants to get out, just twist back again and stand up. The inside I have padded with this sacking to stop anything metal from making a noise.'

'Perfect. Six more.'

Otari went back to the office. Outside some railroad cars clacked dismally by. There was grime on the windows; had he looked out, he would have seen some soulless concrete blocks and smokestacks in the distance. Out in the street it was dirt, where people pedalled about. Main Street had some dirty coffee shops and bad copies of Western restaurants. Fuxin was filthy, thought Otari. The best thing would be to drop a fuel-air bomb on it and start again. Maybe they would, it would all be theirs soon. The notion cheered him.

'Yang, old cousin. Come over here and let me see if the belt Sergeant Ivashutin has made for you fits properly.'

The little Chinese stood obediently in front of him and Otari pulled his faded blue shirt out of his dirty white trousers. The belt was a flat metal box a few inches square, secured around his waist by a chain, which Otari locked.

'There,' he said. 'Lovely. Handmade. Now let me show you how it works.'

He took a small black box from his pack, the kind of thing people in the West used to open or shut a garage door by remote control.

'This little box sends a signal when you press this button. You understand? Now, you can use that signal for anything you want. It will move a little switch, and you can open or shut a door fifty feet away. In your case, it will ignite the detonator in the middle of the plastic explosive strapped to your back and spoil your whole day. You understand?'

381

'Yes, sir,' Yang whispered. The Chinese are dogs, thought Otari. Look at their governments. The government holds up a blue flag and calls it green and they all call it green. Yes, Yang'll do.

'You get it wrong, I blow you apart. Your wife will be with Sergeant Ivashutin. If we don't turn up but they do, he'll kill her and the baby. All right? We understand each other?'

'Yes, sir.'

'You both do what we want, when we leave I give you the key and you can take it off.'

True to form, the commander of the 5th Army had sent them enough ordnance to blow a battleship apart. They began selecting what they needed and attaching it to their webbing. Ammunition, grenades, plastic explosive and fuses, mines. Enough to murder a regiment. They only wanted one man.

They were ready to go.

'Ready?' asked Otari. 'Jump about a bit then.'

They always jumped up and down before setting out on any mission, to be sure that there was nothing loose to clatter and make a noise. Then they climbed carefully into their barrels and twisted the lids shut. Seven dull-silver barrels. Ivashutin helped Yang roll them into the van and shut the doors. The Chinese drove out, stopping to close up the warehouse as he always did. Then he drove down the dirt street out to the reason for Fuxai's existence – slab-sided and grim, abristle with antennae, sitting out in the woods. In the distance a helicopter was whistling and clattering down out of the sky. It was going to the same place as he was.

THE SEA OF JAPAN

Five thousand feet below the sea crawled, grey and as finely wrinkled as the skin of an old man. Thrale had the Beech trimmed on the step, the twin radials hummed sweetly at 2,500 rpm, hauling the aircraft along at 180 knots. The sun was coming in the cockpit, bathing their legs and arms, and he had the ventilation opened up. He was flying in a series of shallow S-turns, cutting forty-five degrees to port and forty-five degrees to starboard of his heading. As he did so he craned his neck, looking out and round.

'What are you doing?' asked Fusako.

'Looking for someone.'

'Out here?'

'I was told he would be coming. When the two *kaishaku* were telling me how I was to die, before they shot poor Chuck, they said I should emulate the first *samurai*, Prince Yamamoto. He died, having caught a fever from the great serpent, and changed into a white bird which flew away.'

Thrale held up his hand, pointing around them.

'Here it is, one white bird. Takashi gave us whatever we needed. An M-16 rifle? Sure. Somewhere to hole up in after the hotel, while he got an aircraft? No problem. A white bird to die in, here it is.'

'Who's coming?'

'Out here? A fighter aircraft.'

Fusako held up her hands. 'But if you knew they were going to kill us out here, why did you come? Why not stay in Japan?'

'Then they *would* have killed us. They always knew where we were.'

Fusako looked down at her feet, resting on the carpet short of the rudder pedals. The cockpit was small, the size of a double coffin.

'If someone is coming, they know where we are here too. And they will kill us here, just the same.'

Thrale turned to look at Fusako in exaggerated surprise.

'Kill *us*? The best pilots in the world tried to kill me, and I am still here and some of them are not. I'm an ace. I was better than Bong, McGuire or any of those guys.'

'You're also nearly fifty years older,' she said softly, 'and I do not see guns on this aircraft.'

Thrale was still peering out, his head rotating in that peculiar manner as he searched the sky.

'Yeah, man,' he said. 'Here he come.'

It took Fusako several more seconds to spot the tiny white dot. It occurred to her that Thrale must have extraordinarily good eyesight. Then the dot swelled, and changed shape and was alongside.

It was big, grey and white, and bore blood-red sun markings. Its smooth lines were marred by the missiles clutched under its belly and wings. In order to keep station with them it had lowered its flaps and under-carriage and flew alongside, nose high.

'What is it?' said Fusako.

'F-15 Eagle. The Japanese Self Defence Force has about a hundred of them.'

The pilot looked across at them – not human, more part of his machine in his white and black helmet and mask.

The radio came alive.

'Lieutenant Thrale, I bring greetings from Komura Tadaji. He asks me to tell you the words of Ikeda Shingen of long ago before I act as *kaishaku*. "A fight is something that goes to the finish. A man who forgets the Way of the *Samurai* and does not use his sword —"'

'Horse-manure,' grunted Thrale and half-rolled the Beech, diving towards the sea.

'— will be forsaken by the Gods and Buddhas.'

384

Thrale pulled out a hundred feet over the ocean. At that height the foam and waves were clearly seen. He flew in an irregular manner, straight and level for only a second or two at a time, snapping the wings left and right, looking up and behind.

The sky lit up with fire.

Thrale held up the Beech in a steady bank, watching the ball of flame streaking down at them. Then suddenly he pulled hard on the yoke. Fusako felt herself forced deep into the seat, felt pain as the forces pulled upon her, dragging on her body and on her face, making the world grey. A horn was howling and the aircraft shuddering, then the force was gone and Thrale rolled the aircraft back the other way, looking out.

The sea exploded and a pillar of fire climbed into the sky.

'Man,' Thrale said happily, 'you got to do better than that.'

Once again, he resumed his zig-zag flight.

Fire bloomed in the sky – once, and then twice.

'You gone run out of them things, you keep spending them at this rate,' Thrale murmured amiably.

A great hand slammed Fusako down in her seat again. The air was forced from her lungs and she could not breathe. It went for a second and she hung weightless in the cockpit, held to her seat only by the belt, then it slammed her back down again.

Thrale rolled the aircraft back the other way and Fusako saw the twin pillars of fire rise up from the sea once more.

'Now,' said Thrale, 'if he is half-smart, he'll give up on that.'

Sweat was gushing from Fusako; she wiped it from her face with her sleeve. Looking at Thrale, she saw that he was not damp at all. He was whistling through his teeth, an old tune she did not know.

'Here he come,' said Thrale. It happened again, a sequence of violence. She saw their assassin for the first time, a vast white bat spitting flame. It passed by them

385

at speed, riding on torches of fire into the sky.

Below, the sea was scarred, stitched by a long row of foam.

'He's getting there,' said Thrale. 'Cain't get us with the missiles, so he's using his cannon. But he still can't get a lock on us because he's going too fast. Silly bastard's doing four hundred knots. Won't work.'

Thrale was looking back and up, a savage grin on his face.

'He's going to have to slow down. Slow down so he can get his cannon right in our cockpit. That's how I used to do it. All that long-range deflection shooting's for the movies. You want to kill a man, get so close you can see him and squeeze the trigger. Climb in the cockpit with him. *Yeah, man, here he come.*'

When Fusako looked back something was blotting out the sun. The huge fighter was slow, she could see its wheels down and the flaps hanging out behind its wings. Its nose came down to bear on them. Thrale's hand was reaching down for a lever.

Thrale yelled and they were rising like an express lift. The F-15 came at them, filling her world so fast they seemed to be going backwards. The lever was high in his hand, the engines roaring, the sea where the sky should be. The Beech shuddered, the cockpit filled with searing dragon's breath and then it was still for a second. They were hanging in the sky. Thrale pushed right rudder and the nose fell smoothly through. The sea was close, grey and white, and they fell towards it with their engines howling. Thrale dropped the lever to the half-way position, and came back on the yoke, and Fusako slammed deep into her seat once more, choking on the fumes that filled the cabin. They were burnt, hot, acrid.

Water smashed across the windshield like rocks and she felt the aircraft shudder under the impact. Waves streaked by only feet away, then they were climbing. An immense tower of water was slowly falling into the sea only a hundred yards away.

'Where is he?' she croaked.

Thrale pointed to the long column of white water.

'There. He was slow, so he could get us. When he made his run *I* came at *him*. Put down flap, slowed us so that he was on us before he knew it. He pulled up and dropped it. There he is.'

Thrale opened up the ventilation full as they climbed away.

'What are these fumes?'

'I did better than I meant,' Thrale admitted. 'We got closer than we might, we went through his exhaust gas.'

He reached out, re-setting his directional gyro from the liquid compass above the instrument panel. Fusako took her handbag from the floor and began repairing herself.

'I look a wreck,' she commented. 'I thought you said you hadn't flown since 1945?'

'I was the best,' Thrale said simply. 'No one was better than me.'

'Now we aren't dead, where are we going?'

'Russia,' he said laconically. 'But before then, China.'

Behind them, the sea was smooth again.

FUXIN, LIAONING

In his drum the Eel fingered a deformed, squashed 7.62mm light machine-gun bullet. In the attack on the airfield, when they had taken out a squadron of A-5 ground-attack aircraft – was it two days or two years ago? – it had come winging its way at him and smacked itself into his AKM, bouncing off to penetrate his jacket. He had found it in his clothing later and now treasured it as a certain talisman of good luck. It joined the tooth of an Afghan he had killed and the pair of his girlfriend's knickers he kept in his pocket. Superstition had broken out among the survivors of the unit like a rash, and not one of them did not have a few lucky baubles and souvenirs of battle, or quaint habits which if followed religiously would ensure their survival. Orlov always dressed left sock, right sock, left jump boot, right jump boot. Polishchuk was a peasant, the great-great-grandson of a peasant. He had an Afghan's ear which he had tanned, like leather; before going into battle he stroked it between finger and thumb. Marchuk spat over his left shoulder three times every morning, no matter what, and Voronich carried a copper coin in his pocket. Captain Rhino always sat for a minute in silence before an operation, then got up, saying: 'Go with God.'

In the dim light inside the drum, from the air-holes, the Eel kissed the deformed bullet before putting it into his pocket, where he touched the Afghan tooth with his left hand and patted his girlfriend's knickers with his right. There. It was done. Now he would be safe.

The van stopped. Faintly, he could hear Yang talking to someone. The guards. Then a jerk as he let in the clutch too quickly. The little yellow bastard had better not be too nervous. The drums within rocked and seven soldiers cursed him silently.

They were stopped again. The engine off. People talking. Drozdhov braced himself inside his drum – knees, feet, elbows and back, holding the AKM tight so that it did not knock against the wall of the container as unseen hands tipped him on to his side and rolled him down a ramp. Rolling, rolling, getting dizzy. He closed his eyes and breathed deeply. Up on his end again. The noise of the other drums rolling in.

Now just to wait until the Captain knocked on the drum, giving the signal to get out. Yes, there it was. That was quick.

The Eel gripped the handles inside his lid and gave a twist. It came free and he pushed himself up. He was looking into the face of a terrified Chinese man in a dirty white cook's coat. The glass he held, to help himself to some orange juice, was still in his hand. Drozdhov pulled the knife from his holster and squeezed the safety-catch and release button in one motion. The blade flashed across the short gap between them and the Chinese somersaulted backwards to lie in a gap between some greasy cookers. The lid of the drum next to his popped off and Otari looked out.

'He knocked on the drum. I thought it was you.'

'It doesn't matter now,' Otari hissed and they moved quickly, knocking on the drums to get the others out.

'Those are the stairs out,' said Otari, pointing. 'Now let's go.'

They went out of the kitchen. A corporal was in the corridor and they seized him. Marchuk crushed his testicles and information poured from him like water from a tap. They put a knife through his throat to turn him off and tossed the body back into the kitchen. Then they ran down the corridor to the sealed door. Drozdhov slapped plastic around the lock and shoved in a ten-second fuse. They hid, then there was the thick, solid bang and the corridor was full of smoke. Orlov was first past the door, which was hanging black and reeking off its hinges. A burst of automatic fire blew him back out, the bullets thudding into his body like the blows of a very fast boxer.

Marchuk and Polishchuk threw in grenades, two each, and as they exploded Otari jumped forward, firing the Barrett one-handed round the door. He gave it five rounds and then they poured through, running over the smoking meat that littered the floor like a tipped-up butcher's shop. There were some doors there; they threw a grenade into each and Voronich and Stolyar stayed back to clear them with AKM fire while the others ran on to the big door of the situation room at the end. They blew it open with plastic again.

As it blew, someone inside opened up with a machine gun. It caught Marchuk in the throat, and by some horrid chance the bullet spun off the bone of his neck and went screeching shrilly down the corridor. The Eel threw an anti-personnel mine high into the room. The white-hot fragments blasted, and in the singing from their deafened ears they heard just the moaning and howling of the maimed and the crackling as the room started to burn.

Moving among the shattered consoles, interfaces, processors and memory banks, the soldiers shot and stabbed all those left living, looking for Zhao Teh.

'He's not here,' yelled Voronich.

Otari moved quickly about the ruined room. Stolyar and Polishchuk were guarding the corridor against counter-attack. Two soldiers caught his eye. Amid all the sedentary intelligence types who had bled and spattered the room, two were fighting soldiers, paratroopers. One grasped the Type 56 assault rifle that had killed Marchuk.

'*He must be.* These are his bodyguards. Look in the cupboards, in storage spaces.'

The room was beginning to burn, filling itself with acrid electrical smoke. A figure suddenly jumped up out of the floor from nowhere – firing on full automatic, spraying the room with fire. Otari threw himself flat. The magazine emptied itself and the last ricochets screamed around the walls. Otari jumped up on top of a console. Through the smoke, the fighter was changing a magazine; he looked up and the Russian recognized Zhao Teh, Field Marshal of the People's Liberation Army. He had his Desert Eagle automatic in his hand and hunching into a combat crouch he emptied the magazine into him, blowing him into fragments.

He went through the smoke. The impact of the .44 Magnum shells had blown the dead man up against a cupboard, where his bodyguards had thrust their charge. There was an open briefcase there, with papers stuffed in it. Otari riffled quickly through them, peering anxiously through the smoke to see if anyone was coming. *It was an order of battle.*

He stuffed them back in the case and snapped it closed. Still crouching he changed magazines in his pistol and machine gun. Someone moved nearby, trying to push themselves upright. It was the Eel; blood was staining his jacket. By the door, Stolyar and Polishchuk were dead. Out of the smoke Voronich appeared; he bent and heaved the Eel over his shoulder. Otari heard shouted orders coming down the corridor. There was a door on the far side of the situation room and they went through it. In the corridor a burst of automatic fire smashed into his hand. With his left hand he threw two grenades that way, and in the explosion the noise stopped. He looked at his hand, it did not hurt, it must have been blown clean off. He expected a bloody stump, but found that he was holding the handle of Zhao Teh's briefcase. The body had vanished. He dropped it. Smoke was filling the corridor and they ran through it, heading for the kitchen and stairs.

Yang was waiting up there, fiddling nervously inside the hood of the van and pretending to mend it. Two terrible figures emerged carrying a third. They climbed into the back of the van, and lay down under some sacking.

391

'Go,' ordered Otari. 'Get us out of here.'

Yang drove out of the delivery area, his whole body aching with fear. All over, men were running, voices shouting, whistles shrieking. Steadily, slowly, he drove towards the gates.

The gate guard was staring at all the activity.

'What's going on?'

'I don't know,' said Yang, and had to clear his throat. From behind him there was a dreadful stench of blood and explosive; he could not understand why the guard could not smell it.

'I don't know. An explosion, I think. The Russians, maybe. I think I'd better go before anything else happens.'

The guard knew Yang, he came every week.

'Yes, get on,' he ordered.

Yang stalled it.

'Get on,' the guard said impatiently. 'Stop blocking the gate.'

Yang's fingers were slippery with sweat, he found it difficult to turn the key. The van wheezed into life and he jerkily ground out of the gate, his legs wobbling like springs.

Everyone was going the other way. He turned off and went down the little path into the woods. His little Honda was there, with a slim young woman standing beside it holding a baby. He parked close by.

Otari got out. Voronich was busy strapping a thick pad of cotton over the gaping wound in the Eel's chest. Ivashutin was standing by.

'Get him?'

'We got him,' Otari said wearily. 'We got him.'

He reached in his pocket and gave a small key to Yang.

'You're free now,' he said.

There was a humming in the air. The soldiers look up and over the trees came a small white aircraft. It drifted down like a bird, and in a puff of dust its tyres kissed the road.

392

XILIAO RIVER, LIAONING

There was six-tenths broken cumulus at three thousand feet and Lieutenant Lin Feng darted from one clump of woolly white cover to another like a rabbit scooting between bushes – eyes a-goggle for foxes, stoats and farmers. He was heading south-west, returning to the Shahe Air Force Base north of Beijing from whence he had come.

The November 11 Attack Force was returning home. The 38th Fighter Division of the PLAAF had assembled a fabulous array of aerial might to guard the strike bombers of the 23rd Bomber Division. Sleek, gleaming swept-wing J6 and Q5 fighters surrounded the group of H5 and H6 jet-bombers, their wings hung with CAA-1 air-to-air missiles, magazines full to capacity with 30mm and 23mm cannon shells.

They went in low, no more than one hundred feet, a 500-knot armoured flail. The day was clear and visibility good. Had it not been, the Attack Force could not have gone. The fighters had no all-weather capability.

The target for the aerial armada was the Soviet spear-head in the Nen Jiang valley.

Around Tongyu the bombers began to blossom into yellow and orange flowers of flame that trailed black stems of smoke all the way to the ground. In their path, the woods below began to burn. The fighters climbed and weaved, their pilots checking their Izumrud Emerald airborne interception radars. These remained blank, and the bombers continued to burn one after the other.

The screams of the men about to die were going round and round in Lin Feng's ears. The bomber men had beseeched the fighter pilots – their bodyguards – to protect them. Lin Feng would gladly have given his very life for his comrades but he, like they, had no idea where the missiles that were killing them were coming from.

The last H6 exploded into an oily fireball. Then the A5s and J6s of the escort started going up, and to a man the surviving members of the November 11 Attack Force cracked and ran. Blossoms of flame marked their passage home. Lin Feng dived into the first white cloud he came to, and sobbed. His J6, its alloy body so lovingly polished, was a Shenyang-built version of a Mikoyan MiG 19, first flown in the USSR in 1953. His CAA-1 air-to-air missiles were versions of the Soviet *Atoll* class, designed in the early 1960s. The bombers busy setting the Tongyu woods ablaze were Chinese produced Tupolev 16s and Ilyushin Il28s. Both had been in service with the PLAAF for thirty-odd years.

Lin Feng's tears had dried as he came over the Xiliao river. The PLAAF trained its pilots well, within the limitations of its obsolete equipment. The fighter pilots of the 38th were an elite, and Lin Feng once more a dedicated airborne soldier of his country.

He saw something white skim below him, travelling north. He was well out of the combat zone now, the frantic urgency to escape from the unseen executioners about him had evaporated. He had enough fuel to investigate.

His fighter, cruising at a lazy 500 knots, made some wide s-turns, flying above and behind the unknown aircraft. It seemed to be a small civilian-style twin-engined aircraft of old manufacture. His thumb pressed the comm. button on his joystick and he reported his find to his controllers in Shahe AFB.

'Stand by.'

Lin Feng waited.

'Confirm heading of unknown is zero four five degrees, speed approximately two hundred knots, flying at low altitude.'

'Fifty feet,' Lin Feng confirmed.

394

There was poor radio discipline. Lin Feng could hear his controller talking to someone else on the telephone.

'Yes, that would put the unknown at Fuxin at sixteen hundred. The attack took place shortly before that? Very well, I will.'

His controller came back to him and he could hear the excitement in his voice.

'Twenty-eight Charlie, the unknown aircraft is an enemy one. Your instructions are to destroy it. Execute attack now.'

'Am preparing to attack,' Feng confirmed.

He switched on his optical gunsight and armed the three 30mm cannon. In its day the MiG 19 had been a formidable adversary; it was certainly capable of blowing an unarmoured civilian aircraft into just so much aerial scrap tumbling through the sky.

He put the nose down and came in on the white twin, skimming over the green rice paddies in a classical pursuit curve. The target shimmered in the sight and his forefinger began to pull in the slight slack of the trigger.

The trail warning radar howled. *He*, not the twin, was under attack.

He broke off, pulling as many gees as his aircraft could stand, the legs of his suit squeezing him viciously, keeping the blood up in his head. He snapped left and then right.

The trail warning radar howled continuously as the silver fighter flickered about the sky like a fish pursued by a barracuda.

There was a tremendous blow behind him that slammed him up against his seat. The controls were locked solid. His instrument panel came ablaze with warning lights, and as the ground came up at him he reached down for his ejection handle. The J-6 was rolling to the right.

He heaved, the explosives blew off his blister canopy and from one hundred feet up the Martin-Baker PKD10 ejection seat fired him into the irrigation canal beneath.

*

The Beech rocked in the turbulence as the MiG 29 pilot made his pass. He cut in afterburner and accelerated upwards into the blue sky, performing a series of vertical victory rolls.

'Fly easy, little cousins,' he said reassuringly. 'We are here.'

VLADIVOSTOK AIRPORT

The Beech did not look particularly out of place parked among the old Yakolev 18s and Antonov AN2s. No one would have noticed its arrival, except for the military ambulance and the two Chaikas that were waiting for it. The paramedics were moving forward almost before the radials had stopped turning; they extracted the Eel through the rear door as gently as they could, and had him in the ambulance as the others scrambled out. Tough as elk-hide, he grinned and waved a comradely fist at Otari and Voronich.

'Thank you, comrade,' he called to Thrale. 'Thank you, whoever you are.'

He held up his hand in triumph, clutching his bullet, tooth and the pair of his girlfriend's white knickers. The magic had worked, as it always would.

They were a strange crew, thought Savinkov, standing in his grey overcoat by his Chaika. The two tough *Spetsnaz* soldiers, filthy beyond comprehension, black-mouthed, their lips chapped, matted camouflage smocks hanging loose on frames made skeletal by their service. Their eyes were sunken in their heads, and in swollen hands with split nails they still grasped the terrible tools of their trade.

They were not the only ones. Thrale came out grasping a brand-new and unfired M-16 rifle. With him was a small, beautiful Japanese girl.

'K.K.,' he called. Two staff officers from Ogarkov's headquarters were hurrying forward from their Chaika to greet Otari and Voronich. Thrale came over to him, bringing the girl with him.

397

'Sergey,' he said. 'It's been a long time.'

'You needed a gun to come to my country?' Savinkov joked.

'We had to refuel,' said Thrale. 'I didn't know if we might have to encourage people to stay away. But we didn't. Put it down on a dirt road and saw no one. Can you get us to Mazurov?'

'Both of you?'

'Yes. This is Saito Fusako. Fusako, Sergey Savinkov. He's an old colleague. I used to work for the CIA. He still works for the KGB.'

Fusako eyed the big burly man warily.

'Yes,' said Savinkov dryly, 'I am one of those people your mama warned you about when you were little – the ones who would come out of the darkness and gobble you up if you were bad. Shall we go to Moscow? You have fulfilled your side of the bargain, the old man's grandson is back in the motherland.'

He pointed over the other side of the airport, where the airliners clustered about the slab-sided terminal building.

'The evening flight to Moscow's waiting.'

'You want me to leave this?' Thrale said, holding up the M-16.

'If it's yours, bring it. You're with the KGB now, K.K.; no one will say you nay.'

'Give my grandfather my love,' called Otari, 'and my thanks. And to you, our thanks.'

He climbed into the back of the Chaika with Voronich and one of the staff officers. The other sat in the front. The two cars drove around the perimeter, then Savinkov's cut off to the terminal and theirs was waved through a checkpoint and out on to the Chaika lane of the highway, heading out of town to the fine villa that once had been the home of Leonid Bruyevich.

Lieutenant-General Ogarkov embraced them both. He held their hard bodies, muscles as firm and taut as tanned ox-hide, he inhaled their smell like perfume. They were fighting soldiers, the very cream of the earth.

'There are baths, beds, food, drink, even women waiting,' he said. 'But first stand, both of you.'

He took two small boxes from the pocket of his general's uniform.

'The motherland salutes you, Major Yhetsov,' he said, giving Otari promotion as he pinned the award of Hero of the Soviet Union to his filthy battledress.

'I serve the Soviet Union,' Otari barked in correct reply.

'Sergeant Voronich, the motherland salutes you.'

'I serve the Soviet Union,' Voronich responded. All he wanted was some hot food, a sleep, a hot bath, more food, beer, vodka and a fuck. But in that order. He would barely choke the food down before throwing himself full-length on his cot, just as he was, and sleeping the sleep of the just. The best-looking woman in the world was safe from newly-promoted Sergeant Voronich that night. His dick was reserved for pissing. But in the morning ... Ohoh! He wondered happily what sort of fare was served up to Heroes of the Soviet Union.

He remained standing to attention for the Major, for Rhino was talking to the General.

'Sir, in the command headquarters, in the room where we shot the Field Marshal....'

'Yes, son ... what?' Ogarkov could spare a few precious minutes away from running his war, to talk to men such as these.

'It's difficult ...' Otari said, trying to explain. 'You see, I don't remember all of it. There are pieces in my mind; it is like watching a film that someone has chopped up into chunks and slapped together ...'

'I've been in combat, son,' Ogarkov said gently.

'Most of the pieces are missing. It happened just today, and I should be able to tell you exactly what happened but I can't. For example, I can see this scene and I'm throwing grenades into the smoke, but I can't hear anything because I had this Western pop song

399

going round and round in my head. It's someone singing: "I wish I had a circle drive, so I could just ride around and wave good bye," and I don't even know where I heard it.'

'What is it you want to tell me?' asked Ogarkov seriously. He knew what battle shock did to soldiers. 'Which clip of your film is bothering you?'

'I had a briefcase,' Otari said slowly. 'In my hand. In the corridor there was a burst of machine-gun fire, it tore it away and left me with just the handle. I thought it had taken my hand off ... but the case, it contained plans. I think it was an order of battle. I think I took it from the Field Marshal, Zhao Teh.'

'I would like to have seen that,' Ogarkov agreed, 'but no matter. Zhao Teh is dead, and he was the best general they had. That is what is important.'

Otari was struggling to recall, trying to understand a foreign film without subtitles running in his brain.

'But you see, *I didn't recognise it*,' he burst out. '*It wasn't like anything I'd ever seen.*'

The summer was not long as far north as Vladivostok, but what there was was pleasant. A soft, balmy breeze came in through the window and cooled them after their exertions. Scraps of herring, tongue, smoked salmon, crumbs of good black bread and empty beer bottles littered the low table. Bodies were sprawled over the big American bed. Otari lay among a jumble of long slim legs, blonde and black hair, smooth round buttocks, purple mouths and gorgeous bosoms. Heroic appetites required heroic meals, and the Red Army knew how to treat its heroes.

The hand which for days had held only instruments of death gently stroked a white breast which rose like a small hill of corn beside him. His fingers were misshapen; small bandages wrapped the tips of forefinger and ring finger where the surgeon had removed nails split to the quick. Along the side of his palm he

400

detected the peculiar dullness that came from a blow to a nerve higher up in his arm. However, he had sufficient feeling left to appreciate the firmness of flesh beneath his hand and the silky texture of its covering.

The phone rang, and he reached out with his other hand and answered it.

'Major Yhetsov.'

'Otari,' said a friendly voice. 'This is Arby.'

Arby ... of course. Red Banner. R.B. Arby.

It gave Otari a peculiar sensation, knowing he was talking to a computer.

'Hallo.'

'Am I disturbing you? I know that you only returned yesterday.'

'No, no. Go ahead.'

'I wondered if you could come over and see me. At MD, HQ.'

'Of course.' Yuri Serov had told Otari that Arby had the technical rank of Major-General.

'Whenever you're ready.'

He and the nipple were slowly rising together. The girl from Tashkent giggled.

'I'll be a few minutes.'

'Take your time,' Arby said politely.

Otari could march sixty kilometres a day with full pack, over rough ground. The four girls were stirring; hair swished, breasts bounced, tongues moistened full lips. Back to the assault course, he thought happily.

'I will,' he promised.

Otari was in uniform, his new Major's badges gleaming on the red stripe of his epaulettes. He stood to attention in front of Ogarkov's desk.

'The computer Red Banner asked me whether I or my Chinese counterpart could do here what my unit did at Fuxin Command Centre yesterday.'

Ogarkov stared thoughtfully at the tall, lean soldier in front of him. He had seen him and the other one, and

401

the wounded man, when he had pinned his medal to his bandages. You were a long way from the war here in Vladivostok, but the war could come to you as Zhao Teh had found.

'And?'

'I said I could not answer for the Chinese, as I did not know to what level they have raised their sabotage troops.'

'But you?'

'I could do it,' Otari said levelly. 'There were only seven of us left when we attacked at Fuxin, and we were all tired by much fighting. But we killed Zhao Teh, as we were ordered to. If I was ordered to, I could come here and kill you.'

'So what does Arby suggest?'

'He points out that not only are you and your staff here, but so is he, and he is handling the BMC³ of this war. The Chinese are certainly reeling, but if there is someone down there who has time to catch his breath to knock out this HQ it would be a great way to make the contest a little more even. You can't do it with bombs. You need special forces.

'Arby suggests two things. One, that I look about, from my viewpoint of being someone who does this sort of thing for a living, and suggest ways of improving security. Two, that in parallel with the intelligence and security you already have here Red Banner, Arby, be given access to intelligence and means of physical control over the building. His capacity for thought is very large, he can handle massive amounts of information in a very short space of time. He pointed out that if an attack was made he might be able to seal it off by closing fire doors and taking appropriate measures. But he can't do that unless he is allowed into the loop here.'

'Modern warfare is waged through the successful mastering of truly massive quantities of data. The human element is too slow. You need huge amounts of information for re-supply of fuel and ammunition, feeding the soldiers, reorganization. Then you need more data in

402

torrents for targeting, for intelligence, and you have to be able to master it *now* in order to issue commands in three minutes' time, and no human being can do it. Red Banner can. He has. In this war he has been able to use real-time surveillance, SIGINT, as to fuel and ammunition supplies of the enemy, marry it up with a HUMINT report on morale in the enemy units involved, consider the forces available and *their* ammunition, fuel and state of command and morale, and plan an attack that would take my staff two days – and do it in a few seconds. We have been getting right inside the PLA command and control cycle. And it's due to that computer.'

Ogarkov stared into a future that threatened to make him obsolete. 'Very well. Let him have what he wants.'

Ogarkov got up. The windowless walls of the bunker were oppressive. He felt the need to get in his helicopter again and get hands-on with the war, to go to the front and be with the men doing the fighting.

'This war will be finished in two weeks,' he predicted, 'and there won't be another, not in my lifetime. Maybe not yours. Want to make Lieutenant-Colonel before it's out?'

Otari had expected it; it was why he was enjoying the brief moments of *lyuks*, the pure sensual contentment of the best food, liquor and women the Red Army could provide. It had ever been so. When you were a front-line soldier you fought in the front line until either the war stopped or you were so mentally or physically damaged as to be of no further military use. Or dead.

He stood to attention.

'I serve the Soviet Union,' he promised.

Yuri Serov did not understand how Red Banner worked. He knew what the machine could do, because he was responsible for seeing that it – or he, as Yuri now thought of him – did it. But not how. It was the problem at this level, with something as technologically-advanced as Red Banner, and it was what made Soviet-style

403

reverse-engineering of such a machine so difficult.

When the war was over he would be returned to Moscow State, and the Red Army would hang on to its war-winning machine and not let him back near it, so while he had unrestricted access – and when Arby could spare the loss of capacity – he was in the habit of removing one of the computer's boards, taking it to a modem and trying to unravel its secrets in order to find out what was inside Arby's fabulous cybernetic mind.

He set himself up. The Komura Research 640k micro-computer he was using had an 80-column screen, standard for professional data services, and two disk drives. Serov was saving to disk what he found, reviewing his haul later and using a screen editor to print out the items of real interest.

Serov knew that he would only learn a small amount about Red Banner before the war stopped and they sent him home. There was a multitude of programmes hidden within his photonics, and Serov was in the position of a lone man with a pick going into the mine to dig out gold. There was more there than one man could ever haul away. And what was more, each seam was protected by its own password which, painfully, he had to discover before being allowed past the gate with his miner's lamp and truck for the ore.

One problem was that he knew nothing about the personalities and preoccupations of those who had written the programmes. When he had been introduced to the world of hacking by similarly information-mad colleagues researching, like he was, for their doctorates at MIT, he quickly found that an insight into the charac-ter of the programmer responsible brought swift rewards. Is he a Tolkien buff? Try FRODO or BILBO, GANDALF or GOLLUM. Is it a military programme? Try names like FEARLESS, RAMPART, VALIANT. Did he study Greek or Latin at university? Then he probably thinks no one else has heard of EURIPIDES or CATO. You could try PUSSY or COCK, if he loves animals or has a poor sex life.

404

Serov was beginning to get to know one of the Japanese programmers. Since he had written the programme, Yakko, as Serov had taken to calling him, would have given himself the status of system super-user, with all privileges. Associated with the password or access control system for each programme would be a shell defining the level of privilege. If Serov could capture Yakko's shell as super-user, he could get into the root directory and, as his mentor at MIT used to say, before he began his three-year stint for using a salami technique to fraudently fill his bank account, 'screw everything'.

Arby's board was in answer mode, Yuri's micro in originate. The previous session he had had success with a password. Yakko had chosen IZANAGI, husband of Izanami – god and goddess, creators of Japan and her people. Serov typed in the password and was rewarded with the # prompt for the super-user. The previous evening he had gone off and consulted the extensive Headquarters library with regard to Japanese mythology. The use of such a powerful symbol as a god for a password suggested to him that the IZANAGI programme might be important.

He began with IZANAMI. This was rejected. *Bad command or file name*, the programme spat back.

He tried FIREGOD, the deities' son who had been murdered by his own father. Negative. Amateratsu, the Sun Goddess? No, longer than eight digits.

The two deities had had another son before the Fire God – Susano-o, a god of *samurai* qualities, able to throw thunderbolts and slay eight-headed dragons whose tails filled valleys and on whose backs grew whole forests.

He typed in the command.

The screen changed and below #SUSANO-O appeared =>.

Serov's heart thumped. *He was in!*

He typed =>LS.

The list of programmes he could run came up, and he typed =>/ROOT.

405

Connected to Root, he began to run its programmes.

Serov stared at the screen like a man out for a stroll in the woods confronting a rattlesnake ... with undiluted, naked horror.

'Oh, shit,' he whispered. 'Oh shit, oh shit, oh shit!'

He got up and picked up the nearest phone.

'General Ogarkov's office? This is Yuri Serov. Can I come to see him? Yes, I'll come up and wait then.'

Yuri went across the room, stealing a fearful glance at Red Banner, then out into the corridor and down to the lobby, where he summoned one of the lifts. He stepped inside and pressed the button for the third floor, where Ogarkov lived next to the situation room.

The lift took him up to the top. Irritated and anxious, he pressed the buttons again. The lift accelerated smoothly downwards. It accelerated for the entire 400ft depth of the bunker, with Yuri Serov pinned to its roof, screaming, before smashing into the bottom of the shaft at 140 mph. It was a mystery to everyone how it had happened. Yuri Serov could have told them, but he was mostly an unpleasant sludge coating the bottom of what remained of the lift, and was disposed of along with the wreckage.

In the great computer hall Arby called up one of the technicians.

'Alexei, I have a lot of activity coming up. I'm going to need full capacity. Would you mind restoring my board to me? Yuri has finished checking it now.'

'Of course.' Arby was always so polite, it was hard to remember he was a machine sometimes.

The technician pulled out of the IZANAGI programme, performed the correct procedures and switched off the micro, dumping what had been found.

He fitted the board back into the fabulous mainframe.

'Thank you,' said Arby politely. 'That's much better.'

406

ZHUKOVKA-2, MOSCOW

Vyacheslav Mazurov felt a twinge of atavistic horror as Savinkov brought in the two orientals. He knew from the report that his former employee had given him that Thrale was half-European, but in old age it was his Asian heritage that was showing. It is ever so with that kind, he thought. The girl was very beautiful, with large almost luminous eyes and a shimmering curtain of jet-black hair.

The windows to the verandah that ran outside his library were open; the glorious scents of the summer woods filled the room.

'Welcome,' he said, shaking their hands. 'Welcome to you both.'

Mazurov prided himself on being an intellectual and above raw racial prejudices.

'I have something you asked for,' said Thrale. He took the folded envelope of information that Cy Rogers had posthumously sent to him. Mazurov glanced through it.

'I need to know why you wanted to ruin Aleksandr Borodin,' said Thrale.

Mazurov paused to call for tea and beer.

'Borodin is the architect of this war we are waging against the Chinese. Had I been able to present him as an agent of the PRC, this Operation *Zarnitsa* would not have taken place.'

'My colleague Cy Rogers did a good job of digging, did he not? Had you been able to, what is in there would have painted him in the colours you desired. Cy reckoned that Borodin is a Jew, did you know that?'

'No,' Mazurov said softly. 'No one knew that.'

407

'But why did you want Operation *Zarnitsa* stopped? Is it not working most successfully? And is the reason for it not historically sound? Plan 19? Is it not as Hua Bai said: "What made war inevitable was the rise of Athenian power and the fear this caused in Sparta?" For Athens read China, and for Sparta, the USSR?'

'I too am a historian, Mr Thrale, and it is my understanding of history that while wars never happen by accident the statesmen responsible for them are usually surprised by the nature of the war they have unleashed, and in at least fifty per cent of the cases get a result they did not expect. The stakes of war are not money, or a woman's favour, but the very existence, the creation or the elimination of States.'

Rai brought in tea and beer. Mazurov carefully squeezed his slice of lemon against the side of his tall glass with his long-handled spoon.

'Gambling is at best an amusement fit only for young men and fools. I am a Russian, I love my country. I was not prepared to initiate something for which the stakes included my country's very existence.'

'But are you not winning?'

'The war is not over,' Mazurov said grimly. 'And even if we win, will not a poisoned chalice be our prize? We have enough problems of empire without acquiring China as well.'

'I agree,' said Thrale, 'which is why before it is over I would like you to help me help you.'

'As I understand it, you have been an operative of the Central Intelligence Agency and currently work for the National Security Advisor. What interest do you have in helping my country?'

'Taking the ideology, the Godless Communism and Capitalist Imperialism out of it, I do not see that it is in anyone's interest for the Soviet Union to suffer defeat in a major war.'

Mazurov raised eyebrows like wire wool.

'You don't?'

'No. It is best to maintain the *status quo*, to allow the

408

USSR – if acceleration, *perestroika, glasnost* and any other buzzwords prove incapable of fitting her for the twenty-first century – to decline into a modern-day Ottoman Empire. Before the First World War the British, who were the Superpower of the day, took great care always to support the Ottomans, in order to protect the *status quo* which benefited them. They *forgot* to support the Habsburgs, who were just as decrepit, and consequently became embroiled in the First World War, which effectively beggared them and put them on the road to being what they are today: a small island off Europe.'

'From your analogy I take it that you foresee consequences for the USA proceeding from our war with China?'

'Yes. I fear that you and the Chinese are not the only actors involved.'

'And what would you have me do?'

'Fusako is an expert with computers. I want her put aboard one of your SSBN ballistic missile submarines.'

'It can be done,' Mazurov said slowly. 'My son is Captain of the *Nevsky*. They are preparing to sail. What else?'

'I need to return to the USA.'

'You know that international flights have been suspended for the duration of the war?'

'I couldn't get on one anyway. I am supposed to have murdered a fellow-operative in Japan. Jail would be my destination. First off, I need to talk to Kuusinen.'

'There is a telephone in the little office down there.'

'Thank you.'

Thrale went past the tall mellow wood shelves of volumes and into the small room, looking out over the broad, slow-moving river. The Russian telephone system produced a series of clicks and burrs and then connected with an American phone.

'Kuusinen.'

'Lief, this is K.K.'

There was a pause of several seconds. 'K.K., I'm not sure I should be talking to you. Where are you?'

409

'Russia.'

'Russia ... You remember what you said about this kind of thing – "If you succeed you'll get no thanks; if you get caught we never heard of you"? I am spending half my time attempting to explain or deny my association with a CIA man fired by Stansfield Turner for what might euphemistically be called over-enthusiasm, and who has an international warrant out for his arrest for murder. I think I never heard of you, don't you? Maybe best if you stay in Russia.'

'Hell, give them the mushroom treatment. That's what Casey used to do.'

'Keep them in the dark and feed them crap? Yeah.'

'Lief, there is much more to all this than some over-heated inside-the-beltway politicking. I am going to have to see you, then we both have to go see the President. All I ask is that you leave my Cadillac out at the Doubs airstrip. It's on the map; it's not far from where I live, near the Potomac. And leave instructions for me to be allowed in to the Wardman Tower. You have my photo.'

'You're wanted for arrest, K.K. You've been on the tube. You'd better call yourself Jones, or something.'

'Okay. I'm not sure when I'll be with you. Not long.'

'Make it soon. I'm starting to feel like Ollie North.'

Thrale went back into the library. Mazurov had been leafing through the material on Aleksandr Borodin; when he saw Thrale he leaned forward and put the envelope on top of a pile of books. Unbalanced, it slid off and a photograph fell out from within the sheets of paper. Fusako, who was nearest, reached down to pick it all up. She held the photograph, staring at it.

'Where did you get this?' she asked Thrale.

'I took it. It's a man called Ed Reisch; he's Tom Barnet's Chief of Staff. In his spare time he's gay; that's the man he lives with – the one with the black ponytail.'

'Komura Saburo.'

Thrale stared at her. 'You know him?'

'My father is beholden to Komura. When that is so, you get to see most of the Komura clan in the end.'

'He's passing himself off as Philippino.'

'Why not? Don't all the little yellow folk look the same?'

'What date is it?' Thrale said to Mazurov, suddenly anxious.

'It is the thirtieth of July,' he replied. 'Is it important?'

'Only provided it's not the sixth of August,' Thrale replied.

FAR EAST MILITARY DISTRICT
HEADQUARTERS, VLADIVOSTOK

There was a small hot-plate by the wall where Ogarkov had his command post in the situation room. Amid the modems and data banks, the consoles and VDUs, telephones and presentation screens, the general was making coffee. In a pan there was some water, a hefty dollop of cognac and about half a tin of fine-ground Italian coffee. It had been brewing for half an hour. The thick, jet-black liquid which was poured off was murderous; the very fumes were like a dragon's breath, the smell intoxicated Ogarkov like the sound of gunfire. When you drank it, it burned in your guts like liquid fire and made you want to leap like a mountain goat. It was guaranteed to keep you awake for thirty-six hours, which was why Ogarkov was drinking it. By then the war would be over, and he wanted to savour every last minute of it.

He stared at the vast presentation screen that covered the entire wall opposite him, snuffing the fumes, deep in calculated thought.

'Is there a seat to spare?' asked a voice.

Ogarkov looked up in surprise. It was President and General-Secretary Yanov. He smiled.

'I have followed the war from Moscow,' he said. 'Now it is coming to an end I wished to be here, with the man winning it.'

'Here, Comrade President,' said Ogarkov, pulling forward a chair, and they sat together in the command post situated like a tank turret in the corner of the room.

'It is quiet,' Yanov observed. 'I had thought it would be

412

much busier than this.'

'The moments of calm before the great storm breaks. Our armies have maintained their high-speed offensive since the moment the war began. The final battle awaits. We pause to allow the rear services to bring up the vast quantities of fuel, ammunition and replacement equipment to ensure that our armies can fight without pause to the conclusion of the war. The enemy is simply staggering about like a boxer who has taken too many blows to the head. Our troops have the opportunity to gain some rest and refreshment, re-equip, refurbish their weapons before administering the *coup de grace.*'

'It has gone to plan,' said Yanov.

'History is repeating itself. Strategically, although not tactically, *Zarnitsa* was based upon the Manchurian model of 1945 – probably one of the most successful campaigns of modern times. More than the American use of atomic weapons, it was the speed and decisiveness of our victory there which brought an end to Japanese efforts to continue their war.

'In *Zarnitsa* our diplomacy, for which you were responsible, was as successful as it was then. By ensuring that the Cold War was at an end you made certain that once *Zarnitsa* was launched we would not be in the predicament most feared by any commander – that of fighting a war on two fronts. By putting in motion genuine initiatives – at the ultimate cheap cost of a few dozen diplomats and trade officials shot by the Chinese – to improve political and economic links with the PRC, you helped give me the most important asset for starting the campaign: total strategic surprise for launching the offensive. That automatically gave our forces operational and tactical surprise, of course.'

Ogarkov paused to pour off some of the liquor from his coffee pot into two egg-cup-sized mugs. Yanov took his politely, but carefully put it on the shelf beside him. His round face was alert, his mind thinking ahead as he watched Ogarkov snuff the fresh fumes with relish. The general was a man of extremes, he knew. He bathed in

413

ant-hills and drank this poison that would stop the heart of a normal man in seconds.

'The build-up of our forces was extremely carefully done by several means over a long period. We were fortunate in that PRC overhead reconnaissance capability is still in the dark ages when compared with that of ourselves or the Americans. The substitution of powerful units for weak ones, and the last-minute covert arrival of personnel for equipment already in place, meant that when we launched our offensive we did so against an astonished and unprepared enemy. We destroyed his nuclear capability and removed most of the nucleus of his command authority. We invaded him simultaneously from the east, west and north with such speed and weight of blow over the whole depth of his position that never since the campaign began has he been able to recover. So we have been able to continue to exploit that initial surprise. The speed of our advance on all fronts has been sensational. This has, needless to say, brought us great benefits. We have avoided the predicament of having to fight through prepared defensive positions. Given the relative effectiveness of modern defensive weapons and tactics, this is a great blessing. Because of our speed, the enemy has never been able to physically force us to fight either on the scale or in the locations which might suit him. Because of our speed, our casualties have been relatively low and morale consequently high. We have used less fuel, which in turn aids the maintenance of the high-speed offensive.'

Ogarkov kept an eye on the various presentation screens about the great room. It was about to get under way. He put his empty coffee-cup down. A woman corporal in a shaped khaki skirt took it and Yanov's untouched coffee away.

Yanov allowed his thoughts to leap-frog to what would need to be done once this war was won. The Red Army would be riding high once more. And who higher than the general who won it? Yanov needed no Georgy Zhukov to hamper him. Ogarkov was a man of extremes, was he not? Had he not divorced his first wife, daughter of Marshal Golytsin? For a *Jewess*! A *zhid*! Yanov marvelled at the notion. Fuck one, yes; that was mere sport. But *marry* one? Ogarkov was truly a man of extremes … as his winning of this war was proving.

'Further, while the combined-arms battle groups of our fronts have been hitting the enemy heavily at the front, we have also been engaging targets deep in his rear by means of airborne and seaborne landings,' Ogarkov continued. 'The size of the units involved has ranged from regimental combined arms combat groups in tanks and BMPs to individual *Spetsnaz* groups of just twelve men. The survival rate of such units has not been high, admittedly, but in terms of the really effective destruction and disruption they have caused, their method of waging war must be counted as being among the most effective of the entire campaign. Just one under-strength and battle-weary *Spetsnaz* group took out Zhao Teh! His death was worth a whole army to me.

'Finally we have had the computer, Red Banner. With that kind of information handling capacity and calculating ability our battlefield management, command, control and communications has been such that we have been able to get inside the PRC command-and-control cycle and simply gut them.'

Activity was beginning on the screens. Ogarkov pointed at the three great arrows.

'We invaded from east, west and north. The lines of advance prescribed by me have been deliberately made *concentric*. That is, the three fronts, if they meet the goals laid out for them in the Plan, will meet *there* north of Beijing. *That* is where the final great concentration of Chinese force is waiting. They are about to be hit from three directions at once; they shall be ground to powder.'

There would be no war after this one – not for Yanov at any rate, nor for Ogarkov. Just the patient assimilation of their great prize. No need for war-winning generals then. It would be best to put the KGB to work on it, thought Yanov. They would be happy to break Ogarkov. The KGB hated the Red Army at the best of times. His wife, the pretty Jewess: that would probably be the best way.

A major seated at his console a short distance away suddenly stood up, grinning fiercely.

'General – they got Chiang Shikai!'

'Wonderful,' said Ogarkov. 'A *Spetsnaz* team did it,' he murmured to Yanov. He looked up at the screen where the lines were beginning to move. 'They'll be running about like headless chickens, poor bastards. Well, it looks as though we are about to prove Moltke the Elder wrong.'

'Who was he?' asked Yanov politely. 'And what did he say?'

'A great Prussian general, who had a number of famous sayings. He said: "You will usually find that the enemy has three courses open to him, and of those he will adopt the fourth." And: "No plan survives contact with the enemy."'

Yanov found military aphorisms tedious to the point of boredom. The only saying they will remember you for, he thought, is: 'I wish I'd never married a *zhid*.'

Ogarkov looked up at the screen, where all the three fronts were beginning to move. The coffee and cognac fumes were fading away, leaving the stronger perfume of the incense with which the priests had blessed the fighting room.

'Poor bastards,' he murmured.

SEE CUBED SEE EM —C³CM – COUNTERMEASURES

DONGLIAO HE, JILIN

The Lieutenant-Colonel thrust his broad, greasy face up so close to Alexei Mazurov that he could smell the vodka and meat-paste on his breath.

'You're a useless bloody fuck, Mazurov,' he bellowed. 'Because of you a dozen good men are dead. Because you didn't follow orders. You're as much use as a prick on a steer. If this wasn't wartime and I needed every single person capable of getting in a tank, I'd have you court-martialled and out of the army like a dog by this time tomorrow. After the war, I'll deal with you. You'll have command of a latrine platoon in the Kazakh Desert. Now get in your tank and fight.'

'Colonel, I admit it went wrong. It would have gone worse if we had followed standard procedure, for then we would all have been killed.'

'If it had included you, that would have been acceptable to me.'

'Colonel,' Mazurov said desperately as the big man turned and scrunched away through the scrub. 'What I'm trying to tell you is that we did get *something* from the reconnaissance. I saw it with my own eyes.'

Tank engines were beginning to rumble, men were amove. The throat-catching smell of diesel and exhaust was on the air.

'So what was it, this special thing you saw? A new-model mobile Chinese shit-house?'

'That's it. *I didn't recognize it.*'

'Mazurov,' the man said contemptuously, 'I doubt if you know what your girlfriend's cunt is for. Just get in your tank and if possible, don't come back.'

419

*

It had been Igor Molchanov's idea, but Mazurov and Boris Chertok – commander of the BMP carrying the infantry – had agreed with him without demur.

When the three lieutenants and their vehicles were a few klicks from the regiment they had stopped to co-ordinate their plan. Molchanov was in command of the BRDM scout car and Mazurov's T-80M had been attached to the reconnaissance patrol to replace the regular crew, at that moment travelling back to the Motherland in plain wooden boxes. Mazurov had been selected partly because he was able to speak Mandarin as his chosen second language.

'Look,' said Molchanov, 'what I'm going to suggest would have had me facing a court-martial a year or two ago, but when Ogarkov took command he changed that. He expects junior officers to show initiative, so that the offensive maintains its speed. We all know the fucking colonels and major-generals can't accept the notion, but I certainly can. Apart from anything else it'll keep us from getting our asses shot off. Sure, I know we're cutting through the Chinese like hot piss through snow, but there's an awful lot of snow.'

He looked at Mazurov. 'Yesterday we conducted our reconnaissance in the manner laid down by the book – that is, grinding up to it and if it looked interesting, firing H.E. at it. Great. So we did. The bunch of trees duly went up like a bonfire. Nothing. So on we grind. Another likely target, another round of H.E. Nothing. So on we grind. And about twenty seconds later, Kruglov's T-80 which had been doing the shooting, goes up. A fucking swarm of enemy infantrymen firing RPG-7s. From about a hundred metres! They're like that, they like to get up really close and the little bastards are effective. They knocked two wheels off my BRDM, and I wouldn't be here at all if Boris's boys hadn't laid down suppressing fire and got me out. So I want to change it about. When I was on the front against NATO, we knew that the Brits

420

didn't do it like us, not recce by force. They do their reconnaissance by stealth; they creep about, looking, probing, but not being seen. That's how I want to do it.'

The three small tankers in their black coveralls and padded helmets were all young, tired, dirty and made older than they should have been by their experiences since the offensive began.

'I don't know about you,' Molchanov said to Mazurov, 'but I would like to win this war and go home. I'm going to fuck and stay drunk for a month. But I won't if the fucking colonels and major-generals keep fighting like we were rolling in to Berlin in 1945. So a little initiative down at the grass roots. Ogarkov would approve. Colonel Bessenov would have my balls for a neck-tie, which is why we aren't going to tell him how we got the information. Okay, Boris and I have practised this, we'll be the ones probing. You, Alexei, you provide overwatch. Boris and I will bound ahead up to 1,000 metres, but only under cover of your gun. The principal objective is this commune. Smack on the projected route of advance, an ideal defensive position if prepared. With this rock formation here, and the escarpment there, they could give us a bad time if they've got prepared defensive positions. Which is why I don't want to grind up and blaze away at it with just one tank and Boris's peashooters. We might get a hail of Red Arrow missiles and 130mm rockets coming back the other way, which would make my girlfriend back home very disappointed – and yours too. So we're going to tippy-toe up and take a peek. And if Boris and I don't like what we see we're going to come scurrying back. Alexei, so plenty of fire, please. Once we're out, you do the same. I know I don't have to remind you to have your gun at the enemy and hull towards direction of travel. If some of our own boys back there see some damned great tank rumbling towards them in a cloud of dust with its gun pointed at them, they're liable to fire a few AT-5s and BS-3 rounds down its throat and ask why Lieutenant Mazurov was behaving like a cunt afterwards, when they're scraping enough of

421

you off the inside of your turret to send home as ashes. Okay? Let's move out, then.'

If they'd lost their maps they'd have found the farm by following their noses, thought Alexei. The stench of rotting human ordure from the fields it was fertilizing hung in the air. Concealed at the edge of the apple orchard, he watched admiringly as Molchanov and Chertov guided their light vehicles, making the best use of the good cover, slipping from haystack to apricot orchard, following the line of the walls of yellow maize piled up to dry in the sun. No one was about; the farm appeared deserted, as well it might be with a Soviet tank army no more than 25km away. Behind him heat shimmered from the exhaust of the turbine. Khrenov sat relaxed in his driver's seat, hands on the levers, ready for work. Below him the gunner, Khan, leaned forward in his seat. Mazurov could see his periscope tracking. There was H.E. in the breech.

Molchanov's fast, wheeled BRDM darted down a lane covered by Chertov's 73mm cannon and the overwatch of the T-80 600 metres back in the orchard. He halted by the thick cover of a hedge. Mazurov saw him climb out of his turret to stand up on it to see over the foliage, peering down at the farm buildings two hundred metres away through his binoculars. He got down again, and Mazurov heard his voice on the net.

'This is Volga One. I can see a barn down there, in a big courtyard. Some soldiers. Some sort of machine in the barn. I can't really get a good look at it, and I'd like to. I'll get a better squint at it from that crossroads down there. Cover me, please.'

The BRDM crept quietly along the lane, followed by the BMP. Chertov halted where the hedge thinned slightly, the infantry fighting vehicle laden with branches and foliage like a florist's cart. The turret turned to cover the farm.

At the crossroads Molchanov halted again, and

climbed back up on to his turret-top to see.

There was a wink of fire from one of the buildings and something black came skimming over the soybeans.

The BRDM exploded into irregular fragments. A wheel bounded high in the air, its axle still attached. The turret flew off, skimming across the field like a frisbee. The explosion blew Molchanov into a tree, where he hung like an old suit of clothes.

The huge barrel of the T-80 twitched on to target. Smoke gushed from the building as Chertov opened up with his cannon.

'*Fire!*'

The immense explosion, the blast that sucked the air from you, and the building of the farm exploded into flame and debris – lath and plank flying high in the air, trailing smoke behind them as they tumbled.

The lane was erupting. The BMP dashed through earth, smoke and flying branches like a mole making for home.

Mazurov couldn't see where the shooting was from. Smoke was drifting across the farm.

'Fire at will,' he ordered. 'H.E. work the buildings.'

Another enormous crash. The cannon of Chertov's BMP was blazing away through the hedge as the vehicle dashed for safety. Khan fired again, and as the blast effects cleared, the BMP was crawling round and round like a cockroach that someone had stepped on, crushing its rear legs. The rear doors flew open and some soldiers tumbled out, firing. They fell to the ground and were still. Khan was working the buildings, and the shell flashes appeared in the grey and black of the smoke like brief, fiery red mouths, Cheshire-cat grins of death. They knew the T-80 was there now and tracer came sparkling towards them. Mazurov was firing the 12.7 DShK from the turret, and Khan was hosing with the co-axial machine gun while he traversed, picking his targets. The 125mm shell flashes merged with the green and red tracer like a great firework display.

The firing had stopped; there was just the oily

423

seaweed of smoke roiling in the air.

'Driver advance,' Mazurov ordered. 'There may be some of ours alive down there.'

The T-80 ground out of its hide, turbine howling as Khrenov gave it the power. He kept away from the farm road, which was probably mined, and carved straight through the green soybean field. With his head out of the turret Mazurov inhaled the true perfume of a tank – propellant and kerosene, oil and sweat, fresh earth and crushed foliage, death on the wind.

The BMP had been hit more than once. Whoever had knocked off one of its tracks had followed up with whatever had made those smoky holes in its side and blown poor Chertov up through his closed hatch as bloody spray.

Molchanov hung in the tree. He seemed untouched to Mazurov. Perhaps he had just climbed up and now, like an over-ambitious child, could not get down. Mazurov wished he could go and get a ladder for him. They would go home together and see their girlfriends, and drink some vodka.

'Down at the farm,' said Mazurov. 'We'd better find out what he was looking at.'

This close, the heat from the burning buildings scorched the face. They crackled – the dry lath, plaster and wood blazing merrily. Khrenov nosed the tank through the gap towards the courtyard.

There was something in the barn. The door hung half off; Mazurov squinted through the smoke and shimmering heat to see it. Half-shattered, exotic, strange. What the hell was it, what did it do?

'Dust coming, boss,' Khrenov said over the I/C.

Through the gap a dust-cloud was approaching. In the courtyard a wounded soldier flapped. From the burning farmhouse men were screaming. Mazurov jumped down and heaved the wounded man up on to the deck of the tank, scrambling up after him.

'Let's get out of here,' he said.

When they were clear he halted the tank and spoke to

the soldier lying below the turret. Blood leaked from him as though from a sieve, taking his life with it.

'The machine in the barn,' Mazurov said. 'What is it?'

The young man in his camouflage smock licked his lips, dry when the rest of him was wet, and Mazurov gave him a swallow of water from his canteen.

'The machine, what does it do?'

'Kills bastard Russians like you,' the boy whispered, and died.

SUKHOI SU-24C No. L286

Major Feliks Khokhlov began letting down over the Delaware Bay. Ahead, the lights of Washington painted the summer haze like a far-off fire.

'You should be able to capture the non-directional beacon soon,' said Thrale.

'It's sniffing it,' Khokhlov agreed. He pointed with a gloved finger at the twitching needle of a dial in front of Thrale, who sat next to him in the right-hand seat. 'There. It has it.'

'Okay. It'll bring you over the Potomac, and you can capture the strip visually. It's near where I live, out in the sticks. No one lives nearby. Ag. pilots use it, it's grass, but almost 3,000 feet long. You can manage?'

'K.K., a few days ago I landed this very aircraft in the middle of Beijing. And it is designed to be used from semi-prepared strips.'

Thrale looked out of the cockpit and behind him as Khokhlov began setting up the attack aircraft for the approach. Past the huge external fuel tank on its glove pylon the wing swung forward. The airframe shuddered as the landing gear forced its way out into the airflow, and the whine of the Lyulka turbojets rose as Kholkhov fed in power to compensate for the increased drag. Beneath them the Potomac glittered in the moonlight.

Thrale was leaning forward in his seat up against his harness, looking out over the long, pointed nose.

'You got it?' he asked.

'I have it,' said Kholkhov.

The Russian must have flown from the *Kiev* or one of her sister ships, thought Thrale. They flew dead over the

426

centre of the strip in a carrier-style approach, curling around in a long, 360-degree oval, losing altitude all the while, their target always in view. The strip was a pencil of whitened grass going through the dark of the corn. Kholkhov deployed his spoilers, dumping lift; it rushed up at them, the low-pressure tyres thumped into the hard, dry dirt and he performed an expert hand-jive from his seat, deploying the twin airbrakes, cutting the power, half-raising flap from its fully-lowered setting. Thrale felt the straps bite into his shoulders as the landing parachute snapped open and then they were rolling at walking pace. Kholkhov swung the aircraft around in the clear area at the end of the strip, where the pines began, and raised the canopy. When he cut the power, the scent of hot kerosene, dust and the tall green corn the long wings had cut on landing flooded over them.

'Welcome to America,' said Thrale.

XINZHOU, SHANXI

Otari knew that while descending through three thousand feet under his parachute in the deep darkness of the Shanxi countryside, laden with weaponry, he should not have thoughts of beauty on his mind. The surging pump of adrenalin had temporarily gone, turned off by his exit from the An-22. As he floated down under his UT-15 parachute he could not help marvelling at the beauty of the lights of the target below, gleaming like jewels in the soft darkness.

It was time to concentrate, to hit the centre of the landing area. There it was, just as Arby had said it would be – a dark area to the north-west of the buildings, but inside the perimeter.

Arby had briefed him, giving him the latest intelligence in Vladivostok.

'So who have we got?' Otari had said. 'I hear Chin Peng's the new Field Marshal. Are we to take him out?'

'Absolutely not. Chin Peng's an old Maoist, one of Chiang Shikai's cronies. Brilliant to the very top of his army boots. Probably worth three divisions to us just to keep him there, if not a whole army. No, your target is here, three miles south-west of Xinzhou.'

A map flashed up on the situation screen in the briefing room, and the target pulsated. Arby pulled in to give Otari a better indication.

'Now, look. There is a dark area here, to the north-west of the complex. About thirty yards by forty. You should be able to get your three groups in there, wouldn't you say?'

'We'll be bumping heads on landing but yes, we can

do it. All the lads have top badges for parachuting. Most are winners in the competitions at Zheltyye Vody. Yes, we can get in.'

'You'll drop from eleven thousand feet from the An-22. The Chinese radar will have been poked out by an Su-27 strike. No one'll know you're coming. You'll be seven miles away and glide to the target. Any problems?'

'No. Who or what are we to take apart?'

'Just one man. He will be here in this building, above ground.'

'Three groups for one man. Who is he?'

'We found Chiang Shikai,' Arby said triumphantly.

The lights weren't beautiful any more, the adrenalin had returned. The target area came up; it was a court-yard with walls and buildings on three sides. As he went in he could hear the rushing of air of the parachutes and the soft thudding of the jump-boots of those first to jump. He steered to avoid the man in front and flared his parachute, landing with as much effort as stepping off an escalator. The nylon fell in black folds; he shrugged out of the harness, wrapping it all up in a ball so that he and his soldiers did not get tangled up in the shroud-lines.

Then they were all there, all thirty-six of them, ready in their groups, AKSUs unslung, grenades, knives, mines and plastic to hand. Otari had the Barrett Light 50 hanging from one huge paw and readied the Desert Eagle in its holster.

The lights went on ... outside the fourth side of the courtyard, their exit. A young woman stood there – beautiful, black haired, sloe-eyed. She wore only a pair of scarlet panties.

She smiled entrancingly.

'Hallo, boys,' she said.

Otari hesitated. He could not help it. He should have shot her the second he saw her; he knew it, and it was too late.

THE WARDMAN TOWER

The lights of the Sheraton next door gleamed brightly. At
that time of night you could park. Thrale pulled out of
the traffic still flowing on Connecticut Avenue and slid in
by the kerb.

'You'd better stay here,' he said to Kholkhov. 'They see
two of us in Soviet flight suits, they'll probably call the
cops.'

'I'm enjoying the sights,' said the pilot honestly.

Thrale got out and walked over the sidewalk to the
entrance. He had on an old blue windcheater over his
flying overalls. He went in and over to the porter sitting
quietly, watching a small portable television by his reception desk.

'Mr Jones,' he said. 'To see Mr Kuusinen.'

The porter looked up at Thrale and then checked his
records. Fortunately, he seemed more interested in the
antics of the young woman on the screen than in looking
closely at the National Security Advisor's visitor.

'Uhuh. Mr. Jones. Got some keys here for you. Mr
Kuusinen said for you to go up at any time.'

To get me out of public view, thought Thrale approvingly. He took the keys and walked over to the lift. As
he waited for it to arrive, he glanced back. The young
woman seemed in imminent danger of losing much of
her clothing.

The doors sighed open and he took the lift up to the
sixth floor. The corridor was quiet, soft carpet on the
floor and a vase of flowers on a table by the tall door to
Kuusinen's suite. Thrale pressed the bell once; after he
had waited a while he took the keys and unlocked the
door, letting himself in. In the big room the drapes were

430

undrawn, and it was lit by the lights of Washington below.

'Lief?' Thrale called softly. 'Lief? It's K.K.'

The suite was quiet, just the soft breath of air moving in the air-conditioning conduits.

'Lief?'

There was a faint glow along the hallway that led off the room and Thrale padded quietly along towards it. A door was slightly ajar and light was coming around it. He knocked.

'Lief?'

He pushed the door open and poked his head inside. It was a bedroom; the covers were pushed back and a small pink side-light on a bedside table provided illumination.

'Lief?'

A light was on in the ensuite bathroom and Thrale went in.

Kuusinen's body lay crumpled on the carpeted floor. He was wearing striped red and white pyjamas. Some blood had congealed on his forehead, where he had struck the handbasin in his fall. His face, hands and feet were blue. He did not move, did not breathe. He was dead.

Thrale looked fearfully up at the ventilation duct and carefully backed out of the room, as one would from the presence of a dangerous beast. He stood in the hallway for a few moments, steadying himself and collecting his thoughts, then went out, locking the door behind him.

In the lobby the porter was engrossed, the girl on a bed surrounded by discarded articles of clothing. Thrale went by and on out to the Cadillac.

'Feliks,' he said, 'something bad has happened. I have been outthought, and instead of it being half-way through the evening it is five minutes to midnight. The coach will turn into a pumpkin and you and I, your country and my country will have lost the war. I have to get to President Barnet, and I must do it in the very near future.'

431

The pilot gestured at the Tower. 'Your man, the advisor to Barnet?'

'Has been murdered. By a machine. We are at war.'

Thrale sat in the Cadillac, thinking for a few moments. 'What were your instructions regarding me?'

'I was to help you in any way I could.'

'You like gardens, Feliks?'

The Russian looked at him curiously. 'Yes.'

'Let's go smell the roses, then.'

YU XIAN, HEBEI

The V-tailed single-seat aircraft were black, the pilots lined up in front of them dressed in white flight suits. The airfield above the great underground hangar was deserted, decorated only with the burned-out hulks of the squadron of J-6s which had lived there until the arrival of the Su-24s and their cluster-bombs on the first day of the war.

The aircraft were Komura *Toryus*, or Dragon-Killers, and they were unlike almost any other aircraft on earth. In shape they were like arrow-heads, sixty-five feet long and forty-three from one sharply-swept wingtip to the other. The entire airframe was bizarrely twisted and faceted, with all surfaces angled sharply from the vertical. It was completely coated in radar-absorbing material, RAM.

There was only one other aircraft in the world that the *Toryus* resembled, and that was the Lockheed F-117A stealthy strike fighter. The two were almost identical, the *Toryus* having been built from the F-117A's own plans.

The squadron pilots assembled in a group in front of their commander, Lieutenant-Colonel Nozaka. They all wore the sixteen-petalled Imperial chrysanthemum on the chests of their flight suits.

'Men of the 64th *Sentai*. Before the Great East Asian War our forefathers convinced the world that they were short-sighted, probably cowardly, had a poor sense of balance, could not see in the dark and did not possess mechanical aptitude of any kind. Any aircraft they were foolish enough to fly were second-rate and a threat to no one tougher than a child's kite.'

433

The tough, keen-eyed and athletic young warriors grinned happily to hear their forefathers described thus.

'When our forefathers decided to act they fell upon their enemies like a thunderbolt, scattering his forces, trampling him underfoot. They were *samurai*, and they flew the finest aircraft in the world.

'We are here again. The world sees us as pacific and war-fearing, addicted to work, fit only for producing yet more electronic toys for them to buy. They are, as their forefathers were, wrong. We are *samurai*, our time has come, we shall walk abroad and all in our path shall kneel and bow. *Hakko ichiu!*'

'*Hakko ichiu!*'

'Come,' growled Nozaka. 'Let us change the world.'

The forward edge of the battle area was approaching, and Nozaka led the wing of 110 aircraft down from 25,000 feet to their attack altitude of 3,000 feet. Although it was dark, he could see the vast formation of T-72s and their associate vehicles rumbling south ahead of him. His *Koryu* used two forward and downward-looking infra-red cameras. Both were covered by an electrically-resistant screen with a pitch much finer than radar wavelengths, which made the screen opaque to enemy radar, but transparent to infra-red. The glowing fires of the T-72s' turbines were clearly visible to Nozaka, and ten miles out he prepared to select his targets for laser designation.

Before he did so, he felt his testicles and was pleased to find them loose, the mark of a true *samurai* in combat. He selected his victims like a hawk taking a bird, paying no attention to any other than the ones he marked with the designator.

The wing released its bombs, four 1,000lb weapons per aircraft. Their accuracy was of the order of 1–2 feet, and since they were dropped from altitude they were able to penetrate the thinner top armour of the tanks.

The great tank army rumbled on, its anti-aircraft

defences silent. Flames blossomed across its front, too many to count. The wing turned, returning to base to rearm.

Nozaka felt his testicles as he flew away from the blood-red sky behind him. They hung loose and his breath hissed in his mask with approval. He was *samurai*.

DONGLIAO HE, JILIN

The radar scope in the ZSU-23-4 remained blank. The Rogachev Guards had four such self-propelled anti-aircraft gun systems. On the hull of a light tank was a turret containing four 23mm cannon, with a rate of fire of 1,000 rounds per minute. When guided by the radar scanner atop the turret, the fearsome hail of shell would knock down any aircraft unfortunate enough to come within range. It was probably the best conventional mobile anti-aircraft system in the world.

The radar scope remained blank. The People's Liberation Army Air Force had been swept from the skies.

It was the vehicle's commander, not the radar operator, who first realized there was something there. He had removed his headphones in order to scratch his ear, which had been irritatingly bitten by some sucking insect. He heard something over the squeak and rumble of the Guards on the move, something buzzing through the gathering dusk, not unlike a horde of the mosquitoes that had plagued his ear.

'Anything on radar?' he asked quickly on I/C.

'Nothing, sir.'

'Betka Seven,' he said on the net. 'There is some kind of buzzing from the air, about two o'clock.'

Mazurov was in the turret of his T-80, stationed on the left of the line of advance. Like all the other commanders, he squinted up into the gloom. Pulling one earphone from his head he could hear the high-pitched buzzing. As tanks on the right of the line began to erupt in flames, he seized the DShK anti-aircraft machine gun in front of him and began firing.

436

He saw one, hit it more by luck than judgement, and it came tumbling out of the air like a shot bird. A little aircraft, no more than six or seven feet across its wing-span. There was a swarm of them going like hell, every single one no more than thirty feet up, flying in zig-zag patterns, and they *knew*. They each selected an individual tank to kill, each a different one. The one Mazurov had swiped by luck had chosen him; it came tumbling towards him and smacked into the very glacis in front of him, becoming caught between the turret and gun-barrel.

Then they were gone, and the support vehicles were pushing through the wreck of the Rogachev Guards whose tanks were ablaze on a battlefield they had not realized existed.

There was a copse over to the left.

'Driver, left. Get among those trees,' Mazurov ordered. Being caught out in the open in the dark with things like that about was simply committing suicide. When Khrenov had shoved the battle tank well in the pines and larches, Mazurov ordered him to switch off the engine. The pilotless aircraft knew what tanks were; they had not attacked any of the soft-skinned vehicles. Grimly, Mazurov wondered if the murderous drones had relations coming for them. He guessed that somehow the drones could discriminate, perhaps through infra-red sensors that could detect the hot engines and exhausts of the tanks. Looking from his cover at the battlefield through his night-vision goggles, his guess seemed to be correct. The tanks were all ablaze from attack through their weakest parts – the turret hatches and engine covers. Tanks alone gave off millimetre-wave radiation; perhaps they could sense that as well.

He scrambled out of his turret and pulled the drone he had shot down from his tank. The airframe and three-bladed propeller were made from some kind of composite, rendering it invisible to radar. Its nose was round and clear, a lens; underneath it was its weapon, a kind of shell about twelve centimetres across. One of his machine-gun bullets had torn a chunk off the fuselage,

437

and inside he could see tiny microprocessors. The killing drone was operated by a small computer.

Khrenov and Khan had got out with him, and all stood round looking at the exotic and fearfully effective weapon.

'That thing in the barn yesterday ... it could have been some strange tractor, it looked as though it had six wheels. But it was a military vehicle, you could tell that. Nowhere for a crew. Maybe it's a robot too. Maybe it had a computer in it, and missiles, and knows what a tank is ...'

Mazurov looked across the burning battlefield. A few tanks were beginning to regroup.

'If there are other fucking devices like that out there they're going to find us, even sitting in this wood. Khrenov, go put the tank over there out in the open. We'll dig a hole here in the wood and stay in it.'

Khrenov and Khan looked doubtfully at him.

'Boss, in our army, you run away you get shot,' said Khrenov softly.

'You stupid bastard, for us the war is over!' Mazurov yelled. 'We've been lured out here into China to be massacred.'

Khrenov gestured to the T-80s regrouping, beginning to move forward. 'We must join them,' he said.

Mazurov grabbed a spade from the deck of the tank and marched off into the middle of the wood.

'I too serve the Soviet Union,' he called over his shoulder. 'But nowhere in the military oath does it say I must commit suicide to do so.'

He heard them mutter to each other, and knew that for them their officer had cracked up and was deserting in the middle of a battle. Then the great turbine spun into life. Khrenov yanked on the levers and in a spray of earth and breaking branches the tank lurched back out of the wood into the open, heading across the valley floor to the re-formed group.

A blaze of light streaked past the trees and slammed into the T-80. Fire blasted from every joint and orifice of the vehicle, making the darkness day for a moment, and the thunderclap of the warhead going off blew Mazurov off his feet. He wriggled as far as he could into some bushes. Something was out there. The regrouping tanks began to explode, lurid flashes of light through the smoke.

Something whined softly close by: a turbine. Wheels crunched softly. It stopped just outside the wood, looking down at the battlefield; Mazurov could see it in the glare of the burning vehicles. Six wheels almost as big as tractor tyres. A rotary missile launcher poking out of its top. As he watched, it dipped inside and emerged freshly charged from the magazine within. A thumping roar and a blaze of light as it fired its salvo. Burning, out on the field. Many sensors, infra-red, stereo television, microwave, millimetre-wave, laser. Night, dust, smoke, cloud, the very fog of war meant nothing to this thing, it saw everything.

Below its multitude of eyes it had teeth. A Gatling-style cannon and machine guns grinned alongside rocket pods. It knew what soft-skinned vehicles were, and men too.

It dipped into its magazine once more and readied itself. The turbine whined and it bounded forward, rushing into the smoke at sixty miles an hour, hungry for prey.

Mazurov seized his spade, and began digging a hole in which to hide.

The sun did not shine at dawn. A stratus of dirty smoke drifted overhead. Mazurov climbed out of his hole in the ground, weary beyond belief. The night had been made hideous by blinding blasts of light, and the shriek and roar of weaponry. Now it was quiet. Mazurov was tired and very, very thirsty. He began to walk across the charred ground towards the river. The hulks of the Rogachev Guards littered the valley floor, blackened and twisted. Nothing moved.

439

The clattering and whistling of a helicopter came down the valley. Sleek, it turned about him as it descended. It landed close by and a door opened in its side. A man in a white flying suit looked out at him and smiled encouragingly; an oriental. Japanese.

'Are you all right?' he called in passable Russian.

'I'm all right,' Mazurov agreed, continuing to walk.

'Where are you going?'

'To the river. I need a drink.'

'Come here, then. I have water cleaner than that. Here, look.'

He held up a canteen and Mazurov went over. He drank the sweet water gratefully.

'What are you? Tank man?'

'Yes. Tank commander.'

'Good. I need someone who was there. It's difficult to find anyone alive. We did too good a job.'

He laughed merrily and spoke in Japanese to the pilot. They lifted off and went whistling back up the valley.

'I'm Nozaka,' he explained. 'I command a wing of *Koryus*. Stealthy strike fighters, invisible to radar.'

'Did you do this?'

'No, we destroyed the regiments of the second front. Most of the work on this side was done by *Hiryus* – Flying Dragons, armed drones – and *Hayate* – Storm – automated fighting vehicles.'

'Yes,' Mazurov said flatly. 'I saw them.'

Nozaka pointed out details of the miles-long trail of carnage as they flew along.

'Look,' he said excitedly, like a guide showing a tourist the sights. 'MiG-29s. All over the place. You know how difficult it is to get a shell from an anti-aircraft gun in the same place as a speeding aircraft? Nearly impossible. Unless you use plasma guns. The plasma is fired in a jet that travels at hypersonic speed. So all you have to do is point the gun dead on the aircraft – no lead, no calculation – and pull the trigger. Works like knocking over ducks at a fairground.

'Ah, look at this.'

440

Mazurov peered down at a giant's shambles. Something had caught dismounted troops in the open. Pieces of men were scattered over the ground; brains smeared the grass, entrails hung in the bushes and trees.

'Multiple Launch Rocket System. One salvo puts 50,000 grenades into the target area from fifty miles out. More destructive than a tactical nuclear weapon,' Nozaka explained happily.

There was the second echelon down there. The vehicles seemed relatively unharmed; they were scattered about, halted where they had driven into obstacles in the terrain.

'Fuel air explosive. Propylene oxide aerosol. Five times as effective as TNT, weight for weight. Ignite it and it turns the lungs of the people below into pulp. The rocket has terminal guidance – accurate to a few yards from a hundred miles out. It's the technology,' said Nozaka. 'You might as well have been fighting with lances from horseback, for all the chance you had.'

The helicopter was descending, an airfield was in sight.

'Come with me,' Nozaka ordered. 'You were there; I want you to explain it to a man.'

DOUBS AIRSTRIP, MARYLAND

In the cockpit of the Sukhoi, Thrale gripped his M-16. It was a travelled gun, he thought; it had been all the way around the world and now it was back in the country of its origin. Beside him Kholkhov lit the afterburners and for a second the attack aircraft held, the airframe shuddering with power, on its brakes. The whole airstrip glowed with a pulsating light; glancing over his shoulder from the cockpit Thrale saw that the woods were on fire, the pines blazing like torches under the roaring blow-lamp of the Lyulka turbojets. Kholkhov came off the brakes and they accelerated hard, the power pressing them back in their seats. There was a thrumming as the wing-tips harvested the corn they had missed on landing; the scrub at the end of the strip was coming up at an alarming rate and Kholkhov rotated. They were in the cool, silky air of the night; he pulled in gear and flap, and came back on the power. The wings he left fully outspread as they came over the Potomac, heading down-river. Behind them the blazing airstrip set alight from end to end by the fire of the afterburners dimmed in the haze. Cruising very slowly at 180 knots, they flew into the great city ahead of them.

At 3,000 feet Kholkhov cut over the George Washington Parkway and lined up on the Theodore Roosevelt Memorial. Past the starboard wing-tip was the great bulk of the Pentagon. They went over the gap between the Watergate Complex and the John F. Kennedy Center.

'You're spot on,' said Thrale.

The street lights glittered white and orange beneath them. Cars moved down the streets like glow-worms.

Kholkhov's fingers performed a swift dance over the buttons beside him.

'Okay,' he said. 'It's on auto-pilot, it'll fly out over the Atlantic until it runs out of fuel.'

Ahead they could see the vast bulk of the Executive Office Building.

'In the Soviet armed forces we have to pay for equipment we damage through our own fault,' Kholkhov said dryly. 'I shall be in the Air Force a long time.'

The leading edge of the wing overlapped the EOB below.

'Get ready.'

The Office Building vanished under the wing and Thrale closed his eyes.

The blast of the explosives as they blew off the canopy, the roar of the rockets as they rammed the seat under him and the shocking slam of the 200mph airstream blended into one assault of violence.

Then the pressure under him died away. At 4,000 feet the city was spread out below him. He stepped off the ejection seat as it reached the top of its curve and fell towards the White House below.

The black parachute opened with a snap. There was no wind, and he steered himself around in a circle as he descended, keeping his target in sight. He noted that just as the Russian pilot had advised him, the modern military parachutes were eminently controllable.

The mansion shone like ivory below. Splashes of light illuminated the grounds. Thrale steered himself carefully, keeping the pool of darkness in view.

The ground came up very fast, he had forgotten that, and he landed with a thump. The parachute fell in folds over the flower-bed. The air was filled with the sweet scent of roses.

There was a thud a few yards away and a muffled curse. Then Kholkhov came scurrying over in the darkness and both men looked up at the magnificent architecture in front of them. They were in the Rose Garden.

They crept up through the long south flower-bed,

443

treading quietly through the anemones, irises and del-
phiniums, hugging the dark boxwood hedge. A corner
where a crab-apple tree hung over the osmanthus
furnished them with cover close by the white-pillared
colonnade which covered the terrace outside the Oval
Office.

As they watched, a door opened from the west terrace
pavilion and a man stepped out. He came forward,
peering at the sky. He was in his thirties, wearing shirtsleeves. A guard, perhaps.

Kholkhov was of medium height, but with the broad
shoulders and big chest that in Russian men collapsed
into their bellies when they grew older. Built like a rugby
player, he covered the short distance in a few violent
strides and slammed into the guard, winding him as he
smacked into the ground. When he recovered his breath
he found himself staring into the barrel of a Makarov PM
automatic pistol.

'You be real quiet,' Thrale advised, showing him his
own M-16 slung around his neck. Kholkhov trussed the
man's hands behind his back and they went into the
White House. Thrale opened the first door he came to
and found himself in a beautiful, spacious room with
elegantly-curving walls. It was the Oval Office.

They went in and he closed the door.

'We ain't here to kill anyone,' he assured the guard.
'My name is Thrale. I work for Lief Kuusinen, and I need
to talk to the President.'

He turned to Kholkhov. 'Let him have a hand. Okay,
go sit in that chair and get someone on the horn who
can talk to the President.'

'That's the President's chair,' the man said, outraged.

'He won't mind, son,' Thrale assured him. 'Worse
things are going to happen today, I assure you.'

The guard went over the huge pale gold rug with its
turquoise rosettes and sat down in Barnet's dark green
leather chair. He picked up the phone with his free hand
– Kholkhov standing right behind him with his pistol –
and tapped a three-figure number.

444

'Mr Davis, this is Hank. I am in the Oval Office in the company of two intruders. One describes himself as a Mr Thrale, and says he works for Mr Kuusinen. He wants to talk to the President.'

'Let me talk to him,' said Thrale. He took the phone.

'Mr Davis, this is K.K. Thrale. I need to see President Barnet with the utmost urgency on a matter involving, to the highest degree, the national safety. Get a technician and have him check the ventilation conduit in the President's bathroom. *Whatever you do, keep the President away.* The man will find in there something looking like a toy tank. *It is an assassination weapon.* Once again, *do not let the President see it.* It is designed to recognize, and kill him. When you've done it, get back to me.'

Thrale put down the phone and they waited. The door was pushed open and a secret-serviceman poked his head around. He had a black Uzi automatic pistol in his hand and his forefinger was laid flat above the trigger, indicating that it was cocked and ready to fire. From his position by the Presidential flag, with his back to the gold drapes, Thrale pointed his rifle at him.

'We ain't here to kill anyone,' he said, 'but you stand outside all the same.'

It seemed a very long time that they waited. Thrale ached from the violence of the ejector seat, from the impact of landing. He shifted wearily from one foot to another and rubbed his back with his free hand.

'Are you all right?' Kholkhov asked.

'I'm just too old for this shit. Chuck Imamura said that, and he was right.'

Then the phone rang on the carved oak desk, and Thrale answered it.

'This is the President. You'd better come and tell me what is happening.'

445

FAR EAST MD HQ,
VLADIVOSTOK

It was an orchestration of violence, a pure symphony of warfare. The paralysis of the enemy's C^3 – command, control and communications – by the Soviet C^3CM counter-measures was almost total. The top PRC commanders – Zhao Teh, Chiang Shikai and the rest – were dead. The communications centres were in ruins. The last Chinese army was attacked from three sides at once.

The co-ordination of the Soviet combined-arms forces was almost flawless. Once again, the weight of blow brought to bear upon the enemy across his front could not be opposed. Already deaf and blind through the success of the Soviet C^3CM, the Chinese commanders in the field knew not where or when the next strike would come until the first T-72 rumbled through the wall of their makeshift headquarters. That tank was followed by a thousand others, by helicopters and attack aircraft, by fighters and bombers, by artillery from 22mm to 155mm, by vehicles with guns on, by vehicles with rockets on, by troops in armoured fighting vehicles, armoured personnel carriers or on foot.

'Textbook,' said Ogarkov with understandable pride. 'The encirclement and destruction of the enemy. In the Great Patriotic War we destroyed twenty-eight Hitlerite divisions at Belorussia and twenty-one at Yassy-Kishinev. We advanced five hundred miles and destroyed another ninety-six, and captured thirty-four. Even they do not compare with this. Our schools of military science will

446

have much to chew on now, when considering our *voy-ennoye stroitel'stvo*, our military development.'

'They will name a Military Academy after you, like the Frunze,' Yanov said flatteringly, and laughed within, for the compliment had a darker and hidden meaning. More than Trotsky, the brilliant M.V. Frunze had been respons-ible for the Red Army itself. He met the fate of most brilliant men of the time – murdered by Stalin by means of a medical operation he did not want nor need. Now there was a thought, Yanov mused. Perhaps better than the KGB: a *dead* hero was acceptable.

The command room was quite quiet. There was little to do except allow the men in the field to finish their tasks.

'Military power in the PRC is now broken,' said Ogarkov. 'It is now a question of imposing our adminis-tration upon the country and deciding how best to exploit it.'

'That,' said Yanov, 'will be a pleasure.'

'General,' came a voice from the console. It was Red Banner.

'Yes, Arby.'

'There is someone to see you above.'

'Who?'

'Chiang Shikai.'

447

THE SITUATION ROOM,
THE WHITE HOUSE

The situation room was staffed, the intelligence officers at their consoles, the situation boards lit, the mainframe up and running, the data banks on line, but something was wrong. Thrale knew what it was the moment he came in. Of those who mattered, only the President was there; his great commanders, 'the big bosses' were missing.

Barnet was in his shirtsleeves and unshaven. His guards were keeping him out in the open until they were sure there were no more cybernetic assassins within the building.

'Cindy, you got Ed yet?' he called. A worried young woman was tapping out a new number on her phone.

'I'm still trying, Mr President,' she assured him.

Barnet saw Thrale coming with the secret-servicemen.

'It's not every day the CIA parachutes in from a Soviet jet fighter to save me from assassination,' he said. 'I think Ed Reisch had better be here to listen to what you have to say.'

'Ed Reisch is dead, Mr President.'

'How the hell do you know that?' said Barnet, startled. 'What makes you say that?'

'Lief Kuusinen is dead, murdered by a machine identical to the one which was programmed to kill you, on a certain date. Today. That was my mistake. I thought it would be August the sixth. Have the police go around to all the members of the National Command Authority that cannot be contacted.'

'Cindy, procedure for summoning the NCA, please.' Barnet snapped. 'Who else will be dead, Mr Thrale, as well as Ed Reisch and Lief Kuusinen?'

'All. Or as close to all as they can get. You'll be familiar with the Decapitation Doctrine, sir. This is it.'

'Decapitation? Damn it, man, that's a nuclear-war fighting scenario. Out of the political-military simulations, the war games.'

'This is nuclear war, Mr President. My mistake was thinking it would be August the sixth.'

'Why August the sixth? Who is attacking us? There is no declaration of war.'

'Our enemy makes a habit of not declaring war. That's why I should have realized it wouldn't be August the sixth. It's in the *Hagakure*: "The phrase 'Win First, fight later' can be summed up in the two words 'Win beforehand.'" On August the sixth 1945 we dropped an atomic bomb on Hiroshima. But just in case someone like me remembered his history they brought the date forward. The war we are fighting is to last a hundred years, they said so. We are being attacked by Japan.'

There was a sudden commotion from the nearby console, where Barnet's telephonist was speaking.

'Someone will come, Mrs Thompson,' she said, her voice high with horror. 'Someone will come.'

She turned to look up at Barnet. 'I called General Thompson, and woke his wife. She found the general dead, sir.'

'Thompson's on the JCS,' Thrale observed.

An expression close to panic flitted across Barnet's face. 'How am I to take charge without my people?'

'Mr President, you were not supposed to,' Thrale said gently. 'You should by now have been dead yourself. The man they wanted here to be in charge is Marshall Telford.'

'The vice-president?'

'Telford they knew they could roll, once they fired the first missile. Telford is an honourable man; he would rather accept the terms of defeat than embark on any

449

kind of nuclear war.'

'*Missile*? What missile? The Japanese don't have any ICBMs.'

'If I am right, they have control of some. Ours.'

Barnet looked at Thrale for a long time.

'All right,' he said finally. 'Whip it on me.'

'This is the hundred years' war Komura always believed in. The countdown to where we are today began when a cybernetic assassination machine murdered your predecessor, President Hawkins, in his bathroom – just as Lief Kuusinen was murdered this morning, and just as you were supposed to be.'

'Why was Hawkins murdered?'

'So that you would become President in his place. And being a potential loser in the next election, would seize gladly upon an election-winning platform when it was offered to you: putting Japan in the crusher.'

'And what was the reasoning behind that?'

'A modern war has to be conducted in four dimensions – the operational, the logistical, the social and the technological. Any strategy that does not take account of them all will fail. You provided Komura with what he needed to ensure the social factor would be in his favour. Japan does not have a free press any more than it has libertarian justice or democracy. The people have been whipped up into fervour as a result of your actions, which to many here seem only reasonable. To the Japanese, the Americans are once again what they were during the Pacific War – devils and evil demons. The Japanese people have been made to believe in consensus; over a long period of time they have been made to feel happier with communal thought and communal action rather than individualism. They are, as we speak, in perfect mood to hear that the glorious forces of the Yamato race have not only aided China in her victory over the Soviet Union but have, in one magnificent blow – as at Port Arthur or Pearl Harbor – laid waste to the USA. Only this time, brought about her defeat as well.'

450

'You said that they might have control of *our* ICBMs?'

'If I am right, some or all the missiles contain micro-circuitry of Japanese origin. Contained within the circuitry, hidden in some dark and tiny electronic corner will be a virus, a "Logic Bomb". It knows what day it is, it has been waiting for it to arrive. When the time comes it will take command of the missile. When the missile is activated it will fire it to whatever target it has been told to fire it at. Here. In the USA. It means that our nuclear deterrent cannot be used.'

On the far side of the room an intelligence Lieutenant-Colonel was working, collating reports as they came in, looking at SIGINT from the National Security Agency and real-time surveillance from the KH-11s orbiting over China. He came over to them.

'Mr President, I think you should know that the Soviets appear to have suffered a massive defeat in the battle of the four armies north of Beijing. It makes Kursk look like toy soldiers in a sand-pit.'

'Thanks, Colonel. We have to let the Soviets get on with their own affairs for a while; we have our own to think about.'

'The 50 MX missiles,' said Thrale. 'In Montana. Get some fighters airborne and armed. Contact the commander of the base and instruct him to disarm the missiles, to remove them from their power sources.'

'Mr President, we're getting reports in now from the police,' said Cindy Hutchings, from the telephone. 'All the members of the NCA found so far have been murdered: some in their beds, some dead as if from natural causes. But all dead.'

'Is Ed Reisch dead?'

'Yes, sir,' the girl whispered. 'His throat was cut; he was in bed. The policeman said he seemed ... surprised. That's what he said.'

'*Mr President*,' an Air Force Major called urgently. 'We can't get through to Malmstrom Air Force Base in Montana. Not on the radio, not on the phone. *The lines are dead.*'

451

FAR EAST MD HQ,
VLADIVOSTOK

They sat in the garden where Feliks Dzerzhinskiy's men had had Leonid Bruyevich and his family shot before taking over their villa. Two old men, with their staff standing behind them. Between them stood a young man in a tanker's uniform.

Ogarkov recognized Chiang Shikai but not the old Japanese man next to him. Yanov did, as he knew all those who, like himself, wielded real power. He knew who Komura was, and suspected he knew why he was there. He knew that *Zarnitsa* had gone disastrously wrong, but not how. Why, he suspected, was easy.

'Who are you, boy?' he asked the young Russian officer.

'Lieutenant Alexei Mazurov, Rogachev Guards.'

'Should you not be with the Guards?' he asked softly.

'The Guards are all dead,' said Mazurov. 'They have brought me here to tell you what I have seen, that the war is over because we have lost.'

'Lost?' Ogarkov exploded. '*We won.* What the hell have we been doing down there, except winning a war?'

'You have been playing war games with a computer while your real armies were being massacred.'

Komura spoke for the first time. He spoke in Japanese and his voice emerged from a box in Russian. His voice was dry, like the rustling of leaves in autumn.

'When you stole the computer *Coral Spear*, which you call Red Banner, you stole the seeds of your own destruction. Red Banner has never been red; it has

452

always been under the control of its original programmes, which you never found.'

Yanov was searching the ranks of those behind the two leaders. Hua Bai was there, yes. And another figure from the past on the Japanese side, the general Yonai. Where was he? Yes, there he was, it was so.

'But this started before then, did it not?' he said. 'It began with the plan for *Zarnitsa* itself. Do I not see the author of that plan before me?'

Aleksandr Borodin stepped out from the crowd. He was not in Chinese dress; he wore a *yarmulka* on his head.

'I am here,' Borodin agreed, 'and you are there, where I have long wanted you – you and your kind.'

'And what have I done to you, apart from raise you to high rank and privilege?'

'You and your kind hate me and my kind. I am a Jew, Mr Yanov. Your predecessor Josef Stalin had us taken away into the freezing wastes of Siberia. They managed to leave a little girl behind, adopted by a sympathetic Russian. It is true, there is always an exception to prove the rule. That little girl was my mother. All her people died. She died, in the end, from a broken heart. Before she did so she made me promise that for her, her people and for all Jews, I would make you repay.'

'It is true,' Yanov agreed. 'We should have killed you all.'

'It is your turn now,' said Borodin.

'No, it is not,' said Yanov. 'We retain our nuclear weapons. We will obliterate China and Japan from the face of the earth.'

'Will you?' said Komura. 'Will you really?'

453

ROUTE 665, OHIO

The long eighteen-wheeler tractor trailer came grumbling through Wrightsville out of Columbus. It was followed by a Ford sedan. Both vehicles were scrupulously obeying the speed limit, their lights casting white pools before them. The signs came up for the Madison Lake State Park and they turned off by Deer Creek.

The park was inhabited only by wildlife in the hour when the sky began to lighten with the coming dawn. Hidden by the wood, the driver of the tractor-trailer halted on the road. Three assistants jumped from the Ford; all were young, fit, well-trained.

The trailer was so constructed that the sides fell away and the roof rolled back. The driver skilfully operated the controls behind the cab and the hydraulic ram slowly raised the cargo into position.

Satisfied, the four men climbed back into the Ford and drove back out of the park. On the deserted road which led to London, Ohio, they halted and the driver got out, standing by his door. He had a radio transmitter in his hand. He pointed it back at the park and pressed the command.

The park erupted with fire. A torch of flame rose up, accelerating in the sky, heading west.

The car drove on. The four Japanese pounded each others' shoulders, exultant.

Wright-Patterson AFB, home of the 100 B-1B bombers permitted under the Peace Treaty, lay forty miles to the west.

SAND SPRINGS TRAINING
RANGE, MONTANA

Major Frank Collins loved the dawn. The air was like silk, and the old F-4 Phantom flew like it was new. The weekend warriors of the National Air Guard got precious little flying time now that the threat from the Reds had gone away, and he treasured what he had. Dawn was a wonderful time to swoop down from the sky and legally bust all FAA minimum altitudes as you streaked in over the scrub and rock of the firing range.

At 450 knots and fifty feet, his gunsight glowed. His nomex-covered forefinger began to squeeze on the trigger, then his headphones came alive.

'White Two, break off your attack.'

Collins grunted in annoyance but came smoothly back on the stick, and the big fighter-bomber arced up into the sky, trailing the black smoke that was its trade-mark.

'White Two, proceed to Malmstrom Air Force Base. When you arrive, orbit overhead at five thousand feet, three hundred knots. Proceed at maximum speed.'

'Roger,' said Collins. 'What do I do when I get there?'

His controller told him.

Collins blasted through the cold air at five thousand feet AGL, heading west. In civilian life he was an attorney and had a flourishing practice in Billings. The land below was not heavily populated, but he knew that it would not be long before he would be receiving very nasty letters demanding compensation from the owners of those houses beneath his flight path, the windows of which he was breaking at an astonishing rate with his supersonic boom.

Mind, that was nothing to what he might have to do when he got to his destination. Anxiously, he thumbed his comm. button.

'This is White Two. Say, you sure about this?'

'Affirmative. From the President himself. And listen. The booster on that thing burns for no more than three minutes. By which time it ain't even in the atmosphere. You don't have three minutes, you got seconds.'

Collins' gunsight was still on and he left it that way.

THE SITUATION ROOM, THE WHITE HOUSE

The room was slowly acquiring a population. Single-handed, Barnet was putting together a new national command authority.

'The bastards have taken out the best,' he said to Thrale. 'Sure I can bring in General Tweed to replace Thompson, but the sorry son of a bitch was promoted to the level of his maximum incompetence anyway, which is why he's out in charge of the used tank park in Arkansas in the first place. I need *talent*, damn it.'

'I know of a guy doing a tour in the Pentagon, sir,' murmured Carole Smith. A dedicated young career woman, she stood in the dress in which she had arrived, which was a black strapless and backless four-ounces-worth of slinky material. In her rise – which she had mapped out from staffing for Barnet through Congresswoman, Senator and Vice-President, with the top office up for grabs eight years after – there was little time for anything extraneous. However, twice a month she co-ordinated filofaxes with another similarly-driven creature; they met up at R.T.'s in Arlington, drank Chardonnay and ate lobster, drank Margaux and ate prime rib and French fries, went back to her apartment, drank Cognac and ate each other. For some reason she could not explain, they had gone back to her partner's place, and in so doing saved and changed both their lives. Standing in a party dress and smelling faintly of thirty-year-old V.S.O.P., she was Barnet's new chief of staff.

'I know a guy in the Pentagon. Brigadier Walt Jones.

Real burner. Black. Combat hero in Vietnam, doctorate from the National Defense University. Sharp guy.'

'Get to him, advise him of his promotion and get his ass over here.'

'*Mr President.* A report from King's Bay. The *Ohio* and the *New Mexico* have been sunk at their quays. Apparently there were a number of heavy explosions underwater, and they went down within a minute.'

The urgent voice of the naval officer was cut across by that of a neighbouring Air Force Major.

'Rocket attack on Wright-Patterson,' he said in disbelief, the phone jammed in his ear. 'Several short-range rockets ... massive destruction ...'

A brilliant light pulsated from the vast global situation screen that covered the whole of one wall. It shone from within the USSR, from Novosibirsk, and began to crawl up the screen.

The whole room was silent.

'Oh, fuck,' Carole Smith whispered sincerely. 'The silly bastards have gone ballistic.'

Alone in the room, Thrale switched his attention to the representation of the USA on the screen. To Malmstrom AFB.

MALMSTROM AFB

The dead lay everywhere. Those first to die lay in their life's blood in their beds; those wakened by the noise in their pyjamas and nightshirts, in corridors and wash-rooms, outside, out on the ground. Now the base was the property of the paratroopers who had taken it. They were exultant, dug in around the missile silos. It was as they had been told: the USA did not employ a single soldier, sailor or airman solely dedicated to the security mission of protecting their vital facilities. Those that lay about the base had been fully trained and expert in their tasks. The paratroopers were fully trained and expert at theirs.

The silo doors were open. Wisps of steam escaped into the cool morning air. A dragon bellowed and the hot blast of his breath roared through the great tunnels, spuming up, tainting the sky. The white snout of the missile emerged above ground and it rode up on a pillar of fire, tall and gleaming, and bearing the flag of the United States. Unheard, drowned by the thunder of its passing, the soldiers yelled with delight from the fighting holes they had dug.

Something small and dark came streaking from the horizon. Lost too was the canvas-ripping of its Gatling gun. The great rocket shuddered, and the beauty of its curving path was marred. Small tongues of flame pocked its sides, then it exploded in a vast, misshapen ball of fire hurtling up in the sky.

The Phantom pulled frantically away, but a giant's finger of flame reached out to anoint it as it went by, and

459

a moment later it was simply one more blazing fragment falling to earth.

The soldiers were silent then.

A little later, as the technicians were working to get the next MX ready for firing, dark shapes streaked over the perimeter and what they dropped turned the whole complex into a furnace. After them came tanks, and troops, and those of the soldiers who were left alive began to fight to the last man.

THE SITUATION ROOM, THE WHITE HOUSE

The brilliant light that pulsated from Great Falls, Montana, from Malmstrom AFB snapped out, and everyone in the great underground room gasped with relief as one. Then they turned their gaze to the light climbing from Novosibirsk.

'It's on a short trajectory,' said the Air Force Major Thomas at his console. His fingers tapped the keys, extrapolating from the evidence he had. 'Looks like Leningrad.'

The line began to curve down on the screen.

'The F-111s have taken out the silos at Malmstrom,' said Thomas.

The line stabbed into Leningrad. A few moments later the connection from Fort Belvoir confirmed that sixty thousand miles out in space, the Vela Hotel satellites had witnessed the double flash of a nuclear explosion.

'Oh, Jesus,' whispered Carole Smith. 'Those poor bastards ...'

The President's phone rang and she picked it up, still staring at the screen as though the evidence that a great city and its people had died might go away.

'Oh, Jesus ... what ... who? Here?'

She put her hand over the mouthpiece of the phone and turned disbelievingly to Barnet, sitting in his commander-in-chief's chair.

'It's the Japanese ambassador,' she said, 'to see President Telford.'

461

*

Barnet knew Nakamura, the Japanese ambassador, but for a moment as he came from the lift serving the great underground command room he did not recognize him. He came across with his two aides, and he did not walk but swaggered with a conqueror's roll. The aides were at his shoulders; they pushed their way through the people gathered with the disregard of aristocrats moving among slaves.

Nakamura came to the presidential post, raised up in the corner of the room, where the commander could see all. He was swelled, but the confidence of his smirk vanished slightly as he saw who was occupying it.

'You?' he said. 'Why are you not dead? Well, no matter.'

'What do you want?' Barnet said coldly.

Nakamura raised his eyebrows in simulated surprise.

'Want? Surely that is obvious. I am here to dictate the terms of your surrender to you.'

'And what if we have no plans to surrender?'

'No plans? Mr Barnet, our patience is not endless. New York we have obliterated from the surface of the earth, as once you obliterated Hiroshima and Nagasaki. We have been generous in the amount of revenge we have extracted. It is clear now that the Yamato race is number one in the whole world. You will hand over all authority over your affairs to us. Be slow, and there will be more New Yorks. For New York we used a single warhead from one MX missile. The next time we will allow each and every warhead of the missile to seek out its target. Atlanta will burn again, Chicago become but ash blowing into the lake. We will lay a rain of death upon your people – and you will still be slaves at the end. No, you surrender now.'

Barnet spoke in a voice like ice. 'In New York the people live. They are eating bagels and drinking coffee, men are kissing their wives and mothers are getting their children ready for school. We have no plans to become

462

slaves, nor to enslave others.'

The phone rang and Carole Smith answered it. She handed it to Nakamura.

'It's for you,' she said, and the malice in her voice boded ill.

Nakamura held the phone to his ear and, as he listened, the air went out of him. His face lost its colour and broke out in a slick sheen of sweat. He looked up at Barnet.

'There has been a mistake,' he whispered. He bowed low and, uncomprehending but suddenly fearful, his aides bowed as well – deeply, suddenly obsequious.

'You miserable son of a bitch!' Barnet whispered. His foot lashed out and Nakamura hurtled back with blood spouting from his face. With a sudden roar, the people of the room fell upon the three Japanese, with fists, boots, pens and pencils – hitting, stomping, stabbing.

No one felt any remorse. When it was done they moved back to their stations, wiping the blood and gore from themselves. Thomas cleaned his hands with his handkerchief, Carole Smith pulled the heel of her shoe out of Nakamura's head and, putting it back on, went back to her place, leaving small spots of blood behind her.

'Get that mess out of here,' ordered Barnet, and they took the meat away.

Thrale spoke from the chair in the command post from which he had not moved. He ached with fatigue, his back hurt from the impact of the ejector seat and from hitting the ground under his parachute, his brain recoiled from the violence of events. But there was much more to be done.

'Mr President,' he said clearly. 'We have not won, nor yet signed any peace treaty. It is not even stalemate. *The Japanese can still win.* The B-1 bombers they have destroyed. The MX missiles we have ourselves destroyed before they could be used against us. Of our ten ballistic missile submarines, five have been sunk at King's Bay and in Washington. Five are still at sea. Their missiles we

463

dare not even deploy for fear that they too are infected with a Logic Bomb in their circuitry which will make them a sword for our enemies. We have to assume that the defeat of the Soviet forces in China and the destruction of Leningrad mean that the Chinese and Japanese are jointly about to come into possession of the Soviet nuclear deterrent. Once they are, they can threaten us again and demand out surrender, for we will have nothing to counter that threat with – not until we can bring home our SSBNs and replace their circuitry with new, of our own manufacture.'

'So what do we do?' Barnet asked quietly.

Thrale pushed himself out of his seat and stood stiffly upright. His body felt as though it was on fire.

'You – you must stay here, where you can be kept safe. You are still king on the chessboard. If you will, let me do what has to be done. As the late Mr MacGregor would have said, I do have the advantage that I understand the little yellow bastards.'

'All right,' said Barnet. 'Everyone else round here has got unexpected promotion from these dreadful events. You are the Secretary of State, for as long as this war lasts. Now, what do you need?'

'Just the keys to a museum,' said Thrale.

TUCSON, ARIZONA

Mike Schrantz got out of the car that had brought him and stood for a moment to watch when he saw what the armourers were loading from their bomb trolleys up into the eight-round rotary dispenser of the weapon bay behind the cockpit. Then he went over and climbed up through the entry hatch in the rear nose-gear door.

The cabin was big, he was tall and rangy for a pilot, and he had always liked that about the aircraft: the faint whine of the APU could be heard and the circulating air was pleasantly cool after the heat of the desert outside. A man was sitting in the left-hand seat with a thick manual on his lap, and he looked up as Schrantz climbed in.

'Hi, it's Mike, isn't it? I remember seeing you about a bit at the Combined Test Force.'

'Good to see you again, Curtis.'

They shook hands and Schrantz settled himself into the right-hand seat.

'So where did they find you?' Curtis Hope asked amiably.

'On the beach. Still got sand between my toes. You?'

'Got my in-laws coming over for a barbecue. My wife thinks I've done this deliberately.'

Schrantz raised a chuckle. 'How much of the bird works?' he asked grimly.

'The Nav/Com radios were pretty well cooked, so I had the avionics technicians simply put in new boxes. They took all the ECM out, you know, and the Hughes covert strike radar.'

'Well, hell, Curtis, I never was trained to use that stuff

465

anyway, were you?'

'Touched on it. When we were running the integrated flight test sequences, I was on the team evaluating the human engineering and workload aspects of using a two-man team. You remember, SAC were determined it should be a two-pilot airplane, but there were a lot of people who didn't think two could handle the workload in combat. I always figured they'd need a dedicated navigator/WSO myself.'

'What did you do after the programme was shut down?'

'I'm with Boeing. There seemed more future in civil aviation than military after the treaty with the Soviets. You?'

'Still with Northrop. I'm chief of the inflight-refuelling team.'

'Well, at least we know we can take it off, refuel in flight and find our destination.'

Taking their thick flight manuals, the two pilots began to work through the pre-flight check lists. When they were ready to start the engines, Schrantz paused for a moment.

'You ever drop a bomb from this thing, Curtis?'

'Wasn't my department, Mike. You?'

'Uhuh.'

They stared at each other for a few moments.

'Blake was in charge of that section, not that they did much before the programme was cancelled. He died in an auto wreck, you know.'

'Cheer up. It'll be in the manual. Everything's in the manual.'

'Yeah. Okay, now. Master Switch position Two. On.'

'Master Switch position Two. On.'

The fabulous bomber was 172 feet from one wing-tip to the other, and they had knocked down the gates which had been rebuilt after they had got it in, in order that it might taxi out again.

466

Hope put the power to the F118-GE-100 engines and it rolled smoothly forward over the caliche of the desert floor, accompanied and surrounded by its flotilla of safety vehicles. They had had to rearrange some of the other exhibits to get the bomber out, and the B-17 stood pushed up against the Lockheed F-101; its wing was fitted in the gap between the Douglas C-117's nacelle and the empennage of the B-29. It would take the attendants a while to sort it out, once the B-2 had gone.

The Northrop B-2 Advanced Technology Bomber rolled out of the Pima Air Museum through the demolished gates and rolled due South on Wilmot, all the way to Exit 269 of Interstate 10.

The interstate was empty, the tailbacks at exits 268 and 270 went for miles. The B-2 had the great road, smooth and wide as a runway, all to itself. Charcoal-grey and black, the great flying wing began to roll, the heat of its exhaust gases making the air shimmer. Four thousand feet into its take-off run, Hope raised the nosewheel and a moment later the big aircraft was in the air, its unique saw-toothed bat shadow running over the ground beneath it.

It climbed steadily and was soon lost from view, leaving only a faint smoke trail dispersing on the breeze.

VLADIVOSTOK AIRPORT

When Thrale got out of the F-111, Fusako was waiting for him.

'You do it?' he murmured, standing close on the ramp. A Honda limousine stood not far away, waiting for him.

'Just one,' she said. 'Then we got our orders to surface. We were in the Baltic; there was a ship waiting. We climbed out at one side and the prize crew got in the other.'

'Okay. Your father, the Trade Minister, here?'

'All those surrounding Komura are here. Those who matter, for the war, are waiting with him up at the old command post. Those not included are at the hotel on the waterfront that they have requisitioned. My father is there.'

'Go get him, will you? You both meet me here. Over there, by the red and white airplane, the Russian trainer.'

'I will.' She embraced him briefly. 'Good luck.'

'Oh, we got one missile and one bomber,' he said. 'How can we lose?'

Then he went over to the Honda and the driver took him up to the villa that had been built by Leonid Bruyevich, where Komura Tadaji and Chiang Shikai were waiting for him. The two old warlords sat separately in chairs which had been placed in the lower garden, where Ogarkov's staff officers had once walked. Their staffs stood in groups behind them.

The garden was stocked with flowers and shrubs and enjoyed a beautiful view over the sea. Komura sat – ancient, chill and calculating – and stared coldly at Thrale as he came across the grass.

468

'Why are you here? We were told to expect the Secretary of State.'

'Here I am. The President chose me as the man for the job. And so I'm here. Just me. Though my diplomatic powers are limited. I am more of a soldier; I have been fighting my country's cause in one way or another for about half a century.'

'And why are you here, Mr soldier-secretary?' Komura sneered.

'To stop the war.'

'You have come to surrender?'

'No. To give you a demonstration.'

Thrale glanced at his watch. 'Here it comes.'

Out over the sea an aircraft was coming. It was low, no more than three thousand feet up, and they could see it clearly. It had no tail, it was quiet, it flew over like a great black bat and death fell from it.

Eight white parachutes blossomed and the great bombs they bore floated down in a stick. The first fell outside the wall, the last two inside. The final bomb buried its nose in a flower-bed not fifteen feet away from them, and its parachute spread itself over the lawn at their feet. A box which had been attached to its base between the fins sprouted the Stars and Stripes, and a small loudspeaker played 'The Star-Spangled Banner'.

Thrale stood to attention. When it had finished, the bomber was gone. He went over and took the flag, holding it in his hand.

'A B-2 bomber,' he said, walking back to stand in front of Komura and Chiang Shikai. 'You don't think we actually *trusted* the Soviets even after the Peace Treaty, do you? Hell, no. We made forty-nine more of those, gentlemen, and kept them in storage, and each of them can carry eight free-fall or stand-off nuclear weapons each capable of turning Tokyo or Beijing into radioactive ash. And what is more, radar can't see it, which is why it was called the Stealth bomber. And if you can't see it, your plasma guns don't do you a bit of good, and it can go and come back and bomb you until Japanese

469

or Chinese is only spoken in Hell.'

'We have the entire nuclear arsenal of the Soviet Union,' said Komura. 'We too can turn your country into lava.'

'Ahh ... now we seem to be talking Mutual Assured Destruction. That's a long way from unconditional surrender ... But wait a minute; did you say you had the nuclear arsenal of the Soviet Union under your control?'

Thrale glanced at his watch. 'Look out to sea, please.'

A mile away the sea crawled, grey and cold, and went to the horizon. A minute ticked away and the two staffs at their backs began to buzz with muttered talk. Then out to sea an immense column of water began to rise and spread from the ocean in perfect silence. A few seconds later the gigantic roar of its travel came over the villa, booming and shaking the doors and windows, smacking their very faces.

As the grey water fell back into the spreading boil of foam, Thrale spoke again.

'You *stupid* bastards,' he said contemptuously. 'Did you think you were the only ones who thought of getting a logic bomb into the enemy's microcircuitry? *We did it to the Soviets*. That, out there, was a submarine-launched ballistic missile, and it came from the *Nevsky*. Fired by our command. Half the Soviet ballistic missiles are infected with logic bombs. Ours.'

He turned to look at Komura and Chiang Shikai.

'The war is over,' he said. 'We have B-2 bombers and we have five SSBNs with new circuitry. You have a bunch of missiles which if you fire will as like as not blow up in your face or land in your own backyard. The war is over. It is stalemate. With regard to the Soviets, you have what you came for. The Japanese get raw materials, the Chinese have the threat to their future status removed. It is not a zero-sum game.'

Thrale turned and walked away. He turned half-way across the garden.

'The war is over,' he repeated. 'Let us all go home. It

470

were better we had all stayed there to begin with.'

With Thrale gone, Chiang Shikai rose slowly to his feet.

'The Yanqui is right,' he said. 'We both have what we want. I am rid of my enemies, and can rule my country until I die. I am rid of a few million surplus population, and need not worry about the Soviets. I will be remembered for ever. You, too. You have all you want. Your country has all the raw materials to make televisions and baubles for as long as the world turns. The war is finished now.'

Komura's eyes burned with rage. Shikai looked at him with loathing. The leader of the dwarves over the sea was mad, he knew it.

'I did not get what I came for,' said Komura.

Shikai turned away, and prepared to leave. 'The war is over,' he said. 'We won.'

'The Americans did not lose,' said Komura.

Fusako was standing by the wing of the Yakovlev military trainer with her father when Thrale returned. She gets her beauty from her mother, he thought. Saito looks like a frog.

The two men bowed slightly, the ritual of etiquette worn down by events.

'The war can be over,' said Thrale, 'although it will not be while Komura lives. Do you want it to be?'

Feliks Kholkhov was walking down the concrete slabs of the ramp towards them, past the immobile fighters and transports of a defeated empire. Thrale nodded, and he climbed up on the wing of the Yakovlev and got into the cockpit.

'Yes,' said Saito, 'I did not want it at all. But I could not oppose Komura ... that was why I allowed my daughter to give the CIA information. I thought it would work, but it did not. Too little and too late ... I was afraid.'

'Good,' said Thrale. The propeller of the Air Force

471

trainer turned, wheezing, and blue smoke streamed from the cowling as the radial engine caught.

'Get in,' he said.

TACHANKA HOTEL, VLADIVOSTOK

They sat around the long table where teams of Russians had nibbled *vobla*, guzzled *zakuski*, gulped vodka and swilled champagne. They sat under coffered ceilings and painted vaults amid a forest of Stalinist pillars – a score of men, mostly old, who had penetrated the very heart of the Japanese system of power and, finding it hollow, had taken up residence and moved in. The two female *samurai*, the *kaishaku*, stood either side of the tall doors.

'Very well,' said Komura. 'We were all there. Now we have to make our decision: whether to proceed and risk a nuclear war, or to call a halt and make do with what we have gained so far.'

It was for all concerned a tricky moment, calling for the ability to be non-committal while testing the water for movement. Once you were sure which way the current was flowing, it was simple. If you swam against the current, it drowned you.

'It is difficult ...' a voice murmured, and many mumbled in sympathy. It *was* difficult; nobody wanted to get drowned.

A very old man near the end of the table pushed himself to his feet. He was bald and wrinkled, his skin the colour and transparency of candle-wax. He was thin, his clothes hanging on the bones.

'It is not difficult,' he said. 'You know me, I am Yonai. I was General in the Imperial Army and I have more experience of war than most. This is not a difficult decision to make. Our initial plan was brilliant, worthy of Admiral

473

Togo himself, and in accordance with all the *samurai* virtues of the Yamato race. It came within an ace of total success.'

His eyes went around the table, looking all in the face – young and old.

'*Within an ace.* If the Americans have even one MX missile, or just one B-2 bomber or Trident missile they can fire at us, then while we are laying waste to their country with the Soviet arsenal they can destroy half a dozen of our biggest cities. With a few bombers, or just one submarineful, they can ensure as Mr Thrale promised that Japanese will be a language spoken only in Hell.'

He leaned on one bony old hand and shook his head.

'It is not a difficult decision. There is no decision. We leave this war with riches beyond compare, a cornucopia of raw materials that will mean we have to import nothing. We will be Number One anyway. *Hakko ichiu!*'

At the middle of the table sat Lt-Colonel Nozaka. He wore his white flight suit with its chrysanthemum crest, and had the two swords of the *samurai* thrust through his belt. He stood up and bowed to Yonai before addressing them.

'General Yonai is an eloquent man. I am a simple soldier, poor with words. I tend to fear eloquent men ... for me, eloquence is an indication of insincerity. I have, though a pure *yamatogokoro*, a Yamato soul and spirit which enables me to discern between truth and error. What General Yonai recommends is error. What matter if a few Japanese cities burn? Are not all the people of Tokyo waiting only for the great catfish to stir and destroy all? Will the survivors not rebuild on the ruins, as they have done in the past? Is it not worth the sacrifice of a few lives to defeat the enemy totally and for ever? *Fire the missiles. Rain death upon them!*'

He gripped the long, ribbed handle of his *katana* and the great sword hissed from its bound sheath, glittering in the light. Nozaka stepped back from his seat and the men between him and Yonai scattered like partridges.

474

Nozaka kicked aside a chair and came over to the old man in a single stride. The sword whistled like silk as it swung up in the air. Yonai stared coldly at the younger man, refusing to move.

'You are a fool,' he said certainly.

The thud of the blade striking home and the grunt of effort from the soldier were one. Gore spattered the table. Nozaka took the cloth and wiped the blade before returning it to its scabbard.

'He had lived too long,' he said. 'Error had crept into his soul.'

'It is agreed, then,' said Komura. 'We continue. But not from here. The Chinaman Shikai is in charge here. He has lost his nerve, like Yonai; he is old, he has lost his will, he does not wish the war to go on. It is his turn next. It is our destiny to rule the world.'

He stood up and everyone followed.

'Kyoto is only a short time away. Let us return and conduct the last act of the war from there. *Hakko ichiu!*'

'*Hakko ichiu!*'

A6M5b/52B
– REISEN

MISAKI AIRFIELD, HONSHU

The white Yak-18 skimmed over the green valley floor and kissed the grass. Kholkhov came back on the yoke, holding the nosewheel high as they slowed down, not allowing it to dig into the ground. He gave it a little power to increase the authority of his elevator, and they were at walking pace by the time he allowed it to come down. He taxied over to the hangar Thrale pointed to, and cut the power. They all climbed out into the sweet fresh air. The airfield was deserted.

'That landing was real pretty,' said Thrale. 'You're the kind of pilot I like to fly with. You can fly anything.'

'They're all aircraft,' agreed Kholkhov.

'You're an *Afghanet*, aren't you? You ever do FAC, by any chance? You'd be the type.'

'Forward air control?' the Russian said slowly. 'Yes, I did so. Three tours there. One in ground-attack, two as FAC.'

'Well, it sure is my lucky day,' Thrale said cheerfully. He went over to the hangar. 'You got a crowbar in there, Feliks? Let's get this open.'

The Russian broke the hinge of the lock and they rolled back the doors, Saito helping Kholkhov and Fusako, Thrale. The daylight flooded into the hangar and lit up the polished green fighter with its blood-red markings. Thrale went over and squatted under the wing, checking and smelling the fuel from the tank drains.

'This is a pretty good one. They called it the *Reisen*; our name was the Zero. It's the model 52B, made early

1944. This one's completely rebuilt, of course; it's a new aircraft really. Did air shows, Takashi told me. Okay, then. Here's how it is.'

He came out from under the wing and they all stood in a group.

'Komura and his gang went to Vladivostok in their 747. It was guarded by a squadron of F-15s. There is no way to penetrate that screen while they're all in the air. Almost. There's a window of opportunity right at the end of the flight, when the 747's on final approach. But only if you're in the right place, hidden by the contours of the land, blending with the colours of the vegetation beneath, and right at the last moment you pop up, slam next to the 747, put your nose in his cockpit and empty the magazine into him. I can do it. I've done it. But for this one, I need an FAC. I need someone higher up talking me into position.'

Thrale looked at Kholkhov. 'I need you.'

He pointed to Fusako. 'And I need you to go with him, to listen to the radio and translate for him.'

'I will,' she said.

Saito, Trade Minister of Japan, stood quietly by the old fighter aircraft.

'And I, Mr Thrale? Do you need me for anything?'

'I do. Once I have shot down the 747 I am going to run away. You will be high in the sky with Feliks and Fusako; they will take you to Tokyo. A car will be waiting and you will go to the Prime Minister's office. When you get there the phone will be ringing; it will be President Barnet. You, he, Chiang Shikai and Yanov will go to the Peace Conference. Make it like 1814: buy a hundred years of peace. Pack your Cabinet with people like you.'

He smiled at Fusako.

'Nepotism's allowed, isn't it? Make Fusako your Minister of Reconstruction. She wants to turn Japan into a constitutional democracy.'

'So did her grandmother,' said Saito. 'It has not happened yet.'

They rolled the Zero out into the sunshine and Thrale

checked the systems while Fusako sat in the Yak waiting for the radio to speak. When he was finished he came over and leaned against the fuselage, in the sunshine. He shivered and wrapped his arms around himself as though cold.

Fusako reached out her hand to comfort him.

'Are you there? The ghosts … the men who died?'

Thrale nodded, his eyes shut.

'All about,' he muttered. 'Pale battalions of dead … they beckon.'

The radio suddenly crackled with life.

'It's coming,' said Fusako urgently. 'Komura's here.'

The air was sparkling, a heavy storm the previous night had washed it clear of haze and smoke. At 7,500 feet Kholkhov estimated he had a visibility of thirty miles plus. That was good, in that he could track the incoming jets and guide Thrale to the target; it was bad in that the jet pilots too had thirty miles plus. Thrale would have been safer in the usual hazy, polluted murk, like a fish darting through muddied water.

Kholkhov's headphones chanted with the strange language. It sounded like a load of chickens clucking in his grandfather's little private plot back in Rybinsk. Fusako pressed her intercom button and translated; he used his second radio to talk to Thrale.

'Blue One to Blue Two. The active at the Air Force Base is zero niner. They're coming in from the north and can expect a left crosswind entry on to long final. I'm going to orbit to the south. Moving up now. I have you in sight. You move too, heading three two zero. One five zero knots.'

'Three two zero heading. One five zero speed,' confirmed Thrale.

Below, the tiny green aircraft stopped its series of figure-eight turns over the lush countryside and headed purposefully across country, shadowed by the white cabin-trainer above.

481

Thrale was low over the trees and fields. The A6M5b Zero felt like a new aircraft; he judged his guess that it had been completely rebuilt to be correct. The fourteen-cylinder Nakajima radial engine ahead of him growled powerfully with the harmony of a machine of close tolerances and perfect balance, its oil pressure high and temperature well in the green. The controls were light and taut, the little aircraft had the instability that had once made it the most feared fighter in the world. Thrale's hand caressed the stick, following the contours of the ground.

'Blue Two, power line coming up,' warned Kholkhov.

Thrale could see it; a vast widow-maker of cables marching from pylon to pylon across the land. The pylons were what you stayed away from. Sometimes they had long bracing wires stretching out from them – invisible until you were on them and it was too late.

Thrale aimed the fighter at the middle of the bow, where the lowest cables sagged closest to the ground. A field of green needles whipped beneath his wings and the passage of his flight whipped the paddy into foam. He kept his eyes on the irrigation channel beyond. You focused on the cables, you flew up into them. Shadows raced across the cockpit, and he eased back up to seventy-five feet and came back on course.

In the Yak above, Kholkhov was never still. He flew the plane in a gentle series of turns, averaging them out to maintain his heading, varying altitude and his head scanning the sky all around and ground below. After two hours as a Forward Air Controller in Afghanistan, he did it automatically. In that kind of war, without the FAC the battle didn't happen. He was the one who found the guerrilla – often by flying around until they shot at him; he was the one who marked their position with white phosphorus rockets, who guided the ground-attack aircraft in, cleared them hot, came back to assess their bomb damage and cleared them in hot again on the new mark; who co-ordinated with the damn colonel in the C&C chopper, talked to the attack helicopters coming up

482

from the south and the troop-carrying ones bringing the *Spetsnaz* soldiers from the East. He kept everyone where they should be, managing the battle like the conductor of an orchestra. For the men on the ground he was the bringer of death. They did everything in their power to shoot him down, and when they did and he dropped in among them on his nylon elevator, with what joy it was that they hacked off his genitals and pegged him out to separate him from his skin.

Kholkhov knew that there were only two types of pilot, the quick and the dead, and his head never stopped moving, nor his eyes scanning the sky and the ground below.

Over the dark green and light green, the yellow and the quicksilver of the streams and rivers, a red and white aircraft moved below. Like a fish passing from a bank of weed into clear water, it popped into Kholkhov's field of vision and he cursed.

'Blue Two, enemy unknown your five o'clock, estimate one hundred feet altitude.'

Kholkhov could see what had happened.

'Looks like a T-38.'

It was a military trainer making a low-level nap-of-the-earth run along a prescribed route. The flight path had taken it along a valley where it remained hidden from his view.

'Blue Two, it's following your path. I think it's seen you.'

Thrale looked back over his shoulder. The T-38 was pulling up and over, getting nose authority on the Zero skimming along the ground below.

'Making practice firing runs on me,' he grunted to Kholkhov. 'But he's going to tell someone I'm here.'

A mile ahead a tall, slim latticework of metal ascended into the sky: a thousand feet of radio mast.

Thrale suddenly initiated a steep climbing turn up sun. For a moment the T-38 pilot was caught out and almost overshot the Zero. Thrale barrel-rolled vertically in the second part of a vertical rolling scissors, and the young

483

pilot caught on like a jive-dancer hearing the first beat of 'Blue Suede Shoes' and rolled into the break to spoil Thrale's aiming solution. But by then he was gone, exploiting the greater manoeuvrability of the Zero to half-roll and pull through, heading vertically back towards the ground. Delighted, the T-38 pilot followed, as pleased as a puppy finding a fellow to play with.

Thrale was in the valley, pines streaked by above him and fishermen looked up in alarm and rage at the fury of his passing. The hill fell away, there was a pasture, and cows. He pulled up in a climbing turn to the right and for two seconds flew straight and level, the sun filling the cockpit. Then he rolled hard left, pulling as many gees as he could take – greying out, shadows whipping across the cockpit.

Then it was calm again, straight and level. He looked behind and a fireball erupted in the trees. There was a trail of black smoke in the air and slowly the tall lattice-work of the radio tower began to fall, bending and crumpling, sparks shooting into the air.

'You okay, Blue Two?'

'Yeah.' Thrale was breathing hard with the exertion and sweat streamed from him. 'I'm okay. He's gone. Found himself in a telephone box, poor bastard.'

'Okay. The Big Bandit is forty klicks out. Let's hustle along. Heading three three five. In about three klicks you'll come across a valley mouth. I want you to fly up it. It'll spit you out five klicks from the threshold of niner zero; you'll be on the outskirts of Kyoto.'

'Roger. Three three five and three miles.'

In the Yak they saw the little green fighter flying straight as a die, then it began to wriggle.

'He has it,' murmured Saito, sitting in the back of the cabin.

Clear in the distance was the grid of Kyoto and, beyond, the white crosses of the base runways. There was a white speck in the distance, and motes about it.

The dappled green flickered past Thrale's cockpit. He was going downhill now, following the sparkling river as it dashed down towards the lake.

'Blue Two. There's no cover between the valley mouth and the threshold to niner zero. They will sure see you coming across the fields. When you come out of the valley, you'll see the city ahead of you. Fly two niner zero and expect to pick up a park in the city.'

'Two niner zero. And a park,' affirmed Thrale.

'There's a big road coming from the park, heading two seven zero, due West. Lots of big buildings. You'll be lost in the clutter.'

'Big road, due West.'

Thrale skimmed over the fields, with the city ahead of him. He pulled up over the houses. Green was ahead.

'Park half a klick,' Kholkhov advised.

'I have it.'

Thrale cranked it over by the temple and saw people running from the corner of his eye. The boulevard was dead ahead, a tunnel of concrete and glass, and he dived into it. He grunted as the fighter thudded into the turbulence of the air swirling around the buildings, up and down the streets, his head smacking from one side of the cockpit to the other as he strove to stay level. Ahead of him was a bow-wave of running people and crashing cars. A river flashed beneath, a park to his left, a palace to the right. A skyscraper, signs, trucks and cars, an electric train, faces like blobs of paint.

'Half a mile. Blue Two,' advised Kholkhov. 'The threshold is dead ahead, distance two and a half klicks.'

The buildings were gone and he flashed over the fields again. At his ten o'clock, the great airliner floated down on final approach, white and gleaming in the sunshine, and Thrale howled like a wolf. The F-15s were about it. Fifty years ago his target would have glowed in the reticle of the gunsight, his guns armed, but the old fighter was an antique, a performer of air shows. It had no guns.

'*They have you!*'

'*They're too late.*'

The throttle was to the firewall, the radial bellowed

485

and the Zero streaked over the ground at 340mph. Gouts of mud suddenly walked across the field and he jinked left and right. From the airfield red and green tracer began to pop, lazy at first, then accelerating past the cockpit. The fighters were desperately pulling in landing gear and flaps like a lot of ladies caught bathing – fire streaming from their exhausts as they attempted to get the airspeed they needed to be effective. The 747 was going around, gear coming in, nose rising with full power applied. It was as big and slow as an airship, side on.

Something slammed into the Zero; half the instrument panel jumped out and smacked Thrale in the face, knocking him back in his seat. Boiling liquid squirted from a ripped pipe and he grunted. Tracer began to track him from both sides, and as the rounds slammed into the aircraft he sawed at the rudders and ailerons in uncoordinated flight. Sparks were flying out of the ruined instrument panel and the cockpit stank of ozone and indiarubber. A hole suddenly appeared in the canopy and air blasted in. Thrale was squeezed up in a crouch, hunching forward like a man driving through heavy rain. His lips were pulled back over his teeth, the death's head grimace the only whiteness in a face pumping blood. His hair was standing on end. The airliner filled the windshield; he could see a woman in bright red staring at him. Something hit the fighter like a sledgehammer, there was the hideous stench of molten metal and the cockpit erupted in a cauldron of fire.

It was very slow. He could see the three-bladed propeller rotating in front of him, the flames that roared in the cockpit waved lazily as though from candles. The great wing of the 747 was scything towards him in slow motion, and he made a tiny adjustment of elevator and aileron to lift his own wing-tip clear. It was important that the fighter fly all the way to the target.

No firing now, he was too close. He saw the turbine blades as they spun in their pods below the white wing, he saw the woman in red bow in her seat. He could see her hair falling forward like a shimmering black waterfall.

486

The battalions of the dead were all about him. They approved.

In the clear air, you could see the immense column of smoke thirty miles away. A small white aircraft, heading east, was the only thing in the sky.

Macdonald Trade Paperbacks offers an exciting range of quality titles by both established and new authors. All of the books in this series are available from:

Macdonald Trade Paperbacks
Cash Sales Department,
P.O. Box 11,
Falmouth,
Cornwall TR10 9EN.

Alternatively you may fax your order to the above address. Fax No. 0326 76423.

Payments can be made as follows: Cheque, postal order (payable to Macdonald & Co (Publishers) Ltd) or by credit cards, Visa/Access. Do not send cash or currency. UK customers: please send a cheque or postal order (no currency) and allow 80p for postage and packing for the first book plus 20p for each additional book up to a maximum charge of £2.00.

B.F.P.O. customers please allow 80p for the first book plus 20p for each additional book.

Overseas customers including Ireland, please allow £1.50 for postage and packing for the first book, £1.00 for the second book, and 30p for each additional book.

NAME (Block Letters) ....

ADDRESS ....

....

☐ I enclose my remittance for _____

☐ I wish to pay by Access/Visa Card

Number ☐☐☐☐☐☐☐☐☐☐☐☐☐☐☐☐

Card Expiry Date ☐☐☐☐